# THE QUIGLEY
# RESCUE

## A DANNY QUIGLEY
## ACTION NOVEL

*To BRUCE ABBOTTS
WITH BEST WISHES
RUSS.*

# E.J. RUSS MCDEVITT

# The Quigley Rescue:
# A Danny Quigley Action Novel

Copyright © 2012 by E.J. Russ McDevitt
Gimli, MB, Canada R0C1B0
www.russmcdevitt.com

ISBN-13: 978-1477608258

# DEDICATION

TO THE UNACKNOWLEDGED
WARRIORS OF SPECIAL FORCES
WHO WORK THROUGH THEIR
OWN FEARS AND HUMAN
LIMITATIONS, TO GO OUT ON
SPECIAL OPERATIONS AND
PERFORM INCREDIBLE FEATS OF
COURAGE, ENDURANCE AND
DEDICATION, IN DANGEROUS
AND HOSTILE ENVIRONMENTS.

*I SALUTE YOU.*

# GLOSSARY

**SAS** - Special Air Service
**LAV** - Light Armoured Vehicle
**CANADIAN 1PPCLI** - First Batalion Princess Patricia's Light Infantry
**SOCOM** – U.S. Special Forces Command
**LAM** – Lazer Aiming Module
**S.P.A.S.** – Special Purpose Automatic Shotgun
**IED'S** – Improvised Explosive Devices
**CAS** – Close Air Suport
**RPG** – Rocket Propelled Grenades
**COMMS** - Communication System
**CSAM** – Crew Situational Awareness Monitor
**FOB** – Forward Operating Base
**ARV** – Armoured Recovery Vehicle
**MI5** – Domestic Intelligence Service (UK)
**MI6** – Secret Intelligence Service (UK) International Operations (similar to CIA).
**CSIS** – Canadian Security Intelligence Service.
**J.T.F.2** – Joint Task Force Two – Canadian Special Forces
**BRITISH COLUMBIA** – North Western Province in Canada
**DEA** – Drug Enforcement Agency
**CIA** – Central Intelligence Agency
**BERGENS** – Packs
**VMO** – Village Medical Outreach
**CQB** – Close Quarter Battle House
**HELICOPTER EXFIL** – Extraction By Helipcopter
**WART HOG** – Aircraft With Fierce Fire Power

# Chapter 1

Flashback - Kabul. Afghanistan

For Danny Quigley and his buddy Scotty McGregor, missing a flight was the start of a journey into hell. In the wrong place at the wrong time, waiting for a flight out, they had been nabbed by the NATO Commander in Kandahar for an urgent rescue mission that called for Special Forces' skills and expertise.

Eighteen hours later, they drove out of Kabul on the main road, in a packet of eight vehicles under the command of the Canadian 1PPCI (First Battalion Princes Patricia's Light Infantry). The convoy consisted of two armored Bisons and six LAV's (light armored vehicles).

Scotty and Danny rode in the third vehicle, an LAV, with three Canadian infantrymen. The LAV was capable of carrying 7 passengers and 10 in an emergency. Danny, with his muscular, six-foot figure had to unwind carefully inside the vehicle while his short wiry buddy, Scotty, grinned at his discomfiture. They both still wore the beards and long hair favored by Special Forces as

7

camouflage, when operating in the Afghan mountains.

The temperature was forty-five degrees Celsius, and with body armor and the heat of the vehicle, they were suffering already.

One of the two sentries up in the hatch, Corporal Bruce Logan, dropped down, choking.

"Christ the smell up there would make you want to puke," he wheezed.

They knew what he meant. They could smell it from inside the vehicle. The stench of the city was overpowering with open sewers, animal and human waste, and burning garbage dumped anywhere with people picking through it. However it didn't stop crowds of people milling about the small meat stalls, with skinned goats and chickens, all covered in flies. The road was crowded with hundreds of bicycles, mopeds, scooters, ancient pick-ups, taxis, pedestrians, handcarts, donkeys, and the occasional camel.

The Afghans believed in decorating their vehicles with all sorts of strobes, lights and ornaments that jingled noisily as they barreled along.

Children ran alongside, their hands out begging, as they edged swiftly through the traffic, the sound of horns, shouts, cries and bleating animals, a constant bombardment.

The convoy had to aggressively push through the crowded street to avoid being targeted, and had to maintain a distance of 25 to 30 meters between convoy vehicles to ensure that no suicide vehicle slipped in between them. People shouted abuse as they drove through.

The drivers of the Bisons and the LAV's were in short range radio contact with each other with ear-phones and mikes strapped to their heads. They kept up an ongoing dialogue to flag up any approaching potential security problems:

"Watch for a white Nissan pick-up coming up fast, two passengers... motor cycle parked on the right up ahead, one man sitting on it looking this way... coming up to a break in the stone wall, an alleyway, six people hanging there, just watching..."

Up on top, in one of the two turrets, the LAV sentry stayed alert with his Co-Axiel 7.62 mm machine gun. It fired in the same direction as the LAV's powerful Buckmaster 25 mm cannon. This traversed left, and right to cover any perceived threats from the ongoing radio dialogue. The LAV also had a 7.62 mm that the crew commander could operate.

The armored Bisons had a pintle-mounted machine gun where the gunner was exposed when firing. It also had a dual role of carrying personnel and acting as an ambulance for the injured.

Scotty and Danny were choosy when it came to weapons. They had to be. Careful selection prior to Special Air Service (SAS) operations had stood them in good stead in the past.

There were some highly sophisticated weapons out in the market place, but if they had any tendency to jam or to be ineffective, they were left behind.

Most of the Brits, stuck to the M16 Bullpup model, which used the standard NATO .223

caliber ammunition. This not being available Scotty had grabbed a U.S. 5.56-mm M16A1 assault rifle fitted with 40-mm M205 grenade launcher, which had a 30-round magazine. He piled a whole bunch of ammo magazines and grenades into his pack as well.

Danny was a big fan of the German Heckler and Koch 9-mm MP5A3 sub machine gun, which also had a 30-round magazine, and was delighted to find that the NATO team had managed to find a silenced version with a laser-aiming device. The silencer reduced its range by about 200 yards, but it was a beautiful weapon.

Both of them claimed a SOCOM pistol which had been designed in 1990 as a special requirement by U.S Special Forces Command, (SOCOM). The laser-aiming module (LAM) and the sound/flash suppressor, made it ideal for covert operations. They would have loved to have taken a heavier machine gun just in case the action ramped up, but the weight of the gun and the ammo would have been too much. Bearing in mind that they were rescuing an Afghan policeman and an American officer, and could use the extra firepower, they threw in three Mini Uzi's and ammo, which didn't take up much space, and five Kevlar frag vests.

Finally, almost as an afterthought, Scotty threw into the back of the LAV, an Italian Franchi 12-gauge shotgun S.P.A.S. (Special Purpose Automatic Shotgun), which had a six-round tubular magazine and was absolutely brutal in close quarter combat.

He had spent some of his youth working at a carnival where his father taught him how to throw knives, and to use both a bow and arrow and a crossbow. He had his crossbow with him from the previous op., and they both carried combat knives and three short-range radios. It was the last item that Scotty placed in the bottom of his pack that made Danny's hawk-like face do a double take.

"A Claymore Mine for Pete's sake! You have to hump that baby up a mountain on top of everything else. You may regret this Scotty."

"That's my problem Mate. I have a feeling that we may need an edge on this one. A Claymore may just do that."

Danny shrugged, his intense blue eyes reflecting his doubts.

"Your problem is right. Just dump it if it gets too heavy. That's a steep bloody mountain!

# Chapter 2

In one way it was a relief for the crew to clear the edge of town but another threat was ever present. The possibility that IED's (Improvised Explosive Devices), might have been planted since the last NATO patrol had come through an hour previously.

The convoy's job was to transport them from Kabul to a Forward Operating Base, re-supply, then run them to a drop-off point for the mission. The mission was complex.

A village that had been over-run by the Taliban had been taken back by a joint U.S. and British Force after three days of fighting.

Once the Taliban had been driven out, the Americans flew the Governor of the Province, the Provincial police chief, 20 Afghan National Police, and a liaison officer for the re-construction team, all back to the village. This officer was a U.S. engineer, a Major Duffy. Unfortunately the Taliban hadn't withdrawn very far and swept back into the village when the U.S. and British Force withdrew to their Base.

The 20 Afghan policemen ran off.

The Governor was a personal friend of President Karzai, and the Taliban threatened to behead all three men if there was any movement by NATO Forces against the village.

Normally the Taliban would remove any high-grade prisoners out of the area into the mountains or across the border. A source in the village, with a cell phone confirmed that they were still there. Hence the speed to mount a mission.

Therein lay Danny's and Scotty's reservation - a number of reservations actually.

One was having an op. thrust on them that had been cobbled together by a mixture of NATO officers who had no Special Forces' experience.

The SAS planning strategy always looked at several aspects of a mission:

First was the physical ground and landmarks of the incursion area in detail.

Next was the estimation of enemy forces in the area, their weaponry, and any possible friendlies, as well as the political implications, if any.

Being clear on the objective of the mission was also fundamental to any task. In this case, to free the hostages and get them out.

The next aspect was how to execute the objective with transport, routes, RV's, proposed action points in fulfilling the mission, and getting out again, known as the 'exfill procedures'.

Then came a crucial decision: what to take in terms of weapons and equipment for the task, plus food and water.

The choice of weapons was dictated by what you could possibly expect to encounter, when you came into contact with the enemy. However quite often that was limited by how much a soldier could carry and how far they would have to hike once they left their vehicles.

The last aspect would be communications. This was a vital component.

Who do you talk to, when and how? Useful to know, if you need to call in Close Air Support or an earlier Helicopter Exfill.

A big concern for Scotty and Danny was the complete lack of intelligence as to the numbers of Taliban who had filtered back, and how well armed they were. More importantly, could they count on any support from the villagers?

Another was the lack of time to really explore and develop a plan that had some chance of success. Traditional military officers had great difficulty accepting lower ranks challenging or questioning their proposals, even if they were Special Forces.

No opportunity, as they usually would have prior to an operation, to challenge, role-play or do feasibility studies, create models of the target buildings, or to work out fall-back positions and alternative extraction options, should things fall apart as they quite often do.

The exfil plan called for a chopper to come in and pick them up once they had released the hostages. The back-up forces on the ground, the Bisons and LAV packet, had to stay well out of sight from the village. That was so as not to alarm the Taliban and start them beheading the prisoners. If things got hairy, with IED's and possible RPG (Rocket Propelled Grenades) attacks, they might not be able to get back to support the rescue attempt at all.

Okay, they had a source in the village that, if they could penetrate it, would guide them to the prisoners. Their translator, a skinny, short, 30 year old Afghan called Abdul, who originally came from the village, would lead them to this contact - his cousin.

Thankfully, Abdul looked and sounded trustworthy, but was this a trap in itself?

How much could they trust him? After all they had seen and witnessed in Afghanistan, they still had doubts, and finally, the idea of sending in only a two-man Special Forces team to infiltrate a village filled with God knows how many terrorists... A sixteen-man SAS troop could deliver awesome firepower and decimate any opposition thrown against it. Two troopers however, notwithstanding their courage and commitment, could be overrun by the sheer weight of numbers in a firefight.

It sounded more like a desperate suicide mission.

It was not the SAS way of doing things.

They did have a satellite picture of the village which showed a layout of some fifty mud and straw-built houses, crisscrossed by stone and mud walls. Part of the village backed into the mountain. The satellite picture was useful.

Ideally they would have preferred to have the reserves in closer proximity. If Danny, Scotty, or indeed any of the prisoners were wounded, they would be in dire trouble.

They did have an effective Comms (Communication System) should they need to lay on Close Air Support (CAS), or an earlier or later extraction. They also carried laser-targeting equipment to call in air strikes, as well as a firefly beacon and colored flares should they need to mark their positions.

General Eisenhower once said, "Plans are useless, but planning is indispensable."

Someone else said that plans only last as long as the first contact with the enemy.

The NATO plan was to drop Scotty and Danny from the column of Bisons and Light Armored Vehicles, on the other side of a mountain that towered above the village. The convoy would then keep going, hopefully, to hoodwink any watchers.

Scotty and Danny were to climb the mountain with their translator Abdul, and go down the other side, hopefully remaining undiscovered by sheepherders or insurgents.

Abdul would then guide them into the village in the pre-dawn darkness. Their proposed route, up the mountain and down the other side, was marked on the map with GPS numbers, but not based on any real knowledge of the terrain. All it would take was some deep gully or sheer rock face to throw their timing off schedule.

On rescuing the prisoners, and presumably killing the guards silently in the process, the plan called for them to move out to a large cleared opium field on the other side of the village, beyond some goat pens.

Once they had set up the Comms and made contact with their controllers, a chopper would drop down and collect them.

In essence it could work. It looked good on paper, however they had no answers to the many 'what ifs' they had seen in numerous operations going tits up through unforeseen circumstances or faulty intelligence.

Danny and Scotty weren't in the suicide business, but again, they were in the British Army and had no option but to obey orders.

# Chapter 3

As darkness fell, the LAV crew fired up the CSAM (Crew Situational Awareness Monitor), and the thermal viewing helped them see clearly what they were heading into.

Scotty had taken a turn in one of the observation turrets and was using a set of thermal binoculars that could spot just about anything in the dark, at great distances.

Suddenly they heard the chatter of small arms fire followed by a loud 'boom.'

Scotty screamed down the turret entrance.

"Enemy up ahead.... RPG's coming in.... the fucking lot!"

Right then a storm of bullets clanged off the roof of the vehicle. The radio crackled into life.

"Call sign Spider one...we've taken a hit...RPG I think... we're on fire...can't evacuate injured crew... incoming fire from wall on right hand side... weapon jammed by RPG round... need immediate assistance... over."

The Bison had been hit and damaged.

Scotty came sliding down from the turret. He thumped the LAV Commander on the shoulder.

"Lower that fucking ramp mate" he shouted. "We're going out. Come on Danny." With that he grabbed the M16 assault weapon, threw a handful of grenades into his belt pack and moved to the back of the vehicle.

The ramp clanged back onto the ground and they rolled out staying low.

Danny reached for the MP5 and some grenades before diving out of the vehicle. Two of the PPCLI infantrymen sprawled out beside them, looking cool under fire.

Once outside, they had a clearer view of what was going on.

The first vehicle, the Bison, was ablaze and slewed across the highway ahead. Heavy concentrated fire was being directed by insurgents from the other side of a stonewall that ran alongside the road. The second vehicle's 25 mm cannon was starting to direct fire towards the wall but was constrained by the damaged vehicle blocking its aim.

The armored vehicles behind were constrained for the same reason.

An RPG round screamed past the vehicle they had just rolled out of and blasted a large tree directly behind them. Danny shouted in Scotty's ear.

"We'll get cut to pieces if we stay here. We have to take the pressure off those guys up front."

He leaned sideways and shouted to one of the Canadians.

"We'll have a go at those bastards behind the wall. You two head for that Bison as soon as we start cutting them down and help get those chaps out. Okay?"

The Canadians nodded, still looking steady and under control.

Danny leaned into Scotty and shouted urgently into his ear.

He gave him a look that clearly said 'You're crazy mate' but jumped up with him and sprinted for the stone wall ten feet away.

Bullets whined off the roadway and the sides of the halted LAV. The two Canadians stood up, carefully shielding themselves behind the vehicle, and started returning fire.

Once they slammed up against the wall, Danny crouched down and Scotty placed his boot in his hand. With one heave Danny thrust him upwards onto the top of the wall, then Scotty hauled him up alongside him.

Luckily none of the insurgents had spotted them but they had a clear view of the battle that raged below.

Heavy fire was being directed from the other side of the wall at the trapped convoy by at least 20 to 30 insurgents who were blasting away with AK-47's and RPG's.

The NATO column had only minutes to survive in the concentrated field of fire. The Bison was on fire and the second LAV had been hit as well. It looked like a wheel had been blown off.

Okay, Danny's plan was crazy. He had planned to run along the top of the wall blasting down on the insurgents hoping their own column's firepower wouldn't rip into them from behind, while Scotty would sweep up on the insurgents' side of the wall, but Scotty had his own slant on the strategy. He leaned close and shouted in Danny's ear.

"I'm smaller, harder to hit. I'll stay on top of the wall!"

With that he pushed Danny off and watched as he hit the ground. Then he crouched down and started giving him the silent count with his fingers that they always used prior to launching into action: 3-2-1.

Danny barely had time to lift up the MP5 when Scotty launched himself along the top of the wall, almost like he was being supported by fairy wings.

His M16 started chattering, and already they could hear startled shouts up ahead. Danny was running parallel to Scotty below and was already sighting in on black-turbaned figures ahead, who were swinging AK-47's towards him.

The concentrated firepower from both of them was like a metal hose inside the confined space as bodies were hurled backwards.

Up above, Scotty screamed "grenade Danny" as he loosed a round from his rifle.

Danny dropped down as it 'whoomped' ahead, then he jumped up and kept running. He heard the whiz of bullets flying past him as he moved forward, firing ...changing magazines automatically... blasting at startled faces who were turning and lifting weapons in his direction. He heard a loud screaming noise and realized it was himself as he tore along, lost in the heat of battle, stumbling to his knees at times over boulders, immune, it seemed, to the flickering weapons coming to bear on him and ignoring scratches from thorny bushes. He just kept firing and changing magazines until the weapon grew hot in his hands. He lobbed a number of grenades ahead, shouting a hoarse warning to Scotty as he did so.

Up above, Scotty fell and Danny thought he'd bought it, but after firing off another grenade, he was up and sprinting along the wall again.

Suddenly Danny found himself out ahead and came face to face with half a dozen insurgents in a compact group, standing on an improvised platform up against the wall. They were all carrying RPG's, which on spotting him, they immediately dropped and started diving for their AK-47's. They were probably the ones who had disabled the Bison and had possibly killed dozens of his Brit colleagues back in the mountains, he thought.

He started ripping into them with the MP5 and watched them pitching backwards.

At that moment his magazine ran out. Two of the enemy turned their AK-47s towards him, triumphant looks crossing their faces.

"Down Danny!" He heard the shout and dropped like a stone as Scotty let off another grenade from the launcher.

The two insurgents were blown apart like rag dolls as he pressed himself into the earth to avoid the blast. They had a fleeting image of the rest of the fighters running off.

They left behind their weapons, a slew of ammunition and 23 dead insurgents.

Several of their wounded were strewn along the path of Scotty and Danny's progress. Scotty let loose a long burst at one of the wounded behind him as he reached for his fallen AK-47.

Just like that, it was over.

On the other side of the wall, one soldier in the Bison had been killed and two injured. No one in the second LAV was hurt.

As they were close to Forward Operating Base the Column radioed for help and waited for a rescue group to come out, to recover the damaged vehicles and the wounded.

The NATO Forces never left a broken down or shot-up vehicle behind them that the Taliban could use for propaganda purposes.

The wounded insurgents were a prize they wanted to bring in too.

Shortly, an ARV (Armored Recovery Vehicle) came out with a U.S. route-clearing package known as an IED-buster and some low-bed trucks. One of the vehicles was equipped with ground-penetrating radar and metal-detecting plates, and the second carried the Explosives Ordinance team, to disarm and blow up any bombs they detected en-route.

The journey gave the two SAS soldiers some time to come down from the adrenalin high they had been on during the action.

Hours later the column staggered into the Forward Operating Base where they got some strange looks and numerous thanks from the rescued soldiers.

The plan was to overnight there, but the question in everyone's mind was, could the mission continue with its reduced capacity of vehicles, firepower and personnel?

# Chapter 4

London, U.K. (Present time)

How do you find someone who has supposedly been dead for 12 months and then sends you a message out of the blue? A rather vague message at that!

"Help me... Indians.  C.C."

The C.C. referred to Clive Courtney, a man who had had an enormous and positive effect on Danny Quigley's life at a time when he desperately needed guidance and help.

Just discharged from the U.K.'s Special Forces, under attack by a faceless enemy, and trying to come to terms with some bad stuff in his past life, Courtney was responsible for stepping in and getting his life back on an even keel.

Later C.C. was kidnapped, and in his subsequent escape he killed his attacker, stumbled off into the night and disappeared. At that time he had been suffering from terminal cancer with only months to live.

After twelve months and with no further communication, it was assumed that he had sought out some private place for his final moments.

An unexpected e-mail changed all that!

The morning after Danny received the cryptic message, his first port of call, by pre-arrangement, was with Rebecca Fullerton-Smythe, the Director General of MI5, in her office at Thames House in London.

He was shocked at the blackened state of the ground floor after a recent bomb blast in the underground garage as he threaded his way through a temporary security barrier. They were expecting him and he was escorted upstairs.

With her main field of responsibilities covering counter subversion, counter espionage and counter terrorism, he realized how lucky he was to get in on her morning schedule. On one occasion they had saved each other's lives, so that was probably part of it.

Rebecca Fullerton-Smythe was an attractive dark haired lady in her early forties, with a tight figure that reflected her passion for hunting and shooting in her free time.

Now she stood up and came around her desk with a wide smile on her face and gave him a long hug.

She turned to the man sitting alongside her.

"Peter, meet my favorite 'Sass' trooper, Danny Quigley. Well, ex-trooper actually" she exclaimed as she stepped back and eyed him closely.

"I didn't get a good look at you last night when I collected you at Heathrow, but by God you look fit Danny. Nice desert tan. The insurance business hasn't completely seduced you I see."

"Yeah, I still work at keeping fit." he mumbled.

He was feeling slightly embarrassed at the effusive greeting, particularly as he saw the other man's jaw dropping when the Director General threw her arms around him.

The D.G. caught Danny's arm and turned him slightly.

"Danny I wanted you to meet Peter Fawcett who works as a communications specialist for us. What he doesn't know isn't worth knowing. Hence him being here today to look at your cell phone."

Fawcett was a slender, mid thirties executive with thinning hair and sharp intelligent eyes. He reminded Danny of a teacher he'd had in high school in Wales, who had encouraged him to join the judo class.

Now he stood up and shook his hand.

In his insurance business Danny was meeting people every day and read a lot into a handshake. In this case he was impressed with the firmness of the man's grasp and the direct eye contact.

"I have to say, Mr. Quigley, that today is the first time the Director General has mentioned your name, but from what I can gather, you can practically walk on water."

He smiled as he said it.

"Call me Danny, please," he corrected. "...and I have to say that there's considerable exaggeration in her opinion."

"Oh yeah" she interrupted. "An attack dog had its jaws around my throat and Danny pulled it off and killed it."

Fawcett looked shocked.

"I thought you never left Thames House Ma'am. By the way, what did you mean by 'a nice desert tan?"

She chuckled. "Don't ask, Peter. Trust me... you know the old saying, 'if I told you I'd have to kill you.' Now..." she turned to Danny. "Show Peter the cell phone."

He passed it over.

"Oh, the sixth message down."

Fawcett scrolled down and examined the message.

After a moment he turned to Danny.

"Did you try to send a reply?"

"No, I had some idea that the message might disappear completely if I did. No basis for this... just a vague notion I had."

Peter nodded.

"Probably just as well, but we could run some tests first, before you try and see if we can locate the origin of the message. Tracing emails isn't rocket science with today's technology. It depends on how determined the sender is to avoid being traced. You can imagine how frequently terrorists want to avoid being targeted and have a drone missile come down the air vent minutes after sending messages. We may end up with a general location such as a landmass from the towers that were accessed in the transfer of the message. You know, South Australia or Eastern Europe... though we can be more specific."

He stopped there, looking across at the D.G.

She took over.

"Danny you have no idea how busy we are. Four thousand young Muslim men go out from the U.K. every year to training Mosques in Pakistan, Egypt and Saudi Arabia. Most of the journeys are legitimate but a number are not, and a lot of our efforts are geared to distilling the essence of voice-mails and e-mails coming and going from the U.K. to those countries. The CIA contact ourselves and MI6 quite a lot as they have the same problem, and we have better intelligence contacts in some of the Arab countries."

He shrugged.

"I appreciate that Rebecca..."

She cut in.

"However, Peter will take you downstairs and work on this for a couple of hours. See if he can point you in the right direction, if nothing else."

She looked down at her diary.

"Now I'm lucky to have some time free for lunch today, and it so happens that I'm at my favorite eating place, so yourself and Peter can join me then and see where we are with this."

She read out a well known and rather up market address.

In a moment Peter and Danny headed down into the bowels of Thames House.

Several years spent in the Parachute Regiment and the Special Air Service hadn't exactly made Danny a connoisseur of good food. The army served basic food and lots of it, quite often consumed in a hurry and in between exercises of varies kinds. Even on training exercises abroad, unless they were attached temporarily to foreign units, they stuck basically to the same fare of steak, chicken, fish and chips, sausage and mash - not forgetting lots of beer. British beer, not the diluted stuff they serve in some countries, which is why Danny felt slightly uneasy following Peter into the French sounding restaurant situated further down from the House of Commons and overlooking the Thames river.

Peter chuckled, spotting his discomfiture.

"I thought you insurance executives were out with clients all the time" he teased.

Danny grinned, relaxing somewhat.

"I try to avoid it as much as possible. I actually escape the obligation by having some lunch brought in to the office occasionally. Dining out is not really my bag Peter, I can tell you."

As they were entering the establishment Peter stopped and held his arm.

"Just a heads up Danny. The D.G. travels with bodyguards now, so expect to be checked inside. They have a special little alcove that they reserve for her when she comes here. Near the kitchen unfortunately."

He nodded. "Yeah, I guess that explosion at Thames House kinda changed things."

"You'd better believe it! Now it's regular protection and she doesn't like it. Sign of the times though. Let's go inside".

As soon as Peter announced to the headwaiter inside who we were dining with, he waved his arm and two large men in civilian clothes bore down on them.

One of them flashed his warrant card.

"Metropolitan Police gentlemen. I understand the Director General is expecting both of you but I need to check your ID's first."

He checked a piece of paper.

"Peter Fawcett and Danny Quigley is that right?"

Peter produced his MI5 card and Danny extracted his driving license, which one of them scrutinized carefully. He frowned.

"Danny Quigley...should I know that name? Sounds familiar."

"I shouldn't think so Officer."

He looked at the second policeman who shrugged.

The one wearing the puzzled look returned his card and pointed towards the back of the restaurant. In a moment they were seated beside Rebecca Fullerton-Smythe, the D.G.

On seeing his expression she chuckled.

"Oh, you met my guard dogs outside Danny. I must say I find them a real pain in the butt. I used to be able to nip out of Thames House and grab a bunch of flowers or a birthday card or just go window-shopping as women do. Not any more I'm afraid."

"It's for your own protection Ma'am," Peter chided her gently.

She made a face.

"Yes, I know, I know. That's what people keep telling me, but it's like living in a bottle. I even have to tell them when I'm going to the toilet. It's like being back in school. There's usually a female bodyguard as well who checks out the washroom. Can you believe it? No female with them today for some reason, so no toilet break, even if I wanted it."

She touched his arm.

"What did you think of the security Danny? That used to be one of your skills."

He hesitated; not wanting to criticize what he knew was a mind-numbing and boring job.

Sensing his reluctance Peter leaned forward.

"No seriously Danny, we're all concerned about the D.G.'s safety. How would you evaluate her security out front?"

He looked down considering. They both fell silent.

Just then a young slim Pakistani waiter came up, placed menus on the table and took their orders for drinks. After he left Peter looked at him and spoke one word

"Well?"

He sighed and looked directly at both of them.

"If I was tasked with taking out Rebecca, she would be dead already. So would the two bodyguards and so would you Peter."

Peter paled, his body wilting.

"Jesus, you don't mince words Danny! Two big cops both armed, accosting everyone coming in. In God's name how would you do it?"

"For starters, their checkpoint is too close to Rebecca. I could take out both with a silencer and my target is just steps away. She'd have no escape route even if she had some warning. Her back is to the Thames River. They never searched or scanned me for a weapon, for example. Their biggest problem is their lack of awareness. They're not expecting any trouble. That's dangerous, because when it happens you freeze. That's it. End of story."

Peter turned and stared at Rebecca.

"My God Ma'am what'd you say to that?" he stammered.

She looked nonplussed.

"Danny's right. I know it. I've known it all along. If I want real protection I'd need a ring of steel around me 24/7 and my life would be pure hell. So I just accept it for what it is, a façade of protection. I do carry a licensed handgun in my purse right there and I know how to use it. If they really want to get me they can, so why worry about it. Speaking of which, let's order some food."

Outside in the lobby the two policemen settled in for the duration.

Eric Winslow was a Detective Constable with expectations of making Detective Inspector before very long. He had the look of an ex-rugby player about him and his shrewd gray eyes were topped with a bushy pair of eyebrows. Right now his forehead was scrunched up. His colleague, Ken Wright, a lanky detective constable also, looked at him with amusement.

"What's with you mate? You've had that look since we checked the two who were meeting with the D.G."

Winslow shook his head in irritation.

"It's just that name, Danny Quigley. I can't place where I've heard it before. It's just dogging me."

"Why worry mate? If he's with the D.G he's been cleared big time."

"Yeah, but it's niggling at me Eric."

"Tell you what, the guy looked in super shape. Army look about him."

Winslow glanced across at him his eyes widening.

"Army. Shit, yeah that's it! Couple of years ago. A guy is attacked in an underground garage and put his three attackers in hospital. Then someone killed all three in a manner that suggested someone from Special Forces had done it. Quigley was suspected and was rumored to be ex 'Sass' but was subsequently cleared. The Director General was involved in that somehow."

His colleague sat up straighter.

"Hell, he's the same guy then!"

"Gotta be. See the way he walks? Like a fucking cat. You don't tangle with those guys from Hereford. See the way he looked at us? He must have been laughing at how pathetic we looked. Bodyguards my ass!"

Danny was glad of the D.G.'s guidance and ended up with a delicious steak in some sort of exquisite sauce and let out a deep breath of satisfaction when he'd finished.

They both burst out laughing.

"He's been eating army MREs (meals ready to eat) for the past eight years" Peter chortled, "and had no idea what he was missing."

Rebecca laughed.

"Yes, and now he knows, I think we have a convert Peter. No more meals in his office. His clients won't know what happened."

Danny recognized that the joke was at his expense.

"When I think of the number of times I was sitting in a jungle or desert situation, eating what I thought was a decent meal, and you guys were dining on this. God, if the word gets out, there goes your recruiting figures! Now, thanks for that delicious meal but can we get back to my cell phone and the message from C.C. Peter and I were working on it back in Thames House."

"And?" The D.G. leaned forward.

Peter answered.

"It appears to have come from the northwest coast of B.C. in Canada."

"B.C.?"

"British Columbia. There's vast tracts of land in the interior that the Canadian Government have given back to the Indians, sorry, we're supposed to call them First Nations. It's possible that the call originated from somewhere in that huge area. The closest telephone tower is at a logging town called Hanlon Falls, but it didn't come from there. Essentially the town is owned by the pulp mill company who recruits in Vancouver and bring their new employees in by ship or float plane."

"Vancouver eh? I'm sounding like a Canadian now." Her eyes took on a faraway look.

"Hmm...there just might be a way we could do a quid pro quo on this Danny. Now..." she turned to Peter.

"Can you contact CSIS in Canada for me and see what resources they have up there in northern B.C, if anything. Explain what we're trying to do and see if they can help."

"Who are CSIS?" Danny asked tentatively.

Peter answered.

"Canadian Security Intelligence Service. The CIA equivalent in that country, but with rather limited resources. MI6 are in touch with them more often than we are, but sometimes we get enquiries from them when they're monitoring suspicious immigration applicants. Now we still have to try to send a message on Danny's cell phone. I vote we do that right now."

They never got around to it.

Some people say that you never lose it. Ex cops, speak about how even after they retire, they still sit strategically in a bar or restaurant and do a continuous monitoring of people coming in and out. It's layered in. Army training, particularly Special Forces training, ratchets it up to a whole new dimension, which is practiced, role played and inculcated.

You could be standing at a control barrier in a market place in Iraq or Afghanistan and peering at each face closely as if your life depends on it.

It does…and your buddies' lives too. You're always operating at heightened tension and alertness. Is there a purpose about the approaching person…. a tension? Are they staring intently at you? Are they bulked up? Are their hands under their clothing? Wild eyed? Perspiration on their foreheads? Though by then it's usually too late.

You have to make a split second decision, and it could be a woman or an approaching child that you have to fire on.

Danny didn't realize at a conscious level that during the meal he had been monitoring the young Pakistani waiter at some deeper level. The challenge of the new environment may have blunted his awareness.

Never the most friendly of people, Danny had found that Asian business men lacked the normal friendliness of British people and often wondered why they were even in the business they were in, which necessitated meeting people on a regular basis and greeting them.

Sometimes they looked like they were doing YOU a favor in selling you their goods. So when the young Pakistani waiter displayed what he considered to be the normal unfriendliness that he expected, he didn't think this unusual.

Something must have started to stir inwardly when he noticed that the waiter's eyes never left the D.G.'s face. Even when taking Peter and Danny's orders, his flicked back to the D.G.

His first experience of dealing with a big wig?

But there was hatred in those eyes too.

Well, those from poorer backgrounds never had much time for those who exuded wealth and privilege. But still...

The metal doors leading into the kitchen slammed open and the young Pakistani waiter seemed to almost stagger through. Suddenly the meanderings of his unconscious exploded into shattering alarm bells in his conscious mind. The tumblers started to click into place.

He was carrying the dessert menus but he was no longer slim. His body was bulked up. His eyes were wild. His white chin suggested that he'd recently shaved off his beard, possibly to help him blend in. Perspiration was streaming down his forehead.

Danny was moving before he even planned it, firing his chair back and leaping forward.

The waiter dropped the menus and his hands started to dart inside his clothing.

At that moment precise moment Danny's hands fastened on his as he leaped upwards and sideways, his legs encasing his neck in a wrestling move.

They both crashed to the floor.

Danny screamed. "Suicide bomber!"

The waiter struggled violently beneath him with incredible power, almost wriggling free.

God, he was slipping out of his grasp!

A shot rang out and the man's head exploded around Danny.

Rebecca!

Danny leapt out from under the body and whipped the voluminous clothing from around the waiter's waist.

He was wearing a thick suicide vest, packed with explosives.

"Your gun quick!" he screamed. " There's more of them." holding his hand out.

She slapped it into his hand like a nurse in an operating theatre and he spun round as the metal doors of the kitchen started to open. All he saw were two black hatred-filled eyes and he didn't hesitate, quickly firing two shots.

The doors slammed shut.

There was a moment's silence and then an enormous explosion and the metal doors flew off like missiles. Danny was knocked flat and lay there his ears ringing. One of the doors was blown out into the lobby and crashed through the front window. The other had flattened their table. Both the DG and Peter were on the ground.

Peter had been decapitated.

The D.G. crawled groggily to her feet, testing her limbs.

She spotted Peter's body lying there and groaned.

"Oh shit...Peter.... for God's sake. His wife just had a baby! Those bastards!"

Danny's ears were still ringing but he knew there might be more violence to follow. Staggering to his feet he peered carefully around the huge chasm that had once been the entrance to the kitchen. It was chaos inside with bodies everywhere.

What he took to be the second suicide bomber was lying back in the entrance. He was already with his seventy virgins. The two bullets Danny had placed in his forehead had seen to that.

As he turned he looked into the shocked eyes of one of the policemen, his weapon raised.

He saw the gun in Danny's hand and tensed.

The D.C.'s voice came sharply from the side.

"It's okay Detective Constable. Danny saved the day. Relax. Now get moving on the rescue teams and evacuate this building right away... and watch for more suicide bombers!"

After a moment's hesitation the policeman lowered his weapon and reached for his mobile phone. That alerted Danny to the cell phone that Peter had been handling.

Quickly covering Peter's top with some loose table drapes, he crawled around the area where they had been seated. It was covered with debris from the explosion.... metal pieces, chunks of masonry and wood. Eventually he found it, or what remained of it. It was completely destroyed. Smashed flat.

Later Danny sat out on the embankment side of the restaurant with Rebecca, which had been completely untouched in the explosion. The sirens were a continuous wail from the street entrance. Black smoke plumed from the building. News helicopters buzzed overhead.

The D.G. was clutching his hand almost frantically, as reaction set in, still immersed in the events that had just happened.

"How did you know?" she whispered eventually.

He shook his head.

"I don't really know. Instinct, training, conditioning, experience. Just stuff layered in that the average person wouldn't ever have accumulated. I think he chickened out in the end and had to be pushed through the doors. It happens quite a lot I'm told. I saw him stagger as he came through so I suspected there were more of them."

"Thank God for it then, wherever it comes from. Too late for poor Peter I'm afraid."

Danny stayed silent.

Eventually he stirred.

"If you hadn't acted so quickly with your gun Rebecca, it would have been curtains for all of us. How did you manage to act so fast?"

"I've worked with you Danny. I know you. You made the call and I followed without question. Thank God I did!"

--

He nodded.

"The cell phone's completely destroyed I'm afraid. We'll never know if C.C. is sitting somewhere waiting for a call. Is this now a complete dead end Rebecca?"

"Let me sort this mess out first Danny, but it probably is. You could get another cell phone of course with the same number and hope that he'll call again. Otherwise I could chase up CSIS in Canada and see if we can get some contacts in Hanlon Falls for you. At best it would probably be a wild goose chase, but..........."

"I owe Clive Courtney, big time. I don't like the idea of sitting around here hoping for a contact from him. If you can set up the contacts, I'm off to Canada."

She looked pleased.

"I thought you'd say that Danny. You remember I mentioned a quid pro quo you could do for me............."

After the medics had finished up with Danny, he looked like he'd had a bad shaving morning with a number of cuts and abrasions on his face and hands. Miraculously the D.G. had escaped any external injuries but had sustained a bruised hip and shoulder that the medics recommended she have X rayed. He borrowed her cell phone and called his ex wife Fiona at work. She worked in a fast-paced interior-decorating firm where she had recently been made a partner. She picked up right away.

"Danny, you got back in last night I believe. I was expecting your call. Allison's ecstatic at the thought of seeing you."

Allison was their ten-year-old daughter. He hesitated.

"Ah Fiona…"

"You're not going to disappoint her again are you Danny? I nearly stopped you seeing her any more after that last debacle."

He had got involved in a shoot-out resulting in two terrorist deaths on his last day out with Allison.

"It's just that…look have you watched TV in the last hour Fiona?"

There was a long silence at the other end.

"Oh shit Danny! You were involved in that? Surely not!"

"Actually yes, but you won't see any mention of my involvement in the news. I was with Rebecca, the MI5 Director and her colleague, when a suicide bomber made an attempt on her life. Luckily we foiled the attempt."

"When you say we Danny, you mean that you were in the thick of it. So what else is new?" Her voice had a bitter accusation to it. "This violence just follows you like a curse. You very nearly got Allison killed the last time, for God's sake, and I foolishly agreed to let you see her again."

She could hear him sigh.

"Yeah, you're right Fiona…look, unfortunately a guy we were having lunch with, Peter Fawcett, was killed."

A note of concern crept into her voice.

"Are you okay Danny? Were you hurt? What about Rebecca?"

"I'm okay. Just some cuts and bruises to my face and hands. I look a fright right now with the plasters that the medics stuck on.

Rebecca suffered a blow to her hip and shoulder that they say should be X-rayed, otherwise she's okay."

Her voice softened.

"I'm sorry about that chap Peter, and glad you and Rebecca are both all right. Why the secrecy about your involvement?"

"The last thing I need right now Fiona is the press camped outside my apartment and office. I asked the D.G. to keep my name out of it and she agreed. Oh, and something else has cropped up."

He went on to tell her about the cryptic message from C.C. Courtney and where they were up to when the suicide bomber struck. She was shell-shocked by the news.

"My God Danny......C.C. alive! That's mind- boggling! I know how much he meant to you in pulling you through, when you got out of the regiment. So what are you going to do? "

"Rebecca's to line up some contacts in Canada. If she's successful, I'll probably be heading out there tomorrow. Yeah, it could be a wild goose chase, but I've got to try. The thought of C.C. out there somewhere and in some need...."

"What about your insurance business and the cost of a trip to Canada? You haven't exactly invested much time in that end recently have you Danny? C.C. would be the first to tell you off about neglecting the business he left you."

She was right. A business takes constant application and focus to grow and he'd been involved in too many other issues recently.

He brightened up.

"Hey, I meant to tell you. When Rebecca was driving me in from Heathrow last night she gave me a name in MI5 to contact about their group insurance and health benefits plan which is up for renewal. I made a call to one of the companies that we have a broker's agency with, and they're going to put a team in there to try and get it. That would be a biggie and could lead to other opportunities. Imagine having MI5 as a client Fiona."

She laughed, despite herself.

"Talk about the luck of the Irish! You almost got blown up and here you are talking about some big insurance deal. Anyway Danny, what are your plans for this evening? Are you coming out to see Allison? Who knows how long this Canadian trip will take."

Not one to look a gift horse in the mouth, he said "yes," counting his lucky stars as he did so.

# Chapter 5

When Fiona opened the door her hand flew to her face and she stepped back.

"My God Danny, you look a mess! All those cut to your face." She looked down. "Your hands too! Even in the military, you never came home looking like that."

He made a face.

"The truth is Fiona, no one's safe any more with those maniacs on the loose. I used to get on a plane with my mates and go over there and take out a whole bunch of them. Now they're over here."

Just then ten-year-old Allison charged through the doorway and threw her arms around him. Just as quickly she jumped back and looked up at his face.

"Daddy what's happened to you? You're scratched and cut all over."

"I had an accident Sweetheart, but nothing serious, okay?"

You can't fool a smart ten year old and she was smart. She cocked her head, a calculating look creeping across her freckled face.

"More terrorists I bet," she said matter of factly. "I hope you killed them all."

Fiona gasped. "Allison, how could you say that?"

"Well last time I was there when they tried to kill Daddy, they were shooting at him. I'm glad he killed them or I wouldn't have a Daddy right now."

She grabbed his hand.

"Come on Daddy, I want to show you what I did in school today."

He tried to look suitably helpless as she dragged him off, actually delighted to be taken away from Fiona's accusing eyes.

Later after he'd tucked Allison into bed and read her a good night story, he plopped down in the kitchen with Fiona.

She pushed a glass of wine across the table.

"Sorry Danny, no beer, this will have to do."

He took a large mouthful and sighed.

"God, I'm ready for that Fiona. What a day!"

"Yeah, not every day you kill a suicide bomber here in the U.K. It could only happen to you Danny. You walk away from all that action in the regiment, into Civvy Street, and this stuff just follows you around like a plague. It's unbelievable! I bet Rebecca is feeling it right now. Shooting that suicide bomber and then seeing her colleague's head blown off. You don't just walk away from that unscathed do you?"

He nodded.

"Even guys in the military find it difficult Fiona. You do pay a price sooner or later. Most of us just park the experience and try to come to terms with it later. A lot of guys struggle with it. Look at all the ex military who top themselves after getting out. The demons just stay with them."

She looked directly across at him.

"What about you Danny? The demons still there?"

He wondered if he should fudge the question, but she knew him too well.

"Want the truth Fiona?" he asked.

"Of course."

He hesitated, trying to find the words.

"You know, when you first get out of the Forces you feel as if you've entered an alien planet. I'm sitting in a pub and looking around at what appears to me to be a whole slew of feeble, soft, pathetic individuals talking about completely inane things. As far as I can make out, they haven't a clue as to what us military guys were doing out there: our lives on the line every day, away from our families and comfortable, safe environments. Then I go down to the job center and some vacuous nitwit starts blathering on about my lack of real experience that would attract employers. I've sat there in a pub many times suffused with a growing rage and feeling like taking out the whole goddam bunch of them!"

"Jesus Danny, you never told me about that! Aren't there counseling programs in the Forces to help you through it. Sounds like you were a walking time bomb!"

He nodded grimly.

"The counseling doesn't amount to much Fiona. I can tell you there's hundreds just like me out there. Okay, from what I just said you can gather that I miss the regiment.... the action.... heading out with my mates on a mission...the adrenalin rush, that you get when you jump out of a plane or chopper, and you know that your life is on the line. The smell of gunpowder and the buzz when you have a close call. There's no feeling like it! You're never more alive than right then! The team work, as you cover each other's butts and tackle enormous odds and come out on top. Living life on the edge. You wanted the truth Fiona, and there it is."

She sat back as if he'd slapped her in the face

"Oh my God Danny! I should never have forced you to get out of the 'Sass', should I?"

"You were right to give me that ultimatum. I'd probably be dead by now if you hadn't and I'd never have seen Allison grow up. I'm just telling you that I miss the action and today I only did what I've been programmed for, and I hate to say it but I enjoyed taking those two terrorists out."

She shook her head soberly.

"And you trying to work as an insurance broker. God help you Danny. I hope you can make the switch because sooner or later these pent-up feelings you have, will kill you, the way you're going, and where will young Allison be then?"

They sat there quietly sipping the wine, both of them lost in their own thoughts.

Then she sat up.

"Danny, I thought Clive Courtney or C.C. as you call him, helped you with this stuff in your background."

"Yes he did some super work with me. However it was initially to come to terms with my anger and hatred of my stepfather, who I blamed for my mother's death. C.C. maintained that was what was driving my violent streak in the Forces. Taking it out on legitimate military missions that allowed me to wreak havoc on others without any repercussions. I did, with his help, come to terms with all the people I'd killed, sometimes boy soldiers all doped up and coming at us with machetes. I found a place of peace within myself and put that part behind me."

She looked doubtful.

"It hasn't stopped you killing people though."

He made a face.

"Okay, fair point. I was quite confused for a while about still using violence, until people I'd come to love and respect were placed in danger and I was their only hope. I somehow rose to the occasion and in using my old skills I realized that I had a gift that I could and should use in helping people.

That I had a responsibility to use those gifts. In fact, I discovered that without the ra, ra build-up to a military mission, I was even more effective and efficient."

"Some gift! Efficient at killing people, you mean?" she pointed out remorselessly.

He shrugged.

"I'm not a killer Fiona. I don't revel in terminating people. I'd avoid it if I could. However there are some evil people out there who won't be stopped any other way, like those suicide bombers today. Did you ever hear that story of the sheep and the wolves?"

She shook her head.

"Nope, but I'm sure you're going to tell me."

"Okay here it is. Over ninety percent of human beings are sheep, incapable of looking after and protecting themselves. About two percent of humans have the qualities of a sheepdog, where their sole role and gratification is looking after sheep. Then there are the wolves that are driven to attack and take pleasure in destroying the sheep. In one sense the sheepdogs and wolves share a common aggression, but the wolves' nature is warped. They just want to kill for the sake of killing."

She interrupted him.

"Let me guess. The sheepdogs are the soldiers and the wolves are the bad guys, like your suicide bombers today. Right?"

"Spot on. The soldiers are those people who can walk into the very bowels of hell, risking everything to protect their fellow human beings. Warriors in other words."

Finally she grinned and reached across, touching his hand.

"And you're our warrior Danny. Allison's and mine. We can always rely on you, I know."

That's what he liked about her. She didn't stay moody for long.

This time she changed the topic.

"I'd love to be a fly on the wall at security in Heathrow tomorrow, when you roll up. You'll be lucky if they let you on board looking the way you do."

He reached for his wallet, extracted a card and showed it to her.

"Rebecca's given me an MI5 identity card so I think my battered appearance might just intrigue the airline people to no end."

"Why would she do that? C.C's re-appearance has nothing to do with the Intelligence Service, has it?"

"Oh, she has a little task for me to do in Vancouver.... a quid pro quo she calls it. I have a feeling I just might enjoy it."

# Chapter 6

Langley, Virginia

Bret Zeitner was hanging up the phone in his fourth floor office when his PA Jean Haycock, stuck her head round the door. She was a wiry thirty-eight year old brunette

"Steve Walchuk's here Sir."

He grunted in frustration at the pile of unfinished folders on his desk, all with 'urgent' stickers fastened to them.

He was expecting Walchuk but had hoped to be further along. Jean smiled seeing his annoyance at the interruption, even though it was expected.

"Yeah, show him in Jean," he grunted.

A moment later a tall, lean, bespectacled, fiftyish individual strode into the room and grasped Zeitner's hand limply.

Zeitner, in his short acquaintance with the man had categorized him as a potentially bad enemy to make. His watchful, steel-gray, hooded eyes looked more like those of a mafia accountant than a man who was responsible for a big chunk of the Middle East CIA operations.

Now he sat down in a chair in front and spun it round until he was practically alongside Zeitner, who never like people coming that close.

He also knew that Walchuk never made social visits.

Chit chat was out too.

"What you got Steve?" he asked, his mind still stuck on the now closed file in front of him.

Walchuk slapped a picture down in front of him.

"This man, Danny Quigley. I believe you had some dealings with him."

Suddenly alert, Bret leaned forward, looking down at the picture, even though he already knew the answer to the unspoken question.

He did indeed know Quigley. He wondered at the extent of Walchuk's knowledge.

"Dealings? In what way?" he asked.

"Dammit man, you bumped into him in New York State a short while ago. Two of your colleagues mentioned it in some conversation they had. Strangely, they've both disappeared since. Dropped completely off the radar. How's the investigation going, by the way? Any clues as to what's happened to them?"

"Nooo…. not so far. I agree it's strange, both disappearing at once. Last seen by myself heading for Detroit airport. They never arrived. The investigation is still on going. I'm in touch on a regular basis with the FBI unit who is responsible for the case. Oh and yes, as you say, I did meet Quigley once in New York

State. His picture had popped up on the cameras at Pearson airport in Toronto, and he was flagged as someone connected to MI5 in London. I'd lost a good friend in London the week before... killed by a rogue CIA Security individual, and when Quigley turned up in New York State I made a point of contacting him. I wanted to find out if he knew anything about his death."

"And did he? Know anything that is? Not that that bitch Fullerton-Smythe in London would give away anything."

Zeitner suppressed a grin. He's always had an excellent relationship with the MI5 official and had enjoyed her cooperation on a number of occasions, though MI6 was his main intelligence source in the U.K.

He didn't know where this was going but he wanted the man out of his office as fast as possible.

"Quigley knew nothing and I believed him. He was in New York State to see some friends and dropped in on an old Delta buddy from Afghanistan. There was nothing sinister about his presence there as far as I could see." He spread his hands.

"That's all I can say Steve. Where is this leading to anyway?"

Walchuk got up and began pacing round the room. Zeitner started to worry.

He waited.

Finally the man paused in front of his desk and stared down at him.

"Bret, I'm aware that you know about the nuclear device that ended up in the Iraqi desert. Mossad hauled it out of there during the last week."

Zeitner looked shocked. "I thought that was compartmentalized...eyes only. How did you find out?"

"I'm the Middle East CIA chief for Christ sake! What made you think you could keep that from me?"

Bret shrugged. "That's the way Mossad wanted to play it. The incident was buried as far as they were concerned. Not my job to reason why."

"Well, it's not buried." Walchuk snarled. "Not by any means."

"Okay, let's have the rest of it. You're not known for your chit chat Steve."

"Quigley was there, in the desert when they extracted that sucker. That's the problem."

Bret chuckled. "A bigger problem if he wasn't there. He was the only one who knew the location of that 'sucker' as you call it. He took the Israelis right to the spot. Where's the problem."

Walchuk avoided his eyes for the first time.

"The people behind the whole thing, who organized it in the first place.... they're concerned," he said lamely.

"Those faceless people in the previous administration you mean, who dreamed up this debacle in the first place? Plant a nuclear device in Iraq and suddenly the threatened legal case by Saddam's daughter in the International Criminal Court would go away. Causing an illegal war, looking for non-existent WMD's and murdering her father and brothers. They should have been more concerned when they started this whole stupid illegal and reckless adventure. What are they concerned about now?" he demanded harshly.

"Quigley."

Zeitner looked startled. "Quigley! Why for Pete's sake?"

"He's a loose cannon. A civilian at that, and right now he's going out with a journalist in London. That's why they're concerned and so they should be."

Zeitner looked bewildered.

"This guy's no loose cannon! I've met him for God's sake. He's ex-Special Forces who has signed the U.K.'s Official Secrets Act so he's well versed in keeping secrets. Anyway, he would have spilled his guts by now if he was going to talk."

"The Official Secrets Act only covers his military actions. This operation in the desert has happened to Quigley as a civilian" Walchuk retorted.

Zeitner stood up, towering over the smaller man.

"So what are you proposing," he asked pensively.

Walchuk looked around furtively, then leaned forward.

"He needs to be terminated, and soon."

"Terminated! You got to be kidding!"

"Not for a moment my friend…and you're going to see to it personally."

Zeitner lifted both hands in the air

"Aha…no way Jose. I don't authorize something like this unless the proper oversight committee signs it off. You can take your little schemes somewhere else Walchuk. I'd be crazy to get involved in this."

Walchuk grinned. He was like a viper before it struck.

"I have recordings of your men before they disappeared. The information on there would make you the number one suspect. In any event you'd be suspended from your present role, and whatever happens, your career would be finished. Now, Zeitner, have I got your attention?"

"You absolute total bastard!"

"Yes, but you knew that before I came in didn't you, and you know I'll carry through on my threat. Now I'm going to hand Quigley on a platter to you. He's on a flight from London to Vancouver as we speak. We still access those Canadian bound flight records through the back door. Much easier to dispose of him in Canada than trying to get to him in the U.K. Now, here's the flight details and I want to be kept in the picture.... and I want action soon. I've even got you some assets."

With that Walchuk turned, opened the door wide, and gestured to someone outside.

When Zeitner saw who was coming into his office, he gasped.

"Pierre La Fonte! Where did this maggot crawl out from? How the fuck did he get inside this building?"

"I see you remember Pierre. Not a nice name you called him. 'Maggot,' you said. He's a bad man to get on the wrong side of, as you may recall."

"Who wouldn't? We kicked him out of the CIA and then for no reason that I can understand, the DEA takes him on. I heard he's now killing more people on the Mexican border than the Cartels!"

Walchuk gave a wolfish grin.

"Pierre has his uses, and with being a French Canadian he can fit nicely into that Vancouver initiative. Eh Pierre?"

La Fonte had stood still during this short interaction. Probably the most notable characteristic about him was his black eyes that had the dead look of a shark. Rumored to be the offspring of an Indian and a French Canadian trapper in Quebec he had a lean coiled body that looked ready to strike, and shoulder length black greasy hair.

Bret knew that he looking at a stone cold killer.

La Fonte now moved his eyes up Zeitner's body slowly as if measuring him for something. Then he thrust his head forward. His voice had a wheezy, hoarse sound to it, as if talking was a great effort.

"Not a nice way to start a relationship Mister CIA man," he whispered. "I don't forget easy... but we got some work to do first...yeah?" He threw a card on the desk. "Here's my contact details. I understand there's people who want this wrapped up fast, so I'll await your call." He looked around. "I don't want to have to come back into this crappy place again."

There was an implied threat in the remark.

He turned and left with Walchuk right behind him.

Zeitner sat there for a long time, staring down at the picture on his desk.

Jean stuck her head round the door.

"Coffee Sir?" she asked.

He looked up. "Yes, and lots of it... please..."

As she disappeared, he put the picture down slowly.

"Quigley, you have no idea what's coming your way, you poor bastard," he muttered."

# Chapter 7

Vancouver, British Columbia (Present time)

Anne Fullerton dreaded going into this eight-grade class, the last on a Friday afternoon. She wasn't the only teacher in the High School to feel that way.

The school was in a deprived area of the city and full of the children of emigrants, some who should have been in juvenile prison rather than wasting educational resources. There were a lot of good kids as well, who wanted what Canada had to offer, and had been told by their parents that education was the key to success in their new country.

It was the small remnant of troublemakers who made their lives a misery, not only in the classroom but out in the hallways as well, and after school was over.

When Anne had told her sister, Rebecca Fullerton-Smythe of her plans to be a replacement teacher for a year in Vancouver, she had been delighted for her.

Still recovering from a divorce, and a marriage that was a mistake from day one, Anne, an attractive, slender, 26 year old, had hoped for a fresh start. There was a quirky, night club British look to her, and her bouncing dark curls made her look more like a model than a teacher.

Now, going into her last class of the day, she wondered if she would even survive it.

She looked down at the group and groaned inwardly.

They were both there!

She had hoped they might have skipped the last period, as they often did.

Trying to start on a positive note, she broke into a big smile and sang out.

"Good afternoon...how are we all? Looking forward to the weekend?"

There was a muted response from the class.

A number of them glanced behind where the two sat together at the back.

'Oh, Oh' she thought. ' Something's up.'

As she reached into her briefcase for her lesson plans for the day, there was a shout in broken English from the back of the class.

"Hang on teach! We haff better idea."

With that the two in the back row jumped up and started sauntering down the center of the classroom.

They were both big.

One was originally from somewhere in Romania, who had adopted the English sounding name of Troy. He was squat and muscular with a gypsy look about him, and long black greasy hair. From the glazed look in his eyes, Anne felt sure that he was on something.

The other was a solid, black youth from Barbados, called Spenser, whose mother had come to Canada as a domestic and then managed to get favorable emigration status and brought her husband and two kids to the country as well. Rumor had it that his family were related to a major crime family back in Barbados and the new emigrants were already getting into the massive drug scene in British Columbia.

Neither wanted to be in school and wanted nothing better than to be expelled

Chuckling they both advanced on Anne, forcing her to back up against the blackboard. She shrank as the Romanian reached forward and laid his hand on her shoulder.

Spenser scuttled forward.

"Yeah man, do her! Do her good!."

Troy reached forward with the other hand and grabbed her breast.

She opened her mouth to scream.

Suddenly a loud voice intruded from the side.

"Well, well, it looks like I'm just in time for my portion of the class."

The class looked up and saw him standing there, a tall rugged-looking character, with a scratched face, casually dressed, not to mention jet-lagged and slightly pissed off.

The two youths jumped back and swung their eyes round.

Danny smiled at them.

"I'm the replacement science teacher and I'm delighted to see that you two lads have come forward to volunteer for this portion of the class. It's about the use of fulcrums and leverage. The theory of science shows that if you have the correct leverage you can move anything, even the world.... for example;"

He stepped forward between the two startled youths and, reaching forward, grasped Troy's hand. The youth tried to pull it back but Danny clamped his grip down on the hand and turned sideways, twisting the wrist and bringing the Romanian down to his knees with a howl of pain.

He turned towards the class, still smiling and speaking loudly

"Observe closely. I'm holding him with just one hand. As I said, the power of leverage. Very important as you'll discover in your science projects."

He gave a twist on the wrist. "You can feel that can't you?" he asked the youth on his knees.

The Romanian muttered something.

"Sorry I didn't hear that. What did you say?" twisting the wrist again.

"Yes, I feel" he howled.

"Would you like me to stop?" Danny asked.

"Yes, yes!" he screamed.

"You're going to have to ask your teacher nicely first. Say 'please teacher, ask him to let me go,'" twisting the wrist again.

The Romanian turned his head sideways towards Anne.

"Teacher please ask... he let me go," he howled.

He did let him go with a slight nudge of my knee sent the poorly balanced thug sprawling back on the floor.

As he turned his attention to the black youth, he obviously decided he wasn't waiting for the same treatment by launching a massive right hand at Danny's head.

The class shouted a warning. The punch never landed. Somehow, Spenser ended up standing on his tiptoes as an immensely painful finger lock was applied to his joint. He danced around the stage screeching in pain.

Danny started singing a dance tune "da, da, da, da, da, da, da…."

Danny looked down at the class.

"Come on join in and help him to dance." he shouted.

In a moment the whole class was chanting 'da da' and laughing as he brought Spenser tripping around the stage on his tiptoes to the sound of music.

He stopped suddenly and looked at the youth.

"Let's see how high you can get your voice. Now I want you to say to your teacher in the highest voice you can manage. "I don't want to dance anymore. Understand?"

"Please teacher, I don't want…"

"Higher voice than that" he demanded. "Higher" applying painful pressure and lifting him still higher on his toes.

His voice was shrill this time. Like a choirboy.

"Please teacher… stop him… I don't want to dance anymore."

Danny let him go and he flopped to his knees holding his hand.

The Romanian was struggling to his feet. Then they both turned and scuttled for the classroom door.

Danny swung round to the class.

"I hope you enjoyed the science class demonstration. After your teacher finishes classes today I'm training her for the weekend in using these leveraging techniques, so be very nice to her in future. You hear me?"

Anne clapped her hands.

"Go and have an early break and enjoy your weekend. Go!"

As they scattered out of the classroom, she turned and looked at him.

"Danny Quigley, I presume? My sister warned me about you! By the way did you know we're not allowed to lay a hand on pupils in Canada?"

"I guess that works two ways. They can't touch you either," he countered.

Anne reached forward and gave him a massive hug.

"Welcome to Canada, Danny. I'm glad you're here."

# Chapter 8

There was an exciting air to Vancouver whose reputation had gained immeasurably from the hugely successful Winter Olympics, and the restaurants were just one part of it.

Anne had taken him to one of her favorite spots, a steak house downtown, and afterwards to her apartment near the Stanley Park area. Not having checked into a hotel as yet, she insisted that he use the pull down settee in her lounge for the weekend.

She surprised him when she went to her fridge and produced a bottle of Stella beer.

"Rebecca told me that the SAS lads all drink this."

He laughed. "You two must have had quite a chat Anne. Anyway it's some time since I was in the regiment."

She raised her eyebrows. "Could have fooled me with how you handled those thugs back there in the classroom. Science teacher indeed! I dread to think how I'm going to explain this to the Principal if she gets a whiff of it, or the parents of those two boys!"

"Boys! I hardly think so. More like two young animals" he rejoined, taking a long drag from the can of beer.

"Well, I certainly liked your animal training skills. Everything but a whip. Liked your child psychology too. I doubt that those two will ever be back after you humiliated them in front of the class. That suits me fine. Oh, and the final touch at the end, when you told the class you were going to train me in the same tactics. Subtle has nothing on you Danny."

He took a half bow but was starting to feel that wave of fatigue that was part of a flight to the west coast, which was 9 hours behind U.K. time.

He must be getting old.

Anne was a lively attractive young woman and he was looking forward to spending some time with her over the weekend, and seeing more of the beautiful city, while he organized his trip into northern British Columbia and Hanlon Falls.

He had to admit he was wired to appreciate beautiful women.

At the same time he had to confess that he'd moved beyond hitting on anything in a skirt for his own gratification. Presently he had a relationship going with Jackie back in London, that was showing promise and a casual 'Now and then' relationship with Siobhan, who lived in Ireland. Oh, and yes, an Afghan girl, who stole his heart and whose name he wouldn't even mention.

So, while Anne was transmitting lots of positive body language that she liked him and that things could develop, the jet lag had started hitting him in waves and he began wishing that he'd gone straight to a hotel from the restaurant. No doubt she was grateful that he'd intruded in a potentially nasty situation back in the school.

He was running these thoughts through his mind when the phone rang.

Anne picked it up.

"Hello"

She listened for a moment and her eyes turned to him.

"It's my sister Rebecca in London. She needs to speak to you urgently, she says," handing the phone over.

He knew something was wrong when he heard the clipped voice at the other end.

"Danny? Listen carefully. Two things… both bad. First, I had an e-mail sent to my personal computer that said 'Quigley has been targeted. Tell him to watch his back in Van', obviously meaning Vancouver, so some organization knows of your movements."

"That was it?" he interrupted. "Nothing else?"

"Nothing else Danny I'm afraid. No name, no source, nothing. However we ran a trace downstairs on the email and it had been sent from an Internet café in Washington, D.C."

"Washington! Who would want to target me in Washington? Rebecca, how many people know your personal e-mail address?"

"Well, not too many as such. My family and friends have a separate e-mail for contact, so you're only talking MI5 business contacts."

"So you're talking the intelligence organizations, police organizations and so on.

People who have the resources to monitor flight information. But why me right now? I'm only on a personal trip to locate a missing friend" Danny exclaimed in frustration.

"I have no idea Danny, but my next piece of news is equally disquieting. Your friend Jackie was mowed down by a car in a hit and run, when she came out of her office after work. She's in a coma right now and the prognosis isn't good. I'm sorry. It happened about three hours ago but I just heard about it. When the news mentioned a Daily Mail journalist had been involved in a hit and run, I checked further and discovered that it was Jackie. I'm going straight round there after this call and will get back to you with an update."

Danny wasn't aware that he had jumped to his feet.

"Rebecca, what's going on here? I just don't understand this."

"I don't either, but both of these incidents must be connected. You've been warned about being targeted and your girl friend is run down. Both of you must know something that's threatening someone or some group. I organized police security in the hospital 24/7 since I made the connection. You may want to postpone your trip into the interior and come back here. Remember I set up that contact with CSIS in Vancouver, who would have facilitated your next step. There's only one more thing I want to say Danny, and don't take this personally. Right now, get as far away and as fast as you can from my sister. Your female friends just don't seem to live very long and I don't want anything to happen to her. Are you hearing me?"

He didn't remember how the call finished. His head was spinning!

Anne took the phone from him and he heard a low murmur of conversation in the background as she talked with her sister.

He sat there in shock. Jackie in a coma! Stuck by a hit and run vehicle! But why? What did they both know that threatened anyone or any organization?

It just didn't make any sense... and he had been targeted! For what? Another hit and run? Some hit man from Washington coming after him?

His immediate reaction was to get back out to the airport and head back to the U.K. There he could monitor Jackie's condition and equally have Rebecca organize some protection for him until he better understood the threat level.

On the other hand...

# Chapter 9

Flashback - Afghanistan

In daylight twelve hours later, the Column sliced through some thick wooded countryside at the base of the mountain and paused momentarily as they hurled their gear out of the back of the LAV. They scurried around dragging their kit and weapons back in behind some brush as the packet motored off out of sight.

Then they waited. Danny swept the area with his binos.

Had their drop-off been spotted?

If there were watchers, would they buy the apparent mini detour of the Column as some sort of defensive maneuver with no serious implications?

Nothing moved. Finally they stirred.

The plan was to head up this side of the mountain in daylight, rest for a couple of hours at the top and carry on down the mountain to arrive, hopefully, in the pre-dawn darkness.

Without any conversation Abdul, the translator, Scotty and Danny pulled on their packs and the rest of their gear. Both Scotty and Danny carried their own weapons, ammo, food and water, while Abdul carried the extra weapons and spare ammo, grenades plus his own food and water.

He was also responsible for the medical kit, raingear for the three of them, spare tarpaulins for shelter and some extra jackets to change into should they get drenched.

Many an operation fell apart when the elements cut loose and members ended up frozen and wet without any change of clothing and no opportunity in enemy territory to start a fire to dry out. Scotty was probably loaded down the most with weapons, the radio and his crossbow, but he was the first on his feet and heading up into the thick brush and shale of the mountain.

Carrying heavy bergens (packs), were old hat to the SAS who were initiated on the Brecon Beacons mountains in Wales, in mind-numbing exercises that broke even the toughest of applicants to the regiment and sent them bruised and sometimes broken, back to their units.

Nevertheless, it still took some time to adjust to the heavy weight and the straps that started cutting into shoulders after only a short distance.

Danny wondered how their translator Abdul would cope, but he was on his feet and moving smartly after Scotty.

He hoped he could keep up the pace.

Danny adjusted a few more straps and fell in behind him.

The terrain maps they had looked at indicated that it was about three to four miles to the top of the mountain, and assuming that they could maintain a direct route, they should be able to make it to the top in five to six hours. This meant traveling carefully and keeping a sharp lookout for insurgents or even sheepherders who could be posted on the mountain. If the mission was blown too soon they would have no option but to withdraw back down the mountain and get extracted.

A further complication was that if they encountered any enemy fighters and had to kill them, they would probably be missed very quickly and the alarm would go up. Encountering non-combatants, such as sheepherders presented an additional dilemma. Even out in the ancient hills of Afghanistan, the insurgents had mastered the use of satellite cell phones and could respond rapidly to any threat.

The first hour went smoothly as they headed up a gradually steepening terrain between large trees and brush with the ground slippery under their feet from recent rain. Then it started to change to rock and shale and Danny caught up on Abdul, who was showing signs of fatigue.

Scotty looked back and Danny indicated that they take a short break and melted down behind a group of fallen rotting trees.

"Hey, you okay Abdul?" he asked quietly as he came up to him.

He looked around and grinned.

"Yeah, no sweat. Just not used to these damn packs."

Abdul was an interesting character. He had a sharp aquiline face and dark intelligent eyes. You had to listen hard to detect an accent in his English. He had emigrated to Canada as a six year old and had graduated from high school. Brought up on the old stories of Afghanistan from his father and his own childhood memories, and despite the fact that he had a wife and two children in Toronto, he had opted to go back and contribute what he could to the problems of the country. Still speaking the Afghan language, he had been snapped up by Ottawa as a translator to accompany the Canadian Forces mission.

Now a year into the assignment, he had volunteered to lead the NATO mission into his old village and rescue the prisoners.

Danny hoped Abdul could make it up over the mountain and down the other side. He squatted down beside him and adjusted some of the straps on his pack.

"Scotty and I have a masters degree in carrying these damn things. Basically, you have to ignore the pain and focus on putting one foot in front of the other. Sure you're okay? We have to keep moving Abdul, I'm afraid."

"Yeah, I'm good. I'm fit enough really. Played soccer in high school. I've even done some hiking. I just find I need some time to settle in and get my wind. Course I've never carried this much weight before either. What do I call you anyway? When I'm with the Canadians I usually call people by their rank, especially the officers."

He laughed. "Call me Danny, and that's Scotty ahead. In our regiment, rank isn't very important. It's being there when you need someone to back you up or bail you out that's important. Speaking of which lets move out, and stay alert for any enemy movement."

It got steeper and harder and the wet slippery ground didn't help. Both Abdul and he stumbled a number of times and occasionally fell to their knees.

The shale surface made tricky going.

The brush got thicker, and up ahead, Scotty had started to take a number of short detours to avoid having to claw his way through it. At one point they came to a hundred foot stone hill and had to skirt around it for a quarter mile, before they could head up again.

At the two-hour point Scotty pointed to a rock overhang that provided some cover and in a few moments all three of them had pulled off their packs and were digging out water bottles and power bars.

Conscious of how voices could carry, they huddled close and spoke in whispers.

Scotty leaned in close to Abdul.

"When you were a kid did anyone come up this mountain?" he asked.

"No, not really. There were a lot of old wives' tales about the mountain. We were told that bad people lived up here in caves and would devour us if we wandered up. I suspect it was really designed to keep us away from some dangers on the mountainside. When I was back a month ago I saw that on the other side of the mountain, near the village, brush and trees had been cleared to make more grazing areas."

Danny thought about that. "We could be spotted then coming into the village."

Abdul shook his head.

"This is one of those Afghan villages where a number of houses are built into the side of the mountain and my cousin's house is one of them. You basically climb over a mud wall and step off the mountain into their top story. Down below on the lower level is where they sometimes bring in some animals at night. So access will be relatively easy, however we have to find out where the prisoners are being held and that's where exposure could be a big problem."

Scotty had some strong views on the country and the people and Danny was hoping that he would keep them to himself.

He should have known better.

Scotty turned to Abdul.

"So how do you feel about us, the infidel, being here in your country?"

Abdul turned slightly towards him as if trying to read beyond the words from his body language. Finally he grimaced.

"Well, let me give you one insight. The Canadians at an FOB (Forward Operating Base) laid on what they call a VMO, a village medical outreach, and brought in a number of doctors, nurses and even veterinarians for the day. Hundreds of men and boys turned up for treatment but not a single woman was allowed. That's what I want to help change in my country and I know that as long as the Taliban are in charge, it won't happen."

He paused for a moment. "Oh, and they treated a large number of animals as well at the VMO."

"And no women at all." Scotty murmured thoughtfully.

Abdul nodded. "I was back in my village recently visiting my cousin before the Taliban swept in and occupied it. My cousin suddenly tore into his wife, shouting and screaming at her. She stood there totally humiliated, saying nothing. Then he went across, slapped her face twice and shoved her out the door. And hear this. Then he sat down beside me smiling and saying "stupid woman!"

He was silent for a long moment.

"I could have killed the bastard right there. However I remembered the dignified way that people in Canada treated their wives and families and I resolved to do all I could in the short time I'd be here, to change the attitudes of my countrymen. Sure, it will take time but, you know, we have to start somewhere... Does that answer your question Scotty?"

Danny raised his eyebrows at him.

Scotty looked at him for a long moment. Then he reached forwards and squeezed his shoulder.

"Yeah, it does Abdul. Thanks."

'Hmmm....' Danny thought. 'Some sound bite!'

With that, Scotty stood up and, pulling on his pack, strode off ahead, leaving them struggling to get their packs on and catch up.

They slogged on. It didn't get any easier. There were no natural paths or animal trails that might have provided a respite to plowing their way through waist-high brush and at times, needle-sharp briars. Danny spelled Scotty twice as they struggled upwards and he fell back into the rear position. Abdul, though his face reflected distress and agony at times, maintained a measured if stumbling pace, and never complained, even when Scotty bitched about the conditions during one of the short breaks.

They were near the top, with Danny in the lead, when he smelled it.

Smoke…tobacco smoke he suspected.

He threw a warning sign back down towards the two men and they sank to the ground.

Crouching low he slipped off his pack and stuck the SOCOM pistol into his belt, then crept forward, picking his route to provide the maximum concealment possible.

It was only a hundred yards or so to the top, but it was an hour before he carefully parted some brush and peered through into what was a small clearing.

He heard them before he saw them: three turbaned Afghans, sitting on a bench outside a small make-shift shanty, with a tattered strip of plastic and branches on top for shelter. Three AK-47's were leaning against the bench as the men chattered away, smoking up a storm.

Terrorist sentries.

Not very good ones at that, but a problem nonetheless.

It wasn't a fresh position that would have indicated that they had spotted the Column dropping us off earlier and were expecting them.

What to do?

No problem killing them, but that could blow the mission. Their replacements might already be on the way up or they might be required to check in regularly, using a cell phone.

He slipped quietly back down the hillside making much better time on his return trip.

When he filled them in, Scotty pulled out the map and laid out some rocks to keep it flat. He did a quick GPS satellite reading as well.

He finally looked up.

"Here's the thing. We're on track so far but the only way now is to detour round those guys, at least a quarter mile or even more to avoid them and any Taliban coming up to replace them. It sounds like they've got pretty sloppy up there, so that's in our favor. I'd guess they might be the only patrol up here. What do you think Danny?"

He nodded. "That would be my take on the situation too. Nevertheless we need to be extra vigilant moving out of our present position. One of them could wander over to the edge of the clearing for a leak, and through sheer bad luck, spot us. So let's watch our step…no falls…try to avoid leaving tracks in muddy places in case those guys wander out into the brush sometime. Let's go."

Collectively they held their breath as they retreated sideways away from that position.

Thankfully, there was no outcry and no AK-47 blasting through the shrubbery at them. Also, when they worked their way further around the mountain they found the going easier when they started back up and over the mountaintop.

They lucked in shortly after that in finding shelter under a group of fallen trees that were well hidden behind some high brush. They intended to have some grub and grab some sleep before heading down the mountainside.

The actual rescue still lay ahead and each of them recognized that they would need more than continued good luck to pull this off.

# Chapter 10

Danny had agreed to meet the CSIS agent in a deck restaurant at the back of one of the major downtown hotel chains. It looked out on the massive Vancouver harbor with mountain ranges reaching for the sky in the distance. He was standing there watching some small floatplanes taking off when he became aware of a figure approaching.

"Impressive view isn't it?" the man asked.

He nodded turning, seeing a tall, slim, black man standing there, with his hand out.

"Wow! It sure is!" Grasping his hand. "I guess you're Leroy Hesseltine. I'm Danny Quigley. Yeah, it's something else."

The man laughed. "You're not alone. Most tourists go gaga, when they see this first. Anyway, you're not here as a tourist are you? Let's go sit down and have a chat."

They moved over to a corner away from a mixture of business and tourist guests and ordered a drink from the waitress.

Danny decided to try for a good cup of tea, When it arrived, he poured it out expecting to be disappointed.

Hesseltine noticed his look of surprise.

"It's the English influence around Vancouver and Victoria. They know how to make a good cup of tea for sure. The Brits flock here for the mild weather. Unfortunately it attracts a lot of undesirables as well - the panhandlers as they're called. So, fill me in on what your objective is out here in B.C. The MI5 director, Rebecca Fullerton-Smythe, asked for a favor in having us look after you."

Danny quickly filled in the details of his hopes for the trip.

A former colleague who had disappeared, presumably dead, had sent him a cryptic text message, and the MI5 people had indicated that it came from the B.C. interior. Hanlon Falls was the nearest town, so he intended to start there. Tenuous at best, it was all he had and needed to satisfy himself that he had done all he could to locate the originator of the message. Presumably it was from Clive Courtney, known as C.C.

Leroy listened intently, occasionally asking some questions.

He frowned finally and spread his hands.

"Most Brits don't appreciate just how big Canada is and British Columbia in particular. You could fit England into the province many times over, so that gives you some idea of how much territory we're talking about. When you say that the message came from the interior, we're talking about a massive piece of territory, a lot of it now owned by the First Nations who aren't particularly happy about the white man wandering around their space. So you can see how difficult your task is going to be. Time consuming and probably expensive as well."

"I'm not too worried about the expense Leroy, and as for time, I'd like to give it a shot. So how can you help me?"

He observed Danny for a few seconds as he drank his coffee, as if evaluating him.

Finally, he looked like he had made some sort of decision.

He pointed to the harbor.

"You saw the float planes taking off. CSIS have a rental arrangement with a local company here and we can fly you up to Hanlon Falls - tomorrow if you wish."

His face must have reflected his surprise.

"You know this isn't official intelligence work Leroy. I'm sure Rebecca made that clear. Why would you go out of your way to help me out like this?"

He thought about Danny's question as if deciding how to answer. Then,

"We have a CSIS agent in Hanlon Falls right now looking into something else. Rebecca told me some stories about an ex Special Forces character called Danny Quigley. If a quarter of what she told me is true, it's possible you can be of some assistance to us up there."

Danny shrugged. His ex-wife keeps telling him that it follows him around.

She was right and here it was again.

"Whatever, Leroy. Anyway what's the agent's name and how do I contact him?" he asked impatiently.

"Pat Tarrant, and don't worry Danny, they will contact you. Now, one thing that worries me even more than that. You're MI5 friend asked me if I could tool you up with some weapons. Apparently some people may be targeting you. I'm not even going to ask who or why. I don't want to know. However the answer is yes, with one proviso. I have to take you out to the RCMP (Royal Canadian Mounted Police), shooting range where you have to go through a vetting, familiarization and licensing procedure before I can provide you with some weapons. If the stories I've heard about you Danny are true, that shouldn't be any problem to you."

Two hours later after traveling on the main road in the direction of a town called Hope, Leroy made a right turn with the 4 wheel drive jeep and carried on for a further mile. He then pulled the vehicle off into a large parking lot in front of an oblong building. Out beyond were numerous familiar mounds that were part and parcel of any shooting range. As they stood there, they could hear the popping sounds of weapons being discharged and spotted various small groups moving out on the ranges.

Leroy nodded in their general direction as he opened the hatchback in the rear of the vehicle.

"We can move outdoors later to sight in the rifle after we get you qualified on short arms inside. Here, have a look at what I managed to scrounge up."

He lifted out a single bundle wrapped in sacking and handed it to Danny.

Special Forces guys are weapons junkies, and he couldn't help whistling when he opened it - a Winchester model 1866 rifle known as the 'Henry Repeater', which he had tried out once and absolutely loved it. He knew the caliber to be 0.44, which took a 16 round tubular magazine. It had ended up being nicknamed 'the Yellow-boy' for its distinctive brass receiver.

Leroy smiled at his reaction. "I don't know what you were expecting. You know we don't sell assault weapons in Canada, but Rebecca mentioned your sniper skills so you can probably do something with this. Oh, a further version of this rifle became 'the gun that won the west', so appropriate for you here on the west coast. We'll leave it in the car until we get you qualified on the small arms range first."

"Beautiful, just beautiful!" Danny breathed, as his hands ran up and down the historical weapon.

He looked across at him.

"Some weapon all right and I'm delighted to get my hands on it but not what a modern sniper would take into the field…. unless you can attach a scope to it."

Leroy shrugged. "I have no idea Danny. This is the only long gun I could get my hands on plus a bunch of ammo. I do have a weapon that we can't take inside but you can take with you tomorrow in the plane to Hanlon Falls."

He reached in again and produced a smaller blanket-wrapped bundle and passed it to him. Curious now, Danny placed it on the floor of the trunk and unfolded the blanket.

This was more like it.

Lying there was a Ruger MP-9mm, an updated and improved version of the Israeli Uzi, which has a detachable chrome/molybdenum steel barrel and can be fitted with a noise suppressor... a silencer. It provided great back up in a firefight with a 32-round box magazine.

"Where the hell did you pick this up?" he queried.

"British Columbia is on the receiving end of thousands of guns coming across the U.S. border all the time. The drug smugglers use them for protection. We work closely with the city police and RCMP who are frequently stopping cars and find this kinda stuff in them. No problem collecting the odd souvenir when I want to. Oh, I got lots of ammo for it too."

He glanced almost furtively around. "You didn't get these from me by the way, if you get stopped and searched. Okay?"

Danny grinned. "I seem to have traveled this route before. A deniable operation or under the radar. Yeah Leroy, I got it. Now what else have you got? I could use a pistol more than anything, if some guys are going to go for me in a city or town."

He nodded to a shoebox on the floor.

"Try that. I think you'll like it."

Danny did like it. Almost an old friend in fact. A Heckler and Koch Universal Self-Loading Pistol, 0.45 that had a 10 round box magazine capacity. It was fitted for scopes, night sights and laser spot projectors.

The U.S. Special Forces, in fact, had ordered an up-dated version of the weapon, called the SOCOM pistol, which he had used with great effect in Iraq and Afghanistan.

Leroy noticed the familiar way he caressed the weapon.

"Not a stranger to it I see" he commented.

"Yeah, I actually used the SOCOM version not too long ago. Let me tell you Leroy, they are effective!"

Leroy raised his brows. "Hmm..... I know you're out of the Forces a couple of years Danny, so I won't give into my curiosity and ask you any more questions. Now let's get you inside and get cracking. We have a time booked for a range so we'd better hustle."

In the SAS regiment they put a lot of time in using small arms...pistols and automatics, in every conceivable situation where speed and accuracy was required to achieve an outcome. They never envisaged surrendering their weapons as a solution to negotiating a hostage's release. Experience had proved this to be a 'no brainer',

So they trained to take advantage of the smallest portion of a live target and make the shot count. A 'double tap' to the head was the ideal to go for.

A suicide bomber could still detonate his vest of explosives even after a number of shots to the body. An Air Marshall had visited the regiment in Hereford and shared how to shoot a suicide bomber on a certain spot on his or her nose that killed the brain instantly and prevented them from spasmodically setting off their explosives.

Danny wasn't the best shot in his troop with a pistol, but his fast reactions compensated for that.

After he had blasted away at targets for some time, Leroy kept stacking up the targets that he was winding back on the pulley, at different ranges.

Now he brought them over, scratching his head.

"Jesus Danny, where did you learn to shoot like that? The distance doesn't seem to make any difference to you, and your speed is amazing! You hardly seem to aim at all man! And you're supposed to be a financial planner for God's sake!"

He hadn't been on a firing range since he left the regiment so he was glad to discover that he hadn't lost it. Saddened too as he recalled his last qualification with his mates around him, cat calling and pulling each other's leg.

Some ex members referred to those times as 'the best years of their lives.'

Danny hoped that wasn't true. He now looked forward to seeing his daughter Allison grow up, get married and have kids of her own, and he wanted to be a part of that without wallowing in past victories or distorted memories.

While he was shooting he was aware of people on both sides of them, separated by thick plastic sheets, all practicing with numerous handguns and concentrating on various targets and distances. At one time he heard some raised voices on one side as two men came in and claimed that the section on the right had been booked by them for that particular time slot. After some back and forth angry exchanges, the people who had been using the range left, threatening to find the range officer to sort it out.

Leroy made a face at him, but with his earplugs they couldn't hear much anyway.

A few moments later Danny removed his earplugs and leaned forward to examine the target. At that moment a shot rang out and he could literally feel a bullet brush past the back of his head.

Leroy screamed "What the fuck..."

Danny swiveled round to the side where he felt the weapon had been discharged from, and saw a face peering at him through the plastic sheeting, a weapon in his hand.

Without thinking he tore round the side of the plastic and leapt forward, grabbing the weapon from the man's hand and slamming him up against the front of the wooden window sill, his elbow on his throat.

"Just what the fuck do you think you're playing at? You almost killed me you moron!" He pushed harder.

The man gasped. Danny started to ease up.

"An accident" he wheezed.

"Yeah, some fucking accident you brainless wonder!"

Right then he felt rough hands grabbing him from the side.

The partner of the man, a tough swarthy-looking individual, stepped forward, shouting.

"Here, get your hands off him!"

Without taking his hands off the man he was holding, Danny launched a back-knuckle strike sideways catching him on the bridge of his nose, and as he staggered backwards spouting blood, he kicked backwards at his knee joint, hearing it break.

He hauled the man he was holding forward, so he could deliver some similar treatment.

Leroy's voice intruded right then as other people from the indoor range started gathering round.

"Danny, for Christ sake, let the guy go. It was an accident. Hey, ease back man!"

He looked around.

Several people were staring at him holding the man and also his injured companion, lying on the floor.

Danny eased up on him and he slipped sideways out of his grasp.

A large man in an RCMP uniform with Sergeant's stripes, pushed inside the small unit. He looked at Danny.

"Have you assaulted this man?"

"Yes, but it's because…" he started.

The Sergeant shook his head. He stepped forward and gripped his arm.

"There's no excuse for fighting in a firing range. For one thing it's downright dangerous, and for another…."

As his voice droned on Danny was aware of the man who had shot at him was marshaling some help to lift his partner, and they both staggered out the door.

He started to push forward. The Sergeant held on to him tighter.

"Look" Danny protested, "These are the two you should be talking to, they…"

Leroy butted in. "Yeah, they fired through the plastic into our side. Look!"

The Sergeant looked baffled, peering from Leroy to Danny, then went over to the plastic sheeting.

He turned to them.

"Well this needs looking into, but an assault did take place here so we need to get the details first before we do anything else. Now…."

Danny shook his head disgustedly and looked at Leroy.

"Follow those two out and get their details. Make sure you get some ID and their car number."

He looked at him blankly.

"Quick!" he insisted.

Leroy turned and ran out the door.

He was back in a moment later.

"They're gone Danny. Disappeared, just like that. That was no accident was it?"

It wasn't.

He still remembered the man's eyes. Dead eyes, just like a shark.

# Chapter 11

The Village - Afghanistan

Major Tom Duffy realized that the screams he was hearing from a great distance, through a haze of pain, were his own. The beating had lasted, it seemed, for hours. Each blow interspersed with shouted questions in broken English;

"How many villages you go?"

"How much money you bring?"

"Who get money?"

"Which villagers you work with?"

His refusals were at first strong and emphatic:

"My name is Major Duffy and my number is... Under the Geneva convention I am not required to tell you anything else."

Now they were whispered through his broken, bloodied lips like a mantra.

The three Taliban standing back by the door, holding their AK-47s were grinning as the beating progressed.

His interrogator, the one he had nicknamed 'The Crow,' because of his black turban and beak-like face, was screaming with rage, spittle flying from his mouth, his frustration increasing by the minute.

"You infidel! Invader of Afghanistan. No rights under Geneva…You die here all of you, like Russians. You speak now…no more beat."

Duffy raised his head and looked directly at him.

"Fuck you Crow" he hissed, marshaling all the strength he had before collapsing back.

The interrogator drew back his boot and kicked him several times, the thumps echoing around the room.

Just then one of the other prisoners, a lean, light-colored 30 year old, whom Duffy knew as the Provincial Police Chief Ibrahim Amin, spoke up, addressing the interrogator in Pashto.

The discourse went on for several minutes.

Then Amin, the Police Chief, switched to English and looked across at Major Duffy, his green eyes filled with concern. He spoke English in the staccato, sing song voice that some Afghans had been taught.

"Major Duffy, bad news. Tomorrow night take you across the border into Iran. This man beating you is Al Qaeda from Morocco, bad man, but not bad like Iranian jailers. You will tell everything, so save yourself all this beating. Everyone talks in the end my friend."

Duffy raised himself up defiantly, but before he could speak the police chief cut across him, speaking to the interrogator again. After listening for a moment the terrorist delivered a viscous kick to Duffy's ribs and stalked out of the room.

Duffy sat up and inched himself back painfully against the wall.

"What was that all about?" he asked, nodding at the door his interrogator had gone through.

Amin grimaced. "I told him I talk to you. Then maybe you tell him information. He come back in one hour."

Duffy groaned as he tried to find a position that would ease his bruised body.

"He'll be wasting his time Ibrahim. I won't be telling that bastard anything!"

He spat out some blood and a broken tooth.

The other man, the 50-year-old Provincial Governor Khaili Taraki, sat there, a terrified look on his face, saying nothing.

Duffy pointed to him. "What's with him?" he asked.

Amin glanced sideways at the Governor and shrugged.

"He thinks we be killed soon. Heads cut off."

He leaned forward and whispered. "He's gone a little crazy I think. Used to be a warlord one time with own militia. He knows what happen to prisoners. I think he's right. When you go, they kill us here."

Duffy writhed around trying to find a position that lessened the pain, but without success.

The Police Chief leaned forward again.

"Have you hope for rescue Major Duffy? From NATO maybe? They know where we are? Special Forces teams?" he asked.

"Not a chance Chief. It's a standoff right now. If a rescue is attempted as the Taliban have warned, we get our heads lopped off."

He looked around the room. "Ironic isn't it? I was involved in building this community center for the village and here I am, a prisoner chained to the door support that I actually measured some time back."

"The irony of Afghanistan has not escaped armies who came here in the past Major Duffy. Now can I do anything for you."

"Actually you can Chief," he said, through gritted teeth. "Tell me about Afghanistan please. Help me understand it"

The police chief looked startled.

"You lie hurt and can speak only in pain and you want history lesson! Surely you have NATO briefing on country."

Duffy nodded. "I need something to take my mind off this" he said pointing to his face and body.

A flash of understanding crossed the Amin's face.

"Ah, of course major. But you must understand that you ask six Afghans to speak this and you get six different stories. I do not claim to speak truth, only as I see it."

He eased along the wall, the common chain they shared, clanking as they moved. He finally stopped beside Duffy's sprawled form, reached behind his back with one hand, and straightening him and with the other; he held a plastic container of water up gently to his mouth.

"Try some water Major for a start. We have to get you strong before Morocco man comes back to beat you."

Duffy choked as the water entered his mouth, stinging his broken lips.

"Shit Chief, I was hit playing football many times but never like this."

He drank greedily from the container. Then pushed himself back against the wall for support.

"Okay Chief, I'm ready for class" he rasped, massaging some sore ribs as he did so.

The Chief told him the story of how the rulers of Afghanistan have always been Pashtuns; the majority of these are Sunnis. The second largest group, also Sunni, were Tajiks.

The Shias, who make up a quarter of the population, traced their ancestry to the Iranian armies who came to Afghanistan in the eighteenth century. This is why Iran supports the Shia sect and Saudi Arabia support the Sunni Walabi faith, both sides supplying a flood of financial and material support, including weapons, to whichever warlord or militia, they think will grow their influence. Both Pakistan and India have continually used Afghanistan as a battlefield in their own power struggle.

Then the Russians invaded in 1980 and the United States poured weapons and money into the Mujahidin resistance and both sides turned the country into a war zone.

According to Amin, prior to the Russians coming in, Afghanistan was starting in small ways to address some of the country's more challenging problems, and given time might have succeeded in making progress.

That all changed when the Russians invaded.

Ten years of suffering and chaos descended on the Afghan people.

Thousands, many the educated elite, fled or tried to leave the country. Those caught trying to escape were shot or thrown into prison.

The Afghan people, in their hatred of the Russians, saw the Mujahidin resistance as their saviors and supported them in any way they could.

The American CIA supplied Stinger missiles to the Mujahidin, which eventually broke the back of the Russians resolve. After ten years they left, having lost fifteen thousand soldiers and causing at least one million Afghan deaths.

The long-suffering Afghan's painful experience, however, had just begun.

The Mujahidin, vying for power, splintered into three opposing groups and all three started shelling and bombarding Kabul, reducing its buildings to rubble. The population left in droves heading on an eight-day trek to Pakistan and refugee camps. Some went on to Iran and countries in the west, those who would accept them.

The Mujahidin were then replaced by the Taliban who imposed an extreme version of Islam on the Afghan population, beating any woman who showed even an inch of skin. Women who ventured out quite often disappeared or were thrown into prison where rape and torture were commonplace.

Then Bin Laden came to the country with his followers.

Then 9/11 happened.

The U.S. with their B 52 bombers chased the Taliban out of Afghanistan, with the help of the northern alliance.

And so Afghanistan had come full circle again.

History repeating itself.

Duffy had stayed silent during Amin's staccato monologue of his country's story, staring straight ahead and listening carefully.

Now, as the Police Chief fell silent, he inched his head around and did a silent hand clap.

"If I was standing in class right now Chief, I would be clapping you. Well done and very succinctly too. Now tell me, how do you really feel about us...NATO that is and all we're trying to do?"

Amin put his head down and scratched his forehead.

Hmm......you ask a difficult one. What you try to do here is good. If you stay too long you become invaders again, and then even I will fight you. If you go too soon the Taliban will come back. What more can I say."

"What do you mean Chief by invaders?" Duffy asked, the importance of the question obvious by his sudden lurch forward.

"Look at Iraq. You have Embassy of one thousand people, the largest in the world, though your troops started pulling out at the end of two thousand and eleven. That not freedom. That's still occupation. The U.S., still protecting its interests. If that happens here, you will be my enemy and my son's enemy in ten years time."

"Christ Chief, you should be talking to the White House! What must we do then? How can we keep the support of people like you who are the future of Afghanistan? Tell me that."

"Allow us to feel that we are in control of our own destiny. Imperfect, stupid perhaps, lacking western ways. ...Let us start to stumble forwards and stand back and just be a friend. Otherwise history shows this will be your graveyard too."

Animated now, Duffy straightened further, his interest piqued.

The door burst opened as the Moroccan stormed back into the room, followed by three armed Al Qaeda.

It was the end of the history lesson.

# Chapter 12

Afghanistan - Pre-dawn

They had made excellent time going downhill wearing night vision goggles and staying alert for any movement in front or to the side.

It was 3 am when they hunkered down overlooking the village. Too late for a group nap. They had to get into the village prior to the Muezzin's call to prayer, when everything stirred.

Danny opened up the Comms to the aircraft, which by pre-arrangement, was up there monitoring them.

"Foxtrot One, this is Charlie Three. Preparing to move into village in figures two hours."

There was a double click in acknowledgment.

They planned to move down at 5am when Abdul confirmed that everyone in the village would be fast asleep, hopefully including any sentries or dogs.

Their strategy assumed that there would be outlying sentries posted in addition to those guarding the prisoners. Once they got to the perimeter of the village Danny would rid himself of his pack and slip forward, taking his knife and SOCOM pistol with the Laser Aiming Module (LAM) and Sound/Flash suppressor.

He would wear his frag vest as well.

Once the sentries were silenced they would have to move at speed to Abdul's cousin's house and find out exactly where the prisoners were being held.

Time was of the essence, as they had no idea when sentries were being replaced, after Danny took them out.

Scotty, having slimmed down his pack to essentials, stretched out and was asleep almost instantly.

Abdul watched him for a moment.

"How does he do that, before action?" he asked in a whisper.

Danny shrugged, saying nothing and started preparing mentally for the battle ahead.

He ran through all the successful actions that he'd been involved in and saw himself strong and invincible, with his superior training and experience, cutting a swathe of steel through any opposition that he came up against.

He saw Scotty alongside him, a formidable warrior, covering him as he moved forward. They couldn't afford any mistakes with a village of terrorists that could spring awake in minutes and encircle them. With only light weapons, and limited ammo, they hoped to get to the extraction site on the far side of the village without any alarm going up at all, though now that seemed highly unlikely.

Dogs were the nightmare scenario of any operation and Abdul said that there were a few in the village. Scotty might be able to use his crossbow on them, or they could use their silenced SOCOM pistols.

They moved out at 4am with Danny leading.

He moved forward slowly and cautiously watching for signs of perimeter sentries.

Again, as before on the mountaintop, he smelled them first.

Their smoke.

Sinking down he gestured back to the two behind and shed his pack, only retaining his knife and pistol. Then he crept forward, conscious of every piece of brush and the shale under his knees. After 15 minutes, parting a small leafy branch, he spotted the first one in a small clearing, sitting with his back to a tree, facing down towards the village and with an AK-47 balanced across his knees. He had a long bony face and was wearing the black head-dress favored by foreign Al Qaeda fighters, and was smoking.

After a brief scrutiny, Danny made a decision that the sentry was on his own. He also figured that there would be other sentries posted further along the perimeter.

This one had to be taken out first. Knife or pistol?

The knife was a more final solution and reduced the chance of setting off an alarm as a result of a bullet that was even slightly off.

He spent the next twenty minutes crawling in a large circle until finally he was behind the tree, which the terrorist was propped up against.

Then he slid the knife out and leapt around the tree grabbing the terrorist by the chin with his left hand and slicing across his jugular with the razor-sharp knife.

He slipped his left hand up from the chin, clamping it savagely on the terrorist's mouth. He never uttered a sound.

Danny lowered the dead body to the ground.

He found the next sentries fifty yards further on, two of them, also smoking.

They were both moving about restlessly as if trying to stay awake.

There was no chance of getting close enough to use his knife. Using the silenced SOCOM pistol was the only option, but because of their movements, taking the second one down was the problem. It might allow the terrorist time to get off a shot.

He needed to get closer.

He needed an edge.

He made a decision and hurried back to where he had killed the first terrorist. It was an iffy plan at best, but he'd pulled situations off before that were equally chancy. He disrobed the terrorist and put on the long caftan and headdress, aware as he did so of the blood spatters on the front of the garment. He tore a hole in the side of the garment on the right side where he planned to produce the pistol at the appropriate moment. He wasn't changing his boots.

He shook his head.

Shit, what were the odds? Probably should warn Scotty to get ready to bolt back up the mountain.

No, they had come this far. It was worth the risk.

Turning he edged back the fifty yards to where the two terrorists were situated.

He watched them for a few moments studying their movements.

Timing was everything.

As one of the sentries moved out of his sight, while the other turned away in the opposite direction, Danny stood up and started walking towards them.

Incredibly, he managed several paces before the second sentry turned and gaped at him, his brain trying to analyze what he was seeing.

He died without knowing as Danny gave him a double tap in the forehead.

As he was falling the first sentry, now alerted and lifting his rifle, stumbled forward.

Danny had both hands extended out front in the shooter's pose and made his next two shots equally effective.

Three down.

He quickly searched the two dead terrorists but found no cell phones or two-way radios. That was good news as it probably meant that there was no regular check in for the sentries.

In a few moments he was back at the position of the first dead terrorist and used his radio to bring Scotty and Abdul down.

He was still unwinding the headdress when Scotty pushed through the brush and froze.

"Jesus Danny, I nearly blew you away you daft bugger, seeing you standing there like that!!

He'd forgotten how trigger happy Scotty could be in combat.

In a moment he had filled them in on the situation and then all three headed down at greater speed towards the edge of the village.

It was the easiest part of the whole trip.

When they were crouched behind a mud wall that surrounded his cousin's house Abdul used his cell phone to make contact.

Within minutes they had clambered over the wall and walked into the top level of the mud and straw built house.

They were in the village.

# Chapter 13

Mohammad Yousuf, the cousin of Abdul was nothing like him. Where Abdul was slim and tall, his cousin was short and tubby. His black eyes widened in alarm as he saw the two troopers push into the small space behind Abdul.

There was a quick exchange of conversation in Pashto.

Abdul turned to them.

"He didn't want the rescue group to come into his house. His wife and kids are sleeping downstairs and if the Taliban find out he's helping us they'll all be murdered."

"Too late now" Scotty muttered. "We couldn't hang around outside for God's sake!"

Danny touched Abdul's shoulder. "Look, we can solve his problem quickly. We need to keep moving. With those sentries lying up there we could be discovered at any moment. Ask him where the prisoners are being held" he instructed.

There was another fast exchange of conversation.

Abdul nodded and turned back to him.

"They're being held in the community center, which ironically was built by the re-construction guy who is being held there."

"Major Duffy" Scotty murmured.

Abdul nodded.

"My cousin says Al Qaeda have been torturing them, especially the Major."

"Those bastards!" Scotty spat.

Danny's eyes narrowed as he considered this.

Would the Major be able to travel if he was in poor shape?

He turned to Abdul again.

"Ask him how many guards are on duty outside and if he has any idea of the numbers inside?"

There was another short burst of conversation. Abdul turned to them again.

"He couldn't be seen to be doing a recce of the place so he managed to walk past a few times without stopping. What he saw was that the community center has two doors, one front and one in the back and there are two Taliban or Al Qaeda guards on each door. On one of his walk pasts he saw four people go inside who looked like foreign Arabs....Al Qaeda, he thinks. A lot of the villagers are pro Taliban but few like the foreign fighters in their village."

Danny and his SAS mate looked at each other.

Scotty said it for both of them.

"Shit, eight people in three different locations. The chances of even getting into the community without raising a ruckus is pretty slim. This is where we needed the full troop Danny."

He nodded, turning to Abdul. "Where exactly is this community center located?" he asked.

Abdul pointed to a rough wooden table in the center of the room.

"Let's sit here for a few moments and I'll show you."

Just then a small person wearing an Arab style burka and headscarf, came up the stairs and into the room. All they could see was a pair of intense looking eyes regarding them.

"This is Suhalla, his wife" Abdul whispered. "She knows what's going on so don't worry. Now I'll get a piece of paper and do an outline of the community center and the surrounding houses. The good news is that it's close to here. The bad news is that your extraction point is on the other side of town, so if we get discovered, you will have to fight your way through the whole village, to get to it."

Scotty shook his head in disgust.

"Bloody NATO Officers and their briefing strategies! They don't know shit about what it takes to pull something like this off. Jesus Danny, we're up the proverbial creek!"

Danny's face was cold.

"Looks bad all right, but we've got this far and I'm not leaving a fellow soldier who is being tortured with these bastards. I'll call in a bunch of helicopter gunships with hellfire missiles and selectively level every inch of this town first. Now let's look at Abdul's outline of the village."

They spent the next several minutes examining the drawing. Mohammad's wife went back down stairs when some plaintive and muffled children's voices sounded. Finally Danny looked across at Scotty.

"Do you see it?" he asked.

Scotty pointed to a place on the map. "Right here. It's a short distance from the back door and those two sentries. According to Abdul, it's used for drying fruit and is empty right now. I could take out one of those guys with my crossbow while you SOCOM the other. If we do it silently we don't have to take out the two other sentries on the front door."

Danny pursed his lips. "Yeah, could work. It means getting inside and taking out the internal guards silently and then sneaking back out the same door."

Scotty made a face. "How do we get in that door after we kill the sentries? Is it locked? Is there a password they use?"

Abdul interrupted. "I've got an idea. You may or not know about Afghan hospitality, even if we don't like our visitors. Mohammad tells me that the villagers have been bringing gifts of hot tea and some flat bread to the guards in the community center on a regular basis. What if I roll up to the door with the tray after you have taken out the guards and have them open the door to accept our gift offering?"

Scotty gaped at him.

"Christ, you're an interpreter man! We don't expect you to start getting involved in something that could get you killed."

He nodded to Mohammad. "His family too, more than likely."

Abdul reached across and caught them both by their arms.

"I want to do this. Remember my story of the village medical outreach? This is my chance to do something meaningful… please!"

Danny and Scotty looked across at each other and then back at Abdul.

"Okay, Abdul, you're in Mate…but no heroics. Just get us in that dammed door and step back. Got it?"

Abdul nodded, a grin all over his face and then turned to his cousin where they engaged in some rapid-fire chatter.

Scotty stabbed his finger down on a particular part of the map.

"Back in the regiment in brainstorming a mission like this, someone would have asked the question Danny? You know what it is?"

"Yep. Fall back options if our extraction point is compromised…and it could very well be in this case. What's your suggestion Scotty?"

He stabbed at the map again.

"Abdul pointed this out as a dried up river bed that runs like a culvert back up into the mountains. It's close and accessible and could get us past perimeter sentries who may be spread along there."

"And we would head for where exactly?"

"On top, where you spotted the first sentries. It's the only cleared area on that mountain where a chopper could do an exfill."

"You're not forgetting those sentries are you? They would be alerted and shooting down on us as we tried to descend."

"Beggars can't be choosers Danny… It's all we got mate."

"Hmmm…. caught between a rock and a hard place for sure…OK, that's our fallback position.

Danny set up the Comms and sent a message.

'Foxtrot One, this is Charlie Three. Extraction in figures thirty minutes. Possible optional exfill point is clearing on mountaintop. Some ragheads there.'

There was a double click in acknowledgment.

Thirty minutes and counting. Then he turned to Scotty.

"Something we haven't discussed. What if we run into people between this house and the community center? They could be innocent villagers."

Scotty made a slicing motion across his throat.

"Collateral damage Mate. We can't take a chance. It could compromise the whole mission"

Abdul started. "Killing innocent people! I didn't sign on for that Danny."

He shrugged. "Reality check Abdul. One shout and we're all dead meat, including the prisoners. Hopefully we won't run into anyone, but if we do, stay back and leave it to Scotty and myself. No ideas about playing the hero please!"

He stared intently into Abdul's eyes until he nodded.

"Now," Danny went on, "what about dogs? You mentioned something before."

"The villagers do have dogs, mainly for herding purposes and hopefully asleep with their masters."

They glanced at each other.

Not exactly a walk in the park.

They needed to be prepared for any contingency.

# Chapter 14

The village was still in darkness. Getting into the fruit shed without being spotted by an early riser would have been a bonus.

It wasn't to be.

They were barely out in the street five minutes when a figure came round the corner twenty feet from them accompanied by a large dog, which immediately made a snarling run at them- at Scotty, to be precise.

Danny got off two quick shots while the dog was in mid air, but it still impacted solidly and sent Scotty sprawling.

The animal lay still.

He swung the silenced SOCOM pistol back towards the figure just as a form darted past him with an upraised arm and slammed something down on the head of the man in front.

It was Abdul, who was now crouched by the unconscious Afghan, examining him with a small pinpoint of light from a torch.

"It's a villager." Abdul hissed. "He's not even pro Taliban."

Scotty had regained his feet and pressed in looking down at the felled villager.

"Abdul, you should have stayed back as we told you. You could have screwed everything up. Now we have to take the time to tie this man up, gag him and shove him out of sight somewhere and hope he won't be discovered. Jesus!"

He looked around at Danny in disgust. "Save me from fucking amateurs Mate!"

Somehow they managed to get the villager tied up, gagged, and stowed away, and the dead dog dragged behind a mud wall.

They made it to the fruit shed without any further incidents.

Preparing the assault was strictly the result of years of training and role-playing, particularly in the CQB (Close Quarter Battle house) in Hereford, where every imaginable scenario was played out. Having worked and fought and thought together made their preparation for the assault seamless.

They stripped down to everything but weapons.

Scotty had his assault weapon with grenade launcher and SOCOM pistol and the SPAS shotgun over his shoulder. His pack was loaded with ammunition. As soon as he used the crossbow he would drop it and have his assault weapon at the ready.

Danny had the MP5 with 30-round mags tucked within easy reach. The SOCOM was out and ready to synchronize with Scotty on the crossbow with which he was going to target one of the sentries.

Abdul had a pack slung over his shoulder containing the UZI's, which they would pass to the prisoners on their release. He also had the tray with hot tea and bread for the insurgents.

A rooster crowed off in the distance.

Abdul looked startled.

Danny gestured to Scotty and they both stepped up to the empty window frame.

"One, two, three' Danny counted audibly.

They both fired.

Two sentries flopped to the ground. One started writhing around making a mewing sound as he tried to reach back for an arrow embedded in his back.

Danny swore and leapt through the door, racing across the narrow street.

He was within ten feet when he fired two quick rounds

The terrorist's chest exploded and his weapon flew out of his hand thumping into the back door.

Scotty was beside him then and they grabbed the two dead terrorists, their rifles, and scooped them off to one side, round the corner of the building. At the same time Danny gestured urgently to Abdul to get over to the back door.

He dashed across holding the teapot in place and reached the back door just as it opened and a terrorist stuck his head out, an AK-47 at the ready.

Abdul immediately started a conversation and after a moment the terrorist stuck his head out, looking around.

Afterwards Abdul said he'd told the terrorist that the two sentries were squatting around the corner having their tea. Danny and Scotty had chosen the back door because it led into a small hallway and not into the main room itself where the prisoners were being held

As Danny, peering round the corner, saw the terrorist pull his rifle back and reach for the tray, he took three steps and pumped two fast rounds into the sentry's face. Scotty, beside him, caught the man's weapon to prevent it from falling noisily to the floor. Abdul made an amazing catch in rescuing the tray.

Incredibly, they were inside, with no time to waste.

They heard voices inside. One of them shouting angrily. Then the sound of a whip.

A man's voice cried out in pain.

They looked at each other. As already planned, Danny was to track targets on the left hand side of the clock and Scotty on the right. They both had their SOCOM silenced pistols out and ready.

Danny did the countdown with his hands. One, two, three, then leapt inside.

They had it wrong. There were five terrorists inside. Four carrying AK-47s the fifth, whom they assumed was the interrogator, was over by one of the prisoners, a whip raised in his hand, over the quivering form, they discovered later, was the Governor of the Province.

Shocked silence greeted their entrance.

The group of terrorists stood frozen.

They started to react, but it was too late.

Two SAS troopers and five terrorists was not really an even fight.

Danny pumped a head shot into each of his targets and ignoring Scotty, kept moving like a cat across the room, slamming the unarmed fifth terrorist, the interrogator, to the side of his jaw, sending him slumping to the floor.

He spun round quickly, arms extended in the shooter's position but he didn't need to. Scotty's two were down as well. All four were dead.

They breathed out together. Whew!

A voice in English came from the corner.

"Thank God you made it. I was hoping and praying...I couldn't have taken much more."

His voice choked off.

Danny went over to the man who he knew must be Major Duffy.

"You're OK now. We'll get you out of here smartish."

The Major stared. "You're Brits! I thought they'd send the Seals or a Delta team. How many of you are there?"

Danny chuckled as he used the cutters on the chain holding him.

"Sorry, you're disappointed. Oh, there's just the two of us Major."

He helped him to his feet. "Are you OK to walk?"

The Major nodded. "Sure, fine. Take more than this Al Qaeda filth to stop me."

Danny patted his shoulder. "That's the spirit. Now here's a weapon you might like to use on the way out of here just in case the village wakes up."

Scotty had released the other two and was handing them weapons as well.

The interrogator was stirring and Danny went over and rapidly searched him relieving him of two pistols and a knife. He gagged him, slapped a set of plastic cuffs on him and pulled him to his feet where he stood swaying.

Danny left him for a moment and went over to Abdul who had been waiting in the hall with instructions to shout the alarm if the terrorists at the front came into the building.

His face was pale and he was shaking.

Danny grabbed him gently. "Look buddy, you did just great back there. Couldn't have done it without you. Now here's the thing. I'm going to take this Al Qaeda thug with me on the exfill. I think he's on one of those lists of high profile Taliban. So can you grab him and hustle him along as we head out?"

He never got an answer.

The community center was filled with gunfire.

Danny spun round.

The Governor was pointing the UZI at the Al Qaeda terrorist he had just unleashed 30 rounds into, and the weapon was now clicking on empty.

They were well and truly up the proverbial creek!

Danny gave a signal with his hand to Scotty, who nodded and started pulling the shotgun from his back as he dashed out the back door and raced around to the front of the building.

Then he leapt across the room and wrenched the Uzi from the shaking hands of the Governor.

"You stupid bas..." Danny started.

Ibrahim, the Afghan national policeman, gently took his elbow and nodded at the Governor's face.

The man was sobbing ... tears running down his face.

Ibrahim said. "You don't know what they do to him."

Before Danny could reply he felt a tug on his arm. It was Abdul.

"Danny give me his weapon. How do I fire it?"

Danny flipped the taped magazine and snapped it into the UZI, making some adjustments to it as he did so. He thrust it into Abdul's hands.

"Just pull the trigger. I changed it to short bursts. Scotty and I have more mags when you run out."

His gaze snapped around. "Everyone out of here now. Out the front door. One of you help the Governor" he barked. "Now move!"

There was one more thing he had to do in the room. He was moving as he heard two shotgun blasts from the front door direction.

Scotty was in gear.

The guards were down.

Danny grabbed the metal cutters and sliced through the plastic handcuffs on the dead Al Qaeda leader and pulled the gag out of his mouth.

Sooner or later the media would be involved, or some human rights group, and he didn't want President Karzai's friend up on charges for slaughtering a handcuffed prisoner.

Danny had to make a quick dash out the back door across to the wine shed to collect the Comms system he'd left there. It only took 30 seconds but as he emerged from the shed two armed terrorists came racing round the corner of the nearest house. Without slowing he blasted at them with the MP5 sending them flying sideways.

Then he raced around the front of the community center where Scotty and the group were coming together.

On spotting Danny, Scotty pointed in the direction of the culvert and dashed off. Some shots were going up in different parts of the village.

"Follow him!" Danny shouted, and managed to get the group stumbling forward. Abdul was up front with the policeman behind him leading the Governor. Major Duffy had fallen back beside Danny, stumbling but still looking comfortable in his new role and holding the UZI in a way that told Danny he was no stranger to action.

Up ahead, Scotty had substituted the shotgun for his assault weapon.

He spotted a group of armed men spiraling out of a large mud hut and let loose with his grenade launcher.

Luckily the grenade flew through the door rather than exploding on the thick mud walls, and blew up with a massive sound inside. The windows exploded outwards, the force of it throwing some of the terrorists into the street on their faces. As they staggered to their feet he hosed the rest of them down with the assault rifle.

Danny and the Major were firing now as fighters were emerging from different houses, some still in disarray, others firing their rifles in the air to awaken the village.

Ibrahim paused long enough to cut down a terrorist who leapt out of a window as they passed, then grabbed the Governor and hustled him along.

Abdul caught sight of another armed figure, who came racing round the corner and pointed the weapon at him, pulling the trigger.

He wasn't expecting the jump of the weapon in his hand and he missed, as the terrorist kept coming.

Danny fired from behind with a quick burst as the fighter was hurled backwards.

Then they were around the corner and Scotty was waving them on frantically and pointing.

They had almost reached the culvert. The dried up river- bed.

The darkness helped.

If they could slip in there without their route being initially spotted, they might be able to get clear of the village and up into the mountain.

Scotty raced back to Danny.

"Get them in there fast and keep them moving. I'll cover from here until you get started."

He then hunkered down beside a corner house, which, despite the darkness, gave him an overview of the main street. He pulled the claymore mine out of his pack and set it up facing back down the main street and waited until a group of at least 20 terrorists came spilling round the corner, heading in his direction.

Scotty then turned and dashed to the edge of the culvert, jumping down behind the hardened mud bank. He was counting in his head as he did so, estimating the proximity of the approaching group.

Now! He pressed the remote.

Boom! An immense explosion rent the air and the mud hut that had been there before was demolished. He didn't see what had happened to the group of terrorists, but he knew that few would survive the hail of jagged metal that scythed up the street.

It had been worth humping it up and down the mountain.

Danny and the group raced up the dry edge of the culvert, the Major at this stage holding the other side of the Governor with Ibrahim.

He ushered them forward pointing in the direction of the lower section of the mountain, and at the same moment heard the sound of, what could only be a claymore mine going off.

He smiled. Scotty had used 'his edge.'

He glanced back and was relieved to see his buddy dashing back towards him, and that no one was following them.

Scotty flopped down beside him.

"Got a bunch of the bastards back there. We may still have a chance." Danny grunted, setting up the Comms.

"Foxtrot One, this is Charlie Three leaving village with package. Exfill on mountaintop. Will advise time. Need support fire now on selected targets especially community center."

"Roger that."

No clicks this time. The beehive had been kicked over.

"Trying to distract them in the village?" Scotty asked.

"Yeah, they may assume some hellfire missile is an imminent assault coming at them and set up to repel it."

"Forget about us for awhile you mean?"

"Hope we can slip by those other perimeter sentries that we didn't kill and make some headway up that mountain. We haven't very much time though. They know by now that the prisoners have escaped and will figure out pretty smartish which direction we went in. They won't want to lose such high asset prisoners, so let's move our asses."

They raced on up the dried culvert.

Abdul, being familiar with the general area had taken the lead and the group had made good progress when the SAS troopers caught up with them.

The Governor, Khali Taraki, was now walking on his own without help, and seemed to be aware of the imminent danger they were facing. Major Duffy and the Afghan policeman were coming up in the rear looking alert and business like.

Scotty immediately took up the lead position dashing ahead, his assault rifle at the ready.

They didn't get far when bullets raked across the river- bed in front of them, sending the group diving for cover.

"Shit!' Danny thought, "This will alert the Taliban in the village. We can't get hung up here or we'll shortly be caught in crossfire.

He felt Major Duffy crawl up beside him.

"Got any grenades?" he panted. "I used to be a pitcher back home. I think I see where these guys are firing from. There's only two of them I think"

Danny thrust two grenades into his hands.

The Major nodded to him. "Give me some covering fire." He started counting aloud. "Five, four, three, two, one."

As Danny started blasting upwards, Scotty joined in and the Major stood up and hurled both grenades upwards in a huge arc into some brush fifty yards ahead.

The grenades exploded almost simultaneously followed by screams from the brush. Scotty leapt up and ran forward hosing down the shrubs and immediate area. Then he turned and gave the thumbs up and shouted back.

"Three of the bastards. Good throw Major!"

"Yeah, bloody good throw" Danny repeated, standing up.

He looked around at the group.

"Honeymoon's over lads. They must know back there where we are now. We may be past the perimeter sentries, so let's ramp it up. We still have some sentries on the top of the mountain, who may be coming down at us. We have to take them out, to get our exfill out of here, so stay sharp and let's move it!"

"Duffy looked at him. "What honeymoon? I hadn't noticed Danny."

Danny threw him a taut grin and the group headed upwards, slipping and sliding in the increasing elevation of the river -bed.

They heard the hellfire missiles start to explode back down in the village.

That should keep them busy for awhile, Danny thought.

Shortly after, they climbed out of the culvert and started threading their way up through the trees, as streaks of dawn slanted down, highlighting the way ahead.

They passed through a narrow pathway where they had to go in single file for twenty yards.

Once through, Major Duffy caught his arm.

"Got a couple more of those grenades Danny? I can set a nice booby trap back there. Give us some warning too and might slow them down once they know we're laying some traps."

"Thought you were an engineer, Major? You know, bridges, buildings and things" Danny teased.

"We blow things up too. Didn't they warn you about engineers in Special Forces?"

"Not especially Major, but I'm beginning to think they neglected my education somewhat."

Duffy slipped back down the pathway as Danny pushed on, frustrated by their slow ascent. He appreciated that the prisoners had been chained up for days and were finding the sudden demands of the climb difficult.

The Major rejoined them a moment later and gave him a thumbs up.

A little surprise back there for the terrorists.

It surprised them too when the grenades went off twenty minutes later.

Scotty came dashing back.

"What was that?" he demanded.

"Major Duffy laid some booby traps back in that narrow place we came through." Danny replied.

Scotty snapped his head back. "Shit, that's too close! We're not going to make it are we? I figure another three hours to get to the top. With this group, we can't go much faster."

He cast a bleak glance at Danny.

"We have to slow them down somehow."

Danny turned to Duffy.

"Major, can you hustle them on up the mountain. Our goal was a clearing on top that would take a chopper. There were some Taliban guards there yesterday so watch for them. Here's the Comms unit to activate the exfill."

He filled him in on the call signs.

He also handed him one of the two-way radios. "I may have you call some air strikes through, if I can get the Taliban bunched up below us. I have a laser targeting device with me, so we can make the bastards pay as they come at us."

The Major nodded.

Without another word Danny and Scotty headed back down the mountain looking for an area that would enable them to make a stand.

They found it a short ways back: a large fallen tree lying in a small grove of trees surrounded by covering shrub and providing an excellent field of fire downwards.

They laid out their weapons, discussed tactics and waited.

It didn't take long.

A file of Taliban fighters raced out of the trees, below.

Danny intended to use all the skills he had picked up on the elite U.S. Marine sniping course that he had attended. He allowed them to get twenty yards out of the trees and sighted the MP5 using the scope then started firing single shots with the sound suppressor.

The first three fighters were down before the rest of the group realized they were under attack. Danny took one more down as Scotty opened up with the assault rifle sending the second tier into broken shambles.

They both hurled grenades, which rolled the last few yards before blowing up with a loud bang. Then they grabbed their gear and ran.

Half a mile up Danny laid a rough booby trap, hoping that the speed of the terrorists would walk them into it - two grenades with the pins out under some loose boulders.

It was a mile further up that they found another spot.

This time the terrain had flattened out and they figured that the terrorists would probably come at them from more than one direction.

'Boom!' Boom!' The sounds of the grenades going off echoed up to them.

Danny gave a thumbs-up to Scotty, now a short distance away.

They got ready.

Shortly, two columns of fighters started racing from the trees below. They had split their forces but were moving with more awareness now.

Danny got in another three shots before the fighters reacted by throwing themselves to the ground and blazing back up the hill with their AK-47s.

Scotty was using the grenade launcher to great effect sending explosion after explosion down on them.

An RPG round blasted the tree behind Scotty.

They had got his range.

Two more RPG rounds came blasting in exploding in the mud bank behind him.

He winced as something stung his back.

The group below Danny rose and started running uphill towards him.

He lobbed three grenades down the hill and immediately RPG rounds and bullets came ripping up at his position.

He calmly started picking the fighters off one by one, only stopping to change the 30 round magazines.

The rest of the fighters dived for the ground.

Then Danny and Scotty turned and headed back up the mountain.

It was another mile before they stopped, breathless. Again they chose a high point but could see that the Taliban fighters would probably spread out on the ground below and sweep up at them on several fronts.

Scotty glanced across.

"We can't hold them any longer mate. It's time to get some CAS (Close Air Support) on the job."

Danny nodded and pulled out the short wave radio.

He didn't worry about the normal frequency protocol at this stage.

"Major Duffy" he barked. "We need some CAS down here fast or we're overrun. Find out what's up there right now. I can start painting the targets as soon as you let me know. There's at least a hundred fighters coming up the mountain below us."

"Roger that Danny. Be right back."

He was true to his word.

"Danny get ready to start lazering in figures five. They've got something up there you're really going to like."

"Yeah?"

"A fucking Wart-Hog man!"

Danny switched off and glanced across at Scotty.

"They got a Wart Hog incoming in figures five!"

"Jesus, those poor bastards don't know what's coming down on them."

The Wart-Hog, or The Hog as it was referred to, was an aircraft with a machine gun that was capable of placing bullets in every square inch of a football field as it swept across. It would decimate the Taliban fighters.

Both of them crouched behind some solid tree trunks and Danny set up the laser-targeting device, pointing it downwards.

Already the Taliban fighters were racing from the trees, firing upwards as they ran. Both of them were out of sight but the enemy was firing blindly hoping to find them.

Danny fired the radio across to Scotty.

"Tell Major Duffy we're ready, and to get the Hog down here a.s.a.p. These bastards are coming up at us right across the whole hillside. They're in the open and pretty exposed."

There was a brief conversation and he turned to Danny.

"One minute to go… I told him we were very close to the targets and he advised us to get some colored flares out to pin point our position and get behind some cover if we can."

Danny nodded to his pack.

"Do it!!" He urged, still holding the laser-targeting device steady on the middle of the advancing group.

Scotty stood up behind the tree and hurled the two flares to the left and right of them.

Just in time.

They didn't hear the plane's burping progress, until it had almost swept past but they saw the ground being chewed up all along the mountainside, casting the Taliban fighters aside like rag dolls.

He held the laser steady moving the target area lower down to take in the area below the tree-line as the Wart- Hog swept past again.

Trees were exploding as if a giant chain saw had run amok down below.

There were no screams below.

Death had been instantaneous.

Amazingly a group of the fighters who had been near the top of the hillside, closest to Danny and Scotty's position, had survived the Wart Hog's fly past and were now on their feet and racing up towards them.

"Scotty…" Danny started to shout.

"Yeah I know mate."

Scotty unslung the shotgun and started sprinting along the top of the gradient, weaving in and out of the trees and blasting downhill at selected targets. The heavy shotgun slugs were slamming back the fighters as if hit by a Mack truck. The remaining fighters started to zero in on him and bullets were raking off the trees and brush around him. An RPG round went screaming off through the trees behind him.

Danny dropped the targeting device and picked up the MP 5, putting it on automatic as he hosed down the remaining fighters, in conjunction with Scotty's booming shotgun.

Then there was silence.

The radio buzzed.

It was Duffy.

"How's that Danny? The controller wants to know if that's done the job?"

"Spot on. The Taliban got their asses kicked. I don't know how many they got but I'd estimate at least 50 to 75 of the bastards. There were a few more at the top end who escaped the Wart Hog, but we sorted them. We're good."

"They'll be delighted to hear that. A body count from Special Forces is money in the bank. Well done you lads too. Now what's next?" Duffy asked.

"Tell the Wart-hog to stand by just in case and get the Exfill set up for one hour. I figure that's how long Scotty and I will take to make it to the top. Any sign of those sentries?"

"We could get the Wart-Hog to hose the top of the mountain down Danny."

"Too late for that Major. They will already be heading down in your direction and may have had some cell phone instruction. Stay alert. We're not there yet."

"Roger that Danny.... out."

He turned and explained the situation to Scotty, after which they grabbed their gear and started moving back up the mountain face at a rapid pace.

Up ahead Major Duffy and Abdul were out in front while the policeman was helping the now exhausted Governor along.

An RPG suddenly exploded, sending metal whining across the clearing.

The Afghan policeman was down clutching his arm.

They all hit the ground.

Fortunately they had fallen into small jagged rut in the ground, which provided some cover, but their luck wouldn't last, once the terrorists keyed in on their location.

Bullets started hissing across the clearing.

Major Duffy was lying beside Abdul, desperately trying to determine where the rounds were being fired from.

"Where the hell are they?" he gasped. "I can't see a dammed thing. We're screwed for sure!"

"Don't worry, I'll find out," Abdul shouted in his ear.

Duffy slewed round. "You'll what?"

Abdul started shouting out from his position on the ground.

The firing stopped.

Abdul then stood up and continued shouting.

Duffy hunkered up on one knee peering desperately ahead.

Twenty yards ahead the bushes parted and three young fighters emerged.

Abdul started walking towards them.

Duffy reached up to stop him but Abdul kept walking.

Then the three Taliban fighters lifted their weapons and opened fire, almost cutting Abdul in two as he stood there with his arms out.

Duffy opened up with the UZI. He heard the policeman's weapon joining in.

In a moment it was over.

The three fighters were dead…. and so was Abdul.

The group was still lying in numbed shock when Danny and Scotty dashed into the clearing.

They took one look at Abdul.

"Ah shit, no!" Scotty groaned. "What the fuck happened here?" he demanded.

Ibrahim the policeman got unsteadily to his feet, clutching his arm, which was bleeding profusely.

He pointed down at the fallen interpreter.

"Abdul shouted out that he was from the village. He thought they were from the village too. He said that all the killing wasn't worth it. That they would only get killed too. He wanted them to let us pass. But they were hard core Al Qaeda and cut him to pieces."

There were tears in Scotty's eyes as he knelt down beside the broken bloodied body of Abdul and lifted him into his arms."

He looked across at Danny.

"He wanted so much to bring his country back from the dark ages. Look what it got him. What every goddamn army that's ever come to Afghanistan gets eventually…killed! I'm not leaving him here near his village Danny. They don't deserve him. I'm taking him back to Kandahar for a decent burial. Get that exfill down here and let's get the hell away from here."

He stood up holding the body of the young man and started walking upwards.

It was over.

# Chapter 15

Langley, Virginia

When his intercom buzzed just prior to lunch, Bret Zeitner listened for a moment to his PA then groaned.

"Shit, he's the last guy I want to talk to, but you told him I was here so put him through."

In a moment he heard the French Canadian accent on the line.

"Did you warn him Zeitner?" the voice rasped.

"La Fonte, what the hell are you talking about?"

"Quigley, we tried to blow his head off at a firing range but he put my partner in hospital and nearly choked me. Someone must have warned him. I could only think of one person who knew about our plans."

Zeitner suppressed a grin. "Why the hell would I warn him La Fonte. My instructions are to facilitate your efforts to terminate the guy. What you just ran into was a goddamn killing machine called Danny Quigley, not just some poor slob down on the border, who

134

doesn't know how to fight back. You're lucky he didn't kill you."

"I was told that he was a financial planner... a Limey."

Zeitner chuckled. "Shows you just how soft you've gotten La Fonte. Barging in there without any research on your target. Quigley is ex SAS with a bunch of decorations from several Governments. The Israeli Special Forces, base their escape and evasion program on Quigley's time in Afghanistan, when he was inadvertently left behind on a joint Delta/SAS mission and killed a whole bunch of Al Qaeda and Taliban."

There was silence at the other end of the line. Finally La Fonte's voice came back, now more subdued.

"Nobody told me that. Anyway I've got a team together to follow him up into British Columbia. CSIS have rented a floatplane to fly him into Hanlon Falls. Lots of space to make people disappear my friend."

There was a subtle threat in the words.

"Okay La Fonte, you do what you have to do. Where can you raise a team up there?"

"Serbs" he replied.

"Serbs!" Zeitner's voice was startled." Where the hell do you get Serbs in Canada?"

"They buried 8000 Muslims in Bosnia. That's a lot of IDs they can use to get into Canada. Hey, you read in the papers, the Canadian Government are looking for thirty war criminals they let in. The bleeding hearts in the immigration department just open the doors to these poor people who have had most of their families shot over there. They don't realize that the people they're letting in are the shooters. Lots of them."

"Where the hell do you get your information from La Fonte? Canada takes three years from start to finish before they finish their vetting and grant immigrant status. They cherry pick for God's sake! We have lots of applicants in the U.S. as well from the Balkans, and for the most part, they're pretty decent people. Where the hell are you getting this team from?"

La Fonte chuckled. "Not as smart as you think Mister CIA. I'll tell you where we get them. They're all involved in the drug trade, and when we squeeze them for information, they sing like canaries. These are people we can use, and do use when it suits us, like now."

Zeitner whistled in amazement. "La Fonte, what can I say? Jesus, Serbs in Canada! Now, how can I help you? Walchuk tasked me with supporting you on this."

La Fonte snorted derisively. "We don't need a desk jockey where we're going Zeitner, and we don't need any of your resources either. I just need you to keep out of my way and we'll finish this in the next few days. Whatever his background, Quigley is history."

He paused for a moment. "This Quigley, was he with NATO in the Balkans?" he asked.

Zeitner wasn't sure where this was going. "Probably... Brit Special Forces were chasing, and killing war criminals in Bosnia and on the ground in Kosovo."

He heard a rasping chuckle at the other end. "My little team of Serbs will love this one then. Those SAS snipers were deadly and they would like nothing better than to have a go at one of the bastards who was responsible."

The conversation finished a moment later.

Zeitner had lost his appetite for lunch.

# Chapter 16

Hanlon Falls, British Columbia

Danny had a bird's eye view of a large sprawled-out township resting on the shores of an inland sea, as Hanlon Falls came into view. Below on the water, he could see a gigantic raft of logs anchored near the shore, with figures moving from one log to another on it.

The pilot nodded down at them.

"Tough bastards those loggers. They hang out at the Maple Tavern. Rough place, but the beer's good."

Danny grunted and continued to check out the terrain below.

The town was dominated by a massive factory complex, which he assumed was the pulp mill, and apparently provided the bulk of the employment.

The seaplane splashed down gently and crept forward to the jetty, where a small group waited.

The pilot turned his head, his earphones now around his head.

"We wanted to make the trip worthwhile, so I'm taking back some employees going on vacation, or whose contracts have ended, and a couple of injured people going down to Vancouver for therapy. Is someone meeting you here?" he enquired.

Danny had been disappointed that the CSIS agent Leroy Hesseltine, was unable to accompany him on the trip, but had enjoyed having the small craft to himself, marveling at the hundreds of miles of lakes and trees sweeping below him.

He nodded. "Someone knows I'm coming all right. Not sure when they'll contact me. I'm staying at a guesthouse in town somewhere."

"Probably the Black Bear Inn. You can walk quite easily from the jetty. The pilots stay there when the weather closes in, as it does often around here with those mountains. Nice place, run by a couple called Fitzgerald. Their breakfasts are to die for!"

Danny grinned. "Breakfasts are my weakness. I'm beginning to like this place already."

They didn't have any more time for conversation as the plane eased up to the jetty and was tied up by some volunteer.

He shook hands briefly with the pilot, grabbed his pack and hold-all, and climbed out onto the wooden jetty. He didn't spot anyone in the small crowd who was paying him any special attention, so he asked directions from a grizzled old guy who was tying up the plane, then started walking.

There was a slight breeze coming down from the mountains surrounding the town and Danny immediately enjoyed the smell of pine trees as he headed off. The village was dominated by small wooden houses, and gardens beautifully maintained. He passed a number of what looked like small businesses, a couple of pristine white churches, some local convenience stores, which appeared to sell a limited amount of groceries and the inevitable lottery tickets. The few people he passed nodded to him and said 'Hello', which made him think back to when he was a boy in Wales.

He enjoyed the short walk, promising himself to get some exercise as soon as he could.

The Black Bear Inn had a large figure of a stuffed bear outside, standing on its hind legs. Danny had no way of knowing if it had originally been a real one, or one of those created one's that he'd seen in tourist shops in Vancouver.

The building was made of logs and swept back into some trees, giving the impression of being a substantial dwelling. Inside, the walls were covered with the heads and antlers of various animals, including one bear's head that looked real, with the animal's eyes glaring ferociously out at all and sundry.

A middle aged, short, chunky man with a speckled red beard glanced up from a window seat where he had been reading the paper.

"Heard the plane come in. You must be Quigley. We got you booked in okay."

Danny set his pack down on the floor, careful not to bring attention to the hold all with the weapons in it.

"Great! I was told that I was booked in somewhere but forgot to ask the name of the place."

The man laughed. "Not many choices around here unless you're with the pulp mill. They have their own bunkhouses. There's a couple of Bed and Breakfasts that get some hunting and fishing guests in season, but most people have to settle for us here. I'm Tom Fitzgerald."

"Danny Quigley." They shook hands.

He was impressed by the firm handshake and steel grey eyes that surveyed him.

"I hear the breakfasts are to die for" he commented, noticing the pleased grin on the man's face.

"That would be the pilot no doubt. Those bastards eat us out of house and home. But yeah, we get comments all the time about our breakfasts."

After he'd signed in, Fitzgerald asked him the question that the CSIS man Leroy Hesseltine had told him to expect.

"So, what brings you to Hanlon Falls? No fishing gear that I can see, unless you want to rent some."

Danny and Leroy had agreed on a story that might answer a lot of questions people might throw at him.

"A U.K. travel firm are looking to expand their adventure holidays for active young people, and have asked me to check out the area south of here. I'm hoping to make contact with some of the First Nations who own the territory. I understand they're pretty business-like these days, building casinos and developing other money-making opportunities."

Fitzgerald's face creased with concern.

"I'd hate to see you heading off on the wrong track here Quigley. For starters you're talking about a massive piece of territory there. Before it was handed over to the Indians... yeah, I'm supposed to say First Nations, a number of hunters used to head down into the territory and got some beautiful game. Since the hand over, they keep running into natives who let them know that they're not welcome. Some of them found their pack animals butchered when they came back into their camp after a hunt. And there's worse."

"Worse?"Danny queried.

"Yeah. A couple of groups went down there and never came back. Disappeared off the face of the earth, you might say. Creepy stuff!"

Danny's face looked puzzled. "Didn't they send in search parties? What about the RCMP?"

"Sure we have some pretty shit hot woodsmen around here and rescue teams who are used to hauling people out of the hills and off their boats when they break down. The RCMP coordinates all these of course. They found nothing of the missing hunters, except one strange survivor."

Despite himself Danny found that he was straining forward.

"Strange? In what way?"

"They found one of the hunters running round out there in the woods... completely naked and totally out of his mind. Deranged... and...."

Fitzgerald looked away. "Jesus, I don't know how to even say this!"

Danny peered at the man's ashen face. "Say what, for God's sake?"

"He had been scalped!" he whispered. "Still alive and scalped."

Danny blinked and stood up rubbing his face. He started moving around the room.

"I can't believe what I'm hearing! Scalped in this day and age? Oh man! Where is this guy now?"

Fitzgerald shook his head. "In a mental hospital in Victoria. The prognosis is, apparently, that he'll never recover. A young healthy man with a family as well. So when you tell me that you're thinking of going into that territory my friend, I'd say forget it unless you have a heavy duty team with you and know what you're about. Adventure holidays! I don't think this is what your U.K. company has in mind Quigley. Hey, don't just take my advice, go talk to the Sergeant at the RCMP detachment. I don't know where you would get a team to go with you anyway. That place is a no-go area as far as anyone around here is concerned."

When Danny wandered back up to his room and lay back on his bed for a well-earned rest, his mind was spinning.

'CC, what the hell have you got me into mate?' he wondered.

Still plagued by remnants of jet lag and feeling the effects of the fresh air, he was soon fast asleep.

He woke up sweating hours later, his dreams haunted by a picture of an Indian chasing him with a raised tomahawk, stained with blood.

He decided to get some exercise and investigate the layout of the town at the same time. Changing into some running gear he headed out through reception, waving to Fitzgerald as he went past. He moved off on a slight incline, that led back up into the wooded hills, passing hundreds of replicas of the small wooden houses that he'd seen earlier. Some more modern residences stood out along the route, which he assumed had been built independently since the company had established the town.

He was struck by the relaxed 'Middle America' air about the village with kids playing in the streets and various people working in their gardens, who stopped and waved to him.

Probably didn't get too many joggers, he thought.

A mile later he came to the top of the hill and stopped to look back.

The village was like a gigantic S shape hugging the water and stretching over two miles across. It was split in two by a medium-sized river that flowed down from the surrounding hills, and he could see two bridges spanning it. The inland sea or 'sound' as it was called was about two miles across to the land on the other side, and disappeared left and right into the distance. He knew that ships came in regularly with supplies and to pick up the pulp mill products. In the distance he saw towering mountains, some still snow-capped, and miles and miles of pine trees. A tug-boat was pulling a small raft of logs in towards the area where the larger raft was anchored.

And that pine-scented fresh air!

He turned and headed out of town, gradually feeling the kinks ease out of his limbs for the first time since boarding his flight at Heathrow. A number of pick-up trucks passed him, the drivers either waving or flashing their lights.

He found a clearing off to one side about two miles out, where trucks probably loaded up with timber, and there went through a Karate Kata routine of firing punches and delivering kicks and chops, gradually increasing his speed and power.

He wasn't aware that he was being watched until he heard a door slam and looked up to see that a pick-up had pulled up on the roadside, with two men, one walking towards him.

He reminded Danny of the stuffed bear: large and furry, with long hair and a beard, wearing a yellow hard hat and a big grin on his rugged face.

"Shit man, you're fast! Me and Rafe been watching you for a few minutes. You a fighter?"

Danny turned, wiping his face on a small towel he carried around his neck when jogging.

"Hey, I thought I was all alone up here. Never heard you pull up. No, I'm not a fighter, just trying to keep in shape." He wiped his hands on the towel and reached out to shake the man's hand.

"Danny, just over from the U.K. Got in today actually."

The handshake was bear-like as well. "Yeah, I recognize the accent. We've lots of Brits up here. Good workers. Dick Sharpe, by the way, one of the contractors that hauls logs from back here down to the mill."

He peered closely at Danny.

"So what the hell do you work at...ah Danny, to move like that? Jesus, you move like fucking lightning, man!"

He shrugged. "It's just a Tai Chi exercise program I'm involved in. I work for a travel company in the U.K. who are looking at this area as a future destination for adventure holidays. You know these danger junkies are always wanting to raise the bar and find new destinations."

"A travel company! Hell, things must have changed since I last booked a holiday. You got a military cut to you Danny. My eldest son is in the Forces."

"Oh, what's he in?"

"J.T.F.2." he replied.

Danny answered without thinking, and could have kicked himself afterwards.

"Joint Task Force Two, good lads."

This was the Canadian Special Forces unit.

Sharp gave him a strange look. "Hmm... they are...they are. In fact my son Rob is home on leave right now. I'll tell you what, we'll be in the Maple Tavern later on tonight and I'd be delighted to buy you a drink, if you care to wander down there."

The conversation ended there and the logging truck tore off down the road.

He turned and started back towards the village.

Three different pick-up trucks slowed down and offered him a lift, but he thanked them and waved them off.

When he got back to the Black Bear Inn, he spent a long time in the shower and then dressed in some new chinos and a long-sleeved outdoorsy shirt.

He lay down on the bed for a short nap.

It was dark when he woke up and he was hungry.

He felt good. His body was adjusting and coming back to normal.

He felt his cell phone vibrate in his pocket.

When he checked it he found a text message with only a bunch of numbers on the screen. He stared at it for a long time.

Another anonymous message.

Finally he stood up.

Time to see what the nightlife in Hanlon Falls was like.

The Maple Tavern was a long low-slung wooden building with a large parking lot full of trucks and pick-ups. A half dozen men were outside the front door pulling on bottles of beer and in various states of inebriation.

Some nodded to him as he went in.

Inside at least a hundred men and women milled around a long bar and various tables, some eating gigantic servings of food, but most standing knee deep around the bar, drinking.

An old style jukebox belted out a country western song, which some of the women were singing along to.

He pushed down to the end of the bar and was surprised to see three empty bar stools. Looking around he couldn't see anyone who might be claiming them and eased himself onto the end one. He wasn't sure if he imagined it or if there was a momentary lessening of the noise around him.

"Not a good idea!"

He looked up into the eyes of a woman behind the bar. She was tall, with dark hair and high cheekbones, not unlike an Indian.

He stared.

She was beautiful.

"Sorry..." he stuttered. "You said something?"

"Yeah, I said, not a good idea, sitting there."

Danny looked around. "Hey, I don't see why not, they're empty."

She shrugged, looking impatiently back up the bar where some people were thumping it with their empty beer mugs.

"Your funeral! Look, what's your poison?" she asked.

"Got any Stella?"

For the first time her face softened. "Yeah, we got some in for the Brits. I kinda like it myself."

He slapped down twenty dollars. "Well, have one on me then."

Her face softened further. "I'll stick it in the tips jar if you don't mind. Thanks."

In a moment she was back and placed a bottle down beside him and some change.

No glass.

It was that kind of bar.

He was half way down the bottle when the noise dropped suddenly.

Danny looked up and through the milling bodies saw four large men who had just pushed inside the room. They looked like loggers, with rough woodman type clothing and high-laced boots.

He was aware that the woman was beside him again.

She nudged his arm. "Told ya... you're sitting in their seats."

He spun his circular seat around.

They were heading right for him.

They looked like they'd been cloned. Four big burly figures, two wearing beards and all with the swagger and confidence that comes from doing hard dangerous work that few people were capable of.

Danny never looked for trouble. In fact most people with his background avoided it like the plague, knowing the possible consequences.

In a foreign country he was quite prepared to accept that he had crossed some invisible boundary and would have had no problem vacating his seat, which had presumably been reserved, in some fashion... except for their approach!

The leading man, a burly redhead, stopped three feet away and pointed at him. His whole body throbbed with aggression.

"Get the fuck off my seat you meathead!" he bellowed.

Danny eased off the seat, standing up.

He could feel the flow of adrenalin start to move down from his head into his loins, alerting him to the imminence of violence.

He automatically adjusted his stance in anticipation.

He had seen too many men cold-cocked, standing face on when it was obvious that they were about to be attacked.

Danny knew he was being stupid, but he couldn't help himself at that stage. The fact that the dark-haired woman was standing there with baited breath might have had something to do with it.

He was also still a trifle jet-lagged, and even if he would admit it, somewhat pissed off.

He smiled now, easing sideways slightly away so that his back was not against the stool.

"Not tonight sunshine. There's two there you can have. I kinda like this one..." Danny said loudly.

There was a collective gasp from the bar.

Shock and anger flashed across the features of the four men.

The redhead stepped forward and slammed his right hand down on Danny's shoulder, grabbing him.

Danny clasped the man's hand tightly with his right hand, and without trying to pull it free, spun sideways and levered downwards bringing the man to his knees. Without pausing, he slammed his boot into the man's gut and as he came forward grabbed his hair and brought his knee up into the man's face, sending him backwards into the second man. The third and fourth men rushed at Danny.

He blocked a roundhouse punch from one of them, and quick as lightning threw a side knuckle strike at the other one, catching him on the bridge of the nose and sending him reeling backwards. The third man threw another roundhouse, which Danny, going with the punch, putting him off balance and snapped a kick at his shinbone. As the man bent forward screaming he chopped him savagely on the side of his neck, poleaxing him to the floor.

The second man had now extricated himself from the first casualty crashing back on him and rushed forward, fists flying.

Danny loved leg sweeps. It was his favorite in the dojo. You grabbed one of his arms, waited until an opponent's forward foot was coming down on the mat, just a fraction of an inch off the ground, where all his weight is being transferred to that front foot, and you then swept it with your foot.

Timing was everything.

Done correctly, it was devastating.

In this case it worked beautifully, and the man slammed down noisily on the rough wooden flooring. Danny finished it off by dropping straight down on his stomach, hearing an explosion of air coming from him. For good measure he slammed his elbow into the man's jaw, and leapt to his feet as the man he had done a side knuckle strike on had now grabbed a bottle and was taking a swing at him.

He never made it.

A large hand grabbed him from behind, tore the bottle from him and, turning him, ran him head on into the bar, splintering it.

A lean crew-cut six-footer stepped forward grinning and stuck out his hand.

"You met my Dad this afternoon.... Dick Sharpe. I'm his son Bob."

He surveyed the bodies sprawled on the floor.

"Nice work. We were all pissed off at these guys swaggering in here. You might have a visit from the Sergeant up at the RCMP detachment, cause I guess a couple of these may be on the next chopper out for medical treatment. Come and have a drink with us. My Dad's over at the top end of the bar."

That was how Danny ended up with a small group who spent the following ten minutes slapping his back and recounting the fight they had just witnessed.

An ambulance with a crew came and all four casualties were taken out, one on a stretcher, the other three staggering out supported by medics.

Finally Dick Sharpe turned to him.

"You never gave me your surname this afternoon Danny" he prompted.

"Oh, it's Danny Quigley."

With that his son exploded a whole mouthful of beer onto the bar.

"Jesus, I don't believe it!" he breathed.

"What?" his Dad asked. The barmaid, who came to wipe up, paused, listening.

"The story I heard in Afghanistan a couple of years back. A Danny Quigley and another Brit Special Forces guy did a rescue mission with the PPCLI. Not only did they save the Canadian column from being wiped out by killing twenty-three terrorists, but also they went on to rescue the Governor of Kandahar Province, the police chief, and an American Major. The tally for terrorists, a mixture of Taliban and Al Qaeda fighters killed, partly in an air strike called in by Quigley and his colleague was up around one hundred."

All eyes swung around to Danny. Even nearby groups fell silent.

"Well Danny, are you the same guy?" Dick queried.

He shrugged. "Yeah, I guess so."

Bob looked in shock. "You guess so! Man you're a fucking legend over there! I don't believe I'm sitting here in Hanlon Falls next to a guy we've talked about many a night in Afghanistan!"

Before he could reply the barmaid leaned forward and whispered in his ear.

"I'm Pat Tarrant, CSIS. I'll see you for breakfast at the Black Bear at 9am."

Then she was gone, leaving Danny in shock, sitting in the midst of a bunch of admirers and free drinks piling up in front of him.

He suddenly thought of something.

Pulling out his cell phone he switched it on and showed Bob the last text message.

"You're a military guy Bob. What would you say those numbers are?" he asked.

Bob glanced at it. "Shit, no question. It's a grid reference number, Man. It will bring you spot on to this very location, wherever it is."

Danny nodded. "Yeah, that's what I thought."

Bob caught his arm turning him sideways. "Look Danny, I dunno why you're here but I'd like to be part of it. I'm on a week's leave and bored shitless. Count me in if you need some back up. Okay?"

He stared intently into his eyes.

Danny squeezed his arm, saying nothing.

He wished he had the troop there with him to help out with all the drink.

# Chapter 17

Danny was ten minutes into his breakfast and enjoying it immensely, when Pat Tarrant joined him. This time she was dressed in a comfortable sweater and jeans tucked into a pair of high top suede boots. She wore a minimum of makeup.

Still beautiful in the daylight, he thought, but in a cool self-sufficient sort of way.

Her steel gray eyes surveyed him with amusement.

"Discovered the secret of Hanlon Falls I see."

He blinked. "Oh?"

"The breakfasts...they're something else aren't they?"

He nodded through a mouthful of home fries. "Hmm... I may just stay on here."

She laughed and then just as suddenly her voice went cold.

"A bit rough on those loggers last night weren't you?"

He put his utensils down carefully. "In what way?"

"Gave them no chance. Put them away so business-like, just as if you were chopping trees."

He breathed in a few times collecting his thoughts.

How to explain?

He took another swig of coffee, sat back and looked directly at her.

"I let a guy get off the floor once and he killed a mate of mine. Lessons learned. Anyway, when you're on your own, with four big lugs looking for a fight, you can't afford to mess about."

As an afterthought. "Actually they were quite lucky."

She snorted in disbelief. "Lucky? No shit!"

"I could have hurt them a lot more... broken some bones and stuff," he said quietly.

She stared at him. "Jesus, just who the fuck are you Danny?"

He chuckled, knowing her reaction to his next answer.

"You may not believe this Pat, but I actually work as a financial planner in the U.K."

She snorted again. "Yeah, sure. Now pull the other one. Anyway, Leroy gave me some background on how you ended up here. Can you run that past me again?"

He spent the next ten minutes explaining how Clive Courtney, known as C.C. had disappeared and had apparently been resurrected with a mysterious text message, which had led to Hanlon Falls.

On completion of this background information he produced his cell phone with the grid reference numbers on it. He passed it to her.

"Hmm…so it seems that this C.C or someone has brought you here and now shown you the next leg of your journey. You know what that means don't you?

"What?" he asked.

Whoever these people are, they know that you've arrived in Hanlon Falls. They're watching you. So what's your next step Danny?"

"Bob Sharp, the young guy at the bar is in the military and is going to get his maps out this morning and tie down that grid reference. Then I'm going to get some transport, gear and supplies and head down there. I'll need a guide too I guess. Bob wants to come along in any event."

"Okay, well let me tell you why I'll be coming with you too."

He opened his mouth to interrupt.

She held her hand up stopping him. "Let me finish Danny. In 2009 the Mounties picked up an Iranian/Canadian in Toronto who was caught trying to ship transducers over to Iran."

"Transducers, what exactly are they?" he asked.

"They can be used as centrifuges that enrich uranium into weapons-grade nuclear fuel. This guy was tried under the United Nations Act and Canada's Nuclear Safety and Control Act, which is aimed at keeping nuclear technology out of Iran."

He nodded. "Okay I'm with you. Now how does this influence the situation here Pat?"

"Well a small light plane, and there are hundreds in British Columbia flying all over the place, crashed in the interior south of here. When the rescue teams found them, the pilot and a passenger were dead, but guess what they discovered on board?"

"I'm dying to hear."

"A transducer, tucked up nicely as freight."

"Holy cow! But going where? Where were they headed?" Danny asked, sitting forward.

"Good question. We discovered that they were way off the flight plan that they'd logged so that was no help. There were no documents on board to indicate where the transducer had originated from or it's destination. No identification on either of the dead. A complete mystery, but as you can imagine, flags went up right across the board, and across the U.S. border as well."

He studied her closely. "Hence your presence in Hanlon Falls. Your cover at the pub must be useful for keeping your ear to the ground."

"Well I come from here originally. I'm part native as you may have picked up, so I was a natural choice, but nothing's happened until you got here and get a grid reference for the area south of here that swallowed up that small plane. That's why I'm coming along with you. Oh by the way, there's a guy called Jeff Wilson, or White Feather, which is his Indian name, a full blooded native who works as a guide for hunters, so if he's free he may take us in there."

Danny was about to answer when a tall slim man, approximately 40 to 45 years of age, in a RCMP uniform, wearing Sergeant's stripes came into the dining room and, on spotting Pat, came over to them.

She managed to whisper to Danny as he was approaching. "He knows I'm CSIS."

He stopped and looked at both of them. "Ah Pat, wasn't expecting to see you here. I'm looking for a Mister Quigley, involved in a fracas at the Maple Tavern last night. You were probably there. I'm here to get a statement and possibly to lay charges for assault against Mister Quigley. Oh the Maple Tavern is claiming a thousand dollars in damage for the bar, bashed in by someone's head."

He looked at Danny. "I guess you're he?"

He was about to answer when Pat reached up and pulled the Sergeant down into the seat beside her.

"Sergeant Phil Dryden, I want you to meet Danny Quigley. Danny is with MI5 in London and is about to crack this whole thing open about the plane crash south of here and so on."

Danny went to open his mouth and protest that he wasn't part of MI5, but Pat winked knowingly at him.

Sergeant Dryden's mouth dropped as if flabbergasted.

He shook his head.

"What is happening in sleepy Hanlon Falls all of a sudden? Here we have a breakfast of spooks going on and I'm not even invited."

She patted his arm. "Forget all about this assault stuff Phil. Danny was attacked in the tavern by four thugs and he laid them out, end of story. There's not a man in there who won't support this, and that goes for me too. The claim for a thousand dollars is absolute bullshit. That bar was damaged already. Now as the top cop around here, we want to clear a trip we plan to make into that big chunk of territory south of here. We already have Bob Steele who is coming, and Jeff will hopefully be our guide. I'm part of the team, and..."

"And me too" the Sergeant interjected. "You're not going anywhere without me. And... I can organize the vehicles and the gear. I can get the jeeps in for servicing right away. Danny, if you meet up with me there at the garage, we can sort out the supplies and gear. Then we could go to the outdoors store and get you fitted up. You're going to have to pay for the supplies and gas."

Danny shrugged. "Sure, no problem. However I should mention another possible problem."

The Sergeant looked from one to the other.

"You mean there's more to this?"

She rolled her eyes. "This is news to me too. Come on Danny let's have it."

He made a face. "It sounds a bit odd in the light of day, especially sitting here in sleepy Hanlon Falls, but here goes. I got a weird text message two days ago that was received in London by MI5 stating that I was being targeted. Nothing more. MI5 traced it back to Washington D.C., to an Internet café."

The Sergeant's face reflected his confusion. "Targeted? In what way?"

Danny drew his hand across his throat. "That way I guess. It's the only way I can interpret it, especially..."

"Especially what?" Pat interjected.

"I was on the firing range outside Vancouver." He glanced at Pat. "With your colleague Leroy, when someone came within inches of blasting a hole in my head. They disappeared before we could determine who they were."

Pat slapped the table loudly. "Jesus Danny, you're a flaming magnet for violence."

He nodded wearily. "Yeah, my ex wife keeps telling me that."

The Sergeant leaned forward. "And you're telling us this, why, exactly?"

"I don't know who these people are or why they're targeting me but we need to tool up for the unexpected and be on the alert. I don't know just how sophisticated these people are or what their resources are."

She finished his thought pattern for him.

"So you don't know if they can mount a mission up into B.C."

She glanced at the Sergeant. "Any strangers come in since Danny got here yesterday?"

He shook his head. "No, just some new employees for the pulp mill. They would have been processed weeks ago in Vancouver, so they couldn't be part of some plot."

She raised her eyebrows at Danny. "I'm beginning to see why she's your ex wife" she murmured.

Two hours later Danny was with Sergeant Phil Dryden in the middle of a bustling garage where two mechanics were working on a pair of jeeps for them.

"Solid looking" Danny commented," should do the job nicely."

Dryden nodded. "Yeah, they've seen a few miles but reliable as hell. With five of us, these two should do the trick, but we need a small trailer to carry gas cans and camping gear. Pat Tarrant has gone off to suss out the guide, Jeff, so if he comes along he might have his own ideas on what we should carry. When Bob meets up with us with his maps and ties down that grid reference, we need to plan our route and leave details with the police detachment in case anything goes wrong, where we need to be rescued for any reason. That's standard practice up here and it's proved it's worth in many instances, especially with skiers, hunters and fishermen. We probably need to plan for five to seven days out in the woods depending on how far we can actually drive."

They left it at that for the moment as the Sergeant took a phone call and Danny wandered round the extensive garage. He talked to a few of the mechanics and learned that most of the people in town owned cars and occasionally took the lone road south to the nearest larger town several hours away. As he drifted back towards the front of the building he became conscious of the hairs rising on the back of his neck. He'd learned not to ignore this sensation in the past.

He stopped and casually looked back, surveying the busy scene.

Twenty yards away a small truck was up on a hoist with two mechanics busy underneath it. It was the third man standing there that caught his attention. He was facing away from the truck and staring directly at Danny. An extremely tall, lean man, with narrow bony features and long black hair tied back with a bandanna, not just staring at him but glaring, with what looked like hatred in his eyes.

At that point the Sergeant wandered back over to him.

Danny caught his arm and casually steered him off to one side.

He was speaking quietly to him as he did so.

"Phil, just eyeball that guy standing over by the truck will you. He can't take his eyes off me since I came in here. If looks could kill…"

The Sergeant immediately picked up the inference and casually flicked a glance backwards.

He grunted. "Oh, yeah, I see who you mean. The guy came up here 6 months ago on contract to the pulp mill. Got fired for being drunk on his shift. Luckily for him the garage was looking for another mechanic and took him on."

"Hmm… know anything about him?"

"Nothing much. He's from Bosnia or somewhere over there. Sticks pretty much to himself and a couple of drinking buddies from that part of the world. What's your concern about him Danny?"

"Radar went off in my skull when I picked up his interest in me. It's kept me alive in the past. Why would a complete stranger look so pissed off when I just walked past him? There's a stillness and competence about the guy that speaks volumes. I'd say he's seen some military action. I can smell it on him. "

Phil looked thoughtful. "Want me to go over and check him out? You know, shake him up a bit."

"Uh Uh. No sense putting him on notice. Shit, I may be totally wrong. Perhaps I just remind him of someone."

"No, stick to your instincts Danny. I've been in this job long enough so that what you're saying resonates with me. It's a flag up, especially in view of your peculiar phone call. Though I can't see the connection between an ex-employee from the pulp mill and the threat against you. Anyway, we're finished here. I want to call in on the gun shop."

On that basis they made a detour to the Black Bear Inn so that Danny could show the Sergeant the small cache of weapons that Leroy had come up with in Vancouver.

Like a lot of cops, he was a gun nut.

He reared back when Danny produced the Winchester model 1866 rifle.

"Oh man.... the old Henry repeater! What a beauty!"

"Isn't it just? However I would be more enthusiastic if I could get a scope for it. As a sniper I like to get them right in the cross hairs."

Phil hefted the weapon. "We can take it round to the gun shop. I'm sure Dave there can fix you up. Now what else have you got?"

The Heckler and Koch Universal self-loading pistol didn't cause much reaction but when he hauled the Ruger MP-9mm updated version of the Israeli Uzi out, he stared mesmerized.

"Jesus, I know you got licensed for the rifle and small arms Danny, but you know of course the laws in Canada when it comes to assault weapons. If one of my Constables stopped and searched you, he'd charge you right away."

"But?" Danny prompted.

Phil sighed. "In view of what you told me about being targeted. I have to look the other way on this one. Could be my ass on the line too when we get out there. Speaking of asses. There goes my career, if this gets out."

They spent a couple of hours in the gun shop, which also stocked outdoor gear and clothing. Danny got his riflescope and was outfitted for the trip, throwing in a wicked looking knife and other essentials. Phil threw in some cans of mosquito repellent with a knowing grin.... and a bundle of ammunition.

Then it was time to meet up with Bob at the Maple Tavern, which was apparently much quieter in the afternoons.


That evening, as dusk was falling, Danny changed into running gear and headed up the familiar road out of town, feeling the smoothness start to flow back into his stride as he bridged the top of the hill. Physical training was very much a part of his life and being fit was an expression of who he was. Sure, he wasn't jumping out of planes any more or going on demanding exercises to various countries, which was part and parcel of being in the SAS, but as a financial planner, he felt more energized and competent in his role when he maintained a high level of fitness.

He passed the area where Dick Sharpe had stopped to talk to him as he was completing some martial arts movements. He went a mile past his previous run but kept glancing back occasionally as he kept hearing what seemed to be a vehicle back down the road. He shrugged it off, not spotting any lights to his rear.

Finally he stopped and carried out ten minutes of strikes and blows and some Tai Chi exercises.

Then he started back, lengthening his stride and breathing easily.

A sudden squeal of brakes and the shape of a vehicle slewing sideways across the road, thirty yards in front of him made him realize that he was in trouble. He dimly made out three figures leaping out of the vehicle on the far side and dived for the verge of the road. He heard the familiar popping sounds of weapons being fired and bullets started zinging past him. As he forward rolled he spotted flashes in his peripheral vision, which told him that three gunman had opened up on him. He took another leap, springing forward, and fell down into the four foot culvert that ran alongside the road.

He was glad that he'd automatically taken his holster with the Heckler and Koch pistol with him out on the run, despite the irritation of it banging against his hip as he ran. Now he pulled it out and snapped off the safety. While it had a night sight and laser spot targeting, he was limited to the 10 round box magazine. He didn't have the silencer attached unfortunately. He couldn't survive a prolonged shootout against three attackers.

He heard shouting and was aware that they were racing to the side of the road.

Firepower started scything down into the shrubs and trees below him as the gunmen assumed that he would keep running back into the woods to escape.

Danny turned and started crawling backwards down away from the position of the attackers. He knew he hadn't long before some of them would leap down into the culvert to flush him out.

He had crawled about thirty feet when he spotted a large pipe coming from under the road, which was obviously for shedding water, and without hesitation he crawled inside. He might be safe here for a while but he doubted if his attackers would give up too easily. He knew what had happened to Qaddafi when he was caught hiding in a large pipe. His best solution was to take the battle to them and he had the ideal opportunity to do this as he could now come at them from the other side. He slithered along through the pipe barely aware as of the mud and grit under his knees.

He came to the end unexpectedly and fell out, jarring his shoulder and almost losing his grip on the pistol.

Then he started moving fast, bending low, so as to be concealed from the three attackers.

He came to within ten feet of where he figured the van was slewed across the road, and peered out cautiously. Still dusk, he could make out the forms of two of the men across the road, blazing away with their weapons into the trees and foliage below them. He spotted a form leaning across the hood on the far side of the van and figured that the third attacker was holding back and covering the road in case he made a break for it.

Danny tested the night scope and got a clear view of the back of two of his attackers. He avoided using the laser dot to avoid raising the alarm if the third man spotted it.

Not wanting to lose the advantage of surprise, and equally wanting to avoid shooting two people in the back, he quickly moved the pistol sideways and, using the scope, put a shot in each of the two tires on the side of the vehicle.

The van lurched forward noisily onto it's rims. As the sound of Danny's weapon exploded, the third man shouted out a warning and started firing up along the side of the road. The other two gunman turned, still not sure where Danny was and started hosing down the opposite roadside.

Without hesitation Danny, using the scope, pumped two fast bullets into the chest of the gunman on the left and moving it slightly, did a double tap to the head of the second one.

The third attacker must have spotted him as bullets started ricocheting off the asphalt around him. The weapon had the booming sound of a hunting rifle.

Six shots gone, four left in the mag.

He could still get killed, if he wasn't careful.

Swinging the pistol back to the van he couldn't find a target as the man had now ducked back out of sight. He moved the scope downwards under the vehicle and nodded to himself.

He spotted legs and fired one quick shot.

Three rounds left.

There was an unearthly scream from the other side of the van followed by the clatter of a weapon falling onto the roadway.

Danny then started climbing out of the culvert.

As he stood up the vehicle engine sprang into life and the van did a quick reverse and swung round back in the direction of town, the motor roaring and sparks flying from the two wheels now down to their rims.

Danny grabbed his cell phone from his waist pouch and quickly speed dialed Sergeant Dryden's office number, which he had pre-programmed in that afternoon.

It was answered immediately.

"Sergeant Dryden here."

"Phil, Danny Quigley. Look, I've just been attacked by three men with weapons on the main road, two miles outside of town. Two of them I've shot dead but the third is heading back your way in a van with two tires shot out and raising enough sparks to be seen miles away."

"Jesus Christ Danny. Sounds like you've brought a fucking war up with you to Hanlon Falls..."

"Look Phil, you haven't much time. This guy coming your way is wounded in the leg and he dropped his weapon on the road here...a hunting rifle. I don't know if they had any other weapons in the van so be careful. He's doing about forty miles an hour and I doubt if he can maintain that speed, but you haven't much time to get a roadblock up."

"Gotcha Danny. Two of the constables are here right now on switch change, so we can ramp up right away and set up a reception. Gotta go."

That left Danny standing in full darkness, which suddenly seem to envelope him.

He carefully moved across to the two attackers who he assumed were dead, though he had seen the enemy in the past who still managed to squeeze the trigger and kill people. One was on the side of the road, with a headshot.

No doubts there.

The other had been thrown back down into the culvert and was lying on his back, his neck in an unnatural position. It looked like he might have broken his neck in the fall, but Danny suspected that he was already dead.

A few minutes later he heard an almighty crash back down towards the village, followed by a series of shots, which died down almost immediately.

It took another ten minutes before a police vehicle, with flashing lights came barreling up the road and slewed to a stop beside Danny, who by this time was out in the road waving them down.

Sergeant Dryden leapt out and ran up to him.

He was breathless. "That CSIS lady Pat was right. You're like the fucking Pied Piper. Violence follows you wherever you go. "

Dryden went across to the edge of the road shining the torch down carefully on the two dead attackers.

"I gotta say it Danny. When you hit them, they stay permanently hit. Looks good…two weapons, lots of empty casings. Shot from the front. It will help with the hearing, which happens anytime there's a suspicious death. Now…"

Danny interrupted. "What happened back there?" he asked impatiently.

Dryden snorted. "We had three cruisers in a road block. The guy wouldn't stop. Came right at us and wrote off two cruisers and then came storming out like Rambo with a pistol blazing. My two constables are experienced hunters. They opened up and dropped him like he was hit with a Mack truck. Dead."

"Ah, so they had more weapons."

"Yeah, and guess who he was."

"I have no idea."

"The guy you pointed out to me in the garage. The one who was giving you the hate look. Oh, and by the way, the two in the ditch, they're his drinking buddies who work in the pulp mill."

He stared at Danny. "Just what the hell is going on here? It's suddenly become like the OK corral since you arrived in town yesterday."

Danny lifted his hands helplessly. "Phil, I wish to hell I knew, then maybe I could protect myself or avoid it completely."

Dryden stared at him for a long moment, then sighed. "Makes me wonder if going south with you into that big wedge of Indian Territory is a good idea, but if I don't go, I'll always wonder. I was complaining only last week about what a tame posting this has been and now………come on Danny, let's get you in the cruiser and get your statement while it's fresh in your mind. There's an ambulance on the way up and one of the constables will have to do the crime scene thing and get lots of pictures. This is going to be a long night. I don't know what my superior is going to say to all of this. The pulp mill isn't going to be very happy either, losing two employees. They may just want you out of town on the first chopper."

# Chapter 18

It was a long night... and a long day followed.

Being involved in a violent death in Canada was no simple matter.

The RCMP detachment personnel suddenly exploded as a team flew in from a town called Williams Lake, further south.

Phil Dryden said that he hadn't seen so much brass since the last police funeral he'd attended.

Danny had to recount his story several times and playing the MI5 card was running a bit thin on closer scrutiny. Rebecca Fullerton Smythe had been on the phone several times and warning him about any mention of MI5 involvement, particularly to the media, which had descended on Hanlon Falls en masse. She still managed to provide some coverage for him by mentioning that he had participated in a number of MI5 operations. She didn't volunteer that most of these were as a serving member of the British Army while in the SAS. But she did confirm the threat that she had received on Danny's life and that the threat still existed.

His pistol was confiscated, as evidence, and his room was searched with his permission. Bryden told him this was just routine to stop speculation that he might have somehow been connected to the drug trade. The CSIS card was a strong one and appeared to deflect further suspicion. At least they didn't confiscate his passport.

Luckily the Uzi was safely stored in Sergeant Phil Dryden's house.

The three bodies were whipped out on a chopper heading for Vancouver for the autopsies and Danny would have to attend an enquiry at some later date.

An exhausted and starving Danny was finally rescued by Pat Tarrant and Phil who hauled him round to the Maple Tavern in the late afternoon where a meal had been pre-arranged.

They started to get stuck in.

He hadn't reacted to killing the two men the night before, but on sitting down at the table he noticed a slight tremor in his hands.

'Damn it!' he thought, 'killing people didn't use to have any effect on me. Killing in the line of duty as a soldier was certainly different from killing civilians.'

Pat noticed, and casually went over to the bar and came back with a mug of beer and placed it in front of him.

"Here, drink this Danny. You've earned it my friend, and none of us have any further doubt that you're on some organization's hit list, for whatever reason."

He took a long quaff from the mug, finally placing it back down.

His face reflected bafflement. "You know Phil, some of your superiors today couldn't accept that I hadn't a clue as to why these guys came after me with the obvious intention of terminating me. I agree it sounds strange, but, I don't!"

"It's weird Danny for sure. Lucky for you the third killer came down that road and came at us like Rambo, and my constables took him out. If you had killed all three back up on the road there, it might not have looked so cut and dried."

Pat looked across at Phil. "So who are these three that went after Danny?

He shrugged. "God only knows. Obviously their backgrounds will have to be checked out carefully."

Danny reached into his shirt pocket, pulled out a note and passed it to him. "This might be a place to start" he commented.

Phil looked down at the piece of paper and went pale. He looked accusingly at Danny. "Where the hell did you get this?" he demanded, "and how long have you had it?"

Pat snatched the note from him and glanced down at it.

"Holy shit!" she breathed, "This is a whole new ball of wax. The immigration department is going to go bananas!"

Danny took another long drink and carefully put the mug down, his eyes gleaming.

"Hmm… interesting isn't it? MI5 passed it to me on my last phone call. They got the message at Thames House in London from the same source in Washington D.C. - the Internet café. As you can see, the message reads:

'The Hanlon Falls killers are Serbs in Canada illegally using Muslim papers of people they butchered in Bosnia. There's more of them and they won't let up on Quigley.'

He glanced carefully at both of them. "So you may want to re-evaluate that trip with me into the bush."

They never managed to reply as the door of the tavern flew open and a woman almost fell into the room struggling with a small suitcase.

Danny's jaw dropped and his chair crashed back.

"Siobhan, what the hell are you doing here!?"

It took some time for the atmosphere to settle down in the Maple Tavern.

After a long hug Danny led her to the table and an exhausted Siobhan slumped into a chair hastily pulled across by Pat from another table.

Phil went and grabbed a cup of coffee for her from the bar and set it before her.

Danny looked helplessly at Siobhan and his two colleagues and managed to blurt out "Siobhan is a friend from Ireland," before asking her again, "Siobhan what are you doing in Hanlon Falls?"

She lifted her head and looked across at him.

Normally a face with almost a beatific glow to it, she was now wan and obviously desperately tired. She was a slim dark-haired woman of approximately thirty years and had been thrown together with Danny almost 2 years previously and they had become very close. Unfortunately their separate responsibilities, hers in Ireland and his in the U.K. had prevented them from developing that relationship.

Now she peered pensively across at him.

"C.C.'s alive Danny. I started feeling that about a week ago. Very strongly. I tried to contact you, but failing that I called your friend at MI5, Rebecca. She told me of the message you had received on your telephone. I told her that I had to be with you on the search. That I could probably help out. She told me to forget it. That it was too dangerous by far and that other implications were involved."

Danny glanced sideways at Pat and Phil.

"Siobhan and C.C. were close friends, more a spiritual connection, but she has a physic gift, if I can call it that, where she can sometimes sense what's happening to him. I actually saw it working once when he was being beaten up, and she actually felt it."

Pat shook her head. "Jesus, that's some gift. How exactly does it work?"

Danny shrugged. "Basically she senses his feelings and pain, as I mentioned, and in some cases his general location. I don't really understand it myself."

He turned back to Siobhan. "So Rebecca told you to forget it, then how come you're here?"

"I told her that I'd call the media and blow the whole thing wide open" she said dryly, a small smile creeping onto her face.

Danny's eyes widened. "You went as far as to blackmail Rebecca Fullerton Smythe? Oh my God! I can't believe you're even sitting here. She's one heavy hitter."

Siobhan sat up straighter and spooned sugar into her cup, some color coming back into her cheeks.

"She got me on a plane out of Dublin to Toronto and another flight to Vancouver. She had her contact Leroy pick me up at the airport and he got me on an RCMP helicopter flight that was leaving for Hanlon Falls. When I got off at the dock I asked for Danny Quigley or Pat Tarrant, a name Leroy had given me, and was pointed to the Maple Tavern."

There was a long silence as the group tried to take it all in.

Danny, sitting alongside her, put his arm round her.

"Hey look Siobhan, I know how brutal these long-haul flights are and how they can affect you. We'll get you to some accommodation and let you have a good long sleep. It wouldn't make any sense to dump everything on you as to what's happening right now. I think you're far too exhausted to take it in."

Pat interrupted him. "Look I can take her round to my place. There's a spare bed there and it's nice and quiet, apart from the pulp mill siren going off at shift change." She reached forward and touched Siobhan's shoulder lightly, as she spoke.

Siobhan just nodded, saying nothing.

Danny helped her onto her feet and gave her a re-assuring hug.

Within five minutes she was off out the door with Pat, leaving the two men sitting there looking across at each other.

# Chapter 19

The two men had barely sat there a moment when Rob Steele came through the door accompanied by another man. His companion was tall, ramrod straight and obviously First Nations. He didn't need the headband with the feather stuck in it to confirm his status. He had long bony features, hair as black as a crow and watchful piercing brown eyes. Danny picked up from his movement that he had been a soldier at some time in the not too distant past.

Competent and dangerous, he thought.

Rob waved to the barman and came over to them.

"Phil you already know Jeff Wilson or White Feather, his native name. Jeff this is Danny Quigley."

Danny stood up and reached across, gripping the man's hand.

He found himself held in a strong grip, noting the long powerful shoulders and the defensive stance. Their eyes were almost level and the Indian held his gaze for a long moment as if measuring him somehow.

Finally he nodded and murmured something, which Danny didn't catch.

If there was a smile there he didn't spot that either.

As they sat down Rob caught Danny's arm. "He said 'a warrior' Danny, I guess you didn't catch that."

Danny blinked. "I recognize the same in Jeff. He turned to him. "You served?" he asked.

Jeff made a small acknowledgment with his head and shoulder. "Crossed over into Washington State and joined up. Marines...were in Panama and Kosovo. Missed Afghanistan and Iraq... glad I did... white man's shit."

Danny chuckled. "I'll grant you that. It was shitty all right."

Jeff nodded at Rob. "He tells me there are stories of some stuff you did in Afghanistan and Iraq. Apparently now used for escape and evasion training with the SAS and Israeli Special Forces."

Danny looked uncomfortable. "Like all stories Jeff, they get bigger and better with the telling. Hell, I was just trying to stay alive. Some people just got in my way" he muttered.

For the first time he saw a flicker of a smile. "The Israelis don't fuck about. Hard bastards. I'll try not to get in your way."

They all burst out laughing and the atmosphere lightened.

The barman brought over Rob's beer.

Phil looked across at the Indian. "Do I gather from your remark that you're coming with us?"

"Try stopping me Phil. I have wanted to go into that territory for the past two years. Something strange going on in that area. I want to see for myself. From a business point of view I'd like to open up some new territory for my hunting and fishing business. Getting harder round here to please the trade, especially the Americans. They want virtually virgin lakes to throw their hooks into."

Rob cleared off the table and laid out a large map.

He pointed to an X marking deep in the middle of a huge chunk of territory.

"That's where the grid reference that Danny received is situated, and we assume that someone wants him to go there. Probably and hopefully his buddy C.C. Courtney, though he says that Courtney wouldn't have a clue about grid references. So your guess is as good as mine."

Phil looked at Jeff. "So the route then is…?"

"Straight down the main road for approximately five hours, then we do a hard right. " He pointed to some narrow lines. "These are small logging and mine roads which we can take for several more hours and then we hook north again until the roads run out. Bear in mind that roads that were used some years ago for logging and mining access get overgrown very quickly, trees fall down across them, river crossings disappear and so on, so we end up hiking in for the last day or so."

"What about animals in there?" Rob asked.

Jeff shrugged. "Probably bear and mountain lion. We can probably shoot a deer if we run short of food. Fish too if you want it, though I gather there's nothing touristy about this trip?"

It was a question.

Phil coughed and glanced across at Danny. "You better tell him."

Danny gave a pained expression. "The more I tell this story, the more crazy it sounds. "He glanced at the Indian. "Okay, here it is. I got a strong warning in Vancouver that some group was out to get me. I barely avoided getting shot in a shooting range outside Vancouver where the people involved just disappeared, and last night three guys tried to take me out on the road above town here. I got two of them and Phil's crew took the other one down. Now today I get another message that these guys are Serbs, in Canada illegally, and that there are more coming after me."

The Indian stared at him for a moment. "No ideas as to what their resources are, what operation they might mount?"

"Nope." Phil answered for him. "But it's a real threat and we have to assume that they may come after us into the woods."

Danny couldn't be sure but he thought he detected a flicker of anticipation on Jeff's face, who continued "We better make sure our Comms are working and that we can call in some back-up if we get hit."

He glanced at Phil. "What could you have on standby. The First Nations of course do their own tribal policing, but the RCMP have Federal jurisdiction."

Phil sighed wearily. "To be honest I've been up to my tonsils in these killings last night. I've been swamped with RCMP top brass, who want this thing put to bed. As for me trying to arrange cover for the trip. I'd have been told in no uncertain terms to forget it. As it is I'm going to be stealing out of town and hoping the brass down south don't notice me missing for a week. Some hope! I can probably kiss my career goodbye after this trip" he said gloomily."

Danny looked thoughtful. "Could Pat get CSIS to give us some back up if needed? Even a chopper if we had wounded to get out. I hope not but I know from experience that preparation is the key. Plan for the worst and you won't have any nasty surprises."

Phil made a note. "Okay, I'll pop over there when we're through here and see what Pat can do. Now tell Jeff about the two women" he instructed.

The Indian's face was inscrutable, but Danny could tell from the slight widening of his eyes that he accepted a trained CSIS agent like Pat coming, but a female who lacked outdoor experience was pushing it, until he mentioned that she was a nurse… and had the gift.

A look of almost reverence crossed his face. "A holy woman… ah… that is good medicine. Yes, she is welcome."

Rob, Phil and Danny exchanged astonished looks.

They arranged to leave in two days time.

# Chapter 20

They walked along the shoreline later that evening as the last rays of the blazing sunset colored the horizon.

She sighed, holding Danny's arm tighter.

"You hear about places like this where nature is so incredibly beautiful. Reminds me of the poem about The Lake Isle of Inisfree..."

"Yes' Danny interrupted... "Where peace come dropping low, dropping from the veils of morning to where the cricket sings. Is that how it goes?"

She stopped in her tracks. "I had no idea, that someone like you, brought up an Englishman, would know any Irish poetry" she exclaimed.

He grinned. "Well, I was born in Ireland and brought up in Wales, so the Celtic influence was there, and that sparked my interest in Irish literature at school. Believe me, that's about the limit of my scholastic achievements Siobhan. Oh, and C.C. brought me out to the Isle of Inisfree, when I was in Sligo. After all the hype, I thought it disappointing really, it was such a small island. Now how are things back in the women's hostel?"

"All going well thanks to your most generous contribution" she replied, giving him a swift peck on the cheek.

Siobhan ran a women's hostel and health clinic in Ireland, where she took in pregnant women and supported them during this time, helping most of them to find adoptive parents for their babies. Some of the women were naive Irish girls who went to England and got sucked into the game of prostitution, a number ending up on drugs. Siobhan's clinic was now helping the women to break the habit and start a new life. They were given direction and support in breaking free, and some decided to keep their babies. The clinic tried to involve their families as well, to lend support and encouragement where possible, and the initiative had amazingly positive outcomes.

It had been C.C. Courtney who had initially underpinned the finances of the hostel until his disappearance. Prior to his disappearance, he had deeded his Financial Planning business to Danny, despite his being new to the business. He had passed on any existing commission accruals to the hostel. Unfortunately they were not sufficient to keep it solvent, and it was on the brink of closing down when MI5 asked Danny to carry out a mission for them, offering a sizable fee, which he passed on to Siobhan.

She looked up at him now. "How are your ex-wife Fiona, and Allison, your cute little daughter doing?"

Danny's face broke out into a huge grin. "Allison is getting more like her Dad every day." He exclaimed. "Much to the dismay of her mother, I must say."

"Oh, how?" she asked.

"Well, I was involved with some terrorists and she said 'I hope you shot him Dad.' Cool as a cucumber she was."

"Are you sure that you should be proud of this characteristic Danny? What about more girlish, gentler traits?"

His grin disappeared. "Yeah, you're right. Fiona says that violence just follows me like a plague and that I'm too dangerous to be around Allison any more. Well, I'm working on this."

"Hmm… not doing too well, from what you told me about this hit team."

He stopped her then gripping her arm tightly. "But don't you see Siobhan, you could end up right in the middle of it out there. I don't know what to expect once we leave here. Hell, I went for a run the other night and was close to getting killed."

She stared him down. "I'm coming Danny and that's it. Anyway that Indian said I'm welcome, so there."

"First Nations, we're supposed to call them that. Indian is something from John Wayne movies." He muttered as he tried to marshal his thoughts. "It's just that any female I come in contact with ends up getting hurt. Look at Jacky, the hit-and-run in London and Sophia getting blown up in Thames house. Apart from that Siobhan, and this might hurt. Having a non-combat person on the trip and a female at that, really makes us all more vulnerable."

"That part I understand Danny and I agree. I can only promise to keep my head down if we get attacked. I may actually surprise you. Remember I worked in a busy ER department in London and that was hell on earth some days, I can tell you."

He'd lost the argument and he knew it.

"Look Siobhan, about us..." He started.

"I'm glad you brought it up Danny. Look this trip is all about finding C.C. Anything we have going for us I want to park until this is over, one way or the other. Getting back into a physical relationship with you right now just wouldn't feel right as my whole spiritual dimension is focused on finding C.C. Can you accept that?"

He nodded, a flicker of regret on his face.

"Sure I understand Siobhan. Sometimes easier said than done, though I can certainly be more alert if you and Pat are sharing a tent together, than lying two feet away from me."

"Hopefully not too far from your tent, in case we need some protection."

He smacked his forehead. "That reminds me, I had my pistol confiscated as evidence. I need to tackle Sergeant Dryden for a replacement, just in case.

"You know Danny; all your fears may be for nothing. The trip in and out might go smooth as butter. We might find C.C. and be back here within the week and without any more attacks on you. Wouldn't that be something?"

"God, I sure hope so!" he said fervently. "But just in case…"

"Yes, I hear you…prepare for the worst. It's no different in medicine Danny. So let's go get your pistol."

# Chapter 21

It was a crisp early morning, loaded with breakfast from the Bear Inn when the column crept quietly out of Hanlon Falls and headed south.

Three Jeeps, one pulling a medium sized trailer.

White Feather (Jeff Wilson) led in the first with Pat as his co-driver.

The lean six-footer Bob Sharpe, from JTF2 was in the 2nd with Siobhan.

The third vehicle carried Sergeant Phil Dryden and Danny.

The first leg was three hours down the straight, narrow, boring road. Then a promised stop at a wayside diner, mainly the haunt of truck drivers bringing the pulp mill products out and supplies in.

Danny was learning fast that coffee time was almost a religious experience to Canadians and had bumped into the famous Tim Horton's, a coffee and donut restaurant, on a previous trip.

He spent the three hours learning more about Phil and the famous and historical RCMP.

When pressed, he admitted that the Police Force was a pale image of what it used to be back in frontier days, with poor management and leadership. He had strong words to say about the selection process for new recruits, and bitched about the people who now ran the organization.

At one point Danny ventured a remark: "you know Phil, you're talking about something that's not just limited to the RCMP. It's in the military, in business at the highest levels, in hospitals and even non-profit and charitable organizations. I bumped into some of the RCMP overseas, training emerging Police Forces and their professionalism was shit hot. Don't under-rate yourselves. You know the world has changed since the frontier days. There's a great lack of respect and let's admit it, appreciation for the job you people do, as well as teachers. It's not easy being a cop these days and yeah, it seems that the brown-nosers get to the top while the decent good guys are sidelined. You're not telling me that you would like to be in Ottawa or Vancouver making policy or sitting on some disciplinary panel or citizen's complaint panel?"

Phil slowed down as a deer shot across almost on top of the hood.

"God, almost totaled before we've had our first coffee break. Nooooo... you're right Danny. It would kill me to be doing any of that crap. I'll gladly leave it to the snivelers, though I take your point. It does seem to the rank and file that the incompetents push their way to the top and then haven't the skills to properly manage the direction and reputation of a Force that we love so much. It just kills the retired members to see that what they built up is being flushed down the toilet, that's all.

But look, thanks for your comments about the lads working overseas. I'm told that one doesn't appreciate just how good we are, until you train overseas and see policemen going out on patrol with no shoes, patrol vehicles or even the most basic of skills."

After some more small chat they both fell silent as Danny took in the miles and miles of pine trees on both sides of the road, a road that went straight south without any deviation.

Before they knew it they were pulling off for the much-anticipated first coffee break. It was a sprawled-out complex and some gas pumps, where a half-dozen trucks were parked, together with a number of dusty pick-ups.

Inside was a bar/ diner, and before long they were grouped around a circular table as Phil made a quick note on orders and disappeared up to the counter.

Siobhan grabbed his arm. "Did you see that bear Danny?' she said, her eyes excited.

"No, but Phil just avoided getting clobbered by a deer. I couldn't believe how fast they move, like lightning."

Bob stuck his head forward. "You should see the vehicles that get hit by moose in Newfoundland. Do they ever smash them up! The place is over run by them. A hundred vehicles written off each month at least. I was posted down there for 6 months on a training course."

Phil just came back and heard the tail end of the conversation. "Yeah, we have a template for deer/car accidents. It's simple. No statement from the deer either. They're usually injured and we have to finish them off."

Siobhan shuddered. "Oh those poor animals! Such beautiful, silky brown coats."

Jeff's brown eyes flickered to her. "Better shot than torn to shreds, still alive, by wolves and coyotes, or the eagles."

The arrival of some snacks and coffee put an end to the small talk as everyone got stuck in. Danny tried a Danish pastry and Siobhan nibbled on a stale Boston cream donut.

Phil checked with each of them as to how the vehicles were performing, and all reported no problems. In two hours they would be turning off the tarmacadam road onto a gravel road and he suggested that they keep more of a distance between them to avoid the clouds of dust flying up. Jeff had previously told the number two vehicle occupants to regularly check that number three was still with them.

When he had finished his coffee, and before the rest of the group were ready, Bob nodded across to Danny, indicating that he come outside.

He followed him out and crossed over to the jeep with the trailer.

He reached inside and hauled out a long bulky object, which he handed to Danny.

"Have a look," he instructed.

He suspected that it was a weapon and unwrapped it carefully.

His jaw dropped. "Where the hell did you get this?" he demanded.

Bob grinned. "Thought I'd surprise you, especially in Canada, with our gun laws."

Danny shook his head. "An assault rifle with a grenade launcher attachment."

"Yeah, thought it might be useful, especially with the news of some possible action. Oh, I brought it back in a military aircraft from overseas. Should have seen some of the stuff we bring back in. Mostly for souvenirs. None of the lads are into selling them. Like it?"

"Well yes, but have you any grenades or ammo?"

A bigger grin. "Got a half dozen grenades I picked up across the border at one of those road side gun places, and got four full mags."

Danny held it reverently. "This could prove to be very useful if we get hit. No one would expect us to have something like this." He looked up at him. "What did the Sergeant say about this?"

More grins. "He doesn't know. He will soon enough if we get attacked and then he won't mind, I'm sure."

Danny shook his head. "Rob, you believe in living dangerously for sure. Keep it to yourself for the moment." He glanced across at the building. "I need the washroom before we head off, though I know there's a million trees out there I can stand behind."

Within ten minutes they topped up the gas tanks and were on the road again.

They had settled into a rhythm.

# Chapter 22

The pace and tempo changed once they switched off the paved highway on to the gravel road. Phil cursed as the dust started penetrating the canvas sides of the jeep and eased further back from the second vehicle.

He flicked a glance across at Danny.

"You must have run into this stuff in the desert over there. I've heard stories of how sand storms can spring up out of nowhere and completely disorient people caught out in them. That could really screw up an operation I guess.?"

Danny caught the inferred question but stayed silent.

Phil wasn't ready to give up. "That ever happen to you?"

"Well, the supply convoys coming from Kuwait into Iraq ran into these sudden sand storms. They had no option but to pull over and hunker down until they passed and that could take several hours. A mate of mine arrived in a camp out in the desert that got caught up in a similar storm and it tore the campsite to shreds. Canvas flapping all over the place and sand up to the windscreen on the jeeps, that they had to dig out afterwards. Of course you can imagine how difficult it was to keep weapons clean and ready for action."

"Speaking of weapons, Pat picked up from Leroy and your friend at MI5, that you'd done some sniping over there. Anything interesting?"

"Well snipers played a big part in Iraq, which didn't get much publicity. I can tell you that those who are in a sniper's section are glad about that. It's all about slipping into a target area, settling down into a hide and waiting for your target to appear. More often than not they don't, and you just crawl out a day or two later carrying your own crap and urine in a plastic bag. The U.S. Marines are past masters of the art and have the best sniping course in the world."

"Which you attended I believe. What was your best shot out there? I've read about the recon units in Vietnam and the incredible kill ratio of the top snipers."

Danny made a face.

Most Special Forces, and especially snipers, who he classed as a special breed, didn't particularly like talking about their experiences. Sometimes they ran into conflicting views as to 'what's the big deal, killing someone from a thousand yards out, well away from personal danger'.

That's because they hadn't a clue as to what they were talking about.

The years of training, the personal deprivation in lying out in a hide for days, avoiding enemy sweeps, who may pass by within inches, and the fear of dog patrols sniffing you out. Not to mention the extraction afterwards, when all hell could break loose as the enraged enemy casts a wide net to find the sniper team.

Reluctantly, and probably because the journey was boring, he volunteered an incident, hoping it would get Phil off the subject completely.

"Best shot Phil? Probably an Iranian bomb maker I took down in a emerging sand storm at five hundred yards, in Basra. I mean five hundred yards is nothing to brag about when you figure that those Marines in Vietnam were killing the Viet Cong and NVA at over a thousand yards."

"In a rising sand storm, probably with the wind velocity ramping up too, I'd say that was some shot Danny. Sorry, I'm guessing that you guys would just as soon not talk about it. Bob's the same. He doesn't say much. I gather he had a few hairy experiences in Afghanistan."

Glad to change the subject, Danny interjected.

"The Canadians adapted very well over there from doing peace missions to direct combat. The U.S. Forces were very cool fighters after nearly nine years at war, but your Canadians were formidable warriors and the Americans and us Brits were always happy to go out on patrol with them. They were always competent under fire and pulled their weight. You could rely on them to be there when things got sticky. More than I can say for some of the other NATO allies."

"Yeah, I read about the caveats some countries would write into their participation.

They would send their troops to Afghanistan as long as they were left out of the hot areas like Kandahar province and others."

"I should say that there were other nationalities that played a significant part as well. I don't mean to exclude their efforts.... soldiers sent home in body bags, and you have to recognize their courage. The Aussie Special Forces were real tough bastards. Loved to fight and were good at it. No Taliban Forces could take them on, and by the way the Canadians were never beaten in any battle with the Taliban. They had excellent strategy and tactics and first class leadership in the field. Their use of field artillery support dovetailed beautifully with their leopard tanks on the ground, as the enemy found out on many occasions."

They had to stop it there as the jeeps ahead were pulling over.

Their first puncture.

Ten hours after leaving Hanlon Falls they pulled off the gravel road onto a narrow logging trail which headed in a northerly direction.

Just five hundred yards in they found a large clearing, pulled over and parked.

Tired, dusty and weary, they planned to set up their first night camp.

Jeff, with his hunting party experience had the camp set up in double quick time with the three-man tents, separated by some distance, sitting snugly behind some trees. The policeman Phil had moved away and was using his satellite phone.

The two women were sharing one of the tents, and they disappeared into it.

Danny and Bob were sharing a second and Phil and Jeff the last.

Before very long Jeff had a fire going and a small gas barbeque set up with a table and camping chairs. He slapped some steaks on the barbeque after shouting "Food in thirty minutes."

Danny and Bob had helped unload the trailer and distributed sleeping bags to the tents. Within minutes they were sitting back in the camp chairs with a beer each. Bob was drawing hungrily on a cigarette.

"Light me one up too Bob." Pat Tarrant had just wandered up. She had changed into a woolen sweater and already looked like she was feeling better.

Danny glanced up. "Siobhan okay?" he enquired.

She nodded. "Just zonked out from jet lag and ten hours of being shaken around in a jeep. I'm not sure she'll eat very much. She's just flaked out on the sleeping bed."

Danny went as if to get up but she waved him back. "Just let her be for awhile Danny. I'll bring her something later."

Phil wandered over. "The media are still on a feeding frenzy and the immigration department is denying that they may have soft pedaled some applicants from Bosnia. Everybody is covering their asses. The good news is that no one knows I'm off on a jaunt in the woods. Long may it last" he said fervently.

Phil grabbed a beer and offered one to the Indian, but he refused.

Pat leaned forward and whispered. "He never drinks on any of his escorted trips.

Booze makes him a little squirrelly... you know, Indians "she hinted, as if that would explain everything. She probably knew, being part native herself.

She didn't refuse a beer herself though, and the rest of the evening settled into a pleasant time of eating good steaks, washing them down with beer and enjoying relaxed conversation.

Pat checked with Siobhan and found her still fast asleep.

They all settled in early.

At Danny's suggestion, they decided that the men take turns on guard duty, changing every two hours.

# Chapter 23

Danny pulled the two to four shifts and spent the time getting familiar with the area. There was little variety. It was all woods and brush. He drifted back two hundred yards to the gravel road they had pulled off prior to camping for the night.

Nothing stirred, apart from the occasional sounds of what he took to be small animals back in the brush. It was a black cloudy sky with the moon breaking through and flooding the place with dim light. It reminded him of a lot of other nights when they waited, not knowing if contact with the enemy was imminent.

In these peaceful surroundings, it was hard to even think about an enemy presence anywhere within a thousand miles.

Long may it last, he thought fervently.

He called the Sergeant who groaned in protest but crawled out and headed outside.

Danny lay down and was asleep in seconds.

Somewhere in his mind, perhaps a dim memory of the past, he heard the sound of choppers and shifted uneasily, then fell back to sleep.

He woke suddenly.

The cold touch of metal on his forehead shocked him into consciousness and he tried to sit up.

"Move and you're dead, Bastard." A voice spat in his ear. "Everybody's cuffed outside, including the women."

Rough hands pulled him to his feet and plastic cuffs were fasted tightly to his wrists.

He looked up, into the face of the man who had tried to blow his head off at the shooting club.

The man grinned.

Somehow it didn't reach his eyes, which soulless, were like dead sharks

"The pleasure's all mine Quigley. We weren't properly introduced back at the gun club. Pierre La Fonte at your service, but not for long, nor for very long my friend."

Two men dragged him outside and hauled him to his feet.

Danny looked around. The first strands of daylight were starting to penetrate the clearing.

He heard a sobbing off to one side.

It was coming from the RCMP Sergeant, Phil, cuffed and on his knees with all the other members of the group.

"Jesus Danny, I'm sorry!" He shouted hoarsely.

La Fonte laughed. "Yeah, asleep in the jeep if you like. Some guard duty."

Danny was pushed forward and forced to his knees beside the group.

Phil started to say something again and was kicked in the face by one of the men and sent sprawling.

Danny glanced sideways. Bob Sharpe was on his knees next to him and was kneeling erect, his face thrust forward defiantly.

Next to Bob was Siobhan, her head down and trembling with shock and fright.

Next to her was Pat Tarrant, crouching silently, her eyes, gimlet-like and fastened on La Fonte, like he was a rattler ready to strike.

Jeff Wilson was alongside her, his powerful shoulders straining hopelessly against the plastic cuffs, his face inscrutable, his piercing brown eyes flicking around the clearing as if looking for an escape route.

There was none that Danny could see.

Several large men in pseudo military gear stood around the clearing, with weapons held at high alert. La Fonte was wearing chinos and a red woolen lumberjack shirt.

Laid out in front of Danny's group was a collection of the weapons they had brought with them.

La Fonte leaned forward and picked up one.

"A grenade launcher. What were you going to do with that out here? Knock a tree down?"

He picked up the Winchester. "Now this, Pierre keeps for himself. Nice weapon and lots of history. I like that, which leads me to the main point here. Quigley, you won't have any more history after today."

Danny straightened on his knees, looking across at La Fonte.

"Look, I don't know you from Adam, La Fonte. Just tell me this. Why have you been trying to kill me, both in Vancouver and up in Hanlon Falls?"

La Fonte chuckled. "You want to talk, yes? Every man I killed wanted to talk. Just to postpone the inevitable. Life becomes so sweet when you know you have no more time left. Whatever... why not? You know about a nuclear weapon placed in Iraq. Some people don't like loose ends. Big people like Steve Walchuk in the Middle East CIA and Bret Zeitner, whom I believe you know. All want you dead Quigley."

Danny flicked his head around at the group kneeling beside him.

"Fine, kill me, but what about these people? They've done nothing. Let them go La Fonte, for God's sake!"

He didn't mind that his voice was pleading at this stage.

"Danny, Danny" La Fonte chided. "A man of the world, and a very violent world at that. We have a lot in common. You think Pierre leaves witnesses? Come on my friend, get real."

Danny's voice hardened. "La Fonte, you and I have nothing in common. I only killed when my country tasked me with a mission, or when my life was in danger. You are nothing but a slime ball and someone who sneaks up behind someone like you did in Vancouver and tried to put a bullet in my head."

Pat's voice whispered beside him. "Don't provoke him Danny."

La Font's cold killer eyes fastened on him.

203

"Oh we have some entertainment planned before the main event, but I don't think you'll like it Quigley."

He nodded to two of the armed men standing back.

They came forward and hauled Danny to his knees.

La Fonte continued talking. "You see, you have some history with these gentlemen. In Bosnia and Kosovo it seems that the SAS snipers took out a number of their colleagues, and when I told them that, according to our information, you were over here, they wanted to come on this little jaunt and meet you personally."

He stopped talking and nodded. The group of men gathered in closer to watch

That was the signal for the beating to begin.

It was systematic and brutal and Danny had little chance to defend himself. His only benefit was that by having his hands cuffed in front, he managed to block some of the more savage blows and kicks.

It went on for a long time.

He heard Siobhan cry out, but his mind had distanced himself from the beating.

He was only still standing, because two held him as one carried out the beating. Then when he was tired, they switched over.

They got angrier when he refused to make any sound or beg for mercy.

Finally they stopped and Danny collapsed to the ground.

Siobhan spun round and tried to lift his head, but was roughly pulled to her feet by two grinning men.

La Fonte continued to speak as if the brutal beatings had never happened.

"You see Danny, these Serbs killed all the men in a village over there. Muslims were nothing but maggots anyway, as far as they were concerned. Then they took all the women and put them in a large building. Every day at their leisure they would stroll over and select some of those juicy young Muslim women and do them the favor of trying to impregnate them with good clean Christian blood. It was every man's fantasy. They claimed that the girls struggled and protested in front of their families but actually loved it when they were getting hammered. Now where's the point you say? Well, I'll tell you."

Siobhan's head jerked up. "You stupid, stupid little man! I've been a nurse for fifteen years and I've never known a woman yet who enjoyed being raped! You bastard!" she shouted.

Danny struggled to sit up, as he felt horror attack his mind. 'Jesus, no! he screamed inside. Out loud he said. "Siobhan, don't provoke the prick."

La Fonte chuckled again. He started moving across to a large tree, shouting back as he did so. "You guessed it right Quigley. The seven here and the three in the choppers are going to have some fun with the girls first, like back in Bosnia. They miss that time, and talk of nothing else when they get pissed. Love to join them, but my tastes run somewhat differently."

He undid his fly. "I'll just have a leak while they have their fun."

With that each of the two women were hauled to their feet by a group of the Serbs who started to drag them across towards the two tents.

Siobhan's voice cut like a whipsaw across Danny's nerves.

"Danny, please, help me... please. Nooooooo, please noooooo" she shouted frantically.

The cold steel of the weapons pressed against the back of his head.

The five remaining Serbs stood there grinning.

The tent canvas had only just closed over the opening when the screaming began.

Then it happened.

A scythe of bullets cut across the clearing, thudding into the Serbs and catapulting them backwards.

There was a stunned moment of silence and Danny, without thinking of his injuries was on his feet and hurtling across towards the tent. He didn't realize that Bob was on his feet also and closely behind him.

He tore into the tent just as the large Serb was starting to pull his trousers up, and Danny kicked him, right in the crotch, harder than he had kicked anyone or anything before. The Serb screamed and dropped like he was pole axed. Danny didn't stop. He dropped straight down on his neck with his knee, hearing it crunch, and knew the man was dead.

He turned to Siobhan. "Did he...?" he started.

"No, thank God, he wanted me to ...." she indicated her mouth.

He touched her head gently for a moment and turning, leapt through the tent opening and ran smack bang into a large, almost naked figure.

His jaw dropped.

It was an Indian in full war paint.

The Indian reached forward with a knife.

Danny tensed.

The Indian cut of his cuffs and placed something in his hands.

Danny looked down. It was the grenade launcher.

The Indian pointed back through the trees.

Danny saw a figure running towards the road.

A figure wearing a red shirt.

He pointed enquiringly to the other tent where he knew Pat had been dragged.

The Indian made a cutting gesture across his throat and then turned Danny around and pushed him after the running figure.

As he hared off he spotted the rest of his group being cut free and raised to their feet by more Indians.

He felt the pain now in his limbs and muscles, but tried to ignore them and focused on closing the distance between himself and what he assumed was a helicopter, which had utilized the gravel road to land on. He heard the sound of chopper blades revving up. They sounded extremely loud.

His hands played along the weapon as he gritted his teeth, his legs hammering beneath him.

He was getting closer.

He saw the red sweatered figure jump into a chopper and knew it would be close. He ran another dozen yards and dropped to his knees as the chopper started to rise from the ground. Just as he pulled the trigger he was startled to see the shape of a second chopper drift across in front of the one that La Fonte had clambered into.

Hell, there were two of them!

The second chopper took the full blast of the grenade and burst into flames, dropping to the ground.

The first chopper rose drunkenly and as Danny frantically tried to fire a second grenade, it turned and headed south, disappearing over the top of the trees.

Danny lay on his knees panting from the effort.

He scrambled to his feet and then ran forward until he was as close to the burning chopper as the heat would allow him. He glimpsed two figures inside in flames and thought about opening up with the assault weapon.

Hell, let the flames do the job.

He turned back towards the camp.

What would he find there?

# Chapter 24

As he approached the group, he spotted one of the dead Serbs sprawled on the ground.

His eyes widened, as he froze in mid-stride.

Just then Bob ran across to him.

He glanced at the ground and then up at Danny.

"They're all the same" he panted.

Danny shook his head.

He thought he'd seen everything. "Scalped, all of them?" he asked hoarsely.

Bob nodded. "All of them. Even Siobhan, the nurse, threw up when she went across to one of them. What about the chopper?"

"There were two choppers. I took down one with the grenade launcher. Two dead in the crash."

"La Fonte?"

"No, the bastard got away in the other chopper, heading south."

"Shit, that little weasel... what a mess! Who could have figured this! Some people back there really want you dead Danny."

"Yeah, and no reservations about how many they take with me." He looked across at the group.

"How are they doing?" he asked.

"Jeff and Pat are solid. Probably hit them later. The Sergeant is shaken but starting to get his act together. Won't meet my eyes...knows he nearly got all of us killed. Feel sorry for the poor bastard... he's gonna live with this one forever."

Danny grunted. "In the troop, he'd be on evac and out of the unit. I feel like punching the shit out of him. Falling asleep on guard duty for crying out loud."

Bob glanced at his body. "Took one shit kicking back there yourself Danny. We need to get Siobhan to check you out. How you hared off up that fucking road after going through that, I'll never know."

Danny knew he'd taken a severe beating and could already feel his body crying out and stiffening up.

"What happened in Pat's tent? You were right behind me when I made a dash for where Siobhan had been dragged to."

Bob laughed. "When I got inside that fucking rapist was impaled on a knife a foot long, wielded by this big Indian in war paint. I grabbed Pat and hauled her out of there. I still didn't know whose side they were on. Were we just going from the frying pan into the fire? I had no idea, until I stepped outside and saw the group being cut loose. I was cut free a second later and the Indians disappeared like shadows, but not before they scalped those Serb bastards."

The Sergeant was just finishing up a call on his satellite phone.

"The RCMP are flying in a whole bunch of stuff. An incident room, forensic lab, a large team of investigators. This is a major incident with possible international implications, certainly the CIA for one, at this stage."

He looked somberly at Danny.

"This is the end of your trip Danny. It goes no further. Too many dead. Too many threads to unravel. I've been instructed to lock down everything and everyone right now."

Siobhan's voice was pleading.

"Danny, what about C.C.? We can't leave him out here!"

He was about to answer when a thought occurred to him.

"How the hell did they find us, all the way out here?"

The Sergeant stared at him for a moment, as his expression cleared.

"That dammed garage in Hanlon Falls! They were servicing our vehicles right there in front of us."

Danny turned to Bob. "Do a search of the jeeps. You're looking for tracking devices."

As he dashed off Danny turned to the RCMP Sergeant.

"We're heading off out of here in twenty minutes. You have to stay, obviously. Tell your brass that we'd pulled out when you got back from checking the downed chopper."

The Sergeant straightened to his full height.

"This is a major Federal event now Danny. You'll have the full force of the Federal

Government coming after you, if you try to carry on. I could stop you, you know."

"No you couldn't." he said quietly, staring him in the eyes. "Here's the thing Sergeant, turn a blind eye for the next half hour, and when we eventually give our statements, as we will have to, there will be no mention of how you fell asleep on guard duty and nearly had us all killed."

"That's blackmail Danny" he protested, his face reddening.

Before Danny could reply, Bob came dashing back, holding some objects in his hand.

"Two of the jeeps had tracking devices. We can check later on in case they planted a second device."

Danny grabbed him by the shoulder. "Load up two of the jeeps and the trailer for the five of us. The Sergeant stays here and is letting us continue despite his superiors telling him to lockdown everything here on the site. I want to be out of here in twenty minutes. Move!" he barked.

He turned back to the RCMP Sergeant.

"Can I make a quick call from your satellite phone?" he asked.

"I can't let you Danny. I'll have to tell them you were gone when I finished the last call. A call from you on my phone now would show that to be a lie. I'm in enough trouble already. Just get your gang out of here as fast as you can."

"Okay, thanks for that. Look, how long have we got before they get here and then start looking for us?"

"How long is a piece of string? How much resources will they pile in here right off the bat? They may want to sanitize this crime scene first and get the bodies out. That would tie up their choppers. I would think about 2 to 3 hours before you hear chopper blades at your rear. When they do catch up Danny, my advice is, don't take any offensive action against them. That would be curtains for you."

Danny nodded. "Don't worry Phil, I've no intention of tackling Canada's finest. However, a favor. Call the MI5 director in London, Rebecca Fullerton Smythe and brief her, and especially pass those three names to her."

"You mean Pierre La Fonte, Walchuk and Bret Zeitner? Don't worry, they're engraved on my mind forever."

A faraway look came into Danny's gaze. "It's a shame really. Yeah, I shot some of those bastards over in Bosnia and Kosovo, but I met a lot of fine Serbs and Yugoslavs as well. People who would make ideal citizens here in Canada. This will start a witch hunt on them won't it?"

"Not your concern now Danny. All I can say is that we don't shoot from the hip up here, unlike our southern neighbor. You'll find a measured response and an enquiry that will still be going on in five years time. Now, for God's sake get the hell out of here."

They tore out of the clearing ten minutes later.

The Sergeant held his thumb up as Danny's jeep swept past.

# Chapter 25

The narrow logging road was slow going. Every ten miles or so they had to stop and drag a fallen tree off the road, and on two occasions, they needed the chain saw.

After two hours Danny felt they were running out of time. It didn't take a genius to figure out that a helicopter could sweep up behind them, and then it was game over.

Driving the lead jeep with Jeff, the First Nations man, he finally waved them off into a brush-covered notch in the tall trees and jumped out.

The second jeep pulled up behind them and Pat, Siobhan and Bob piled out.

"Problem Danny?" Pat called.

He looked at them, frustration covering his face.

"I figure they'll be on top of us at any time. We need to get the jeeps under cover with good camo. Hopefully they won't spot us, so do a good job covering anything reflective and break the form and shapes down. Bob and I will show you how."

Jeff looked around. "So are we camping here? It's kinda soon isn't it?"

"I figure that they'll do one sweep up this track for another 20 miles or so and then come back down. Though obviously, the first tree they see across the road will tell them we're in this catchment area. However back down the road, every battle scene takes on many dimensions. Bodies to get out, more people to fly in... the crime scene itself, gathering brass and taking pictures and measurements... every one of the top RCMP brass will want a piece of this so more demands on their transport. In essence we may be a loose end, and when you think about it, haven't actually committed any crime. We're witnesses in effect and will eventually have to be scooped up. The Sergeant back there may downplay any view that we are trying to flee the scene. If there are any leaks to the media, and there always are, you'll have choppers all landing up and down the gravel road out there with the need to contain them and keep them at a distance."

"A bit of wishful thinking Danny. No crime, you say? You killed three people back there.... again" Pat said drily.

He sighed. "Yeah, you got it in spades. But if I'm right, as soon as they sweep back down that logging road, I suggest we get moving again. We may have to camp early and travel at night or abandon the jeeps entirely further up."

Jeff nodded. "If we can get another day on the logging road, that would position us nicely to walk in the rest... no roads up there, even for jeeps."

They exploded into a flurry of activity as the vehicles were pushed in under overhanging brush. Jeff went back and brushed out the jeep tracks leaving the road.

Twenty minutes later they heard the chopper, as it swept low over their site, heading north.

It never wavered in its flight.

A half hour later it swept back down the road again.

They all stood up again from where they had been hunkered down.

"Got that one right Danny." Bob remarked.

He made a face. "They're not fools those guys. Apart from discovering fallen trees, they probably landed further up, if they found somewhere solid enough and checked the roads for tracks. They may know now that we're contained somewhere in this area and may be back for a more careful reconnoiter, and with more choppers. So let's try and make some tracks and try to break out of the area. We can pull off early, back into the deep woods." He glanced at Bob, a grin playing across his face.

"No steaks tonight my friend. We can't risk any fires."

They stuck to the plan and eventually, after pushing it hard for several hours, they nosed into a thick batch of brush, surrounded by tall majestic trees. It was a perfect camping place and even had a small twenty-yard size pool of water that Jeff figured was home for a beaver family. It had a crystal clear creek flowing into one end and out the other. After they had done their camo and set up the camp, Danny had gone across to the pool, stripped to his shorts and eased his body gratefully into the water.

There was a gasp from behind him.

"Danny, your whole body is bruised black and blue."

It was Siobhan.

He smiled crookedly. "Yeah, it's been stiffening up all day. I took some bad punishment today that jeep ride was brutal."

"I don't even have anything to rub on it. You must be in absolute agony" she said looking around desperately.

"You do now." Jeff had walked up and thrust a large jar into her hands.

"This'll do the trick Siobhan, along with those healing hands of yours."

She unscrewed the jar cap and looked at the black sticky grease inside. She touched it tentatively and sniffed it.

"God, that smells terrible! What is it?" she asked.

He smiled faintly. "You don't want to know." He produced a blanket and laid it on the ground.

"Let's get Danny out and dry him off and then you can apply this ah...stuff all over those bruises. Believe me he'll be a new man in a few hours time."

Whether it was Siobhan's gentle hands or the ointment doing its job, he fell asleep on the blanket and woke some hours later feeling remarkably fitter. Someone had thrown another blanket across his body.

A form loomed up out of the gloom. It was Pat carrying a paper plate with some cold cuts, buttered bread, and a can of juice.

"Orders from the nurse. You're to eat." She sat down beside him.

He sat up groggily. "Wow, I don't normally go off like that. Went out like a light."

He wriggled sideways up against a small oak tree.

"We all saw your bruises while it was still daylight. Some beating you took Danny. How do you feel now?"

He stretched and moved his body left and right.

"Surprisingly better. Whatever that stuff is, it really works. What's in it exactly?" he asked.

"Melted dog. An old Indian medicine."

"Oh Christ" he exploded. "Don't tell Siobhan. Whatever would it do to her nursing ethics? Melted dog!"

She glanced down at his shape. "Where's the worst pain?"

He pointed. "My right thigh. I used it to block a lot of kicks directed at my crotch."

"Not that I'm interested, but did you sustain any injury there?"

He grinned. "You're something else Pat. I could almost say you're half Irish instead of Indian...sorry First Nations."

A smile flickered across her high cheekbones.

She shook her head. "The guy's half dead and he's flirting with me."

She made a shushing sound and hunkered down beside him, placing her hands on his right thigh.

"Just try and relax the muscle Danny. I want to knead that muscle and do some work on it. Again, something I picked up from my native background. If we can get that muscle sorted early, it'll heal faster and keep you from hobbling around for the next week."

An hour later he was sitting further back in the brush with the rest of the group.

# Chapter 26

Langley, Virginia

Bret Zeitner leapt to his feet as the door to his office burst open.

It was Steve Walchuk, a desperate, haggard look to his face.

Zeitner saw the apologetic look on his secretary's face behind him.

"I tried to stop him Sir but he was like a man possessed." she said.

He came round the desk and moved across to Walchuk, whose chest was heaving.

Zeitner nodded to his secretary and she quietly closed the door and left.

He lightly caught Walchuk's arm and led him across to a chair, which he slumped into.

He studied the man. His clothing looked like he'd slept in them and there was a streak of what looked like green toothpaste stuck under his bottom lip.

"Just what the hell is going on Steve? Why not call me first if you have a problem? We could have met outside somewhere. Wandering round the building looking like

220

that will start all sorts of rumors and speculation."

"Doesn't matter now... anyway. I'm screwed... you're screwed too," he mumbled.

Zeitner felt his stomach tense.

"For God's sake tell me what's happened Walchuk!" He reached down and shook the man roughly.

Walchuk suddenly seemed to get a grip on himself and straightened in the chair.

He took a few deep breaths and peered up at Zeitner.

"Pierre La Fonte, ran an op across the border into British Columbia."

Zeitner froze. "Ran an illegal operation over the border in a another sovereign state? You got to be kidding! You'd better be."

Walchuk waved his hands as if to quite him. "There's worse. He had two choppers and ten men...those Serbs he was talking about. They caught up with Quigley and his group. Six of them. Took them unawares while they were sleeping and had them on their knees in handcuffs."

Zeitner went back round the desk and dropped heavily into his chair.

"I don't think I'm going to like this" he whispered, almost as if he was talking to himself.

"You won't, Zeitner. La Fonte had the Serbs put a severe beating on Quigley and the men were going to pleasure themselves on the two women."

"That bastard La Fonte! Why the hell did you ever get that butcher involved Walchuk?"

"Wait till you hear the rest. Just as the women were about to be raped, there was a sudden blast of weapons from around the clearing and the Serbs were wiped out. Quigley got loose with an RPG and took out one of the choppers with the pilot and one man in it. La Fonte manage to escape in the other chopper."

"Why do I feel that there's more to this debacle Walchuk?

He nodded. "There is. When the prisoners were on their knees, Quigley started asking questions…. why? Who? Where? Probably to prolong their lives. La Fonte couldn't help being expansive."

"Oh Jesus, he told him our names? Tell me it's not true!"

A desperate look took hold of his features as he leaned forward and peered at Walchuk.

The man nodded several times.

"Oh, it's true all right. Both our names will be on the wires as we speak. The word is probably filtering out there already. Big RCMP incident room set up in the woods. An RCMP Sergeant was a witness to the whole thing. This is coming back down the tubes as we speak."

Both men sat there for a long time staring at each other.

Finally Walchuk stirred.

"What do we do Bret?"

Zeitner got up and wandered across to the window and looked out.

"Took me years to get here, and you and you're little plots have put me back out on the street. Probably in some federal prison when all the ducks line up on this operation. They'll have you singing like a canary before you know it and your friends in high places may be in the slammer with us. Have you told them yet?" he asked.

"First call. There is some scurrying going on back there right now. I'm meeting someone after I leave here down by the Potomac River, who wants to try to salvage something from this."

"You can't give them La Fonte that's for sure. Where is he now? Gone into hiding somewhere I'll bet."

Walchuk shrugged. "He's got a dozen places he can disappear into. Probably has lots of cash stashed away from his drug enforcement work. Pierre works both sides of the street."

Zeitner groaned. "You sure know how to pick them Walchuk. Okay, how long have I got?"

"Ottawa won't mess about on this. They'll be onto the CIA pronto. I'd say you'd be pulled in for questioning sometime today. You better have a story ready."

"But there is none I can give...." he paused, thinking. "Unless..."

Walchuk's head snapped up, desperation written all over his face.

"Unless what?" he demanded.

"Nothing that concerns you Walchuk. Just a private thought" he answered casually.

Walchuk's eyes narrowed suspiciously. "Look, if there's a way out of this you need to tell me."

"I don't need to tell you anything you bastard. You waltzed in here with that killer La Fonte and started this whole thing. I should have kicked your ass out the door and took my chances with any so-called rumors you had about those two agents who disappeared. Now it's too late. Too late for either of us."

He looked around his office as if drinking in the whole façade and layout, then shook his head.

"Let's get out of here."

They both headed for the door, Zeitner ignoring some urgent calls from his secretary as he brushed past her desk.

Thames House-London.

Rebecca Fullerton Smythe raised her eyebrows on hearing her PA's voice on the intercom.

"A Mister Bret Zeitner from Washington is on the phone for you Ma'am."

"Fine, put him through."

She hit the switch which put the call on speaker, as well as starting a recording device.

"Mister Zeitner, can't say it's a pleasure after the call I got some hours ago. You've been caught with your pants down, haven't you?"

"Ma'am, I won't kid you. It would appear that you're right. Now, if you give me five minutes I may be able to show a different side to the story and my motives."

Rebecca tried to feign indifference.

"I'm sure it will be a good story, but shouldn't you be talking to your colleagues at Langley? I hear you've gone missing in Washington and your usual haunts are being checked out, including your home. You should know that Danny Quigley is a friend of mine, and any plot to kill him makes you my enemy."

She heard a deep breath at the other end. "Listen, hear me out first before you jump to judgment. I was the one who sent you the warnings about a plot to kill Quigley by a bunch of Serbs. Also the follow up call after Hanlon Falls."

She leaned forward, her face perplexed.

"How come you were involved in this Zeitner? What exactly are you trying to tell me?"

"That I got wind of the plot and wanted to stop it" he retorted.

"So why not inform your colleagues at the CIA and get them to stop the attempt? Why this sneaking around Washington, sending emails from an Internet café without any identification. As it turns out, your emails, if it was you who sent them, were a dammed ineffective method of stopping the killers, wouldn't you say?"

She heard him sigh. "Okay, Walchuk blackmailed me into being involved. I had no choice but to go along, but I tried to make sure that Quigley would not be hit."

She shook her head tiredly. "Look Zeitner, I've had a brutal day and I don't need your crappy situation piled up on top. As I say, why the hell are you calling me anyway? Go wash your CIA dirty washing back in Langley. Nice talking to you."

She went to hang up.

His voice sounded panicky. "No, no don't hang up! Look you're the only one who can support my story that I tried to stop the plot to terminate Quigley. I need you to send copies of those emails to Langley for starters. Secondly, I need to find Quigley up there in

B.C. and make sure he'll come back and testify as well that he received those emails. I need you to find out where Quigley is and I'm going in after him."

She laughed. "Sure, you expect me to tell you where Quigley is right now. How do I know you're not still working for that little faceless group who ordered this killing, and who want you to go in there and finish the job?"

"For Christ sake Ma'am, I want to keep him safe now so he can support my story."

"Look Zeitner. Just to get you off the phone, I'll forward those emails to Langley. As far as giving you Quigley's location or destination, I have no idea, and even if I did I certainly wouldn't give you the information. Now Good-day to you!"

She went to hang up and froze.

"Hang on Zeitner, the computer screen has just come up with some information from Langley. Hold on a second."

She leaned forward reading rapidly as the information spiraled down the screen.

Her voice sounded shocked when she spoke again a moment later.

"Zeitner, your friend Walchuk has been found down at the Potomac river. He's dead. It looks like suicide."

There was a gasp at the other end.

"Suicide? Yeah sure!" he said cynically. "When he left me earlier he was meeting up with someone from the group who ordered Quigley killed. That leaves me as a loose end and La Fonte, unless they have unleashed that mad dog on us. They're cleaning house Rebecca and I better get moving."

This time he did hang up.

She sat there for a long while, thinking.

She shivered, feeling goose pimples on her forearms.

"Danny, just where the hell are you?" she whispered. "This thing is far from finished. For God's sake take care of yourself and come back safely."

# Chapter 27

If it wasn't for the threatened violence surrounding them, it could have been a pleasant sit down in the woods after a hard days driving. They were blessed with a full moon and starlight in lieu of a campfire which enabled them to have a good view of each other's faces as they sat in a circle and chatted.

Danny had been feeling much better and made his way over and sat down amongst them with Siobhan on his right, Bob on his left, and Pat and the Indian Jeff directly across from him.

Bob tapped him on his knee. "We were just talking about the beating you took back there, and the state of your body. You had two beautiful ladies ministering to you Danny, so I don't know if that makes it all worth while."

He smiled, appreciating Bob's attempt at levity. "Yeah, the ladies were terrific but I'm sure there's an easier way of getting some TLC. Anyway, now that we are heading into the last lap of our journey, I was going to ask Jeff and Pat, to tell me about the First Nations. As a Brit, I haven't a clue, to be honest. Apart from John Wayne movies, that is......."

Bob cut in with a fake John Wayne accent. "The only good Indian..."

"Is a dead Indian." Pat finished for him.

Danny smiled self-consciously. "Well yeah, exactly... I stand convicted. Apart from hearing about stand offs between First Nations and the white population over land disputes in the past few years, I have a very limited knowledge of the subject."

Jeff's voice cut through the conversation.

"You know Danny, if you were standing in the dock right now as a symbol of the British nation, and charged with your country's treatment of the red man over the centuries, and pleaded ignorance on the subject, you'd be laughed out of court."

"Hey, come on Jeff, give Danny a break. He's just asking you to fill him in on the background issues." Pat thumped Jeff on his arm and glanced across at Danny.

"Just ignore him."

"No, no, let him talk. Sounds like an interesting approach. We role-played a lot in the army and it was a brilliant learning process. I don't mind playing the bad guy, as long as I can ask questions as we go along. I confess to always having sympathy with the natives I met in other countries. They were always the poverty stricken and the underdog."

Jeff nodded. "Fair enough. Okay, speaking of armies, have you ever heard of Pontiac's war?"

He shook his head. "No sorry. Doesn't mean a thing to me" he answered.

"Not surprising. The war happened in 1763 to 1764 when the British were fighting an alliance of tribes. The British Commander, a Captain Simeon Ecuyer, gave blankets to the Indian warriors he was fighting."

"Sounds like a very human gesture towards the enemy" Danny commented.

"It does, doesn't it?" Jeff's voice had a dry resonance. "Unfortunately, the blankets were infected with small pox which caused an epidemic and gained time for the British re-enforcements to arrive."

"Oh shit! I didn't see that coming Jeff. That's fighting dirty. I thought it was a modern invention. I was in a Sierra Leone village where ten and twelve year old boys had cut the hands off everyone to stop them voting. I live with that to this day."

Pat's voice picked up the story. "Danny, it has to be said, it's not just the Brits. Since Christopher Columbus, five hundred years ago, the Indian tribes have signed treaties with Holland, England, Spain, France, Mexico, the U.S.A. and Canada. Four hundred treaties in all, and all have been broken by the white man."

"Aren't the Russians in there too somewhere?" It was Bob's voice.

Pat nodded." Yep, the Russians came to Alaska in 1741 to the 1800's. The Aleut Indian population was around 18,000 at that time and by the 1820's there were only 1500 of them left. That was as a result of small pox, measles, scarlet fever, typhoid, TB and influenza, as they had no defense to the white man's diseases. In fact by 1825, 80% of the North West coastal Indians were wiped out."

Jeff leaned forward. "It wasn't just diseases. Many fell from musket fire from European armies. The French, British and Spanish bribed the tribes to fight each other. Crop failures played their part too."

Danny straightened, trying to ease some pains in his back and thigh.

"Why do I feel that there's more finger pointing coming up? No sorry, I'm not belittling all the history. It's actually interesting and probably says a lot about the present state of affairs, I imagine."

Jeff nodded, though with the moon scudding behind some clouds, no one noticed.

"A lot of bitterness is still held by First Nations because the Canadian Government in 1884 outlawed one of the more important events in the Indian culture, the Potlatch, and made it a criminal offence. That was their greatest feast and held between mid-winter and mid-summer. It celebrated certain events such as raising a totem pole, ancient stories were enacted, masked dancers participated, colorful costumes were worn, women's societies and the winter solstice were celebrated."

Pat cut in again. "The law was repealed in 1951 as a spiritual right, and the act included some hunting and fishing rights. No doubt everyone's heard of the terrible mission schools that the Brits brought in, both in Canada and Australia. They were only allowed to speak English and were forbidden under threat of jail from practicing their cultural traditions. Effectively, the nail in the coffin of Indian culture, as it existed for thousands of years. In Canada most native Americans were not granted citizenship until 1960."

Bob shook his head. "God, just listening to this makes me feel real shitty as a Canadian and Danny must think we're a bunch of bastards, but there is good news as well. In 1992 the B.C. treaty commission was established, putting in place a negotiation procedure by which individual bands could begin the treaty process- the culmination of nearly 100 years of native conflict over native rights. However conflict is still ongoing over natural resources and salmon fishing rights."

Pat made a face. "Yeah, I think the Government's heart is in the right place. Pass responsibility back to the natives and support them with money and resources to help them achieve this."

Jeff grunted sourly. "Yeah, after tearing the very heart out of the Indian. He's now a lost dysfunctional soul, who will never again re-capture his true spirit. It's Humpty Dumpty all over again. The white man knocked him off the wall and now wipes his hands of any responsibility and expects the Indian to somehow stick himself back together again."

Pat thumped him again. "Oh come on Jeff, don't be so melodramatic. The Indian is doing quite well thank you. Look at all those profitable casinos and large billion dollar land settlements. Even a First Nations university with Indian teachers. They have self rule over their tribal lands, using Indian laws and have their own tribal police. The Federal Government has given them complete autonomy. That's progress for Pete's sake!" she exclaimed.

"Perhaps, but it's got a long way to go yet. And there's still a lot of unforgiveness in the Indian heart" he responded gloomily.

Pat wasn't willing to let it stop there. "Well, I think it's time the Indian stopped blaming the white man and got on with life. They have all sorts of opportunities opening up to them. Look at me for instance. I had no one block me or discourage me when I went into law enforcement and the intelligence field."

On that note they all broke up and stole off to their tents.

They still made sure to allocate sentries for the night and they knew that no one would ever fall asleep again while carrying out that duty.

It was a peaceful night.

In the pre-dawn light the campsite was a hive of activity as they had a quick breakfast and prepared to abandon the vehicles. Jeff and Bob laid out the essential items that they had to take with them, and allocated them to various packs.

Danny and Pat were moving the vehicles deeper back in the woods and doing their best to camouflage them from discovery by air. That meant cutting numerous pieces of shrub and bushes and making sure that no reflective glass was exposed. Then they went back and did their best to eliminate any tracks leading into the camp- site.

Siobhan had taken on the job of cleaning up the breakfast dishes and hauling out all the material, including food, from the trailer and the jeeps. She placed the weapons off to one side for the men to sort out.

Danny was feeling much better and moving around without the severe pain in his leg that he'd experienced the previous day.

He wasn't sure if it was 'The melted dog' or the ladies first aid that had brought about the mini miracle.

Initially he'd had some reservations about Siobhan's ability, trekking back into the woods, but discovered that she had been in a walking club back in Ireland and also had knowledge of treating and preventing blisters.

In the selections as to what to take and what to leave, Jeff had the final say and the loads were distributed around the group in accordance with their size strength and experience. They dumped one tent as Jeff said he'd sleep outdoors anyway, and Bob had to abandon his assault rifle with attached grenade launcher.

He felt better when Danny passed him the mini Uzi while he held onto the Winchester repeater. Jeff figured it would take them a day and a half to hike in to the location of the grid reference that Danny had received.

What would they find there? Was C.C. Courtney actually alive and well?

It was anyone's guess, but they might have to fall back on Jeff's survival skills if it turned out to be a dead end.

Danny spent some time adjusting Siobhan's pack, and Jeff was moving round like an old mother hen making sure that no one was carrying too much weight, which could affect the progress of the group, should injuries occur.

They did a last scour round the site, and then headed out.

They were now into the last stage of the journey.

# Chapter 28

They stopped after three hours.

Jeff had slipped back after they had been on the route for half an hour, to check on how they were managing their loads, and their general foot comfort.

Even Bob, with his military experience, grunted in satisfaction as he tightened some straps and adjusted his pack, which wasn't comfortable.

Now they flopped to the ground in various stages of mental and physical need.

Siobhan was pleased that her previous walking experience was paying off.

Danny too, was starting to feel his muscles easing up and his thigh ligaments were no longer forcing him to hobble.

Pat had the beginning of a blister, which Siobhan looked at and decided that a bunched up sock was causing the discomfort.

Bob looked like he could walk all day without any problems, and Jeff was his usual inscrutable and competent self.

He had a small fire and a coffee pot going in no time.

"These tall trees will disperse any smoke" he commented.

"Doubt if they'll be looking this far inland anyway, if they are still looking at all" Danny agreed.

Pat came over to Danny, enquired about his injury and kneaded the muscles as he lay there for a brief moment.

After she had finished, Danny spotted Siobhan off to one side with her head down, and he went across to her.

"Hey, you okay Siobhan? He asked.

She nodded. "Sure... yes," she whispered. "Just thinking back there, those men."

He put his arm around her. "It was a close call...too close, if the truth's known. Hey look, we're past that and moving on. Hopefully we'll see C.C. shortly."

She eased herself gently out of his embrace.

"It's just..." she started.

"Just what?"

"The way you killed that man... so efficient... so precise."

"For God's sake he was about to rape you Siobhan! I had my hands cuffed in front of me and didn't exactly have a choice of methods of killing the bastard. Hell, you've seen me kill before: in Ireland when they were about to assassinate Gerry Adams. I would have thought, if anyone deserves killing it was that animal who was about to rape you and then murder all of us, including yourself!"

Her face twisted in agony. "I'm sorry Danny, I guess I saw you in a different way somehow. It's hard to explain."

He shook his head in disgust. "You don't have to explain Siobhan. You remind me of all those do-gooders back in the U.K. who are happy to put us on a plane to go off and kill their enemies in some foreign country, but aren't comfortable when they actually see up close what we do. Next time I'll walk away and see how you like the alternative!"

He turned and stormed off.

Jeff as if sensing the dispute, produced some thick bread sandwiches and steaming cups of coffee for each of them, and led them back to the fire.

"So this is the kind of treatment your clients get Jeff, when you take them out" Bob teased.

He chuckled. "Yeah, they come up here for some backwoods experience, just as long as they get three square meals a day presented to them, tent showers set up and goose down sleeping bags to keep them warm at night. Oh, and not TOO close to the animals they shoot, in case they bite back. Which they do sometimes. Still, it's a living!"

Pat waved her sandwich. "Doesn't always work though does it? You read all the time of bear incidents where hunters come too close to their cubs and they get nasty. That must take courage Jeff, facing down a bear."

"You can't outrun them, that's for sure" he said. "Though as the joke goes, you only have to outrun the guy running with you."

They all joined in the laughter and fell silent as they got stuck into their lunch.

It was Pat who started up the conversation, looking across at Bob and Danny.

"Speaking of courage. You guys in the military must have it in spades, the situation you confront every day. I always worry that I'll chicken out if I'm in that situation. Make a right fool of myself and perhaps get my partner killed or injured."

Bob and Danny glanced across at each other. Danny nodded to him to go ahead and answer her.

Bob cleared his throat. "Well, military and police training have the same goal. To break groups down and get them working and pulling together so that when something happens, they respond automatically and with precision. Sure you've grown close to your buddies and wouldn't want to let them down, or yourself for that matter. I'm not sure I'd call it courage. It's more of a conditioned response. You suspend your conscious thoughts and just react as you were trained to do. I was shaking like a leaf an hour after my first engagement with the Taliban, and a number of the guys were the same. What do you think Danny?"

"You got it in one Bob. Look I think it takes more courage for parents to have to walk into the hospital ward after finding out that their five year old daughter has terminal cancer, and they somehow have to share that with her. Or a woman who is lying on a trolley, going willingly into theatre for a mastectomy that is going to brutalize her beauty. Or take a ten year old kid who heads off to school knowing he's going to be bullied again. Now that's what I call courage!" he said intensely.

There was silence for a moment and Pat reached across and clasped Danny's hand.

Jeff coughed discretely. "Okay, change of subject. You two military guys, answer me this. Is Iraq and Afghanistan worth it? All that treasure and blood that could have been used to pay for education and healthcare, or taking care of the terrible situations on the native reservations, the violence, broken families, drunkenness, and dysfunctional young people?"

Bob jumped in immediately. "If you saw how the women are treated in Afghanistan you wouldn't even ask the question. We've started something and you know, perhaps they have a chance, but it's not a four-year stint and everything's hunky dory. This is a long haul project, twenty-five years at least, if we want to really change the country. Iraq? Well Canadians were not there. Danny might have some thoughts on that."

He did, but, along with most of his ex-military mates, preferred to stay out of conversations like that, but he could see that some reply was expected.

"Okay, Iraq was a mistake. After nine years the Iraqis want the Americans out of there. After over four thousand plus American dead and a massive future cost looking after all the wounded and disabled. Now, the Iraqis are cozying up to the Iranians, who are on the verge of producing a ballistic missile topped with a nuclear weapon. What the invasion of Iraq did, was create a massive recruiting campaign and training ground for Al Qaeda. You know, infidel boots on the ground in Muslim lands. Sure Osama Bin

Laden is dead but these people have dispersed back to their own countries to create mayhem without his leadership ...

The Iraqis? They're showing an amazing adaptability for corruption and opportunism. Hell, the people still only get two hours electricity a day after all this time. They had it better under Saddam"

"Whew...." Siobhan exclaimed. "You call a spade a spade. I'm not sure the U.S. Congress would like to hear your views."

There was a babble of conversation as others joined in.

In ten minutes they were off again.

Somehow, they were becoming a more cohesive group. Not exactly getting broken down military style, but getting more comfortable with each other.

The following morning they headed out early.

It happened in a split second.

One moment Jeff was leading the group through some mid size trees with Pat behind him and Siobhan a couple of steps to her rear.

There was a flash of a fawn object leaping from an overhanging limb and colliding into the back of Jeff, sending him crashing to the ground.

It was the screaming sound from the animal that froze them to the spot. A catlike sound. In this case a cougar or a mountain lion as they referred to it on the west coast.

Jeff immediately felt the claws tearing his shoulders and teeth attempting to grip the back of his neck.

Thirty feet, further back, Danny and Bob both tried to get their weapons off their shoulders, but they were hampered by their packs.

Pat stood mesmerized, as if unable to take in what she was witnessing.

Surprisingly, it was Siobhan who sprung into action.

She grabbed the frying pan sticking out of Pat's pack and raced forward, screaming at the figures of Jeff and the cougar writhing in the grass.

Coming up on them she lashed out at the animal with an overhand swing that caught it on the back of its head, making a clanging noise. The animal's head shot sideways and glared back at her. She continued screaming and kept hitting it several times. It released its hold on Jeff and leapt sideways facing back towards her.

Siobhan stepped forward and slammed it again, directly on its nose.

It screamed, scuttling backwards, it's eyes flickering left and right. Then it turned and disappeared into the foliage at an incredible speed.

Like that, it was over.

Now it was Siobhan who stood frozen to the spot and who suddenly, as if realizing what she had done, burst into tears, and dropped slowly to her knees.

Pat was beside Jeff in a moment helping him sit up.

Danny and Rob were both standing looking at the useless weapons they had managed to release, too late, from around their shoulders.

They both raced off in the direction the cougar had taken, to make sure it wasn't lying in wait for another attack.

When they returned Siobhan was fully back in control, and with Pat, was treating some deep scratches on Jeff's upper back and one shoulder. Fortunately, no stitches were needed. He also had some minor cuts on the back of his head that Siobhan dabbed with antiseptic ointment.

Bob called an unofficial halt and insisted on a medicinal shot of whiskey for Jeff who rarely, if ever drank. There was little conversation, until Jeff was back on his feet and waving off their attention. "Hey, I'm okay. No damage done" he insisted.

He did however, go over and give Siobhan a long hug.

"When they asked me to take you with me, it must have been my ancestors, looking after me, who said 'yes.' Thank you for what you did. In view of what we talked about earlier, that took courage."

"I was just doing my E.R. thing. You know, when trolleys come flying in with people injured, you just act" she protested.

"Yeah" Bob retorted dryly." A little different though, when a mountain lion jumps on someone. I'm sure that wasn't on your curriculum when you were training to be a nurse."

Danny noticed Pat turning away, her face stricken.

# Chapter 29

The incident with the cougar seemed to give them new energy, and they made excellent progress during the afternoon. The woods provided a variety of terrain, from tall trees to tight brush, a couple of years after a fire had passed through. However one section of several miles bore the blackened evidence of a recent fire and they all ended up at the end of the day looking like chimney sweeps.

Apart from one brief stop, when Siobhan checked out Jeff's scratches, they forged ahead, and when Jeff finally called a halt 20 yards from a fast flowing creek, they all sank gratefully on the ground.

Bob and Danny took over setting out the camp, while the two women went across to have a quick wash and get rid of the soot on their hands and faces.

Danny squatted down beside Jeff who was sitting with his back against a broad pine tree.

"Hey, how're you doing?" he asked, closely monitoring his features.

Jeff waved him away. "If this is the worst that will happen to me on the trip I'll be a happy man. I know it's very un-Indian like, but those scratches that cat gave me hurt like hell!"

Danny nodded. "I noticed the same with wounds. A gut shot is of course the worst, but small wounds, like a piece of metal slicing a leg, or something like that, can drive you demented."

"Unusual for mountain lions to attack people like that though. From what I could see it wasn't scrawny and starving, which might have provoked an attack. I stood off a bear once that was deliberating making a meal of a hunting party I was escorting, long enough for a member of the party to shoot it, but like today, it took a few moments for the group to get their weapons operational."

"Yeah, well Bob and I had our weapons at the ready after that attack. Actually, there would have been no chance to shoot that cat when it landed on you. You were all tangled up with it on the ground and the women were blocking my view."

"Thank God for that feisty Irish lady! The fighting Irish they say. Now I see it's the women too! She's something else!" he said fervently.

"You got that right."

Jeff peered up at him. "I saw you watching Pat afterwards. Can you do something there Danny? You know..." his voice trailed off.

Danny tapped him on the arm, saying nothing as the two women came strolling back.

He stared at them. "My gosh, I can recognize you two again. You reminded me of putting on that camo stuff before a night exercise."

Siobhan stiff-armed him. "You can talk Danny Quigley. Right now I might just shoot you if I was on sentry duty and you wandered out of the brush. You look like one of those Yeti legends."

"Yeah" he retorted, "just as long as you don't use that frying pan on me, girl. Oh, even I know the Yeti are somewhere else in the world. Snow-capped mountains and places like that."

Then he cursed to himself as he saw Pat's expression.

It was a subdued group that sat around finishing supper, and Danny washed up the dishes at the creek and rejoined the group.

Bob came across and filled up his coffee. "Danny, we were just speculating about tomorrow. Jeff says we should hit that grid reference late morning or just after noon depending on the terrain of course, and no detours or rivers to cross. Right Jeff?"

Jeff leaned forward grimacing. "Yeah, that's what I figure. The question is, what will we encounter, once we get there? What's your best guess Danny?"

He considered that for a moment.

"OK, best guess scenario my old friend Clive, known as C.C. Courtney, who was supposed to have died of terminal cancer over a year ago, has contacted me from back in the bush here somewhere.

A rather cryptic message which makes me wonder why he didn't fill in some details on his whereabouts and how he got there. Is he a prisoner, forced to make that telephone call, and for what purpose? He mentioned Indians. We were rescued by Indians when Pierre La Fonte and his little playmates had us handcuffed back there and close to death. Does that mean that they are friendly? I have no idea. But they must be connected to C.C. somehow and want us to come to their location."

"Sure, come into my cave said the spider to the fly!" Bob offered.

Danny glanced across at Jeff.

"Look Jeff. I'm totally out of the picture when it comes to the native movement here in Canada and indeed the U.S., probably like most Brits. Is there, for example, some sort of organized military wing that has emerged over the last few years. La Fonte's men were blown away by some sort of cohesive and planned attack, using assault weapons with deadly accuracy."

"Organized military wing? Not that I'm aware of. Something called The Red Power movement began in the 1960's in the North West, influenced mainly by the African American civil rights movement coming out of their urban ghettos. In B.C. the Indians believed that they should return to the values of co-operation and communal living, and that they had to fight for their land rights; that peaceful protests and legal battles were not enough.

Out of that came something called AIM, The American Indian Movement, and they went on to occupy Alcatraz in 1964, which got a lot of public support.

In 1974 AIM and other native groups formed The Indian Treaties Council in

Canada, to correlate efforts at lobbying the Government and land reform. There's been a mish- mash of results over the years. Still a lot of resentment on the native's side as a result of the neglect and destruction of the their culture over the past one hundred years. Oh, and today there's something called The Native Brotherhood of British Columbia, which acts as a kind of trade union to protect the interests of commercial fishermen."

Bob cut in. "Didn't some tribal chief a few years back encourage his people to cross the border and join the U.S. military, with the objective of building up an Armed Resistance Force?"

"Didn't amount to much" Pat added. "CSIS had an alert out on that, but we couldn't detect any surge in natives crossing over and joining up. You know that all they need to cross the border is a tribal card. Unfortunately the Indian talks a good fight but doesn't think beyond the next bottle of whiskey or drug fix."

Danny turned back to Jeff again. "I'm trying to get a handle on this Jeff. I mean how many tribes are there up here? What about languages? Is there a common tongue among the tribes? I understand they have their own tribal police and the Federal Government basically leaves them to it. Effectively, in a huge tract of territory like this, they could get involved in all sorts of things, and no one would have a clue. Is that right?"

Jeff nodded. "Well, let me see if I can answer some of those questions. In the North West the tribes are The Chinook, Coast Salish, Haida, Kwakiutl, Makah, Nootka, Tlingit and

Tsimshian. There are probably three dozen separate identifiable groups in the pacific North West, with languages and cultural life ways orientated towards maritime and what we call, a riverine environment. You're talking about a massive area here and basically there are five native cultural areas that stretch all the way from Northern and the central B.C. coast, coastal and southern areas, South West B.C. and western Washington. As for languages." A flicker of emotion momentarily crossed his normally stoical features. "English is probably a common language, but along the Columbia river, from it's mouth to the Cascade mountains, are several groups of Chinook an speakers. What could the natives in this chunk of territory get up to without any independent eyes to alert the outside world? Basically anything, if the truth's known."

The group fell silent after that and Pat silently stood up and walked across towards the creek area. Jeff gave Danny a slight nod, angling his head in her direction.

He waited a few minutes before getting up and casually strolling after her.

He found her sitting beside the creek, her arms folded.

"Join you?" he asked and sat down without waiting for an answer.

She glanced sideways at him. "You're not here just to enjoy my female company Danny are you?"

"Well… you are an attractive lady Pat, and why wouldn't I want to spend some time with you?"

She laughed. "Yeah, and what about your on-again-off-again relationship with Siobhan back there? She'd kill me if that were the reason you were here... and probably use that damn frying pan to do it!"

He fell silent for a moment, recognizing that he had been given a cue.

Finally he stirred.

"I'd like to tell you a story Pat. I don't know if it will help you or not. Two stories actually. When I joined the British army, it was the Parachute Battalion that I chose. The basic training is tough, really tough. This day we were practicing throwing grenades for the first time and I was standing behind a Private Tomkins in a trench, waiting for my turn. The training Sergeant was on his left. Tomkins pulled the pin and drew his hand back to make his throw, and the grenade fell out of his hand... directly in front of my feet."

"Holy shit!" she whispered. "What did you do?"

"Absolutely nothing. I froze. You've heard the saying that time stood still. Well I can testify to that for sure."

"So what happened?"

"The Sergeant screamed "grenade," bent over, picked it up and tossed it over the sand-bagged wall. I swear it exploded within seconds."

"Oh my God, you froze? You could have all been killed!"

"Well, you should have heard the Sergeant. He was some pissed off! Actually kicked Tomkins in the butt and hauled us straight off the firing range. He was screaming in both our faces for at least an hour afterwards and we were in a lot of shit with the Commanding Officer. Lost our next weekend pass to boot."

"You froze? The great Danny Quigley that Rob keeps talking about! Did it ever happen to you again after that.?"

He shook his head. "Thankfully no. I can't explain why, but I just moved on somehow. A bit like getting over nervousness in speaking in front of people. It just goes."

"Hardly anything like that Danny" she said dryly, "but anyway, what was the other story?"

He looked away for a moment. "Shit, I thought I'd got over this. Son of a bitch!" he exclaimed, smacking one fist into his palm.

She reached across and held his hand. "What Danny? Got over what?" she asked.

He sighed. "Okay, we were dropped into Sierra Leone, during an uprising, to rescue British Embassy staff and some charity people working for NGO's. We were escorting them under fire from the Embassy out to a bus, a Trooper Davis directly in front of me, his assault weapon at the ready. Suddenly a figure jumped out of an alleyway, swinging a blood stained machete, and Davis froze."

Pat sat there, her face riveted on his. "Oh my God! But why, a trained soldier?"

"It was a kid about ten years old, red eyed from drugs and whatever"

"What happened?" she breathed.

"I shot him. The kid. Blew him away. Then we got out of there."

"Afterwards I talked to him. He had a son back in England about the same age. He couldn't shoot that kid, even though he was about to de-captivate him."

He fell silent.

Finally. "I thought I'd got over it, shooting that kid. But you never do. Not something like that. I'll probably take it to the grave with me."

"Was Davis okay after that? In action I mean" she asked curiously.

"A brick. A rock in any firestorm we got into. I did several missions with him and I chose him for my team without a second thought. Saved my bacon once or twice as well. Trooper Davis... yeah... at least I saved his life, and his son in the U.K. still had a father."

She slowly turned her head.

In the fading dusk he could just make out her high cheekbones that left her eyes in a mysterious shadow. Her lips were slightly parted.

He knew all he had to do was press his lips to hers and they would both be catapulted into a new dimension of relationship.

He turned his head away, thoughts of Siobhan nearby, and Jackie fighting for her life in London, filtered into his mind.

As if sensing that the moment had passed, she leaned forward and leaned her head on his shoulder.

"Thanks Danny" she whispered.

# Chapter 30

They had been moving for about three hours the following morning when Jeff dropped back and strolled alongside Danny and Bob.

"Notice anything this past hour?" he asked them.

Danny nodded. "We're being shadowed. Nothing very obvious just shades and shadows where they shouldn't be. Thought we were being stalked by another cougar for a while."

Rob looked mortified. "Shit, I didn't spot anything. But I was just head down, putting one foot in front of the other. What is it Jeff?"

"It? It's who, and they are shit hot at flanking us, whoever they are. Danny, I want you up front with me and I'd suggest weapons at the ready, though fingers off the triggers until we know what's what."

With that they both speeded up until they caught up with the two women, with whom Jeff had a brief word before heading out in front of the column.

Five hundred yards further on, they came into a wide clearing and Danny bumped into the rear of Jeff who had stopped suddenly.

"Will you look at that Danny!"

He stared and whistled.

Standing in the middle of the clearing was the tall Indian who had handed him the weapon that he had used to down the chopper.

He was still dressed as he was on that night, with a loincloth and some Indian feathers. He looked bigger than ever, at least six foot four, his body, looking like it was carved out of ivory. He was unarmed.

They exchanged glances. "Okay, here goes. Let's do it." Danny said quietly and they both strode purposefully towards the figure in the clearing.

When they were twenty yards away, the Indian held his hand up in a halting gesture.

Behind him, in his peripheral vision, he spotted the women enter the clearing and come to an abrupt halt. Bob came alongside them almost at once, his weapon at the ready.

"That's far enough for now!" The Indian's voice was loud and authoritive.

They halted, spreading out slightly.

Danny thought he saw a flicker of amusement in the Indians eyes as they did so.

What to say in such a situation?

Doctor Livingstone I presume? Or something equally insane.

Danny settled for. "You saved our bacon back there some days ago. I didn't get a chance to say thanks."

The Indian inclined his head in acknowledgment.

Then he spoke again. Impeccable English.

"You must put your weapons down. We don't allow strangers to bear arms in our territory."

Jeff spoke quietly. "Your call Danny, though I suspect they have lots of support all around us. Remember those heavy caliber weapons they used when they blew away La Fonte's hard-ass Serbs.?"

Danny looked across at the Indian again. "I'm here to see my old friend Clive Courtney. I guess you know that anyway, or we wouldn't even be here. We come with peaceful intentions."

As he said this he carefully placed his rifle on the ground and stepped back, pulling his pack off his back and extricating the pistol that he was given in Hanlon Falls, to replace the shooter confiscated by the RCMP. He placed that on the ground as well.

Jeff did the same thing.

With some hesitation Bob followed suit.

Almost immediately, four figures shot out from behind some trees and took the weapons away. They were dressed in full battlefield equipment and camouflaged bush jackets and wearing green berets.

Danny gestured to the packs on the ground.

"Don't you want to check the packs?" he asked.

"If you are not honest with us now, there is no point in even leaving this clearing. What is that Christian saying - your sins will find you out."

He moved his gaze back towards the two women. "Your women have done well. We have an hour to go to our camp. We can carry their packs if they wish. If not, follow me."

Both women wanted to finish the journey carrying their loads as a matter of pride, and so they set out.

As they moved out of the clearing a group of fully armed natives fell in behind them.

Jeff glanced back at them.

"Lucky we didn't decide to tough it out. We'd be toast by now."

"They didn't bring us all this way to kill us....at least not yet. Wonder what Sergeant Dryden would have done - pulled the Federal card on them?"

Jeff laughed.

"Yeah, sure. A lot of good that would have done us. At this stage, it's that old English saying.... in for a penny, in for a pound. Is that how it goes Danny?"

"For an Indian, you have quite a sense of humor, did you know that Jeff?"

That was the end of the conversation as the big Indian set a cracking pace through the tall trees and rolling countryside.

They reached the camp in exactly one hour.

Was this the end of his search? Danny wondered.

The first thing that amazed them was the sheer size of the encampment, if that was the word for it. It was laid out like a square. The center of the village had some log longhouses stretching 50 yards, and some smaller buildings, also made of logs. On one side of the village was a series of tepees, at least 50 of them, made of camouflaged material, and laid out in what looked like an organized military formation. A long wooden building flanked them.

On the other side of the village, was an even larger series of tepees, made of faded white material and laid out in no specific formation, interspersed by some medium sized buildings. Beyond the tepees, on both sides and looking strange in the surroundings, were what looked like blocks of temporary toilets that you might see at a modern fairground or sporting event. Directly ahead were two massive, solid, squat log buildings. Danny's eyes were drawn to what appeared to be armed guards, around these.

In the distance, he could hear the sounds of what he interpreted as small arms fire, probably coming from some sort of firing range.

The center of the village had several large totem poles dominating the area.

He stopped at the centerpiece and looked at it, then groaned.

Jeff was standing beside him. The totem pole showed what was plainly an 1800's uniformed British Officer, bending forward and handing a blanket to a native kneeling before him.

Danny nodded at it. "If you hadn't briefed me on this I'd have said that it showed a compassionate British Officer, providing warmth and comfort to a lowly native. Shit, if this is the main symbol in this place, we've jumped from the firing pan into the fire!"

Jeff grunted assent. "Yeah, Pontiacs war. Infecting them with smallpox."

He pointed to two totem poles looming up on each side, showing the faces of two savage Indians.

"I should point out that the Haida, the main tribes people of the North West coast, are renowned for their carving abilities. The first figure you see is of the Apache Chief Geronimo, who was a prominent Shaman, or holy man in the late 19th century. He hated the Mexicans, who killed his wife and three of his children. He lived until 1909 when he died at 80 years of age."

Danny moved across to the second pole. "And this one?" he asked.

"That's Cochise, another Apache leader." He waved at both of the totem poles. "Both fierce warriors."

Danny was moving to the next totem pole, which looked like a small white animal, and was turning to Jeff, when he noticed their big Indian escort, gesturing impatiently to them.

The group speeded up until they came up to him.

He pointed to the entrance of a medium sized squat building.

"The Chief and the council of elders are waiting for you inside. Be respectful when you enter. Now follow me."

With that he stepped through a low entrance to the building.

Glancing with some trepidation at each other, they followed him inside.

Danny was the first inside and he glanced around.

It was a wide spacious room but it was the people inside that immediately drew his attention.

Sitting cross-legged in the center of a semi circle was an imposing, craggy-faced First Nations male, wearing a bonnet of feathers and with a colorful blanket wrapped around his shoulders. He was middle aged, but with a powerful upper frame, and piercing yellow eyes, which were now focused on the group entering.

To his right was a muscular young male, equally wearing a bonnet with a few feathers. It was his visage that struck Danny like a spear: His eyes glared, with what he took to be murderous hatred. There was a strange cast to his features. He wondered who the Indian reminded him of, and then it came to him. He was almost a twin for the killer Indian in The Last of The Mohicans. His taut sharply boned face, looked hungrily at the group as they filed in. To his right stood an exact replica of him, presumably his twin.

The six foot four Indian who had escorted them there squatted down on the left of the Chief. In the semi circle were two further male Indians and three females. It was the third female that made Danny gape. She couldn't have been more than seventeen years of age, but her exquisite, glowing beauty seemed to filter out and fill the whole tent.

Her shiny black hair hung almost to her waist and her finely boned features had an oriental cast to them. When she looked up at them he felt almost enveloped by her deep green eyes.

Beside him he heard Bob gasp and he nudged him warningly, while at the same time, he drew his eyes back to the Chief, who was watching him closely.

The Chief now gestured to them and pointed to the mats on the floor.

The group shuffled forward, dropping their packs by the entrance, and, despite the unsettling scene in front of them, sank with relief onto the floor.

Almost immediately, two younger males came through a side door with jugs of water and mugs, which were offered to the group.

No one refused.

'No pipe of peace', Danny thought.

The Chief's voice sounded North American. It sounded confident, like he was used to being obeyed, and totally in charge.

Canadian or U.S.? Danny couldn't tell the difference.

"I am Black Cloud, tribal Chief. Which one of you is Quigley, the British soldier?" he demanded.

Danny hesitated. "Well, I'm Danny Quigley. However I'm not a soldier any more. I'm a civilian."

The Chief waved his hand dismissively. "Once a soldier of the crown... In 1763 a British officer came to our land, also serving the crown, during what's known as Pontiacs war. He offered his hand in friendship to my native and naïve brothers, and you know what happened?"

"Yes I saw the..." Danny started.

The muscular Indian on his right jumped forward, until his face was only inches from Danny's.

"Shut up until the Chief is finished," he snarled, looking like he was on the verge of smashing him across the face.

Danny had had years of experience handling jumped-up young officers, who let their shoulder pips drive their ego. He shrugged and sat back, waiting.

He had noted though, a peculiar inflection and accent in the way he spoke English.

He filed it away.

The Chief continued. "Now another British Officer enters our land. Are you bearing gifts as well, I ask?"

Danny wasn't answering any theoretical questions right then.

He stayed silent.

It was one of the others in the semi-circle, a large, fat and heavily jowled woman who shot a question at him.

"Why are you here, in our land?"

He glanced at the Chief, who nodded, so he sat forward.

"I'm here to find my old friend Clive Courtney, who disappeared some time ago, presumed dead. However, I have the distinct feeling that your people have been encouraging me to come here. I certainly wouldn't have made it to the village without your help. By the way where is my old friend? Is he close by?"

The Chief coughed, and leaning forward, pointed his finger at Danny.

"Your old friend is responsible for you being here. We have sat together many an evening around the campfire and told stories to each other. From Courtney, stories of his soldier friend Quigley. Stories that, I'm told, are now legends around your campfires. How you overcame enormous odds and slew hundreds of your enemies, almost single handedly. How you walked away from each battle without any wounds, as if the spirits were with you."

Danny's face reflected his puzzlement. "What has that to do with me being here? I can't see the connection."

"Our warriors are nearly ready for the great task at hand...but not quite. They lack that cutting edge that someone like you can give them. You are right. I brought you here to provide the final battle training to them."

"What great task? What battle? What exactly are you readying them for?"

One of the other Indian woman, cut in with a singsong voice, as if recounting a tribal myth that had been told and re-told time and again.

"In August 1994 a female albino buffalo calf was born in a Wisconsin ranch. She was named Miracle, as she was the first calf of her kind, born in the last 100 years. Female white buffalo are sacred to the plains Indians. Lakota prophesy holds that the birth of such a calf heralds the healing of the earth and of the Indian nations."

Pat's voice cut in. "Hey, you lost us here. How does this healing take place exactly?"

The Chief nodded. "The greatest destruction and contamination of the earth has been, and is, being caused by the people south of the border."

Danny's voice reflected his complete bafflement. "The United States? I have to say chief, greater minds than yours and mine have tried to solve the problems of the environment."

The muscular Indian jumped forward and lashed out at Danny's face.

Danny had anticipated his move and was on his feet in a flash, his hand blocking and holding the man's arm.

The Indian struggled and drew back his other hand as if to strike at him again.

"Striking Hawk, enough!" the Chief's voice thundered.

Silence fell on the tent. Danny loosed his grip on the Indians arm, who stood there glaring at him until the Chief steered him back to his previous position.

In a lower tone the Chief continued. "You may scoff but we cannot of course, divulge our full scale plans to you. I have said enough for now, however, there is a problem. Since we initiated this plan to bring you here, we have had a change of heart. Not good news for you or your group."

There was an ominous threat in his voice.

Danny's group glanced uncertainly at each other.

It was Pat who asked the question in all their minds right then.

"What do you mean by change of heart Chief?"

The Chief nodded to the large native who had escorted them to the village.

"Tell them, Little Bear."

Little Bear, Danny thought. Somebody had a sense of humor!

Little Bear stepped forward and pointed at Danny.

"We send for a warrior and what do I find in the deep forest? A man on his knees, handcuffed, waiting to be slaughtered like a pig. Is this the warrior we need to teach our tribes. I have much doubt, but still we bring you here."

He stepped back.

The Chief spoke again. "First you must pass some tests tomorrow. Fight Little Bear hand to hand. Before you fight we will have Striking Hawk give a demonstration of our skills by fighting one of your men. "He pointed to Bob. "You look like a soldier who can handle himself."

Danny held his hand up as if to push Bob into the background.

"Look Chief, it's me you brought here. Let me fight my own battles. Leave the rest of the group out of this. They just volunteered to escort me here."

Bob jumped to his feet. "I'm not scared of the bastard. I'm quite prepared to fight him!" he said strongly, looking directly at Striking Hawk, whose face looked venomous with anticipation.

Danny felt himself tighten inwardly. He didn't like what he had seen in the man Bob would be fighting. Something from his past combat experience sent warning bells off in his head.

He held his hand up. "Chief, let me fight Striking Hawk and Bob here can fight Little Bear" he argued.

Bob glared at him. "Thanks a lot buddy. Have you seen the size of Little Bear?"

The Chief clapped his hands.

"Enough! It is decided. Now one more test. You Quigley, also have the reputation of being a sniper. You must prove that too. A shot from five hundred yards out....but with a difference."

"A difference Chief?" Danny asked.

"One of your group will be fastened to a target and you must strike four designated points around their body. One inch from each side of their head and one inch from each side of their chest.. You, Quigley, can choose who your sacrificial lamb will be, so to speak"

"I'm volunteering. " Pat's voice cut through the meeting.

Danny hesitated. "Now look..." he started.

She caught his arm and pulled him sideways towards her, looking directly at him.

"Danny, let me do this please. You know why I need to" she pleaded.

He hesitated a moment then nodded. "Okay..."

Siobhan jumped up. "It's not okay! You can't let her Danny. Say something for God's sake! This is murder!"

Rather than get into an argument, he turned back to the Chief.

"What weapon will I have for the shot?" he asked.

A small smile curled around his features. "Why, the rifle you brought with you of course."

Danny stared. "The Winchester? That's not a sniper rifle" he protested.

The Chief nodded. "Then you better be good, hadn't you?"

Jeff spoke up for the first time. "Chief, what happens if they don't pass these tests tomorrow?"

Striking Hawk stepped forward. "Then you all die!" he snarled. "You are no further use to us."

There was a stunned silence in the room.

It was Siobhan who finally stirred. "Chief, when can I see my old friend Clive?."

"Little Bear will take you there now."

It was the end of the meeting.

The Chief and his group stood and silently walked through a door leading into the rear of the building, leaving a mute group who were led out by Little Bear. There they were passed over to an escort of two tribal policemen…

# Chapter 31

They were led back into the forest for approximately five hundred yards, to a tepee set up on its own between a small group of trees. There was no one around.

The tribal policemen pointed wordlessly to the tent.

It was Jeff who suggested that Siobhan and Danny go in first.

When they ducked inside they stood up and it was then that they saw him.

C.C., alive and well, standing tall with a large beaming smile on his face.

They both gasped.

"You look ten years younger!" Siobhan cried out, throwing herself forward into his arms.

C.C. staggered back at the force of her embrace.

They clung to each other for a few moments and Danny could see that they were both sobbing quietly.

He turned and slipped out through the entrance.

The group looked up at him.

Danny couldn't help smiling. "It's C.C. all right. Bigger and better that ever and even younger that I remember him." He gestured back at the tepee. "It's kind of personal in there. They're both in tears. I'm just giving them a moment."

The group, forgetting the sinister group they had left some moments previously, dissolved into relieved laughed.

"So, it's not a wild goose chase after all. I was worried that this whole thing was going to end in a huge disappointment for both yourself and Siobhan."

Pat's reaction echoed all of their feelings right then.

"I can't believe it myself!" Danny said fervently. "Last time I saw him he staggered off into the night and disappeared, with a life expectancy of three months from terminal cancer. Speaking of such, I'd better get back in there and find out. Hey, the rest of you can come in now as well."

With that they ducked back inside and it was Danny who walked across and wrapped his arms around the large figure of his old friend.

C.C. grasped him with both arms and hugged him.

"My old friend Danny Quigley... come all this way to rescue me, even though I don't want to be rescued. Well if that isn't friendship, I don't know what is. Here, let me look at you."

He pushed him backwards and examined him closely.

"Ah ha" he exploded. "A civilian now, but still with bruises all over your face like back in

Sligo in Ireland." He shook his head. "Same old Danny. It follows you doesn't it... trouble?"

"That's what his ex wife keeps telling him" Pat interjected.

C.C. then turned to the group and the various introductions were made.

Within minutes they were seated in a semi circle in the tepee, and after some initial small chat it was Siobhan who brought the conversation around to what the whole group were dying to find out.

"C.C." she begged. "Put us out of our misery and tell us how and why you ended up here, and how come you're still alive. Delighted though we all are that you're hale and hearty, and looking younger than ever."

C.C. looked around at each of them, like a good storyteller, gauging the mood of his listeners.

He smiled. "Hmm... and quite a story it is my friends. Yes, I was a prisoner at the MI5 camp in the U.K. and was tortured by a man whose name I won't even mention. At the same time that Danny and his crew attacked the camp where I was being held, this man cut me loose and started beating me again. All my life I've been a man of peace, and my life was based on that principle. Suddenly I found my hands around that evil man's neck, and before I knew it he had slumped to the ground, the life crushed out of him."

He paused, looking away, as if reliving the moment.

There was total silence in the tepee.

C.C. sighed and continued. "I was a dead man walking, with my cancer, but I wanted to go somewhere and find that core of peace inside myself again. I'd seen National Geographic films on the First Nations people back in the deep woods of British Columbia, so I traveled to Canada and headed north along the coast. I foolishly struck off into the hinterland of this huge chunk of territory, ceded to the Indians by the Canadian Government some years previously. I stumbled across an injured young Indian lad who was out in the woods, supposedly completing some manhood test, and who had been attacked and mauled by a bear. He was close to death and I nursed him back to health over several days and eventually got him back into this camp where, as you can imagine, I was made most welcome. He happened to be the old Chief's son."

"But this group we just met..........." Bob started to interrupt.

C.C. waved his hand. "I'm coming to that... okay? They kept me on and had some idea that I was something of a holy man sent to them. Perhaps I was able to help them in some ways."

"I'm sure you were C.C. knowing your skills" Siobhan offered, her eyes glinting with excitement. "Go on, tell us the rest. How did you get your health back?"

A smile flickered across his face. "Yes that... well, the old Chief had this beautiful young daughter, Little Dove, you may already have met her. She has something of a healing gift, if you like. She's no doubt, a spirit-filled creature, and one day, as if she was led to do it, she arrived at my tent with her father. She came inside, walked straight across and laid hands on me, speaking in what I presumed was an Indian dialect. I felt waves of light passing down from my head to my toes, and the last thing I remember was keeling over into the hands of the Chief. I don't know how long I laid there, an hour, perhaps longer, then found myself completely alone."

"Holy cow!" Siobhan breathed. "That's some story, and were you better from that moment on?"

"Interestingly no, but something undoubtedly happened to me because from that moment I started to get better. Gradually, I got stronger and felt my health improving day by day. I started walking in the woods, quite often with that beautiful young daughter of the Chief. She pointed out things in the forest that I should eat and I brought them into my diet. Six months later, I knew I was back to full health."

"That is some story!" Pat said fervently." What about the young daughter of the Chief? Do you still see her, now that you're fully better?" she asked.

C.C. smiled. "That's the beautiful thing, you see. She comes to my tepee regularly, with a female member of the tribe as escort, and we work together as a team. A healing team. She has taught me and I have taught her about some of the stuff I do."

Siobhan turned to the group. "C.C. is a Master Practitioner in Neuro Linguistic Programming. He used it to help Danny back in Ireland with some baggage in his past life."

"Neuro what..." Bob started to say.

Danny tapped his arm. "I'll fill you in later Mate." Turning to C.C. "You keep saying 'the old Chief.' What about that gang we just met across in the camp. What we just encountered doesn't sound like a healing community to me C.C."

He sighed. "Yes, the nightmare began a year after I got here. Up to that time the tribe was peaceable and lived on fishing and hunting and some crops. One day a group of strange Indians came to the camp and started agitating the young braves about the evils of the white man. More and more of them slipped into the village, some very peculiar looking Indians, who didn't even speak English. The Chief came and asked me for advice, and what I said probably got him killed. I told him to chase these people out of the camp before they corrupted their whole way of life. He disappeared that same night with his elders, and the next thing I know I'm summoned to their long house and told that the tribe had elected a new Chief, Black Cloud. All the familiar faces had gone. He told me that he was keeping me and the Chief's daughter, Little Dove on as an offer to the spirits for the good fortune of their plans. Striking Hawk is the devil incarnate and wants to take Little Dove into his tepee as his squaw, when she comes of age, which is quite soon."

"So, what have you observed since then in the camp? Comings and goings and so on?" Danny asked.

"Well, there's an old logging road that has been expanded by them out to the coast twenty miles from here and they've been bringing truck loads of equipment in on a regular basis. There's some big new port out on the West coast, where this material must be coming in from. They also have a small landing strip where they bring in other stuff as well. They were waiting for a plane some months ago that didn't arrive and the Chief and Little Bear were quite angry about it."

"I wonder if it was that plane with those transducers on board, the one that crashed? Jesus, this is getting hairy!" Pat exclaimed.

She took a moment to explain her remark to C.C.

He looked thoughtful. "More to this than meets the eye" he commented.

Danny went back to his question. "What else have you seen?" he demanded impatiently.

"Military training, day in and day out. Marching, shooting on the firing ranges, Exercises out in the forests for days on end, unarmed combat in the forecourt."

"They're training for something serious here for sure. This is heavy stuff coming down, buddy," said Bob, looking at Danny.

Siobhan went across and touched C.C.'s arm. "You said something about not wanting to be rescued. Was it you who sent the email to Danny asking for help?"

He grimaced. "I gave Black Cloud your email under the threat of his handing Little Dove to Striking Hawk right away. She would have killed herself first. A year ago I would have sent you all packing. I had a life style I would never have walked away from, but now, I'm torn. This is all going to end badly. I would go now, but Little Dove would have to come with us. But we can't." He said sadly.

"Why can't we?" Siobhan begged him.

"They won't let us. Oh, we could make a run for it, but we wouldn't last a morning before they caught up with us. They're like ghosts in the forest. They would slaughter all of us on the spot, for trying to escape, believe me."

Danny moved across to him. "Look, they want me to train their men in combat. Won't they let us go then?" he asked.

"What do you think? Whatever they're up to, they won't want any witnesses who could possibly sound the alarm."

The group looked silently at each other.

It was Bob who put their feelings into words.

"We're screwed, whichever way you look at it. If we don't pass these damn tests tomorrow, perhaps sooner rather than later."

C.C's face perked up. "What tests?" he asked.

When it was explained to him what they had to face tomorrow, his face paled.

"I don't like the sound of this. They look like they want an excuse to finish you off tomorrow. I'll go and talk to the Chief, if he'll see me, and see if we can reduce these tests to something where you stand a chance. Once you chaps are out of his way, Striking Hawk will finish me off and take Little Dove for his squaw."

He ran his hands through his hair as if in desperation. "My God, I never thought it would come to this! My little piece of heaven on earth has turned into a virtual living hell."

He turned and ducked down as he strode from the tent.

Danny went swiftly after him, catching his arm outside.

"Look C.C. Bob is slated to fight with Striking Hawk. I have a bad feeling about that. Could you get the Chief to cancel that bout or let me fight him instead?"

He looked doubtful. "The Chief doesn't like to look like he made a bad decision. I don't believe I can sway him, but I'll see what I can do. Leave it with me."

He strode off through the trees.

# Chapter 32

C.C. was back within 20 minutes.

He grasped Danny arm, looking directly into his face.

"No go. I'm afraid Black Cloud has made his mind up and that's that. The tests start at 9am tomorrow, with the shooting challenge first. Your Winchester will be available for you to sight in, out at the firing range, any time you want to head over" he pointed. "It's directly through the trees in that direction."

He looked around. "Where's Siobhan?"

At that moment Siobhan, Pat, Jeff and Bob, ducked out of the tent.

C.C. looked excited. "Siobhan, I want to show you my favorite place, over by this small lake. When we get there you have to fill me in on the hostel in Sligo and how it's getting on. I'm dying to know."

Siobhan laughed delightedly. "Now that's a good sign C.C., wanting to know about things back home. I'd love to come with you."

Pat wandered over to them as they were starting to leave. "C.C., where's that airport located? I'd like to take a sneak peek at it."

"I'm not sure you should be wandering around over there Pat. They take a dim view of strangers snooping around. Even I'm careful of where I go since the takeover in the village."

She shrugged. "Okay, I hear you. I'll be careful, I promise."

He examined her face for a moment. "Well, if you must... look, head over towards the lake with Siobhan and I, and I'll show you where to branch off."

He looked at the rest of the group. "Meet back here in three hours and we'll go into one of the long houses where food will be laid out. Oh, the grub here is excellent. Black Cloud believes in feeding his warriors well... though we'll be in a sectioned off part of the building. As a group, you'll be sleeping in the back end of that long house."

He turned and headed off with the women in tow.

Danny turned to Bob and Jeff. He grasped Bob by the arm. "Let's go back inside C.C.'s tent. There's something I need to discuss with you."

When they were inside he turned to Bob.

"Look, I want to talk to you about your fight with Striking Hawk tomorrow."

Bob looked annoyed. "What was all that about back there, trying to match me with Little Bear? That guy's a fucking giant!"

Danny nodded. "Yeah, he's that for sure. However, I'd say he would be easier to handle than Striking Hawk."

Jeff had been standing there, looking puzzled. Now he cut in.

"Yeah Danny, what do mean by that? If I had a choice I'd sooner face Striking Hawk than Little Bear, though either would still beat the crap out of me, I've no doubt."

Danny thought for a moment. "Here's my take on this and I'm a bit puzzled myself by Striking Hawk. I used to spend most of my leave time in the Forces, travelling to Dogos in Korea, Japan and Honk Kong."

"Dogos?" Jeff asked.

It was Bob who answered. "Places where you train in Karate, Judo, Kung Fu and all those related self defense crafts."

Danny nodded agreement. "Exactly. Anyway, to cut to the quick, I recognized in Striking Hawk, that he moves like someone who's frequented such places, though how a Canadian Indian would get exposure to that environment I can't imagine. As far as reading his skills, it's hard to describe…the defensive squat he moves with, the way he holds his body and moves his arms. I'd say that he's one tough nut of a fighter to crack. Notwithstanding your training in Canadian Special Forces Bob, which I know is excellent; I felt that I would have a better chance against him. No offence meant."

Bob sighed. "None taken old buddy. I just couldn't figure out what you were up to back there. Okay, how can you help me Danny, or is it too late to teach me a few tricks?"

"It's never too late. However I am guessing that Striking Hawk is trained in Karate so you need to watch for high kicks and really fast powerful punches coming at you. What I can do is show you some blocking tactics and a few tips on anticipating his moves."

Bob looked askance at him. "But you think he's going to take me out, regardless."

It was a statement, not a question.

Danny shook his head. "You know, fights are unpredictable and it's never over till it's over. I've seen some strange outcomes in the parachute regiment where a small guy was supposedly going to get the crap beat out of him and the exact opposite happened. Don't underrate the stuff they taught you in your Special Forces training. It's designed to stop an enemy and fast, without any Bruce Lee leaping around. So focus your mind on that buddy, it works."

With that Danny squared off with Bob, while Jeff sat over in the corner.

After an hour they stopped, both breathless.

"Shit!" Bob exclaimed. "We could have used you on our advanced training Danny. Some nice moves there and nothing too complicated to take in. Thanks a bunch."

"Yeah, you helped me too. I'm out of training myself and that sharpened me up as well. The pain in my thigh is practically gone, so that's something."

Jeff chuckled from the corner. "Could have fooled me Danny. You move like that goddam cat that jumped me back in the forest." He glanced at his watch. "Let's get over to the firing range and sight in that Winchester. If Danny doesn't get this shooting test right, there may not even be any fights in the morning. They might finish us all off right then."

On that bright note, they left the tent and headed off towards the sound of weapons being fired.

When Pat split off in the direction indicated by C.C., she followed a well-defined path through the woods for about a quarter mile. Then she spotted a windsock on a tall flagpole ahead and figured that she must be near the small airport.

Rather than proceeding on the path, she pushed through some low bushes and shrubbery and peered off towards some sprawled out wooden buildings. Four pick-up trucks were parked outside and one appeared to be unloading fuel from some drums on the back of the vehicle, into a large tank.

Several people were moving around, dressed in coveralls. From where she was, it was impossible to determine if they were First Nations or white people.

She was about to slip on through the shelter of the trees surrounding the airport and get closer, when she jumped, hearing a voice directly behind her.

"I wouldn't go there, if I was you. They will kill you if they discover you."

She whirled around, gulping in air. It was Little Dove standing there.

"Whew, you scared the hell out of me!" she gasped.

The Indian touched her shoulder. "Oh sorry, I didn't mean to frighten you. You are Pat aren't you? A strange name for a woman."

"Oh, it's short for Patricia. I always thought my father wanted a son not a daughter, so I called myself Pat."

"Did it work? I mean, did he look on you as a son?" Little Dove enquired, smiling as she said this.

Pat returned her smile, somewhat pensively. "Unfortunately not."

"And you've spent all your life doing man things to convince him."

Pat stared. "How do you know that?"

Little Dove shook her head. "Oh, I know things. I don't know how. I know why you volunteered to be a target tomorrow."

"Oh, why?"

"You worry about your courage and want to prove yourself. "She held out her hand. "Here, let's walk. I will tell you what I'm feeling for you right now. "

With that they turned and started walking back together through the forest.

Little Dove started talking again. "You are, of course, part Indian and I can feel that in you. Your forefathers were great warriors...strong and courageous. You have that blood in you. Let it flow over the whiteness in you. As we walk, concentrate on my hand and feel the flow of the earth and the forest and your ancestors as they cheer you on. You are the continuation of their walk here on earth. They pass on to you all their power and courage and strength, and their proud legacy. You will never let them down...never disappoint them. They are all around you and above you and beneath you, embracing you. Feel it...feel it."

Pat felt her head swirling and it seemed as if all the sounds of the forest manifested themselves in one roaring sound in her head. She dropped to her knees, swaying from side to side. She was aware of Little Dove guiding her gently onto the soft leaves on the ground.

"Rest now," she heard a gentle voice in her mind.

She felt herself floating downwards, downwards, ever downwards, as if many hands were supporting and drawing her. The she saw in front of her gaze, an Indian encampment where some sort of ceremony was taking place. A woman was standing naked by the campfire and was being painted in different colors by the women of the tribe.

She gasped. It was her!

An Indian Chief strode up to the fireplace and the women withdrew.

The Chief produced a bonnet with feathers and held it up in front of her. He spoke loudly.

"This war bonnet was worn by the most courageous warrior in our nation. The black and white feathers of the young golden eagle denote his courage, the owl for his skill in stalking silently, and the hawk for his attack ability. We now pass this on to you, our worthy tribal champion of the future, who will never shrink from any challenge. Henceforth you will be called, Soaring Eagle... and the sun will never set on your courage."

He leaned forward and placed the bonnet on her, and in her dream she felt herself bend her head. She reached up and pulled the war bonnet down more snugly.

Next moment she was sitting up and staring into the smiling face of Little Dove.

"Come Soaring Eagle, a warrior shouldn't be seen lying on a forest floor" she whispered, helping her to her feet.

Pat was glad that there was no one in C.C.'s tent when she got back.

Little Dove supported her as she went inside and left her sitting there on the mats, a beatific smile on her face, her mind still swirling at the incredible and incomprehensible experience, she had just come through.

She wished the afternoon would never end.

# Chapter 33

Danny was awake at dawn and moved silently past the sleeping forms of Bob and Jeff, into a separate section that was empty. He started with some loosening exercises, gradually ramping up the speed and exertion until the sweat was pouring from him. He finished with twenty minutes of short snappy punches and kicks and was pleased that his injured thigh muscles were no longer causing a problem. Then wrapping a blanket round his shoulders, he squatted cross-legged on the floor and went through visualization process of past battles and training. He saw the linkage between his first four years of judo at the school in Wales, and his eventual qualification as a 4th Dan black belt.

His next training in unarmed combat was when he joined the parachute regiment and the brutal hand-to-hand program that taught him to disable and kill an enemy as efficiently and silently as possible. Joining the SAS moved his level of expertise up by several notches. On his training for an MI5 mission, while still a serving member of the SAS, he had been introduced to a Korean instructor who taught him how to disable an opponent through the application of pressure to nerve centers.

This only increased his hunger for further knowledge in martial arts and resulted in him spending a lot of his leaves at dojos, to further his knowledge. He had been beaten in bouts, and welcomed the opportunity to increase his skills.

His incredible speed, combined with powerful upper body strength and fast reflexes, made him a force to be reckoned with.

He figured that Little Bear would be an equally challenging opponent, and suspected that he would take advantage of his height and physical strength to crush him as quickly as possible. He visualized the fight and ran through several counter moves in his mind. Finally he rose and proceeded across to an ablutions building where he heaved a bucket of cold water up into a makeshift shower and washed himself off.

When he came back inside, the two men were standing up and getting dressed.

"Hey, where you been man?" Bob asked.

"Oh, I did some warming up stuff and visualization techniques. It has always helped me in my build-up to fights on the mat."

"You could have woke me Danny. I'd have done it with you."

He shrugged. "It's kind of a personal routine Bob. Not one I can do and lead you through at the same time. I'm happy to work through some of the stuff we did yesterday. Sharpen you up and get your reactions going. It's why you see boxers coming into the ring already sweating.

They've been ramping up their reaction speed so that when the bell goes, they're ready to go and not caught by surprise. I have to say, neither of us will get any time to warm up today. Sorry, don't mean to be a pessimist."

His answer seemed to shock Bob fully awake. Danny went next door with him and they worked through some moves together until he was satisfied that he was using the techniques that he had taught him yesterday.

By this time the camp was stirring and they grabbed some food in a nearby log house, joined by Siobhan and Pat.

Danny sat down opposite Siobhan, looked across the table at Pat and did a double take.

He could see a suffused glow to her face and her eyes had a distant focus to them.

"Hey, you okay Pat?" he asked. "Still willing to be my target this morning?" he asked.

She turned her eyes to him as if tuning in to him for the first time.

"Am I okay? Never felt better Danny.... and as for being your target.... bring it on! In fact, believe it or not, I'm looking forward to it." She leaned forward and squeezed his arm as she spoke, looking directly into his eyes.

Danny looked askance at her and then around the table.

"Am I missing something here folks?" he pleaded.

It was Jeff who answered him. "As First Nations, I can tell you that she has found her native spirit, just by looking at her. Young boys in the tribe fast for days and go out into the forest to meet their spirit and discover which animal they are aligned with in life. Pat has had that experience without any of that. Quite impressive, and for a woman too."

Siobhan, who was sitting beside her, put her arm around her. "Gosh, I can see a difference. I have a gift too, so I understand how this works sometimes. Oh, how beautiful for you!" she exclaimed.

That filled the next ten minutes as Pat tried to recount her experience with Little Dove, the previous evening. Two tribal police appeared in the doorway and gestured to them.

Shortly after, they made their way out to the firing range where the Tribal police handed him the Winchester and a separate 16 round tubular magazine. Danny had been reluctant to part with the sighted-in weapon with attached scope the previous evening, but was consoled when the policemen wrapped it carefully in a soft blanket, appearing to understand his concern.

It was Bob who was ecstatic about the weapon, being somewhat of a weapons junkie himself. He pointed out to Danny that it was called the 'Yellow Boy' because of its brass receiver and it was the later updated version, the 1873 model, that was known as 'the gun that won the West.' He'd heard all this back in Vancouver already, but didn't comment.

He had already familiarized himself with the weapon in Hanlon Falls. It was 39.0 inches in length, weighed 7.8 lbs. and used 0.44in caliber, and the feed was by a 16-round tubular magazine, now with an added scope. They had spent two hours the previous day, sighting the rifle in.

It was now party time.

Already the whole tribal population of the village had created a funnel along the route of the firing range, with the main body crowding as close to the target as possible. He estimated that there were close to five hundred men and women, waiting impatiently.

The tribal police loomed up again and nodded at Pat.

The whole group walked back up the five hundred yards with her, Siobhan holding Pat's hand. As they came abreast of the first Indians, they were aware of the intense stares directed at them. They were also aware that their lives were at stake from the outcome of these tests.

Chief Black Cloud was squatting off to the right of the target, at least six feet away, with his two warriors, Little Bear and Striking Hawk.

Danny was aware of the sneering, triumphant look directed at him by Striking Hawk who gave a measuring, hungry look at Bob as if already savoring his victory.

C.C. and Little Dove were also there, and gave them a reassuring smile.

Little Dove rushed forward and embraced Pat, clinging to her for a moment.

They fastened her up to the target, a circular object with crisscrossed oak planks in the middle, which strangely resembled a cross. Her hands were fastened first and then a band placed around her forehead to keep it still.

One of the policemen hammered in four small metal circles, which looked very much like the tops of cans that one would cut out with a can opener - one on each side of her head and one to the left and right of her breasts.

Shit, the targets looked so close to her, Danny thought.

As if sensing his disquiet, Siobhan squeezed his arm.

Danny looked back down the funnel of bodies to where he would shoot from. It looked a long way back. Then he went over and paused beside Pat, and looked at her.

He'd never seen her look more beautiful. She had dressed in the best gear she had brought with her, and her hair was combed out and looked glossy.

He looked at her for a long time.

The crowd stilled as if sensing the moment.

She smiled at him. "I'm in your hands now Danny. I have every confidence in you. God bless you" she said, speaking quietly but clearly.

He was tempted to give her a hug but wanted to keep his detachment.

He just nodded, turned and walked back down through the crowd, leaving Bob to signal back as to the accuracy of each shot. Siobhan stayed with Bob, and Jeff came back to the shooting area with him.

Inexplicably, a roll of drums started up. It reminded Danny of the Mexicans playing their oppressive music in the film The Alamo.

He lay prostrate on the ground and Jeff carefully passed the weapon to him.

Thankfully there was no wind to factor in.

"Take your time Danny....just settle in...there's no rush" Jeff murmured, having knelt down beside him.

He looked through the scope, and for a moment let it dwell on Pat's serene face.

Then he moved it to the first target, to the left of her head.

He settled the point where he wanted it to rest, held it steady, breathed in, gently let the air out of his lungs, and squeezed the trigger.

The shot sounded loud in his ears and he wished he had earmuffs.

You right idiot, he thought, worrying about your hearing when you might be dead in a few moments.

The flag shot up from Bob. There was a roar from the crowd and the drums stopped.

A hit!

Jeff clapped him on the shoulder. "Good shot buddy! Now the next."

He moved the rifle over slightly. The drums started up again.

A brief pause and he fired again.

Another hit!

The crowd roared its approval and the drums fell silent.

He moved the rifle down to the target near Pat's right breast and fired.

The flag didn't shoot up as it had on the first two shots.

"Oh, sweet Jesus." Jeff moaned.

There was a flurry of movement at the target area, and through the scope Danny saw Black Cloud had moved across to the target.

Then the flag shot up again.

They both breathed again.

Danny got up onto his knees.

"Jeff there's a very slight breeze has started up. I need to know how I placed that last shot, before I fire again. Head up there and measure exactly where I hit the target."

Jeff hared off up the field and the drums fell silent.

Jeff arrived breathless at the target.

"I need to inspect that last shot" he barked to Bob. "A slight wind has kicked in. What happened on that shot?"

Bob pointed.

Jeff was shaken. The last shot had been well over to the right of the target and had nicked the side of the circle, almost hitting Pat.

Black cloud made a judgment that there was more of a hole in the target than outside. Only just.

Striking Hawk disagreed. He wanted the test to stop right then.

Jeff took out a small pocketknife, which had a short measuring tape and held it against the target.

He checked her eyes. "You okay kid?" he asked.

"I'm fine. Tell Danny just to shoot. Not to think about it. Trust his judgment" she whispered.

He turned and ran back down the range again.

Danny was already on the ground, in the firing position.

The drums started up again as Jeff squatted down.

"You shot an inch too far to the right Danny. Can you factor that in? I know it's not one of those highly sophisticated scopes that would do that for you. Those fucking drums!" he muttered. "Oh, Pat said just to shoot and trust your judgment."

Danny didn't reply. He settled in bringing the scope onto the center of the target and then moved it one inch closer to Pats left breast.

He went still, held it steady, breathed in and out gently, then fired.

The flag shot up.

The crowd gave a long roar of approval and the drums struck up louder with what sounded like a happier rhythm.

Jeff helped him to his feet. "You did it you bastard. You fucking did it."

Danny was already racing back up the firing range, his gaze on Pat who was being released by Black Cloud himself.

He finally reached them and stopped momentarily as the Chief led Pat away from the target and pointed to her and to the crowd.

They roared in appreciation.

The Chief then pointed to Danny.

Another roar.

Danny grinned, and seeing that the Chief had finished, went up and swept Pat into his arms. He felt tears springing into his eyes.

"You little beauty you!" he exclaimed, swinging her round a number of times.

"Hey, put me down you ape. You didn't shoot me, but don't now break my flipping spine!" she cried.

He stopped and lowered her to the ground. Then Siobhan, Little Dove, Bob, Jeff and C.C were all crowding round and thumping them both on the shoulders.

Bob grabbed Danny by the arm. "That third shot, Buddy, I thought we were all goners!"

Danny shrugged. "Yeah, it happens Mate. I lucked in on the fourth shot." He glanced at the fourth target. Almost dead center.

"Yeah, sure.... luck. Like hell Buddy, it was sheer bloody marksmanship! Luck had nothing to do with it."

Siobhan came over to him then and whispered "Danny, I can see now how these terrible skills you learned can actually save lives as well. In this case our lives. Thank you, and sorry for my outburst back in the woods after you killed that man. I was wrong."

'Hmm' he thought. 'It's all in your point of view. Civvies back home have no objections to soldiers doing the killing for them, as long as they don't have to clean up the mess afterwards.'

The Chief broke off the meeting and instructed the group that the unarmed combat would take place directly after lunch.

None of them had much of an appetite.

Danny lay down in the long house and went to sleep, to the amazement of Bob who was bracing himself for the fight.

Little Dove took the two women for a walk and Jeff took off on his own, into the woods.

The tribes' people had laid on a slew of food, having what Jeff referred to as a mini Potlatch, or Indian celebration.

There was a building sense of anticipation among them for the event still to come.

Danny wished he were an onlooker rather than a participant, or possibly a victim!

# Chapter 34

Fights were unpredictable.

Danny had seen over the years where someone with all the attributes of a dangerous fighter, was taken down by someone half his size. He'd seen four military police struggling to arrest a small skinny Commando, who nearly wiped the floor with them.

Following the sport of boxing, during his time in the parachute regiment, he was disappointed a number of times, seeing a hyped up match where the fighter's styles resulted in a messy unexciting bout.

He knew he was beatable and had suffered defeats in the past, thankfully in gyms and not in military combat. He had tremendous respect for the highly qualified judo opponent who could slam you down to the mat with a hip throw or a leg sweep. Karate and Kung Fu experts didn't worry him too much, as his fast reactions helped him in attacks, and provided openings to retaliate in deadly fashion.

Today, he was as ready as he would ever be.

He didn't pray or bless himself as a lot of boxers do, prior to a fight. However, he grudgingly acknowledged that there was some power out there, and mentally asked for his strength and skills to be accelerated.

Arriving at the fight location and maintaining his focus, he was only dimly aware of the whole village standing in a large circle, with Black Cloud, Little Dove and the elders, seated at the top end. Little Bear was already standing out in front, glistening with oil and war paint.

He looked formidable.

Danny moved to the bottom end of the circle, where C.C., Bob, Jeff, Siobhan and Pat stood waiting.

Bob looked closely at him.

"You okay Buddy?" he asked.

He nodded, saying nothing.

Sensing his mood, the rest of his group lightly touched his arms and shoulders and then stood back.

Black Cloud moved out to the center of the square and gestured to the two opponents to come closer. When they had done so, he placed an arm on each of their shoulders, looking at each of them for a long moment. Then he spoke.

"Little Bear and Quigley, today you bring honor or disgrace to your tribes. You fight until one of you is killed or injured so you can't go on. If you stop before that, I will instruct Striking Hawk to kill you himself. Understood? Now fight"!

He turned and walked back to the elders and sat down.

Little Bear launched himself straight at Danny, his arms sledging down as if to pummel him into the ground in the first few seconds of the bout.

Standing slightly balanced and bowlegged, Danny blocked the downward blows with his elbows and used his footwork to let other blows slide past him. He backed up as he did so, as Little Bear's aggression and momentum drove him backwards to the edge of the circle. He'd seen openings to strike back but wanted to get more of a feel for his opponent's style.

Almost on top of the crowd, Danny snapped a kick to Little Bear's shinbone and slammed his elbow into his jaw as he leaned forward in pain. Danny quickly turned away from the crowd as Little Bear came after him, lashing out with his long muscular arms. Danny continued to back up as he blocked the onslaught. The crowd had fallen silent now.

As one of the blows slid past his shoulders, Danny grabbed the arm, twisting it, and as the Indian was forced to lean forward with the pressure on his elbow, he drove his boot straight into Little Bear's gut, sending him flying backwards onto the earth He could have kicked him in the head as he scrambled to his feet, but Danny let him get up. Almost disbelieving what had happened to him, the Indian growled and hurled himself at Danny again. He stood his ground until Little Bear was almost on top of him, then he jumped forward and up, placing both his boots on his opponent's thighs, at the same time grabbing Little Bear by his hair, and threw himself backwards.

Little Bear's forward momentum sent him flying over Danny's head onto the ground with an audible 'thump'.

Danny kept rolling, up and over onto the top of the Indian, then chopped down on the side of his neck with tremendous power.

Little Bear lay still.

It was over.

The arena fell into a stunned silence.

Black Cloud and some of the elders came bustling out into the center of the ring, gazing down in shock at the fallen giant. Finally Striking Hawk gave a snort of disgust and drove his foot into the side of the defenseless Little Bear.

"You're a useless coward" he snarled, "letting a white man beat you."

He drew his foot back to kick him again but Danny shoved him sideways, almost knocking him over.

"Leave him alone, you Bastard. He fought a good fight."

Striking Hawk went for Danny, his face suffused with rage. It looked like another bout was about to start until Black Cloud stepped in between them.

"Maybe later you two, not now. Striking Hawk now fights for the honor of the tribe. Bring the soldier forward."

Striking Hawk gritted his teeth and pushed his face forward. "Maybe later? I make sure it happens. Believe me. Now I break your friend into pieces."

Danny shrugged. "Whatever..."

He turned to the Chief. "Our custom is to take care of a fallen fighter. Give me five minutes to take Little Bear to our tent where our healer Siobhan, can tend to him."

Black Cloud threw up his hands in anger and frustration. "Do what you must. But be back here in ten minutes for your friend to fight."

Danny, C.C., Little Dove and Siobhan gently lifted the big warrior and staggered off towards Siobhan's tent. Bob was going to follow, but Danny shook his head.

"Stay here and get your focus" he cautioned.

Back in the tent, Little Bear was starting to come round and struggling to sit up. Little Dove spoke softly to him in her language and he settled back down.

Danny went back outside with C.C. Little Dove joined them a moment later.

Without a word they headed back to the arena.

It was time for Striking Hawk and Bob to battle it out.

# Chapter 35

Bob handled the first onslaught very competently.

Striking Hawk, true to his name, struck first, with a flurry of punches, kicks and hand strikes.

Having been primed by Danny, he stayed strong under the attack, backing up as his opponent went for a quick finish.

Striking Hawk took a deep breath, his black eyes narrowing as they looked at Bob, measuring him with new respect.

Bob's gaze flicked to Danny in the crowd, as if to say 'thanks, you warned me about this.'

It was a mistake to even momentarily take his gaze off someone like Striking Hawk. Danny started to shout a warning, but Striking Hawk was already in the air, his right foot slashing across Bob's chin, felling him.

He stumbled to his feet but it was obvious that he was stunned by the kick.

Danny knew that the Indian could finish Bob right then.

But that wasn't his plan.

Satisfaction glinted in his eyes as he moved in and started on Bob. First savage kicks to his legs and punishing body blows to his stomach and rib cage. Then a leg sweep put him down again. When he fell, Striking Hawk went after him, raining kicks to his side and head. Then he caught Bob by the head as he attempted to get up and smashed his knee into his nose, breaking it and sending blood spouting out like a geyser.

Bob crashed back down and Striking Hawk knelt across him and raised his arm preparing to deliver a killing blow to his windpipe.

For a moment, Striking Hawk raised his head and gazed directly at Danny in triumph.

Danny was already running as the arm started descending.

He was too late, but C.C. wasn't. He had dashed in from the sidelines a moment before, sensing the ending and grabbing Striking Hawk, hurled him sideways off Bob's still form.

Like a snake Striking Hawk was on his feet and lashed out at C.C. felling him like a tree and then moved towards him.

A small figure intervened, and Striking Hawk froze as Little Dove waved a feathered circle in his face, then, pointing to the sky, moved the circle from the west to the east, calling out in a sing song voice.

Everyone went silent except Striking Hawk.

"That Indian crap doesn't worry me Little Dove" he sneered; yet an uneasy look crept across his face.

Black Cloud's voice rang out.

"Little Dove say Striking Hawk die before sun cross the sky tomorrow. If Striking Hawk still alive, then Little Dove medicine not work and she must die. I have spoken."

Within minutes the crowd had dispersed leaving the small group gathered around Bob and C.C. who had now been helped back on his feet. With Siobhan supporting C.C., the rest of the group carried Bob back to the tent where Siobhan and Little Dove started ministering to them.

A while later they emerged.

Siobhan looked grim. " C.C. is okay. Just a bruised face. He saved Bob's life though. Another minute and his throat would have been smashed. Striking Hawk meant to kill him. Oh, Little Bear, who we brought here to recover, is gone. .

"How's Bob?" Pat asked.

"Not so good really. As far as I can determine without ex rays or a scan, he has two or three broken ribs, a broken nose, some terrible bruising on his thighs and arms and I'm worried he took a kick in the kidney which might have caused some serious damage. He's conscious right now and his main regret is letting Danny down."

Danny shook his head. "For God's sake he managed to hold his own for a while. That Striking Hawk is obviously a master in his own right at this stuff. Bob didn't stand a chance from the outset. I had a bad feeling about that guy."

"Yeah, you tried to get Black Cloud to switch opponents" said Jeff. "Could you have beaten him Danny?"

Danny shrugged. "Who knows? I wouldn't, if I were you, put a bet on me to come out on top. That Hawk is one mean piece of business...as good as any I've seen, and I've seen a few."

Pat looked around at the group. "So where does this leave us now? I mean, are they going to use Danny to train their people, giving us some more time to try to get out of here? Or are we for the chop tomorrow?"

Danny nodded to her. "Let's take a walk Pat, and talk through a few things. We need to figure out some strategy rather than waiting for something bad to happen."

He nodded at the tent. "As if this isn't bad enough. We certainly can't make a dash for it now with Bob in the shape he's in, and I suspect that there are going to be other casualties before long."

He turned and Pat followed him.

Danny walked into the brush and forest at the far end of the camp, aware that the permanent guards posted outside the sizable longhouses were keeping an eye on them. He was curious about those closely guarded buildings and wanted a better look.

As he moved carefully through the trees he stayed alert to any of the tribe either following them or involved in some activities. Fifty yards into the forest he stopped, turning to Pat.

"I don't think anyone is following us. Have you spotted anything?"

She shook her head. "No, I think we're pretty much alone out here. They're not concerned about us making a run for it, what with the rest of our group back there. What have you got on your mind Danny?" she asked.

"I'd like a closer look at the back of those big longhouses. The fronts are guarded 24/7 as far as I can see. I'd like to know what's inside those buildings, perhaps tonight when the Pot lash celebration booze takes the edge off their vigilance. I'm hoping the rear might show some way to get in, and they're near the forest, which gives me a chance to get closer."

She whistled through her teeth. "Shoot Danny, you could be putting the whole group at risk here if they catch you."

He nodded. "We have no other options at present. Sure, they may use me for a few days to do some unarmed combat with their people. If I'm right, we haven't got much longer before Striking Hawk wants our heads. I need an edge. I need to find out what they're up too, and their timelines, if possible. From experience, I've found that attacking an enemy before they hit you, can turn the tables."

She looked at him for a long time, and then stepping forward, she placed her right hand on his chest.

"Danny, I recognize and I salute the warrior in you, and wherever it takes you, I want to be part of it. Please don't think of me right now as a woman, but a fellow warrior."

He had debated using her in a less action-orientated role, but the look on her face and the intensity of her gaze told him not to pursue that route.

Without uttering a word, he reached across and momentarily laid his hand on her shoulder, then turning, started moving off at a tangent that would take them around the back of the longhouses.

It took the best of 30 minutes for them to creep up as close as possible to the back of the buildings without being spotted. Fortunately, with the washrooms and toilets set up in the camp, there were no Indians wandering out into the brush to relieve themselves. Already they could see activity around two massive log doors set up in the back end of one of the longhouses.

Something was happening.

Black Cloud, Striking Hawk, his twin brother and a number of other natives were milling around.

Suddenly Pat squeezed his arm. "Look what's coming in. I spotted that pick-up truck at the small airport they have outside the camp. What on earth are they up to?" she whispered.

He still had the set of field glasses, which had not been confiscated, and he focused in on the approaching vehicle, as it swung round, reversed into the door of the building and disappeared inside.

"Dammit!" he whispered, "I can't see a thing inside that longhouse. I'd love to see what they're delivering. Could be a key to this whole operation. Look at the way those tribesmen are now lined up protectively around the entrance, not to mention Black Cloud and his top people too."

He rotated the glasses upwards, carefully scrutinizing the building then he lowered them and started easing back.

"Let's go," he whispered.

She turned her head, surprised. "What Danny? What have you seen? Why don't we hang around here for a few moments and see what happens?"

He shook his head as he continued to ease backwards, indicating that she should follow. When they reached the cover of some of the bigger trees and brush, he stopped and turned to her.

"We've been gone long enough already. They may be looking for us to return or start tracking us. I've already seen a way in for us tonight. Tell you more about it later and then we'll plan our move. It could be dangerous Pat, so you might be better to stay out of this. If I don't come back, you might be needed to try to make a run for it with the group."

She straightened to her full height. "If you go down, we're all sunk Danny. I'm coming along to watch your back and make sure that you do come back. If you go down, I'll go down with you, you hear?"

A small grin crept across his features.

"You're something else Pat, especially since Little Dove did a job on you." He turned and started retracing his steps back to the camp.

The next four hours seemed to flash by.

Both Danny and Pat dropped in on Bob who was still lying flat out on the ground inside the tent, obviously in considerable pain.

He managed a grin when they ducked inside the tent.

"I can tell that you two are up to something" he whispered, indicating that they should sit down on the floor beside him.

They complied and quickly brought him up to date on what they had observed and

Danny's plan to try to get inside the longhouses.

The thought of the imminent action seemed to energize him and he sat up, grabbing Danny's arm for support.

He looked from one to the other. "I guess you know that if you're caught, it's pretty well curtains for the rest of us."

Pat touched his other arm gently. "Look Bob, Danny and I talked and we agree that we're running out of time anyway. They'll finish us off in a couple of days for sure. We have to get a handle on what they are up to. Possibly get our hands on some weapons in case we have to shoot our way out of here."

Bob grinned ruefully, nodding down at his injuries. "Yeah, and a lot of help I'll be if we have to make a run for it."

Danny squeezed his arm. "Don't write yourself out of the party yet my friend. There are apparently vehicles over at the airport, and from what I've heard, a road out to the coast, so with transport we could possibly make a break for it, even with some wounded or injured."

Pat nodded. "Danny's right Bob. Now if we are missed tonight by Black Cloud or his group, just hint that we're having a romantic tryst in the forest."

He glanced from one to the other. "Any truth in that?" he enquired, a slight grin on his face.

She struck his arm, not too forcefully. "For crying out loud!"

Danny grinned too. "Not my type Bob anyway. Too much Indian. I couldn't handle her."

Pat looked from one to the other. "God, I don't know about you two. We're a couple of hours away from maybe getting the chop and listen to you!" she exclaimed.

Bob preened himself and sat straighter. "Well, you know, Special Forces, comrades in arms and all that. Laugh in the face of death and all that..."

"Crap!" she interjected.

Danny chuckled, but a puzzled look crept across his features. You know, there's one thing that puzzles me about this camp. It was full of good Indians, according to C.C. who didn't want any part of this new bunch who came in and took over. They didn't kill all of them. But where are they now?"

Bob groaned in pain and eased back onto the blanket.

Pat looked up at Danny. "Why don't you go and talk to C.C. about it. Oh, and by the way, I'd suggest you both keep our foray to night to yourselves for now."

He glanced at her, measuring her words. "Um... okay. Something you're not telling me?"

Her eyes had a distant cast to them. She merely pursed her lips and shook her head slightly. Danny waited for a moment, but seeing that she wasn't going to share any further, he shrugged and ducked out of the tent.

Outside he bumped into Jeff who was walking quickly away from the village.

"Oh Danny, the Chief was looking for you earlier and he grabbed me and took me across to the meeting tent. Apparently they now want to use you for a few days showing them some hand to hand combat. Striking Hawk was the trainer before and is one pissed off guy, to say the least. Wanted the Chief to agree to a bout with you to see who is best, but I think the Chief thinks you may be a better teacher. Striking Hawk's high kicks and style takes years to learn and he wants his warriors to take on board some moves that they can use right away. He may also figure that Striking Hawk would beat you anyway and you wouldn't be up to much training after that."

Danny made a face. "Glad I have my uses after all. So we may have a few days grace left. Any hint as to what happens to us afterwards?"

He averted his eyes. "Your guess is as good as mine Danny. Go figure" he said gloomily.

"Yeah, I hear you my friend. I'm just heading over to C.C.'s. Pat's inside there with Bob, who's not feeling too good right now."

"Okay, I'll leave you to it and pop in and see Bob for a minute."

Danny was on the verge of telling him about his plan for the night but bit his tongue, remembering Pat's caution.

When he ducked inside C.C.'s tent, Siobhan and Little Dove were standing up, showing signs of leaving. C.C. was sitting back on some sort of roughly hewn chair contraption.

"The one thing I never got used to Danny, is sitting on the dammed floor. I need something to lean back into."

Siobhan laughed. "Yes, he told me he instructed one of the Indian wood carvers to make a chair for him, and that's the result!"

Danny laughed. "Well, it's functional at least. I wanted to talk to C.C. for a moment. I hope I'm not interrupting something," he prompted.

Siobhan shook her head. "No, Little Dove and I are just leaving. Off for a brief stroll in the forest. C.C.'s all yours" she said smiling at him.

Danny started to squat down but turned, as they were about to leave.

"Oh, Little Dove, where is Little Bear's tent? Can I go and see him sometime?"

She frowned. "Little Bear is in disgrace. No one visits his tent right now. You, as a stranger could try it, but I wouldn't expect any great welcome. After all, you defeated and humiliated him in front of his tribes people. It's the tent over near the longhouses and has a bear sign on the outside material."

Nothing else was said so they turned and left.

Danny gave a great sigh as he sank to the ground. "God C.C. it's just suddenly catching up on me. I could close my eyes and be out in two minutes."

C.C. stared at him for a moment.

"You know lad, you did a super job out there today, beating Little Bear, and you made it look so easy. I wouldn't be surprised if you could take down that big bully Striking Hawk. He's too full of himself by far."

"He's good, I can tell you that. Showing all the signs of a highly skilled fighter, and extremely fit and confident."

"Ha!" he spat. "You told me once Danny boy, back there in Sligo, that a fight's never over till it's over. Too many factors come into play you said. So don't go psyching yourself out when it comes to Striking Hawk. My money's still on you if it comes down to it. Now what did you want to talk to me about? Not that it isn't great to have a chinwag about things anyway. Just to satisfy my curiosity, how is the business going, back in the U.K., Danny?"

C.C. had signed over his insurance business to Danny, in anticipation of his imminent death from cancer.

Danny was silent for a moment. "Asking the question like that, with some time and distance away from it, I'd have to say, not great C.C."

"Go on" he prompted.

Danny shook his head. "It's hard to put into words. My past history is hard to escape. At times it haunts me."

C.C. nodded. "The action, the danger, the adrenalin rush that's now missing. Yes, a big difference between sitting in some chap's house trying to sell a policy, and jumping out of an aircraft in the darkness, over enemy territory, with your mates ready to kill or blow up something when you hit the ground."

"You knew?" Danny queried.

"Oh sure, that was my biggest concern. Could you make the switch? At the time you were my only option, and a good one, I thought."

" Oh, don't get me wrong C.C. I looked after your client bank and earned some nice commissions. Have even arrived at an appreciation of how much I could impact on peoples' lives...."

"But.........?

"MI5 pulled me back for a mission that involved a lot of action and I found my old skills kicked in, like I'd never taken off the uniform. Hell, I was even better, without the ra ra you get in the regiment before a mission. I've no desire to go back into the military, but it made me realize where my true core is."

"I hate to be so brutal Danny, but you mean, killing people don't you?"

Danny swiveled his head from side to side as if in agony.

"No, you don't understand C.C., not just killing people, though that happens of course, but helping to bring closure to situations that call for the kind of skills-set that I live, breath and taste, every waking moment. This rescue attempt, which admittedly looks pretty chancy right now, is a good example. Sure, I did okay at the insurance business, but I realize, as the saying goes, that I'm not being true to myself. I'm only truly alive when I'm out on the edge and metaphorically jumping out of that aircraft again."

C.C. sighed. "So what are you telling me Danny?"

"When and if we get back C.C., I'd like to hand the business back to you. I hate to say it, but your dream here is finished my friend, whether we can safely get all of you out of here or not, wouldn't you agree?"

He nodded slowly. "You're right Danny and thank God for those skills of yours which I didn't mean to denigrate. They may be all that stands between us and being murdered here shortly. Now, was there something else you came over to see me for?"

"Well, yes. I suddenly realized that there were a large number of good Indians, if I can call them that, who didn't fall into line with the new regime under Black Cloud and his elders. What happened to them? I didn't pick up that all of them were butchered?"

"Quite right Danny. There must have been at least a hundred and fifty who protested the new direction of Black Cloud, but they were surrounded and threatened by high caliber weapons and hustled away into the forest. We didn't hear any long drawn out firing, so we assumed they're prisoners out there somewhere. Especially as extra supply trucks come in all the time and the stuff isn't dropped off here."

"So they could be out there somewhere, and if we could rescue them they might turn the tables on this bunch, assuming we could get them weapons." Danny said excitedly.

"A lot of assumptions Danny, if you don't mind me saying so" C.C. responded gloomily.

"Well, yes I agree, but it's something to think about, just the same."

He stood up. "I'm going to try and speak with Little Bear."

C.C. lifted his hand warningly. "You heard what Little Dove said Danny. You may not be very welcome."

He waved back at him and ducked out of the tent.

# Chapter 36

The guards at the longhouses regarded Danny suspiciously as he headed in their direction, but relaxed when he veered off to the section of the camp outlined by Little Dove. Passing a fresh water pump he filled a wooden pail and carried it with him towards a tent with the telltale bear insignia outlined on the canvas.

He stopped outside and shouted Little Bear's name.

Hearing nothing, he looked around to see if anyone was showing an interest in him or hurrying towards him as if to prevent him from entering the tent.

Nothing.

He lifted the tent flap and ducked inside.

The first thing he spotted was Little Bear sitting cross-legged at the back of the wigwam, facing the entrance, almost as if he was expecting someone.

He regarded Danny with an expressionless face, and yet...did he see a flicker of something in his demeanor?.

Surely he couldn't be pleased at seeing him!

The Indian nodded to the space in front of him, and Danny placed the bucket of water off to one side, and then squatted down opposite him.

They regarded each other in silence. Strangely, a comfortable silence.

Finally Danny reached his hand across and Little Bear met it and gripped it tightly.

"You fought a good fight Little Bear" he said.

Little Bear shook his head, a slight smile creeping onto his features. "Not good enough. I'm afraid. I lost."

Danny returned his smile. "I've lost in the past as well, but I learned more from those fights than the one I came out the winner."

"My father said the same thing to me as a boy. Learn from everyone you fight. Keep your strength a secret until you need it. Accept that everyone you meet is your master in something, even the wise old women of the tribe."

"He was wise, your father, Little Bear. What was his name? Is he still alive?"

"His name was Great Owl. No, a tree fell on him when he was cutting it down to make a new canoe for me, for my coming of age. My uncle finished it for me, but it was never the same. He had a good life and a good death. It is the circle of life. I feel his spirit with me."

Danny thought carefully about what he was going to say next.

"What would he think of your present situation here? Would he approve?"

For the first time the Indian's eyes glanced sideways, avoiding his gaze.

He suddenly looked uncomfortable.

Finally he looked back at Danny again. "He would tell me to learn from you until I could beat you, or until we could fight together against an enemy."

Danny chuckled. "With your power and strength Little Bear, I'm sure that wouldn't take too long. No, I actually meant what would your father think of your association with Black Cloud, Striking Hawk and the tribe here planning something terrible, that will only amount to total disaster for your tribe?"

"We start on a path, and once started, it must be followed through. The white man has..."

"Yes, I know, all those treaties broken. I can tell you that the white man has unbelievable military power and no small Indian revolt will even make a dent in it. Sure you can make some surprise attacks, but once they ramp up their forces, there is no doubt how it will end. The total slaughter of your tribe, and quite possibly the loss of quite a number of benefits, even this huge tract of land. This land was passed over to you by the Canadian Government, who, according to my colleague Bob, are genuinely trying to understand the First Nation's needs and are working with them to create a better life. The past is over Little Bear. Now it's time to learn from it and move on" Danny urged.

Little Bear changed the subject. "Little Dove tell me you stepped in to stop Striking Hawk from kicking me on the ground."

"You fought like a true warrior Little Bear. In my world we always treat a defeated fighter with respect, not kick him and humiliate him. Striking Hawk would be barred from fighting in our club if he tried to kick a defeated opponent."

The Indian watched him gravely for a moment, and then nodded.

"Yes, I like that. All a warrior has is his dignity. When you take that, you destroy him."

Spontaneously Danny reached across and grabbed the Indian's elbow.

"Little Bear, you are not destroyed but a great warrior who will win many fights in the future. Listen to your father's voice now. Learn from it and move on. His advice is already working. I believe we are now friends, and who knows" he looked steadily into the man's eyes, "we may yet fight a common enemy together."

He stood up and pointed to the water bucket. "I brought you some fresh water."

The Indian's eyes stayed with him all the way across the wigwam.

Danny paused, turned, and looked at him again.

Then he was gone.

Deep in thought, he walked through the camp, and without shouting out, tucked his head inside C.C.'s tent.

Then he froze.

Siobhan and C.C. were locked in a passionate embrace, completely oblivious of his entry.

His jaw dropped and he wasn't aware that he whipped his head back out and took a couple of unsteady steps backwards.

C.C. and Siobhan! Impossible!

Back in Ireland she had told him that they were just spiritual friends, nothing physical about their relationship whatsoever, and from all the signs then, that was really the case. Of course C.C. was suffering from terminal cancer, which the diagnosis had confirmed. Perhaps logic dictated that they shouldn't get involved, with that hanging over them.

Danny wasn't sure if he was shocked by this apparent betrayal, or his own ego getting bruised. He had thought that Siobhan and himself had something going for them. Okay, so they only got together once a year because of his commitment to building C.C.'s business, but they kept in constant touch by telephone and e-mail. Sure, he had had some other dalliances in the meantime, but in the back of his mind he had thought that there could be a future for them together. Now this, and to discover it in the midst of a situation where they might all meet with death at any moment.

He shook his head dazedly.

"What's up Danny?" He turned and Little Dove stopped beside him.

"Oh, nothing Little Dove. I'm just leaving."

He turned to push past her.

"I'm just going in to visit C.C.," she continued.

He stopped and gripped her arm. "Oh, I wouldn't right now, if I was you" he said.

She gave him a puzzled look, then her head whipped around to the tent of C.C.

Her face flashed understandingly, as she turned back to him.

She hugged him suddenly. "Oh Danny" she whispered. "I'm sorry, so sorry."

Despite himself, he felt tears in his eyes.

Her sympathy and understanding brought home to him what he had just witnessed; the end of a relationship that was special to him. His little Colleen, with the black hair, tinkling laugh and her Irish ways. Gone like a mist on a hot summer's morning.

She spun him around, facing away from the tent.

"Come on Danny, you and I will go for a walk, to a special place that I have not brought anyone else to, until now."

Still recovering from the memory of the two people inside, who in an instant had mentally whipsawed his emotions, he caught hold of her hand as she led him off into the forest.

They walked for about half a mile, and all the time Little Dove chattered away, pointing out various plants and herbs that she used in her healing ceremonies and which she had learned from her mother. He suspected that her motivation was to take his mind off his recent stunning discovery in C.C.'s tent.

Finally she pushed through some dense brush and edged cautiously down a steep slope. She paused half-way down and turned her head back towards him.

"I discovered this place some two years ago when I tumbled down this slope. When I got to the bottom... oh well, you'll see in a moment."

He still couldn't see anything, but she grabbed his hand, laughing happily and pushed through some tightly woven branches hanging down from a massive pine tree. Once through he spotted the mouth of a cave ahead.

Still laughing she pulled him along with her until they entered the small opening in the cave entrance. Once inside, it widened out until he could stand fully erect. As his eyes adjusted to the semi darkness, he could spot a glow ahead, coming from a tunnel. She pulled him forward, and he followed tentatively, not wanting to stumble on the uneven surface.

As they progressed, the glow got stronger and when she finally emerged after about fifty yards, she pointed ahead proudly and stepped aside.

He stopped in amazement and his jaw dropped.

Ahead of him was a pool of azure water about thirty feet across, and he estimated, about five feet in depth. The glow seemed to come from a tiny opening way up in the roof of the cave, and reflected down onto the water.

The only thing he could compare it to was the azure green of the Jamaican waters, but even they paled in comparison to this idyllic pool.

His head moved around slowly, taking in the beauty and almost sacredness of the scene.

"My God Little Dove, this is incredible! The colors........."

"Yes, yes, aren't they amazing! I often come here to renew myself, and just to be."

"And no one else has ever been here but you?" he queried.

"Not until now Danny, with you...our chosen warrior."

He spotted what seemed to be a soft bed of pine branches at the edge of the pool.

"You sleep here too?" he asked.

She nodded. "Sometimes the spirits want to speak to me and then I lie down and sleep. Come."

She led him to the bed of pine branches and indicated that he should sit down.

Then she walked to the pool and, leaning forward, removed her moccasins and stepped in, until she was ankle deep in the soft glowing waters.

She bent down and cupped some of the glowing water and carefully washed her hands and face. Then she turned and filled her cupped hands again and walked carefully towards Danny. As she came up to him he started to rise.

"No, stay seated Danny. I can reach you better."

She leaned forward and gently poured the water on the crown of his head. It sluiced down his face onto his clothes.

At the same time she reached and placed her hands on his head and started speaking in a strange language. At that precise moment his mind blurred and he felt himself falling and spinning into a vortex that had opened up beneath him. The descent seemed to last for a long time but quite suddenly came to a stop.

He found himself lying on the floor in what appeared to be the throne room of a castle.

Seated on the throne was a majestic figure surrounded by an aura of brilliant light and wearing a crown. Danny could barely look at him, so blinding was the light.

A large angelic figure came forward and helped Danny to his feet.

Though no words were spoken, in his head he heard the angel say:

"You must put on the armor of the Lord."

With that, two smaller figures came forward and swiftly helped him into an incredibly light suit of armor. As they fastened it around him, it seemed to mould to his form and he understood at some deeper level that despite it's lightness, it would not only provide physical protection, but mental and emotional as well.

The large angel stood in front of him again.

"You must now put on the shield of faith."

He reached behind him and one of the smaller figures handed him a solid silver shield, which he slipped on to Danny's left wrist. Danny hefted the shield and was amazed at how it blended perfectly with his weight, size and strength.

Still something was missing.

The angel's voice rang inside his head.

"You must now put on the sword of the spirit."

The angel took his arm and led him across to the throne.

Without being told he fell to his knees, head down, unable to gaze directly at the majestic figure on the throne.

Danny was suddenly aware of something touching his shoulder. Half looking up and slightly off to the side, he saw that the figure on the throne had reached forward and touched him with a jeweled sword, first on one shoulder and then on the other. He experienced a bolt of lightning shoot down through the top of his head and straight down through his body, exiting at his feet. He felt his muscles turn to steel and his heart throbbed with an incredible strength and courage.

The large angel helped him to his feet and pressed the sword into his hand. He looked up and saw that the figure on the throne was gone.

The angel looked directly into his eyes.

No words were spoken, but Danny heard his voice.

"You are now the anointed of the Lord. Go forth and conquer evil."

With that, Danny felt himself spiraling back through the vortex, and found that he was sitting up dazedly on the bed of pine trees by the azure pool.

Little Dove was sitting there smiling sweetly at him.

"We'd better get back. Black Cloud will notice our absence" she said.

Danny rose groggily to his feet. "Oh my God, what's happened to me!" he exclaimed.

"The spirits have blessed you Danny. You are now our chosen warrior. You are now prepared for battle. Come, we must make our way back into camp separately."

# Chapter 37

It was a black night with a full moon occasionally scudding out from behind the clouds.

Pat and Danny had blackened their faces earlier with some mud and wore dark clothes as they slipped out of camp and made their way round to the rear of the longhouse that they had seen earlier. The only weapons they carried were a sharp knife each that C.C. had managed to get for them, plus a good length of rope he had removed from a cache that the Indians kept for trapping. They had checked the front of the longhouse and dimly made out one guard sitting down with his back to the building. Hopefully sleeping off the celebrations.

Danny had slept for an hour after the group had supper together. Now he felt refreshed and alert.

He dismissed the amazing time he had spent in the cave with Little Dove that afternoon, his mind now focused on his goal to see what was inside the longhouse.

They reached the vantage point they had discovered earlier and sank to the ground.

After a moment he whispered "no guards out back, that's good. Let's get in closer."

It took a few minutes to cover the open ground between them and the large forbidding longhouse.

Reaching the rear doors he quickly ran his hands over them and checked the locks with a penlight.

"As we suspected. Not a chance of breaking in here" he whispered. "Come on, let's go round the side."

They moved quietly and cautiously along the side of the building until Danny reached what he thought was the central point.

He leaned close to her ear. "Let's see if my mountaineering skills have deserted me."

Danny's plan, that had been hatched in his mind as he viewed the building earlier, was that he could use the rough-hewn log indents to climb up the sloping side of the building. Once there he could drop the rope to Pat so she could scale up. There, the large traditional opening in the top of the longhouse, designed to allow smoke from the fires inside to escape, would facilitate their entry... he hoped!

He scrambled up the sloping roof without any difficulty.

Tying the rope to an abutment, he tossed it back down to Pat.

He need not have worried about her. She was beside him in a moment, not even out of breath.

He patted her back and pulled her across to the opening.

There was room for both of them to stand alongside each other and look inside.

He cursed.

There were no lights inside. He glanced back up at the sky.

"Where's that flipping moon right now? I'd like to know what I'm dropping into" he whispered.

"We haven't time to wait around Danny. I'd suggest you get down there a.s.a.p., and perhaps the moon will break out for you as you go."

He thought that good advice and dropped the rope down the opening.

"I'll shake the rope when I get down, for you to follow, if everything looks okay" he said, as he started to descend.

Danny hadn't slid down a rope since his SAS, days but surprisingly, it went smoothly, and he was joined smartly by Pat a moment later. He hooked the rope off to the side wall, to make sure it wasn't spotted if anyone came into the building while they were inside.

When the moon did deliver some light a few minutes later, they were amazed at what they saw; two large totem poles standing in the middle of the building and surrounded by stacks of wooden crates, piled up around the sides of the longhouse.

Danny took his penlight out as the moon went behind the clouds again, and moved over to the totem poles.

They looked like regular Indian totem poles with all the carvings of eagles, fish and bears. Pat borrowed his torch and went around them, examining them closely. At one time she attempted to rock them back and forth, without success.

She came back to where he stood waiting.

"Well?" he asked quietly.

"They're bigger than the standard totem poles. Their circumference for example...and heavier. I couldn't even shift one of them. I haven't a clue what they're about" she whispered.

The moon flashed it's light inside again and he pointed to the crates, stacked ten feet high.

"Let's climb up on top of these crates and see if we can pry the top off one of them. It might be difficult without a lever of some sort."

Danny scrambled upwards onto the crates, reached down and helped Pat crawl up beside him. The torch showed wooden slats covering the top, with one-inch gaps in between. He could make out sacking covering whatever cargo was inside and hefted at one of the slats in frustration.

"We could sure use an iron bar right now" he murmured.

"Could we risk a bit of noise. That door where the guard is, must be between twenty or twenty five yards away?"

"Probably... what did you have in mind?" he asked.

"This" she said, standing up and driving her metal-heeled boot downwards into the wooden crate.

Two of the slats broke under her foot.

They both froze for a moment, watching the door and listening for the sound of locks snapping back.

Nothing.

Danny let his breath out and shone the torch downwards, then started bending back the two slats. Pat stood up and gave the crate another kick, smashing two more slats. He was furiously breaking off pieces of wood until finally he had two foot square cleared off.

Pat reached down and ripped off the sacking, which had been covering the cargo.

The smell reached him first, gun oil.

A moment later, Pat's voice rose a number of decibels.

"Weapons for God's sake! If the rest of these are the same there must be enough weapons here to outfit an army and start a war."

"He put his hand up to his lips. "Shhh, keep your voice down. You're right, this is mega. Probably lots of ammo in some of those other crates and who knows all sorts of different types of heavy weapons and explosives. This beggars belief!"

"So what do we do now, it's..."

She never finished the sentence as they heard noise and activity from the direction of the front door of the longhouse, where the guard had been posted.

The both dropped down flat on top of the crate and Danny turned off the mini torch and stuffed it into a pocket to make sure it didn't roll off and make a noise.

The lights in the building flashed on and Danny risked a quick glance from his prone position, barely moving his head.

He wasn't aware that he made a hissing noise between his teeth.

"What?" she whispered.

"Striking Hawk on his own. He's pushed the door closed again and the guard is back outside. Stay absolutely still" he cautioned.

Hearing footsteps coming closer, they pressed themselves down, as close as they could to the crates. Danny was glad he had moved the rope off to the side of the building.

The footsteps stopped just below them at the totem poles.

They waited a moment and Pat very carefully edged her face up a fraction. Almost immediately she poked Danny and gave him a nod to join her.

When he gazed down from the top of the crates, he saw Striking Hawk directly below them, his hands rubbing against one of the totem poles.

There was an audible click and a section of the pole swung outwards, revealing a cylindrical device lodged inside.

Pat barely suppressed a gasp. She leaned close to Danny's ear. "It's a transducer" she whispered.

He recalled their previous conversation back in Hanlon Falls.

Transducers could be used in centrifuges that enrich uranium into weapons-grade nuclear fuel.

There was more to Striking Hawk, he thought, than just being a militant Indian.

The man below moved to the second totem pole and with one quick movement of his hand, a section came open revealing a second cylindrical device.

In her eagerness to get a closer look, Pat tried to lean slightly forward. She didn't see the broken slat and instead of support for her hand, it crumbled underneath her and she pitched forward down onto the ground, with a resounding crash.

Striking Hawk swung around, at the same time drawing his knife.

"Infidel bitch" he hissed, moving towards her. "Now I kill you."

As she struggled to her knees, still stunned from the fall, she saw Danny's figure leap over the top of her directly into Striking Hawk's path.

The Indian was momentarily surprised and Danny took advantage of it to shout to Pat. "Get to the door."

She nodded, understanding immediately, and shaking her head to clear it, staggered off.

Striking Hawk's face broke into an evil joyous grin.

"Now I kill both of you infidels" he snarled, and hurled himself at Danny, his knife raised.

Danny blocked it and stepping aside he managed to slam the Indian into the stack of crates. His mind was trying to factor in the words that Striking Hawk had uttered, both to Pat and himself.

Infidels! Where the hell did that come from? he wondered.

Striking Hawk's knife hand had caught one of the crates and luckily for Danny, his knife clattered off.

It didn't seem to concern the Indian.

He strode confidentially forward, with the bowlegged stance of a trained fighter.

"Now we see who is best. I crush you with my bare hands" he grated, launching a series of high kicks and rapier-like punches, as he drove Danny backwards, towards the far side of the longhouse. Almost there, Danny stopped and started trading blow for blow, blocking and striking, blocking and striking, and moving sideways trying to avoid becoming a stationary target.

By the door, Pat's eyes were drawn to the battle that raged up and down the building.

Danny at one time cried out in pain, as he was caught with a short body kick.

Almost immediately, the heavy door started to swing open and she stepped back behind it. A large form leapt inside, halting for a moment, as he took in the scene in front of him.

Pat realized she only had a moment to act, knowing that a shout could sound the alarm and wake the camp.

She knew Danny was relying on her and was now out there fighting for his life.

For both of their lives.

She felt a power flow into her limbs and her mind. A power that was new and beyond her comprehension. She didn't hesitate.

She still had her knife and had extracted it when she went forward to guard the door.

Now leaping forward, she brought the knife stabbing down into the side of the Indians neck, almost as if all the knowledge of her ancestors had directed her attack.

He howled and swiveled sideways, his startled glazed eyes taking in her figure.

Then he opened his mouth as if to scream and she leapt forward, plunging the knife again directly into his heart. As she did so, a plume of blood spurted from his neck artery and splashed over her.

The Indian slumped to the ground - dead.

In a split second Pat caught the door and closed it, casting a quick glance outside as she did so.

No movement out there, as far as she could see.

Then she stood silently by the door her eyes closed. She felt the acclaim of her ancestors and knew that the blood that washed over her was recognition from them of her new warrior status.

She turned to see what was happening out on the floor.

Danny had just thrown his opponent down with a high hip throw, and he moved forward aggressively, but the man leapt to his feet instantly.

"You not get that one again" Striking Hawk mouthed, and leapt forward to the attack.

Danny was driven back again, aware that the wall of the longhouse was coming closer to his rear, and would provide the Indian with an opportunity to catch him with a serious kick or blow.

The Indian missed him with a high sweeping kick and Danny stepped in, slamming his head with a wicked elbow jab.

Striking Hawk staggered momentarily and now it was Danny's turn to leap forward and deliver some solid body blows and another elbow to his nose.

Striking Hawk screamed in pain for the first time, but the pain seemed to energize him as he fought back with two savage sidekicks to Danny's thigh, making him gasp.

"Now I get you!" he hissed triumphantly.

He caught Danny with a high kick to the head that was similar to the one that felled Bob, and like Bob, he dropped to his knees.

The Indian moved forward and lashed out with another kick to Danny's head.

He heard Pat's voice ring out. "Watch it Danny!"

Whether that penetrated his head or not, he would never know, but his crossed hands instinctively blocked the kick, and he heaved his opponent backwards, sending him thumping to the ground.

Danny staggered to his feet and re-focused, calling on all of his past combat experience, and closing on Striking Hawk, savagely drove sledging blows into his face and body.

"Atta boy Danny!" Pat's voice rang out as he renewed his attack, driving Striking Hawk backwards into the crates near the totem poles.

His last technique, a leg sweep, slammed the Indian down onto the ground and he moved forward to finish him off, but the Indian was delivered a lifeline. On his knees, his hand had encountered the knife he had dropped earlier.

Now he leapt to his feet and slammed the metal handle of the knife into Danny's forehead, dropping him like a stone.

As he lay there totally dazed, Striking Hawk leapt on top of him, grabbing his hair and raising his knife hand backwards in the air.

"Allah Akbar." The Indian screamed as his hand descended.

Danny knew he was seconds from dying.

Unaccountably, he felt a cascade of liquid fall on his face and felt the heavy body of Striking Hawk slump on top of him.

When he opened his eyes, he looked into the dead eyes of Striking Hawk and beyond into the face of Pat, who had sliced her knife across his throat.

She looked calmly back down at him.

"Good job you brought a fellow warrior with you tonight" she said.

With that she heaved the body of the Indian off him and helped him to his feet.

Without a word, they clung to each other for a long moment.

Finally Danny stirred.

"Thanks for that, and the guard too. You are some warrior Pat, and God am I ever proud of you Mate."

She grinned. "You were doing pretty good yourself out there... Mate." She was using the British word, he noticed.

"Now look, we have things to do. Someone might come along anytime, and the game's up. I still have to figure out why he shouted 'Allah Akbar' an Arabic Jihad mantra, when he's a flipping Indian."

She looked at him strangely. "Jesus Danny, this could be the key of the whole freaking thing, but I got an idea while you were fighting. I assumed that you were going to win out there."

He looked thoughtful.

"Little Dove predicted his death yesterday, and here he is lying dead. Makes you think, doesn't it? Okay, what's your idea?"

"We saw the second transducer arrive here yesterday and there are only two totem poles, so this must be the shipment that they intend sending out and probably soon."

"And your idea is?" he prompted.

"It would solve two problems actually. We have two bodies to get rid of and I don't want those transducers shipped out of here. Who knows where they might end up. Probably Iran. We just switch the transducers with the two bodies and hope the rest of the tribe here don't open up the totem poles prior to shipment."

"Hmm, I like it Pat. But where do you propose hiding the transducers?"

She pointed towards the back end of the longhouse where the crates were stacked.

"If we can manage to pull out a couple of crates near the ground, we can shove the cylinders back in their place."

"...And hope no one is sharp enough to notice it. A lot of assumptions Pat, but I can't think of anything better to do. As you say, it could solve two problems for us. Let's try it."

It took both of them to pull the cylindrical devices from the totem poles and drag them to the rear of the building.

While Danny was pulling out some crates, Pat managed to drag both bodies across to the totem poles and shove them inside. It was a tight squeeze and it took all her strength to get the panel shut, with a loud click.

Danny had more difficulty with his task. He had to remove a section of crates, stacked three high, before he could shove the transducers out of sight. Even then it meant leaving some crates on the floor, which he hoped wouldn't be noticed.

Finally they were finished.

"One more thing to do" he said breathlessly.

"Oh my God, what else?" she asked impatiently.

"That goddam rope, it's a dead giveaway" he said pointing.

"Seriously Danny, you're in no shape to climb up that rope, and neither am I."

He nodded. "I know.... look, we slip out the front door, getting rid of Striking Hawks' knife and any signs of the guard you killed, weapons, blood, etc. We close and lock the door, leaving the key in it and then slip around the side of this longhouse to where I climbed up originally. I'll climb back up again. I think I can do it without any problem. Once at the top of the longhouse, I can pull the rope up and Bob's your uncle."

"Bob's you're uncle! You Brits do talk funny. Okay let's do it. Oh, do you want us to take some weapons with us from those crates?"

He shook his head. "Take too long to locate the ammo, and if they search our quarters and find weapons, it'll tie us into this building. No, let's go."

They were on tenterhooks for the next half hour, expecting to bump into someone. But it all went like clockwork. Going back through the bush, Pat and he even managed to stop at a small creek and wash the blood off both of them.

When they finally made it back to their sleeping quarters, it was Bob who sat up.

"You two look like you were having fun" he muttered drowsily.

Pat glanced across at Danny. "If he only knew!" she whispered, grasping both his hands in hers.

"I found myself tonight, Danny. I really know who I am now. Thank you"

She kissed him on the cheek and turned, heading back into the building.

He stood there for a long time as he felt the adrenalin draining away.

There were things he had to think about.

He was glad he'd killed Striking Hawk, because now Little Dove would live.

# Chapter 38

The following morning they were eating breakfast in the longhouse. They were all there except for Little Dove and C.C. Bob, still in a lot of pain, was on his feet and had gone over to the door to peer outside.

Now he called out. "Hey, have a look at what's going on over by the big longhouse."

As a group they straggled outside, some still eating their breakfast.

Pat and Danny had moved slightly off to one side and now she caught his arm.

"Would you look at that Danny!" she exclaimed.

Across at the longhouse, a large truck was backed up to the doors and already one of the totem poles was stacked up on the right-hand side, and anchored down with large cables. As they watched, a group of twelve male tribesmen came staggering out of the building, with the second totem pole, and wrestled it up onto the left-hand side of the vehicle. Half of the crew then started securing it with cables and ropes.

The remaining six Indians had noticed Danny's group and started moving towards them. Black Cloud, who had just emerged from the longhouse, followed them.

As they came closer, Pat gasped, seeing what she thought was Striking Hawk striding towards them, with an angry look to his face.

Danny leaned slightly down towards her.

"Take it easy Pat. It's Striking Hawk's twin brother. Probably missing him. Play it cool."

The Indian they had been talking about came storming up to Danny and shoved him backwards.

"Where my brother? You kill him, I know! Where he?" he snarled, shoving him further backwards.

Danny didn't want to start another battle and moved backwards, keeping his balance.

He raised his arms in apparent bafflement.

"What the hell are you talking about? Striking Hawk's missing and you are blaming me for it? What is this all about?"

The twin pushed him again and started spluttering "you kill... I know... I kill..."

Just then Black Cloud moved up and pulled the Indian backwards.

"This is not the way. The soldier Quigley probably has no idea what you are talking about. Remember Little Dove predicted his death yesterday. He may be off in the forest killed by a large animal or by his own hand. We may never know. We should be asking Little Dove."

The twin shook his head stubbornly. "No, I know my brother dead. This man kill him" he stormed.

Black Cloud sighed audibly. "Right." He turned to the remaining five Indians around him. "Go over and search their sleeping quarters and see if there are any signs of Striking Hawk being there. Look for signs of a struggle or weapons, and remember, we have a guard missing too. Two bodies will be hard to hide.... and bring Little Dove to my longhouse immediately with the man Courtney. Now go!" he instructed.

Pat touched Danny's arm slightly as the group dashed off, and nodded at the truck, which had started up and was slowly making its way out of the camp.

The search party could look all they wanted now.

Striking Hawk and the guard were already started on a long journey.

'Hopefully to Iran!' Pat prayed.

Black Cloud looked at the group. "All of you come now to my longhouse. We see what Little Dove say."

Tribal police were dispatched to fetch both C.C. and Little Dove, and the rest were escorted across to the Chief's longhouse. They went inside.

Danny was aware of the smoldering looks being directed at him by Striking Hawk's burly brother.

As he was sitting well back from him he leaned forward and whispered in Pat's ear.

"What's with him?" he asked. "He can't know anything about last night."

She glanced quickly at the Indian and whispered back.

"Twins sometimes have a connection that's hard to explain. Perhaps he senses that you were involved somehow. Who knows? He can't take his eyes off you right now."

Little Dove and C.C. ducked into the tent. Spotting the Chief, sitting up front in his usual place, Little Dove went forward and sat beside him.

The Chief nodded to the tribal police.

They turned and went outside, closing the door as they went.

Black Cloud flicked his yellow eyes around the group and cleared his throat.

"Yesterday Striking Hawk strode the earth like a hungry bear. He was strong and had defeated many enemies in battle. Only yesterday he smashed the soldier you called Bob, into the ground and would have killed him if he had not been halted by Courtney and myself. As a result Little Dove predicted that he would die before the sun crossed the sky again today. This morning Striking Hawk has vanished, and strangely, a guard from the big longhouse also.

Two men are missing. The brother of Striking Hawk feels that somehow the soldier Quigley is responsible. Our tribal police have searched their quarters and found nothing. No sign of a struggle, or weapons of any kind.

I now ask you Little Dove, to tell me what the spirits tell you about this. Is Striking Hawk dead, and how did he die? By someone's hand here or has a demon entered the camp and taken him away?"

Little Dove looked around the longhouse, taking in each face, and continued on until her gaze came back to the Chief.

"Chief Black Cloud, it grieves me to have to say, with his brother present, that Striking Hawk is dead."

There was a loud murmur of disbelief from the Indians present.

Little Dove went on: "As we speak, his body is being taken away from here by an enormous spirit, bringing him to his ancestors. He died as he lived, fighting his demon, but alas, when they come, no one can defy them. As to the visitors here present: No one could defeat Striking Hawk in battle and overcome him. Neither the man Quigley, nor anyone here present is responsible for his death. I only ask that we declare a time of grieving for Striking Hawk and suspend your military training for three days to honor him. The spirits have spoken."

Black Cloud looked around at his elders. "The spirits have spoken. Does anyone have any information to add or wish to speak?"

Striking Hawk's brother rushed forward and stopped in front of Danny pointing at him.

"Not believe Little Dove. No spirits take my brother. Him kills him. I feel it here."

He thumped his chest as he finished.

Black Cloud's face flushed with anger. "To doubt the spirits is to invite bad things to come on your house...and on the tribe. I say now, stop these words and accept that your brother is dead.

As Little Dove suggests, we will honor him for three days and then training starts again. The women of the tribe will organize this thing. I will speak later with Quigley to tell him of my plans for his training of our warriors. Now go!"

Danny's group filed out and moved off.

He caught up with C.C. outside.

"I want to talk to you about something C.C. Just myself and Pat for the moment. Is that okay?"

Courtney directed a searching gaze at him and nodded.

"Hmm…why did I feel back there that you knew something about Striking Hawk's disappearance. Anyway, you can tell me inside. That big twin brother of Striking Hawk is still standing back there and glaring after you."

Nothing more was said until they got back to C.C.'s quarters, where he had a brief few words with the group, then escorted Danny and Pat inside.

When they sat down, C.C. in his improvised chair, Danny and Pat ran quickly over the events of the past night.

C.C. never commented, occasionally his eyes widened, as he looked from one to the other. Finally, they had finished and Courtney let out a long breath.

"Oh my God, this is beyond belief! Transducers being smuggled out in enlarged totem poles, to God know where! Pat thinks to Iran. Weapons stockpiled in the longhouse and probably ammunition and explosives as well.

This is serious stuff! And what's in the other longhouse? More of the same, or something equally dangerous? I don't know what to say. I had no idea what was in those longhouses. Black Cloud instructed me to stay inside on certain days, when presumably, they were trucking the stuff in, and storing it inside the longhouses."

Danny caught his arm to stop him.

"A question C.C. Just how well do you know these tribes?" he asked.

"Know them? What do you mean?"

"Here's the thing, would you know the facial characteristics of different tribes. I understand there are over twenty tribes or more up along the B.C. coast, for example."

Courtney shrugged. "Like you Danny I'm a dumb Brit when it comes to First Nations. I wouldn't know one from the other. Where is this leading?"

"Here's where it's leading C.C. In the longhouse last night, Striking Hawk called Pat and me infidels, and as he was about to kill me, he screamed 'Allah Akbar'! Not exactly an Indian battle cry, is it?"

Courtney's jaw dropped as he looked from one to the other.

"Oh Christopher, some of these people are genuine Indians, but you're suggesting that..."

"They're Arabs...probably Pakistanis. I've had some bells going off in my skull over the last couple of days. There must be some tribes up the coast who have a resemblance to the thin Arab faces I've encountered in Iraq and Afghanistan."

Courtney gasped. "Now that you mention it, I too wondered at their use of English. Their accents. Hell, I should have known. I was on enough Virgin rail trips in the U.K. to have heard the train announcers, mostly Pakistanis, announce the next station coming up. Whew! This is mind boggling!"

Pat jumped in. "There's something else. As First Nations, they can cross the border with just a tribal identity card, so they could filter a whole army of people across into the U.S.A. at different crossover points."

Danny shook his head. "Yeah, but how would they get the weapons and other stuff across. They have all sorts of radiation and explosive detector units installed on those border bridges Pat."

She shook her head. "Danny, it's an eight thousand mile border we're talking about. You can bet your boots that the genuine Indians out there will know where to smuggle all that stuff across."

C.C. and Danny stared at her, their faces shocked.

"Oh Christ!" Danny finally whispered, "this could be worse that 9/11. Is there any way we can warn the proper border authorities? Have you still got that cell phone that you summoned us here with?"

C.C. shook his head. "Black Cloud confiscated it as soon as he forced me to send you an e-mail."

Danny looked from one to the other.

"Okay, here's what I propose as an interim plan. C.C. try to find out if Little Dove knows where the good Indians are being held prisoner, and if she does, see if she'll take you there.

If she will, don't let yourselves be discovered, but bring back as much information and detail as you can, without exposing yourselves."

"What sort of information Danny"? C.C. asked.

"For starters, it's location and distance from here. Rough directions if you can. Where are they being held prisoner - a building or a compound with possibly barbed wire around it? A sketch would be terrific. How many guards and where are they posted? Any visitors or trucks coming in? Things like that."

C.C. nodded. "Otherwise tell her nothing about last night?" he enquired.

"The less she knows the better, for her sake. Though she may already have a good idea with those spiritual skills she has."

"And what will you two be doing?" Courtney asked.

"I'll be visiting Black Cloud to discuss training, and I want him to get used to Pat moving around with me...doing the organization for the unarmed combat and so on, so if he sees us drifting off together, he won't be too curious. As to what else I'm planning, that's enough for now."

C.C. smiled for the first time. "I know very well how you work Danny and I'm glad to see that you're up for this. Somehow I don't feel as concerned as I did when you came in here a few moments ago. God bless you both."

With that they broke up and Pat and Danny headed off towards the food hall.

Striking Hawk's brother was nowhere in sight.

# Chapter 39

C.C. and Little Dove were frequently seen together and created little interest when they walked off together into the forest. Indeed as they went along a well-worn path, they passed, and were greeted casually, by a number of the tribes' people, some who stopped to talk to Little Dove or ask advice about various topics.

Gradually, as they went beyond the normal boundaries of the camp, the tribes' people they were encountering reduced down until finally they appeared to be alone.

Two miles outside of the camp area she stopped.

"If we followed this road we would come to the area I'm looking for, which is some miles from here. However, as you can see, this is a well worn route, used by supply trucks, so we would raise suspicion if we were seen this far out."

"Wouldn't we hear them coming in time to get off the road?" C.C. asked.

"Yes, but some of the people on the truck walk ahead in the hope of catching a deer or some other game for the cooking pot" she replied.

With that she moved at a tangent down a slope and started following a parallel route that occasionally meandered off, as they made their way around nests of thick shrubs and large rocks.

After an hour C.C. stopped and put his pack down. "Hey, can we stop to get our breath for a few moments?"

She laughed happily. "You're showing your age Clive," she teased as she rested on a mossy mound.

He looked closely at her. "Am I imagining things or are you somehow different this morning? What is it Little Dove?"

Her eyes sparkled and she reached out and touched his arm. "Oh, Clive, you can see it?"

She plucked a wild flower and smelled it's delicate aroma.

He leaned forward. "Don't keep me in suspense my Little White Dove. Come on, we share everything" he urged.

"The spirits instructed me to take Danny to a special place that I go to for renewal. While he is already a fearsome fighter, I was to initiate him in the warriors' rite for the fierce battle ahead, but something even more powerful intervened and he had an incredible anointing. Oh C.C., don't you see? The spirits have brought me to a new place and confirmed me in my role as a healer!"

He nodded, not fully understanding. "I can't see...." he started

She caught both his arms in and looked directly at him.

"Do you know that he saw you and the woman Siobhan, locked in a loving embrace in your tent yesterday?"

He looked shocked. "Oh my God!" he breathed. "I had no idea. It…it just happened. We were trying to figure when to broach it to Danny" he finished lamely.

He thought for a moment and then went on. "How did he take it?"

"What can I say? He was standing outside your tent, white as a ghost and looking stunned."

C.C. stood up and started wandering backwards and forwards, looking distressed.

"We came through so much together. Now, I betrayed him in the worst possible way! I need to go back and talk to him Little Dove."

She caught him gently. "Danny is with Black Cloud right now. He has a lot to figure out and the last thing he needs is you trying to explain the unexplainable. You can help him most by carrying out the task he gave us to do, which is to get information on the prisoners further back in the forest. Wouldn't you agree?"

He was silent as he thought about it, then he nodded.

"I could always rely on you Little Dove for wisdom, when I needed it. The spirits, from what you've just told me, still speak to you, and of course you are right. Let's keep moving."

Some forty minutes later, Little Dove raised her finger to her lips and led him through some thick shrubs to a small hillock.

She gestured to him to follow her and crawled under some low hanging branches for about five yards. Then she stopped and pointed through the thick screen of low grass and branches, so he went forward and carefully pushed his head through.

Ahead of him was a cleared expanse of ground.

What he saw in the middle of the area caused him to draw his breath in.

A stockade had been erected, surrounded by a high fence with a barbwire mesh encircling, what he took to be a prison. In the center of the stockade he sighted some squat buildings, with a small number of Indians milling around. Off to the side he could see a small parking lot with two pick-up vehicles in it.

He couldn't see the entrance to the stockade from where he was kneeling and, conscious of Danny's request for all information possible, he decided to move off to his left in order to get a better view.

He whispered his intentions to his companion and apart from a worried look she made no comment. She was already sketching an outline of the stockade on a sheet of paper. He stood up and remaining half-bent over, started out along the edge of the cleared area, still keeping well back in the trees.

C.C. was no woodsman, but he knew that discovery could mean curtains for the group, so he took his time, moving branches slowly out of his way and carefully placing his feet where he wouldn't catch any loose stones.

After about 30 yards, he started hearing voices shouting ahead and dropped to his knees again. The voices were not coming towards him, so he started moving forward again.

Finally, he parted some tall grass and ferns and peered through.

What he saw below had not been in view where they had first stopped.

A group of approximately 20 Indians, clearing brush and trees away from the edge of the clearing. He knew immediately that they were the prisoners, because they were working silently and were surrounded by four heavily armed Indians, who continually shouted at them, carrying on a running dialogue with each other.

'My God!' he thought, 'the chain gangs of the Deep South that he had heard about.'

The guards were totally relaxed and obviously not expecting any trouble from the listless prisoners, all who exhibited the appearance of people who were being starved of proper food.

Despite the risk, C.C. decided to slip further down the slight gradient, which appeared well shaded with cover. It took 20 minutes, but then he had slipped quietly up to the very edge of the clearing and peered round the base of a large tree.

He didn't learn any more from this angle but just as he pulled his head back, he caught a flick of one of the prisoner's head, turning in his direction.

He cursed. "Shit, I've blown it now!" he berated himself.

He heard some shouted words and his heart sank.

Peering round the side of the tree he saw the prisoner who had spotted him making his way across to him. The man was holding his gut and was bent over as if sick.

Suddenly C.C. understood.

The Indian had asked for permission to use the toilet at the edge of the trees, claiming sickness, probably staying in plain sight of the guards.

C.C. froze, hoping the guards would not move closer.

In a moment the Indian had come up to the tree that he was crouching behind, dropped his rough trousers and squatted.

His face was turned away from the guards.

C.C. heard his whisper. "Who are you?"

He made a quick check on the guards. None of them appeared to be coming any closer or were concerned. This probably was a regular occurrence and the poorly fed prisoners, would have no strength to attempt an escape.

He decided it was safe to answer.

"C.C. from the camp" he whispered back.

"Can you help us?" the Indian asked.

"Not now, but in two or three days time. How can we break in?" he asked.

The Indian crouched lower as if concentrating on his sick stomach. C.C. couldn't see, but one of the guards had glanced over with some curiosity.

Finally, the prisoner raised his head slightly.

"At the back of the stockade. We have a section of the wire cut, but are too weak to break out and would be caught very quickly. We'll leave a shoe lace tied there to mark it."

"Okay, be ready, we won't let you down" he whispered back.

He went to move off but the man raised his voice urgently. "Wait, I spotted you, the guards may too. Wait until I get back out there and collapse. Then go. May the spirits guide you back."

With that the Indian pulled his trousers up and shambled back across to the group of prisoners he was working with. Suddenly he gave an agonizing cry and fell to the ground, writhing about and holding his stomach. C.C. could see with a quick glimpse, that all the guards were now concentrating on the prisoner.

He turned and swiftly and made his way back up the gradient and on along the route that took him back to where Little Dove was anxiously waiting.

When she spotted him, relief flashed across her face.

"Thank goodness C.C. I thought you might be discovered."

He chuckled, despite the situation. "I thought you knew everything Little Dove," he teased.

She made a displeased face at him, and then grabbed his arm.

"Let's go C.C. I feel that we've been here long enough. We need to get going and we need to be careful on the way back. We could still be in danger."

Cautiously, they started in the direction of camp.

# Chapter 40

Danny and Pat emerged from the longhouse of Chief Black Cloud, looking somewhat bemused.

"What was that all about?" Pat asked. "I was expecting a whole bunch of do's and don'ts. You know, able to carry out offensive and defensive tactics in specific situations, and stuff like that."

Danny shook his head. "Yeah, instead, I'm basically instructed to take twenty of his warriors and teach them to be body-guards. I'm just wondering…"

"What?" she asked.

"When I was carrying out body-guarding duties in the 'Saas', we were generally escorting VIP's in and out of buildings. I'm talking here, about politicians and visiting dignitaries, who might have been targeted in exposed areas like Iraq, Afghanistan, the Sudan and so forth."

"So your thinking is?"

"Their role may be to escort the ones with explosives, into specific target buildings. If they can manage to steal police or army uniforms prior to the operation, it cuts down the reaction time of the security staff, and perimeter guards."

Pat stopped in mid-stride. "They have over two hundred trained warriors here in camp. That's a formidable force by any measure. If we can't get the word out by cell phone, can we sabotage their material in that longhouse? Blow it up, I mean?"

"Hmm...we'll have to try and sneak into that second building tonight and see what's in there. Probably more of the same, but we might spot something that could serve our purpose."

They had just come around the side of the building when Pat caught his arm.

"Uh, Uh" she muttered. "I think we got trouble Danny."

Almost as if they had been waiting for them, Striking Hawk's twin, eased into sight.

On his own Danny wouldn't have worried but he was surrounded by three other mean looking warriors who strode forward with aggression oozing from their bodies.

There was no mistaking their purpose.

It appeared that there would be no dialogue either.

"Keep back and give me space" Danny grated, pushing her off to one side.

"Now look Danny...." she started.

Danny didn't believe in the Marcus of Queensbury rules, when out-numbered and facing opponents who meant to seriously hurt you.

As the group came up almost on top of him, the twin was slightly behind one of his men, who was on Danny's left.

One of Danny's advantages was his incredibly fast reaction time, almost like a computer that could read an opponent's move even before they had thought it out themselves.

Without taking his eyes off his primary target, Danny stamped down with his left boot on the knee-joint of the Indian on his left, smashing it and sending him screaming to the ground. The man behind him stumbled across the legs of the fallen soldier and Danny, seeing the opportunity, slammed a solid elbow into his jaw, felling him like a stone.

Two down.

He still didn't ease up, but spun sideways and parried a sweeping blow from a club wielded by the twin, who had put all his strength into it.

Danny didn't block it directly with his arms or elbow, as the power of the blow would have shattered his limb. Instead, he stepped sideways getting under the sweeping club and used the momentum of it to spin it, stabbing it backwards into the stomach of the fourth Indian, sending him to his knees, gasping. The club flew off to the side, dropping almost at Pat's feet.

Danny couldn't stop.

The twin was still dangerous.

He didn't think that he was of the caliber of Striking Hawk, but he wasn't taking any chances.

There was no doubt in the twin's mind, as to who was the superior fighter.

Without hesitation he hurled himself at Danny, catching him with a surprise back kick to the rib cage and following it up with a series of straight punches, delivered with savage intent and power.

"Watch it Danny!" Pat shouted.

In backing up from the twin's onslaught, he hadn't noticed that he had backed into the first Indian he had felled, who grabbed him round the legs.

At the same time the twin delivered a massive blow to the side of his head sending him flying across and away from the Indian on the ground.

As he clambered to his knees, he was only dimly aware that Pat had grabbed the fallen club and smashed it down on the head of the Indian with the damaged knee, who was now trying to hobble to his feet.

He fell back, unconscious.

The twin backhanded Pat sending her flying, as he leapt across the prostrate form on the ground trying to reach Danny before he could get back onto his feet.

He jumped back, just in time to block the brutal attack by the twin, who drove him forward with a series of kicks and blows, some of which connected.

Danny breathed in deeply and felt himself settle down under the attack.

He'd been there before.

He felt the strength surge back into his limbs.

He'd taken the best that the Indian had in him.

It wasn't enough.

Time to finish it.

As the twin sent another blow towards his face, Danny fielded it, and then turning, let the elbow slide across his shoulder before levering it down, snapping it.

The Indian screamed, and dropped to his knees, clutching his broken arm.

Danny turned to walk away from him and stopped in his tracks as he heard the sounds of clapping.

He looked across and saw Black Cloud standing there, a big grin on his face.

"That's what I want you to teach my warriors, Quigley."

His expression changed as he observed the beaten warriors.

"You have left me four short now, so you'd better train them well. They have disobeyed me during this time of grieving, so they must pay a price."

He waved his hand and a dozen tribal police hustled and carried off the injured and beaten warriors.

Without another word the Chief turned and walked away.

Pat breathed a sigh of relief. "Shoot, I thought for starters you were in for it with those four." She suddenly looked angry. "Why did you tell me to stand back out of the way?"

He shrugged. "Just the way I fight. I need space to move. Also the last thing I needed was for them to grab you and threaten you with a knife, unless I stopped and let them beat me... probably to death, from the looks of the twin's attitude. Well done with the club by the way. Just goes to show you. As I've said repeatedly, you never know with a fight...anything can happen, and quite often does. Are you okay, by the way? He gave you quite a belt."

She was about to reply when she caught a flicker of movement behind them.

It was C.C. and Little Dove.

They nodded urgently to Danny and Pat and headed off in the direction of his tent.

They obviously had some important news to tell them.

It didn't take them long to recount the details of their exploration back into the forest. C.C went over his conversation with the prisoner, and they talked around it. Little Dove had drawn some sketches of the stockade and it's surroundings, plus an outline of how to get there.

Finally Danny sat back. "So in effect, even if we free the prisoners, they wouldn't be able to make the journey back here to help us?" he asked.

C.C. nodded. "Spot on, but you may be missing something here. I would say that they would fight like hell if we could get them back here to the camp. That Indian I talked to looked highly pissed off, and I would say, far from beaten."

Little Dove leaned forward. "C.C.'s right. If we could get one of the trucks that they use to bring in supplies, and just take those people out that are strong enough to fight, we might have an edge. We saw two trucks there when..."

Pat cut in. "Listen to you for crying out loud! There's two hundred trained warriors here in camp, and you're talking about some weak, sick Indians taking them on! Come on, get real!"

C.C. caught her arm. "Look, give Danny a moment to think this through. He has a trained military mind and I've seen, probably more than most of you, what he's capable of. Why don't one of you get some tea on and leave him alone for a few minutes."

They all sprung into action, leaving Danny to scrutinize the sketches of the stockade and to think through how they might, as a group, extricate themselves from their present dilemma.

It was in fact twenty minutes later, after someone dashed off to get some wild honey for the tea, that they all sat back.

All eyes were on Danny.

"Okay, first off, I'm conscious that Jeff, Bob and Siobhan are missing from this meeting, and their lives are equally in jeopardy here. So the question is, can we make decisions that could seriously impact their lives, without them being present? Do we have that right, is all I'm asking?" He looked around the small group.

There was a moment's silence.

C.C. cleared his throat. "With respect Danny, you're the remaining military tactician we have now that Bob is injured. Siobhan is a nurse, and a competent one at that. Jeff could certainly be useful in this with his hunter guide hat on, especially, if we have to make a break for it. Let's tease this through and get your thoughts on it first."

Danny looked around and could see that the rest were in agreement.

"Okay, first of all, there are no soft options here. There's a large trained and armed Force in this camp who have a plan, it appears, to deliver another 9/11-style attack into the U.S. If you were taking odds, what would you say our chances are, the few of us, unarmed and without any way of summoning help, to reverse this set of circumstances?"

He looked around, his expression grim.

"Pretty slim I guess" Pat muttered.

Little Dove smiled, saying nothing.

C.C. chuckled. "Yes, but they haven't got Danny Quigley on their side. Come on; let's get to it. You've never been beaten yet!"

A faint smile crept across Danny's face. "C.C. you have more confidence in me than I have in myself" he started, but Little Dove interrupted.

"No Danny he's right." She looked off to one side. "I see you as the avenging angel in this situation. The Gods are smiling on you."

"Fair enough Little Dove, but now that you've spoken, I'll throw a particularly difficult task at you. Impossible perhaps. What chance would you have to find the cell phone that Black Cloud took from C.C.?"

She looked stricken. "Oh Danny, if only I could! When C.C. sent you the message, Black Cloud confiscated his cell phone. We even discussed the chance that I could somehow get my hands on it. I decided it was impossible. If it exists at all now, it would be in Black Cloud's private tent which only his two squaws are allowed into."

He held his hand up.

"Okay, enough said. However if the balloon goes up around here and we can get our hands on some weapons, the diversion might allow you or some of us to go in there and look for it. That way we could summon some help, probably too late to help us, but we might get a warning out to the U.S. border people. Enough on that for the moment. Now, my thoughts are this. Tonight Pat and I will try to get into the second longhouse to see what's there. It may fill in some blanks for us and possibly give us some tools to fight back with."

C.C.'s face reflected his deep concern. "Such as what for example? And if you're caught in there, what then? The rest of us wouldn't have a hope in hell of surviving this."

"Fair comment. As I see it, the first longhouse has weapons and we suspect, lots of ammunition. The second one may have vehicles, ground to air missiles, explosives and God knows what else. It could be a key to their whole strategy. If I can get my hands on some explosives, I could possibly blow up the ammo in longhouse number one, and a grenade launcher could help me blow up some trucks that they might load up with material, before they head south. Oh, I know it all sounds gobbledygook, but sometimes these things come together, especially when an enemy is reacting to stuff coming at them.

They may be thoroughly familiar with the tasks they have to carry out south of here, but how would they react to a totally unexpected attack right here in the camp? I'm not planning on moving on this tonight, just scouting the place. However, we have three days of virtual inactivity in the camp during the grieving for Striking Hawk."

C.C. pursed his lips. "And the rest of my question?"

Danny looked from face to face. "Little Dove may get through this, but barring a miracle, the rest of us are toast, I'm sorry to say."

Pat's face grew taut. "Before they take me Danny, I'll take a number with me."

He grinned. "Atta girl Pat. I know what a warrior like you can do. Now the rest of my thoughts."

Little Dove looked stricken. "Those of my people in the prison camp, suffering and probably dying. We can't leave them there Danny" she pleaded.

"Nor, do we intend to" he replied. "What I envisage, is that the next time the supply trucks head out of camp for the stockade, Little Dove and I, or C.C. if he knows the way, will cut through the forest to the camp. The trucks will obviously get there ahead of us. The timing of this is vital. If the trucks pull out in the late afternoon, then we could be in place, as it gets dark. That gap in the back of the fence should be easy enough to find and I'll slip into the camp."

Pat looked uneasy. "But what will you do when you do get inside? What if the guards are actually patrolling the outside fence?"

Danny looked at C.C. "How long has this camp been taken over?" he enquired.

C.C. considered. "Oh, just about two years." He looked at Little Dove for confirmation.

She nodded. "Yes... about that."

Danny nodded. "So the guards out there have been doing this for two years without any problems. They've got sloppy, which is borne out by the fact that the prisoners have a hole cut in the wire and they never spotted it. They'll be nice and cozy inside, I'll bet you."

"I'd say you're spot on with that Danny. What about my question, when you get inside? Remember you don't have any weapons?" Pat queried.

"You're right, I don't, and I couldn't use them if I did" he answered.

C.C. filled in the missing details for her.

"God help those guards in there" he whispered. "They don't know who is coming after them. Don't worry about weapons Pat, Danny will have all the guards' weapons within five minutes of going in there. That's why he can't discharge any firearm and warn the guards, when he gets into the stockade."

Little Dove shuddered. "I don't like killing....but these are evil men and we now find, they have come from a far country. They're not even brothers."

"Okay, I get it. So, what do you plan to do after you liberate the camp?" Pat prompted.

"I'll select the strongest of the warriors and take as many as I can, depending on how many trucks are there. I will have the guards' weapons, of which I'll keep one and divvy out the rest to those who feel strong enough, and who have some training in whatever weapons there are. Then we head back to camp."

"And do what exactly?" she asked, concern creeping into her voice.

Danny shrugged.

"I haven't got that far yet. Possible scenarios could be that I manage to smuggle some arms out of longhouse number one, over the next two nights and store them outside the camp. If I could rig up some explosives while in there, some of you could set them off, from outside the building, to coincide with the prisoners coming back. That could provide cover for Little Dove, to try and find the cell phone, if Black Cloud hasn't already disposed of it. It's a very fluid plan at present, but what I like about it is that we're being proactive, and the enemy will have to react to our initiative."

Pat still looked unhappy. "So Danny, tell me, have you a doomsday scenario, if all else fails?"

He avoided their eyes. "You asked the question. Yes, I could cut the head off the snake and hope this would disrupt their plans somewhat, Doomsday plan? Go through the camp, kill Black Cloud and as many of the leading members of his army as I can locate. Look, these warriors are highly trained and react instinctively to being attacked, so my success might be very limited. It would give you guys time, with Jeff as a guide, to make a run for it in the confusion."

Nothing more was said. Danny rose and left the tent.

One by one they followed him, in silence.

# Chapter 41

They waited until it was dark.

The longhouses had two guards standing at the front entrances.

No sign of additional security since the disappearance of Striking Hawk and the guard.

Neither Danny nor Pat spoke a word as they traversed the distance around the perimeter and reached the rear of the buildings. There was no sign of any guards posted at the back. Still, they waited for a short while to make sure there was no roving patrol going round the building.

Danny touched her arm briefly and they both crept forward, staying low until they reached the side of their target building. Again they paused and listened.

Nothing... not a sound.

They were following the same plan that had got them inside the first building, so Danny crawled up the side without any difficulty.

In a moment he was joined by Pat, and they both peered down into the second longhouse.

It was as black as the ace of spades down below.

He leaned across close to her ear. "Don't like dropping into something I can't see" he whispered.

He felt her breath on his ear. "Could you use that bigger flashlight you brought with you? Just a brief flash. Highly unlikely there are guards below, sitting in the darkness" she whispered back.

He nodded, forgetting that she couldn't see him in the darkness, and carefully removed the light from a small backpack he had with him. Not wanting any of the light to be seen from the top of the building, he leaned well forward into the opening and clicked it on.

Just for a moment.

In that moment they both saw that large amounts of material were stacked about ten yards directly below them, in what appeared to be cardboard boxes. Beyond that were individual blocks of material, scattered around the floor of the building.

No sign of life inside.

They wasted no time in sliding down the rope. Once down, they paused momentarily to make sure they hadn't disturbed the guards at the front.

This time Danny used his pencil torch.

Pat withdrew a sharp knife that she brought with her and started sawing through the top of the stiff cardboard box.

Danny waited impatiently, not knowing how long they had to investigate, or if the guards made checks inside during their sentry duties.

Pat tore off a large piece of cardboard, exposing a cavity in the box that she was working on. She reached in and felt around, finally settling on something firm, and hauled it up, laying it on the top. In the dim light, it looked like a life jacket.

"Jeez, what the hell is it Danny?" she whispered, handing it to him.

He felt his heart freeze at the thought that crept into his mind, as he hefted the item and turned it over.

'Oh shit!' he thought.

He was silent for a moment.

"Well?" she prompted. "You know something."

"You're not going to like this as an Intelligence Operative. It's a suicide vest, for crying out loud."

Her voice went up a number of octaves. "What?" she demanded.

"Shhhhh... Keep your voice down. There's no doubt, I've seen these in Iraq and Afghanistan. It's a pretty high-tech vest for a suicide bomber" he reiterated.

"Oh my God!" she breathed, "All this pile in these boxes are suicide vests? There must be hundreds of them!"

"Yeah, and there's hundreds of so called warriors outside, who plan to head south wearing them" he added.

"Sweet Jesus!" she whispered. "This could be worse that the Twin Towers, and at numerous locations. What in God's name can we do Danny?"

He hauled out his knife and slit a hole in the vest, seeing black powder spilling out.

"We can slice up a number of them and expose the powder in this box and maybe, just maybe, I can rig something up later to blow it up and the surrounding boxes in this pile."

She caught his arm. "While you're doing that I'm going to slip down and see what's in the other stacks of material down there."

"Okay, but watch your step, don't knock anything over, and be watchful for guards opening the door for a check. Careful with that torch, they might spot the glare through the wooden doors" he warned.

While she slithered down the rope to the floor, he opened a second box and, as he suspected, it was also full of suicide vests. He tore open a number of them and seeded the rest of the box with the powder.

He hadn't told Pat that if he couldn't find some fuses and timers, he might have to drop a lighted torch down from the opening above, but that would blow him up as well.

He was hoping she was successful in finding some useful material.

Pat was conscious as she cautiously scurried around, that she must not leave any evidence of their break-in, so she went to the rear of the next stack, which was just three feet from the back wall. Her eyes, by that time, had adjusted to the darkness, and she only needed to use the pencil torch to examine things more closely.

Again there was a small stack of cardboard boxes and she attacked one with gusto, all the time keeping her ear attuned and her eye towards the door.

In a moment she had loosened a chunk of cardboard and pulled out what appeared to be an item of clothing. She switched the pencil torch on and gasped.

A police uniform! So that was part of their evil plan. She probed again and extracted an army uniform.

She wanted to dash back to Danny and tell him but she had to see what the other boxes contained. Just as  he crept up beside her making her jump.

"What did you find?" he asked.

"Police and army uniforms."

"Ah… that tells us quite a lot. Shove them back in and let's keep moving."

She did so, trying to stick the piece of cardboard back up again, then moving after Danny to the next stack.

This time there were small wooden crates, and he had to carefully use the metal bar he had brought in his pack

The crates were crammed with hand grenades.

They hurried on. The next crate contained grenade launchers, and the following one he identified as shoulder to air missiles.

"If they get close to an airport, just imagine what damage they could do" he whispered.

Oh, my God Danny, this is mega! We've got to stop them somehow" she urged.

"You got it in spades" he replied.

The following crate stopped both of them in their tracks.

"IED's for Pete's sake. Imagine what these would do on those U.S. highways or big city turnpikes."

He took a closer look. "I'm not a hundred percent sure, but we were briefed in Bagdad on what the Iranians were bringing in, and this looks like their stuff. It's the best, I'm afraid."

Danny found what he was looking for in the next crate.

Blocks of semtex, in separate boxes containing all the necessary fuses and timers to rig explosives.

Feeling that they had pushed their luck to the limit, he grabbed some blocks of semtex, timers, fuses and wiring, stuck them in his back-pack and clambered back up to the crate which contained the suicide vests.

With Pat holding the pencil torch, he laid the blocks of semtex across the top of the boxes, and busied himself for the next several minutes.

Finally he held up what looked like a TV monitor.

"I've hooked up the semtex with the fuses, a timer and this small device. Everything is linked into this little beauty. Once the button's pressed, this stuff will blow up in five minutes I don't know just how much of this material it would take with it, but it would be one hell of a bang."

"Could I set it off Danny?"

He glanced at her. "Sure, no problem. You just press this little button here and make sure you are nowhere close when she blows."

"Right on! Why don't we hide it outside somewhere nearby, in case we run into any guards going back. I could set it off, if you're otherwise engaged. Now let's get the hell out of here. We've been lucky so far."

Their luck held. With a superhuman effort, Danny, still feeling pain from some of his injuries, managed to climb back up to the opening. Then Pat tied the rope around her chest under her arms and he hauled her up.

Once outside, they decided to store the few implements they had taken with them under some moss by the trees. The 'little beauty' that would blow the building, they hid up in the fork of a large tree nearby.

Their luck held…. almost.

As they emerged from the forest near their tents, Pat saw a guard coming towards them and immediately threw herself into Danny's arms kissing him.

Startled, but not displeased he put his arms around her, and almost at the same time spotted the guard coming towards them.

The guard stopped and pulled his weapon off his shoulder.

"What you do here?" he demanded, his glance going from one to the other.

Pat giggled, pulling back from Danny.

"Oh nothing, just a walk in the woods, you know?"

"Walk in the woods?"

Suddenly his face cleared. "Ah, walk in the woods, ya, ya."

He laughed and moved on, pulling his rifle back onto his shoulder.

They both breathed out again.

"That was close" she said meaningfully.

"In what way?" he asked.

She reached into her jacket pocket and handed him two chunky items.

He looked down and gasped.

She had given him two hand grenades.

The following morning as they emerged from breakfast they had a surprise. It was a shock really.

They had assumed that nothing would happen in the camp until the three days of grieving were over. It seemed that there was either a change of plan, or that prior timings had dictated a certain initiative.

In front of the Chief's longhouse, two trucks had pulled up and a group of approximately fifty men in civilian clothes were climbing aboard.

They carried no weapons, just small backpacks that could contain a change of clothes. The normal type of pack that any traveller, away overnight, might carry.

"What'd you make of that Danny?" C.C. asked.

"Hmm... at a guess, I'd say these are the advance guard that they intend to slip across the border using First Nation tribal passes. They probably have their various target areas that they go to once they're across."

"I agree" Pat volunteered. "The material they need, will be slipped across through the many gaps in the border. It's bound to be well planned. A smooth operation."

Bob was now back on his feet and he and Jeff had just emerged from the quarters.

C.C. explained what they were speculating about.

Jeff still looked puzzled. "I heard you mention material. What material is that?"

Danny's paranoia about secrecy, and Pat's suggestion about keeping events to a smaller group, meant that Jeff, and Siobhan, were not fully in the loop. Danny feared that if any of them were tortured or threatened, they might divulge any plans they were hatching up.

Now he threw a questioning glance in Pat's direction.

Reading his mind she turned to Jeff and Bob. "Oh, we figure they must have lots of stuff in those two big buildings that they guard 24/7. You know, weapons etc."

"Yeah" Bob butted in. "That's what I figure as well. Wish I was a fly on the wall in there."

Jeff pursed his lips. "We're running out of options here folks. If we could get our hands on some weapons we might be able to make a run for it. Especially if we slipped off at night when everyone is sleeping."

"We noticed a guard up around here late last night "Pat volunteered, "So they may be checking up on us."

"Aha," Bob interjected, "you two out late! Now what was that all about?" he demanded, but with a grin on his face.

Pat belted him on his good arm. "None of your damn business!" she retorted, making the rest of the group relax.

Danny decided right then to bring them all into some of their discoveries.

Taking advantage of being out in the open, where no one could overhear them, he recounted C.C.'s trip to the prison camp and their plans to help the prisoners escape. He left out the two nighttime sorties into the longhouses for the moment.

It was Bob who looked skeptical.

"Bringing back a bunch of starved and possibly sick Indians, and pitting them against a camp full of highly trained soldiers, even with the possibility of capturing the prison guards' weapons, is the stuff for a Hollywood movie Danny. So hey, reality check here, even with the infamous Danny Quigley leading them. No offence buddy" he offered.

"None taken either Bob. We're just scavenging around for some morsel of hope here. If anyone has any better ideas, I'd like to hear them."

He looked around.

No one spoke.

On that note, they broke up and went their various ways, Bob to have his wounds dressed by Siobhan, and C.C. to visit Little Dove.

Danny asked Bob if he could have a moment with Siobhan inside first and ducked inside.

Siobhan was laying out some first aid material and looked up.

"Oh, I was expecting Bob back" she said.

"Yeah, he's outside. I asked him to give me a minute."

She looked away. "Yes, I expected that you'd want to talk to me. Look…"

He lifted his hands. "Hey, Siobhan. We both got involved a couple of years ago and I very much enjoyed our time together."

She looked deflated. "Sure but no one was expecting this…C.C. to be still alive."

"Well, I'm glad he is alive. You know, you and I, just seeing each other once a year and not expecting other people to pop into our lives, was totally unrealistic. Either one of us could have fallen for someone else, and we'd have understood it. And guess what? I had that girl from Afghanistan, that I told you about, appear back in my life again."

She perked up looking interested. "Oh, you didn't tell me" she remonstrated.

"Siobhan, I'm sorry to say she went back to her people in Afghanistan. If she'd stayed, I'm afraid you would have been getting a 'Dear John' letter or phone call, so don't feel too badly about C.C. He's a great guy and I love him, which is why I'm here I guess."

"Thanks for saying that Danny and making it easy on me, on both of us. C.C. feels bad about it too."

"Yeah, he's that kind of guy. You know, if we get out of here I wish you both all the very best for the future."

She sighed. "What future Danny? There's no way out of this, is there?"

"Who knows? Where there's life there's hope," he said strongly.

"This isn't the SAS Danny and you don't have a regiment behind you. If there is any way out of this, it's going to be a miracle intervention of some kind."

"There's an old saying Siobhan, God helps those who help themselves, and we're not beaten yet by a long shot so keep your chin up."

Without another word he ducked outside again, nodded to Bob, and headed off in the direction of C.C.'s tent.

# Chapter 42

It was an hour later when members of the tribal police came into C.C.'s tent and hustled them unceremoniously outside, that they saw Little Dove, Bob, Jeff and Siobhan, being marched ahead of them.

They were thrust into Black Cloud's tent, and two of the tribal police stood up front with AK 47's at the ready. The rest of the tribal police backed outside.

'Something's going on here' were Danny's first thoughts. 'And I don't think I'm going to like it."

Little Dove was no longer up front with the Chief, who sat with three of his elders and one of his squaws. Normally the Chief wore an inscrutable expression on his face, but today he was virtually smirking.

Now he turned to the group. "I know all your plans...your foolish attempt to free the prisoners, which Little Dove equally foolishly showed you where they are. She is now a traitor to her tribe and must die, but not before all of you die first, for you are no longer of any use to me.

My plans to wreak punishment on the land to the south can no longer be delayed, and have to be launched immediately. So your services, Quigley, no longer matter. In the meantime you will be held prisoners in the guardhouse by the tribal police."

Danny looked around at the group, going from face to face.

Pat said it for him. "Someone betrayed us. Someone standing here right now among us!" Her voice was bitter.

Danny stood still, realizing that once they were locked up, there was zero chance of making a break for it or sabotaging the material in the longhouse.

He started speaking softly as he pushed his way to the front, where he was stopped by the two tribal policemen, who held their weapons directly on his chest.

"Look Chief, we forced Little Dove to take us there. We threatened her and..."

Black Cloud sneered. "Quigley, you may look on me as a stupid Indian, like all you British did when you ransacked our land and..."

At that moment Danny moved.

Weapons held directly on one's chest are the easiest to deflect without any risk of a shot being fired. Especially when the weapons still had their safety catch on. At the regiment, back in Hereford, they had spent countless hours practicing how to disarm an opponent, in various situations.

Danny's arm swept across both rifles, swinging them down and to the right. Without a pause in the movement, he struck back at the side of the neck of one guard, and savagely head-butted the other, sending both to the floor.

Then he grabbed both rifles, throwing one across to Bob.

Both of them, being of the same mind, snapped off the safety and jacked back the breech on the weapons. One up the breech. Locked and ready.

Danny turned the weapon on the Chief, who stood there with his eyes popping out.

"Now chief, we have a little negotiation to do. We get together a little party and start heading back to civilization, with you and your group as hostages. When we get through the forest, you and your little gang here can go free. If anyone tries to stop us you get a bullet in the head first, but we don't want that to happen do we?"

The consternation on the Chief's face slowly turned to a grin.

He actually smiled.

Danny's mind reeled. What had he missed?

The Chief nodded his head. "You're not going anywhere Quigley. You or your group."

"He's right Danny."

It was a voice off to the side. A voice he knew.

He swung around.

Jeff was standing with a pistol held against the back of Little Dove's head, his left arm around her throat.

"One false move and I blow her pretty head off Danny. Now, slowly place those two weapons on the floor. I'm going to count to five...one..."

"You rotten traitor Jeff...how could you..." Pat's harsh voice rang out.

Jeff's voice remorselessly continued counting "two... three... four..."

Danny nodded to Bob and they slowly reached down and placed the weapons on the ground.

As Danny did so, the Indian that he had chopped in the neck, grabbed it and swung the butt savagely at his head.

His whole world exploded into darkness.

When he came to, he found himself lying on a mud floor. He had no idea how long he had been unconscious.

His head was being supported by Siobhan, and Little Dove was holding his hands.

Siobhan's voice was soothing. "Take it easy Danny. That was some blow you got and those two guards gave you a right kicking once you were down. You're going to hurt in several places, and perhaps have a broken rib, from what I saw."

He sat up, groaning.

"Where the hell are we?" he demanded.

It was C.C. who answered. "It's a small log prison where they throw people who break the tribal laws. Oh, and there are two guards on duty directly outside."

"The prison is usually used for drunks" Little Dove interjected. "There are some facilities, in that small room there." She pointed. "Not much, just a rough dug toilet and a half-full rain barrel. Enough for you to wash your face off."

He pulled himself onto his knees, and then with C.C.'s help, managed to get to his feet.

His head swirled and he was prevented from falling by others in the group who were gathered around him.

He grimaced, holding his side. "Yeah, got me here for sure. It's a sharp pain."

Siobhan gently touched his side. "Could be cracked Danny. We need to make sure it doesn't penetrate your lung if it is. I can't even bind it up for you to give you support. Just move very slowly for the moment and see how that feels."

Pat and C.C. helped him across into the small room, more like an earthen cubbyhole, and Pat splashed some water over his face.

He straightened up blinking. "Must have taken a mean beating back there. Crimes, my thighs, arms and back feel like I've been run over by a truck. Those bastards!" he muttered.

"Can't blame them Danny. You sure showed them up in front of the Chief. It was pay back time" C.C. grunted.

"Didn't do us much good did it?" Danny retorted. "Here we are locked up and our only way out is feet first."

"Oh, I wouldn't say that" Pat replied "After all, we know who the traitor is now."

Danny started walking tentatively back into the main room, feeling stronger with each step.

Siobhan met him half way. "I have no x-ray to go by, but I think you may be lucky. The way you're moving makes me think you don't have a broken rib after all. Possibly a badly bruised one, but it will bother you for some time."

He smiled ruefully. "Time is something we don't have much of do we? Now has anyone figured out why Jeff is in with those guys?"

It was Pat who spoke up. "I think perhaps I do. When we were coming through the forest a few days back, before we met up with the reception party, Jeff told me his father had been abused in the school system, that all Indians were forced into. Lots of bad stuff happened in there. Even though compensation was paid out, Jeff said they stole his father's manhood and pride. He was very bitter about it."

"It all makes sense now. He was the contact person as far back as Hanlon Falls, conveniently available as a guide to shepherd us here. That's why Little Bear knew exactly where to find us."

"There's probably more to it than that. I'm rarely involved in tribal matters, but it wouldn't surprise me if he was promised the hunting and guide rights to this massive Indian territory," Little Dove interjected.

Bob snorted. There won't be much hunting out of here after they carry out their attack on U.S. territory. This place will be decimated, and the land taken back by the Canadian Government. This will put First Nations land settlement claims back fifty years!"

The conversation continued, but Danny lowered himself to the floor and went instantly to sleep. In the past, sleep had been his greatest healer.

It was dark when they shook him awake.

"Wake up Danny, someone's here to see you."

It was Bob's voice, as he helped him to his feet.

Still in pain, Danny felt that his strength was returning and his mind was clearer.

"To see me! Who...?" he looked around him, making out some vague shadows.

"At the door, man" Bob said pulling him across to the barred structure.

When he looked out through the bars he thought he was dreaming for a moment. In the reflection of the flames from the fires out in the center of the area, he saw the figure of a large, bulky Indian.

He peered closer.

"Little Bear!" he exclaimed.

He heard the lock in the door turning and a strong pair of hands drew him outside.

The big Indian leaned forward and peered into his face.

"I think my father want me to help you Quigley" he started off.

"But how?" Danny asked.

Little Bear pointed to the ground.

Looking closely, Danny spotted the still forms of two Indians.

Little Bear nodded. "The guards.... they just changed them, so we have four hours before they're replaced. Enough time for us to get to that stockade and free the prisoners. Yes, Black Cloud told us of your plan. I want to help you succeed."

"I'm not in good shape for walking Little Bear. I just took a beating..."

"I know that... I've pushed a jeep out some distance in the forest. If you can make it that far, we can drive to the stockade. I know there are two trucks there already, if we can break the prisoners out and transport them here, then it's up to you."

Danny drew Little Bear back into the small building and explained the most recent development to the group.

"But can we trust him?" Pat demanded.

"We don't have any other option. For what it's worth, I've spoken to him prior to this and felt a kindred spirit in Little Bear. Now I believe he's on our side. So yes, I do trust him."

"That's good enough for me." C.C. exclaimed. "Now Danny, what's the plan?"

It was rough and ready.

Little Bear would take Danny, Little Dove and Siobhan, out to the stockade where the rescue would take place.

If successful, Little Dove and Siobhan could minister to the health needs of the prisoners, while Danny and Little Bear took the healthy remnants back to the main camp.

Once the noise of the approaching vehicles was heard by C.C., it would be his job to push the button and blow the second longhouse. In the confusion, Bob and Pat would try to take out the two guards and get into the first longhouse.

Once inside, they would hold the building at all costs and wait for the arrivals from the prison break. Danny reached into his pocket and withdrew a grenade, which he passed to Bob. The Indians hadn't even searched him.

"This might help."

Bob's eyes widened. "Where on earth…?"

He shrugged and went back to outlining the plan.

Danny would then seek out Black Cloud, try to locate the cell phone and call for help. In the process he would neutralize any opposition he came across. Later he would probably try to make it back to the longhouse, unless he managed to find a nice secure sniper position, where he could continue to harass the enemy. He would wear a white armband, which those firing back from the longhouse, needed to look out for.

Danny thought of the carefully rehearsed approach of his SAS regiment prior to operations, which included building full-scale models and mind-numbing rehearsals.

Then again, he recalled operations that were cobbled together at a moment's notice, and which succeeded brilliantly.

As someone once said, - it was Showtime!

# Chapter 43

In previous exercises in Germany, Danny had got used to flying along in jeeps using the small needle-pointed lights that just barely stopped you from flying into large objects, like trees!

Little Bear took it a point further, coupling the tiny lights with an uncanny sense of direction and a total disregard for their safety. Danny could hear the gasps of the two women in the back as they hurtled around corners, tore up steep hills and down sloping grades.

'There's a future for this guy, driving a taxi in Cairo or Morocco' he thought drily.

Little Bear's three passengers breathed a sigh of relief when he coasted to a stop a short distance from the stockade.

Danny turned to him. "Okay, what's the plan Little Bear?"

The Indian reached back and drew an automatic weapon forward onto his lap.

"You three get out here and I drive up to the door. Normally there are no guards outside, but with the alert, who knows. Certainly, the hole that the prisoners cut in the back fence has been discovered and repaired now, so I have to get you in the front door. As I drive up, you'll have to make your way carefully to the edge of the building near the front. When I go inside, I'll try to wedge the door open for you.

Otherwise, when I take out the front guards, hopefully silently, I'll step out and wave to you to come in. Then we'll have to locate the other guards, some sleeping and quite possibly, some now posted out back in the stockade. I already mentioned where the guard's sleeping quarters are on the left and right hand side as you go back into the building. By then you'll have taken one of their weapons, so between us we can take care of the rest of them, without too much trouble."

"Total surprise would help us avoid a fire-fight" Danny commented.

Little Bear glanced across at him. "Those men won't surrender, and don't be misled by any of them putting their hands up. They're trained to trick the infidel, as they call them, in any way possible. Remember that."

"What about us?" Siobhan asked.

The Indian craned his neck backwards. "Follow Danny almost up to the building, staying in the bushes, and wait until you see him go in. If you hear gunfire stay back until it finishes, then come on in."

"What if you don't overcome the guards Little Bear?"

He shrugged. "It will be a good fight regardless. If I go to my father fighting for this cause, it will be a happy homecoming. Which reminds me…"

He extracted a knife from its sheath, in one swift movement, making Siobhan gasp.

Reaching across he took Danny's hand, made a small incision in his palm and did the same with his own. Then he pressed their hands together.

"We are now blood brothers Danny, fighting together, so I'm not betraying my own tribe. Those fighters in there, and back in the camp, have come from a far country, and will destroy this place for us forever. I know this now."

Siobhan looked at Little Dove. "If you think that I as a nurse am going to slit my wrist, you've got another think coming. Those men of ours might not die from fighting, but from some dammed infection from their cuts."

Nothing more was said as they alighted from the jeep, which the big Indian then drove off in the direction of the camp.

Danny and the women started walking fast.

When Little Bear drove up to the front of the building, he found one guard standing outside, who drifted around to the driver's side of the jeep.

"Why you here?" he demanded, "and driving in this black."

Little Bear climbed out.

"Yeah, stupid driving in darkness. Black Cloud suddenly decided he wanted me out here, in case the prisoners caused trouble. He worries like an old woman."

The guard snickered. "Prisoners no cause trouble. We beat for cut hole in wire."

Little Bear reached back into the jeep and pulled out a bottle of whiskey.

"I don't know if I offend your religious beliefs or not, but it's such a cold night I brought this."

The guard's eyes glinted and his hand shot out, grasping the bottle.

In a moment he had unscrewed the cap and threw his head back taking a long swallow.

He never finished.

Little Bear stepped sideways, snapping his head back with the curve of his arm and slicing across his throat with the knife.

While the man's body was still writhing, he pulled him backwards behind the jeep and dropped him to the ground.

He picked up the man's rifle and looked back at the tree line.

'Was Danny there yet,' he wondered.

He waved, and was relieved to see him racing towards him.

He arrived breathless and the Indian pressed the weapon into his hands.

"We go to the door now. I try to go in as planned and surprise them, otherwise..."

He shrugged.

"Yeah, we wake everybody up and it's a fire-fight. Okay let's do it.... brother."

Little Bear smiled faintly, and they both strode towards the front door, with Danny sloping off to one side, taking cover behind one of the trucks parked there.

Little Bear hammered on the door, shouting out.

Within a few seconds the door opened partially and Little Bear crowded in, not wanting to give the guard any chance to look outside and try to locate his colleague.

There was no one else in the room with him. The guard backed up.

"Where, where... other guard?" the man started to say.

Little Bear shrugged.

"Oh, he's out there" he pointed. "Wanted you to have some of this. He's coming in, in a moment" he said, reaching down and casually wedging a magazine that had been lying on the counter, in the door.

He held up the bottle, now half full, having fallen on the ground outside.

The man refused to take the bottle.

He looked at Little Bear suspiciously. "I no drink...he know this."

He glanced down at the wedged door and went to swing his rifle up.

The bottle dropped with a crash on the floor as Little Bear grabbed him and they both staggered back colliding with a metal table, containing mugs and coffee-making appliances. It toppled over with an enormous noise and door shot open behind them as another guard stepped in, his rifle at the ready, sighting on the struggling pair.

At that moment Danny dived through the doorway in a forward roll, right into the center of the room. As he started coming out of the roll he blasted the guard hurling him back into the corridor.

Little Bear had his arms around the guard's neck and he gave a mighty wrench, hearing it snap.

There was shouting coming from down the corridor.

Both men said nothing, but turned and jumped through the door, Danny slightly in front.

He spotted a door opening on his left side and two men spilled out.

It was Little Bear who fired first, sending them flying.

As they raced up parallel to the door Danny could hear shouting from inside.

He extracted the second grenade that Pat had given him, pulled the pin, tossed it into the room, and slammed the door.

An enormous explosion followed, blowing shreds of wood and dust into the corridor in front of them.

The door on the right opened slightly. An arm holding a weapon poked out and started firing blindly. Little Bear gave the door an enormous kick and the weapon was dropped, followed by a scream.

Both Danny and Little Bear sent a fusillade through the wooden panel, hearing more screams. Danny looked quickly at Little Bear who pointed him towards the back of the prison. He nodded as the Indian opened the door cautiously, and jumped inside, firing.

As Danny went through a door further down, he was confronted by a series of cages, in which the now awakened prisoners were crowding up against the bars.

He didn't have time to stop and free them but raced past.

As he did so the prisoners in the end cages started pointing towards the back and shouting.

He made out some of the shouts.

"More guards... more guards... watch out..."

He waved briefly to them. Coming up to another solid looking door he started reaching for the handle when shots were fired from the other side of it and holes appeared just inches from his head.

He dived back sideways, and squatted down, analyzing the situation.

The prisoners couldn't be massacred now, because he was between them and the guards. He couldn't wait too long as the guards might get out through the back of the stockade, take one of the jeeps drive back and warn the camp, before the group were ready.

He crawled back to the nearest cage where faces were staring out at him.

"How many guards back there?" he shouted.

There was no reply. The prisoners just stared at him.

"Look" he shouted urgently "we're here to rescue you. How many guards back there?"

One man stepped forward. "Are you C.C.'s friend? I saw him outside two days ago."

"Yes, yes, I'm C.C.'s friend. Now how many guards?" He pointed backwards.

"Three guards, very mean. They beat us half to death here."

Danny stood up, noting the lock on the cage.

"Stand back!" he cautioned. The Indians inside pressed backwards.

Danny held the weapon to the lock and blasted it off.

The door swung open.

He stepped to one side.

"Now...." he started to say. Then all he could do was stand and stare. Like an avalanche, and without a word, the inmates poured through and turned right. When they reached the door they never stopped. Just opened it, and hurled themselves through. Weapons exploded from the other side, cutting a number of them to pieces. They never stopped, just kept leaping through the opening.

The guns fell silent and then the screaming started. It seemed to go on for a long time.

Then those who were still alive started to straggle back to where Danny stood mesmerized.

At that moment Siobhan and Little Dove came through into the caged area and stared.

"Oh my God!" Siobhan. "What utter carnage! Was there no way you could stop them?" she whispered.

Little Bear strode up. "These are First Nations warriors. Nothing could stop them seeking vengeance for what they have gone through. Let's get those cages open and see what we've got. We can't waste any time. We need to get back and take the camp. From what I've seen, you don't have to worry about fighting ability with these warriors."

He reached into his trouser pocket. "A little present for you Danny" he said, holding something up.

Danny stared and reached for it. "Well blow me down!"

"What is it?" Siobhan demanded.

"A bloody cell phone, for crying out loud." He looked at Little Bear. "Where did you find it?"

"In the front office. Makes sense in a way. They must have needed communication between the camp and here. I was never aware of that arrangement."

He smiled. "Any help to you Danny?"

"Any help! My God man..."

He turned and raced back in the direction of the office, staying alert in case any wounded guards might still cause trouble. He needn't have worried. Little Bear didn't believe in taking prisoners.

He grabbed a chair and sat down, thinking hard.

He had to assume that it was a satellite phone.

His mind was churning, trying to recall numbers, which he was normally quite good at doing.

For the life of him he couldn't recall the numbers of MI5 in London.

Then a name edged into his mind: Brett Zeitner, the CIA man he had bumped into on his last trip to the U.S.

He shook his head. Wasn't that the man who sicked a termination team on him that had made an attempt on his life in Hanlon Falls, and back in the forest when they were tied up, and at the shooting range in Vancouver?

The leader of that team had clearly mentioned Bret Zeitner.

Confused, he stood up and walked to the door, looking out at the trucks.

Then he came back and sat down.

He could still remember Zeitner's cell phone number. The time zone in Washington was not in line with British Columbia time...but anyway.

He dialed it.

A gruff voice answered. "This better be good."

"Danny Quigley here. Look, I know you tried to have me killed but…"

"Quigley? Where the hell are you? Oh shit, I better explain…"

"Explain what? That you sent a hit team after me Zeitner?" he said cynically.

"To cut to the chase Danny, it was me who sent you those warning e-mails about the team…I recall, I mentioned Hanlon Falls at one time…ring a bell?"

"You sent those warnings? But how…"

"Danny, I'd be happy to brief you fully when I meet up with you again, but I suspect you're not calling me just for a chat."

"You got it in one and you may think I've been eating magic mushrooms when I recount what's happening up here. Anyway, here goes".

It took twenty minutes, during which Zeitner interrupted with numerous questions and requests for clarification. Finally, Danny fell silent.

Zeitner let out a long breath.

"You know of course, what you've just handed me? It involves everyone from the President on down, and a sovereign country Canada, which we can't just breeze into. The initial urgency for us is the people who are either heading for the border or are across already. Then we have all those suicide vests and IED's that would create absolute panic down here if they got across. Now you've given me the GPS figures for the camp, which you received in Hanlon Falls originally.

What's your plan right now Danny? Can you do anything to slow them down?"

He sighed. "I'm heading back in there with a small bunch of Indians, some pretty sick, and about ten weapons, but they badly want to kick ass. I may be able to blow up one building but I can't guarantee my handiwork, having set it up in the dark and in a hurry. We can try to take out the leaders in this but these guys are fanatics and they'll go down fighting."

Despite the situation Zeitner chuckled. "From past experience Danny, you have a habit of coming out smelling like roses. I wish you luck. Give me your cell phone number and I'll keep you posted."

That was it.

Danny felt a great sense of relief knowing that whole sections of the greatest military complex in the world would be springing to life, south of the border.

Whatever happened back at the camp, the plan was foiled, but could they survive, long enough for help to reach them? Time to find out.

Inside there was chaos.

Some might say organized chaos because Siobhan, Little Dove, Little Bear and C.C.'s contact had managed to break them into groups.

The Indian dead were treated with tender reverence.

The pseudo Indians were tossed out by the wire, to be buried later.

Inside those injured with bullet wounds were lying down at the end of the prison corridor and were receiving some basic first aid, though some of them wouldn't make it. The sick from the prison were sitting or lying at the other end of the corridor. None of them would go back in the cages, even though there was more room in one of the larger cells.

Little Bear and C.C.'s contact had crammed twenty people into a provisions room where some of them had already broken open cartons of food and drinks, and had ferried some of this outside to the sick and injured.

When Danny pushed his way in, Little Bear called a halt to the comings and goings, and pointed to Danny.

Silence fell on the room.

Danny looked around.

On the faces of the twenty men he could read pain and deprivation, and one other thing...determination.

"Okay, my name is Danny Quigley. I'm a friend of C.C. who most of you know. I came here to rescue him, but Black Cloud had other ideas. He now has a trained Force of about two hundred warriors, some of them your brothers, who were misled. We thought initially that Black Cloud's army were First Nations, but apparently they are Pakistanis from a far away country, who have a passing resemblance to an Indian tribe, north of here. They intend to attack the United States, and have already sent fifty warriors to cross the border. The longhouses are stacked full of explosive vests and bombs, which they intended to get over the border at illegal crossings, and pass on to the fifty men already dispatched. The other fighters will, I believe, follow on their heels. You can imagine what effect that would have on the many good people in your tribe."

"C.C.'s contact exploded. "That would finish us as a tribe. We would lose all this land that we have fought to get back from the Government."

There was a murmur of agreement around the room.

Little Bear held his hand up, pointed to Danny, and they fell silent again.

"Here's the thing. If we can take the camp and hold it until help gets here, I'm sure the authorities will be more than willing to look at all the facts. Now who's with me to take on Black Cloud and his people?" he asked.

Everyone in the room raised their hand.

"Right, the plan is that twenty of us head in from here on the trucks. We managed to get our hands on ten rifles and six handguns, so that's a start.

As soon as we storm into camp, C.C. will attempt to blow the second longhouse. I've set up some explosives, but as I did it in virtual darkness, it's possible there might not be the explosion we hoped for. In any event, we can try to take the first longhouse, which has lots of weapons and ammo in it, and we can hand out these to your people. It makes sense that we can't take on Black Cloud's highly trained soldiers head on. There are too many of them and we know that they are not scared of dying."

"I'm quite happy to help them out!" C.C.'s friend shouted out.

Danny smiled, despite the grimness of the situation.

He held his hand up.

"Look, I know all of you can't wait to get your own back for the degradation you've suffered at the hands of Black Cloud. You will get your chance believe me. However your first job is to take longhouse number one and hold it, no matter what they throw at you.... and they will. They'll badly need to take it back because they probably only have limited ammo with their weapons. There may be some stored out on the firing range, for everyday practice. Now you can set defensive sniper positions in that hole in the roof, which, as you know, is there to let the smoke out when you have a fire. However, they'll try to clamber up the sides of the building and come at you that way. You need to be ready. Now help is on the way, but I don't know how soon it'll get here, so at all costs, we have to hold that building. Any ideas?"

One tall, skinny Indian stood up. "I was involved in building that longhouse. We can chip out the mud between the logs and make some holes for shooting out at them."

"Excellent idea!" said Danny. "Anything else?"

Another man shot up on his feet. "What if they try to burn us out. That building is made of logs after all."

"Little Bear snorted. "They need what's in that building to launch their plans of attack down south. They won't try to burn it."

C.C.'s friend stood up again. "What will you be doing Danny? Shouldn't you be with us in the longhouse?" he asked.

Little Bear answered. "Danny fights and moves like a tiger. You don't confine a tiger when he's hunting. He can do more good hunting down Black Cloud and his leaders out there. He told me he will wear a white piece of cloth on his arm, so watch out for him when you're shooting."

He looked at Danny. "Anything else?" he asked.

"Yes, one thing. When you hear choppers, helicopters that are coming, you'll know its help coming in. Don't whatever you do, rush outside, either to greet them or join them. They'll be hosing down anything that moves out there, and they won't be able to tell you from Black Cloud's men. Don't worry about missing the action. You'll have your belly full just trying to hold onto that longhouse. Okay with that?"

The group looked from one to the other, and nodded.

Without any further discussion, Little Bear hustled them outside, handed out the weapons and ammo, and assigned them to their trucks.

Danny made a fast run back to where Siobhan and Little Dove were busy tending to the sick and wounded.

"Right, we're off!" he shouted.

Both women rose and gave him a quick hug, and then he turned and raced back outside, jumping into the driving seat of the second truck.

Little Bear led off and the other two trucks raced after him.

# Chapter 44

Pat had taken C.C. to the location near the second longhouse, and showed him the device that Danny had hooked up to create an explosion. She impressed on him not to hold it or fiddle with it until it was time to set it off.

"So I listen for the trucks in the distance, probably a couple of hundred yards out and press the switch. In five minutes it will blow, right?"

"If all goes well with what Danny's rigged up, yes" she replied.

"Okay, what do I do then?"

"I'd suggest that you make your way over to the first longhouse, where Bob and I will be trying to take out the two guards, once the explosion goes off. We could use you inside, tearing open those crates and divvying out ammunition to Danny's group coming in. If the explosion fails, we're still having a go at those two sentries. We have to get inside as it's the only place we can make a stand."

"Okay Pat, leave me to it. What are you going to do now?" he asked.

She showed him the rope that Danny and she had used to get inside the longhouses.

"I have to shinny back up longhouse number one and drop this rope down inside, assuming no guards are there. When Danny's group fight their way inside the building, they need to be able to climb up to the opening, to guard against an attack from Black Clouds people, coming up over the roof. And also, on Danny's instructions, to set up sniper positions on top, to cover the perimeter of the building. Black Cloud will need what's in this longhouse and will throw everything he has at it."

"My God, let's hope he brings back some of those prisoners, and that they're well enough to fight and climb up that dammed rope!"

Without another word, she turned and crept off.

She did have considerable difficulty getting up the side of the building, without the rope that Danny had dropped down for her on their previous attempts. At one point, when she was only half way up, she almost slipped back off the roof, but managed to wedge her foot in a groove and save herself.

Finally, exhausted, she reached the opening and sat there for a brief moment trying to get her breath back. Then she peered down inside, listening attentively for any sound of movement.

Nothing.

She tied the rope securely round the end of a log section and lowered it slowly down.

She hadn't discussed it with Danny, but now she wondered if it might have been better for her to go down into the building and somehow support Bob when he attacked the front.

Hmm... better not.... Danny was the tactician. Anyway, she didn't even have a weapon and the door was locked from the outside. Bob would also start worrying about her if she didn't turn up as planned.

If Danny's plan worked, he and his prisoners and Little Bear, should be pretty close by now.

'If' she thought. 'God, if it didn't work...'

She shook her head. Better not even thinking that way.

Danny would come through for them.

With that she clambered carefully back down, and made her way through the trees and brush to where Bob had agreed to wait, and from where they intended to launch their attack.

When Danny's three jeeps finally roared into the camp, Bob looked desperately back at the second longhouse.

"Blow, you bastard, blow!" he pleaded.

"Oh, sweet Jesus" Pat breathed. "Those guards are swinging their automatic weapons across and will cut Danny and his group to pieces before they can even get out of the trucks."

Bob's breath stilled.... then he leapt to his feet, and despite the pain from his injured ribs, hobbled out into the open square close to the two guards. He swung the grenade in a high arc towards them, thanking the years of baseball practice he's had.

The grenade landed right beside them and exploded, blowing them both to pieces.

Unfortunately, the front door was blown in as well.

Pat raced out into the square, gesturing urgently to Danny and his group, to make a dash for the longhouse.

She met him as he came forward. "Bring a jeep to block the door she screamed," then turned and ran for the longhouse.

He hesitated, ran back and jumped into the first vehicle.

The prisoners, as instructed, started haring towards the longhouse.

Almost immediately, single shots started coming at them from the surrounding buildings. One or two of the prisoners were hit and fell to the ground. The remainder grabbed them and started dragging them towards the longhouse.

Danny tore past in the jeep and slid to a stop near the door.

He leaned out. "What happened to that dammed explosion?" he roared at Bob.

Bob opened his mouth but whatever he was about to say was drowned out in the sound of a massive explosion from the second longhouse.

It was followed by a series of secondary explosions, some even louder than the first one...and streams of the flares shot into the sky, in all directions.

The prisoners had slowed down in awe, watching the spectacle.

"Keep moving them in Bob!" Danny screamed, leaping out of the truck and grabbing the prisoners, right and left and thrusting them through the door.

Bob and Pat were doing the same. Suddenly, they were all inside.

"The vehicle Danny, the vehicle" Pat shouted. "Block this door for God's sake!"

Without a moments delay he swung the truck around and sent it crunching sideways into the doorjamb, sealing it.

He clambered out the other end of the truck, almost falling as the pain in his chest shot through his body.

Pat was beside him in a second. "You okay Danny? I saw the pain on your face."

"Yeah, okay, I guess, where's C.C.?"

"He should be here now, he was only a few minutes away," he answered.

"That bloody Englishman! Probably lost his way in the forest" he rasped.

Just then C.C.'s big form showed up on the other side of the blocking vehicle. "How do I get in here?" he demanded.

"Crawl across the dammed seats for Pete's sake," Bob shouted, reaching across a moment later and hauling him through.

In a moment C.C. was standing beside them.

Danny and Pat pounded him on the back. "That was some explosion. At first we thought it had failed to blow."

He looked sheepishly at them. "I waited too long. Wanted to be sure it was your vehicles I was hearing. Sorry"

Danny grabbed Bob. "I'm heading out. Get some concentrated fire across at those buildings, where the shots are coming from. Oh, good news." He held up the cell phone. "I've called for help...the CIA, so we have to hang in here, but I've no idea how long until they get here."

He turned and headed towards the jeep again. As soon as Little Bear and three of the prisoners started returning fire, Danny crawled back through the jeep and out onto the ground.

Shots were still pinging off the jeep and sending chips flying from the longhouse. Danny figured it wasn't going to get any better and crawled back around the side of the building. He kept moving completely around until he was looking across at the main encampment. It was a hive of activity with fighters spiraling out of buildings, half dressed. Everyone was shouting and the leaders were screaming instructions at them. Without too much success at first, it seemed.

He risked giving his location away by taking two single shots at some of the leaders, and saw them fall down.

No one had appeared to notice that they were taking incoming fire.

Danny had to figure where to find Black Cloud.

Perhaps the meeting longhouse, but did he sleep there also? He wondered.

The meeting longhouse was about fifty yards away, with some smaller log houses in the middle. Danny knew that one of them was a washing house for the warriors. He changed the weapon from single shot to automatic, and then jumping up from his kneeling position, he made a dash for it.

Not a shot was fired at him but when he crashed through the door he bumped into three fighters who were peering through a small window, across at the longhouse door. They were firing at the jeep, which was now jammed in it's doorway.

Without hesitation, he caught all three of them with a burst, sending them crashing backwards. He quickly relieved them of the magazines in their weapons and was glad to see that they were not carrying spares with them. That could mean they might run out of ammunition soon. One of the weapons had a grenade launcher attached to it. He pulled the dead fighter's body back and gave a sigh of relief when he spotted a nylon pack of grenades attached to his belt. He tore it off and slung both the pack and the weapon over his shoulder.

Tipping the other rifles into a standing rain barrel, he shoved a wooden lid on top, partially covering them, then ducked down as some bullets came flying in, almost taking his head off.

His own group firing back!

Better get out of here!

Opening the door slightly, he could make out that the warriors were lining up in groups. The chaos was gone and some order was settling in.

They were running out of time, he thought. Once they got organized and attacked, the prisoners and Danny's crew wouldn't last very long.

He heard firing coming from the roof of the longhouse.

Good, Bob had got them organized and they were inflicting casualties.

That could have an effect on morale and make the enemy more cautious. Unless there were more suicide bombers in their midst!

At that moment he heard the sound of truck engines starting up in the square and risked a quick look.

What he saw galvanized him into action.

The two trucks they had driven in on, were now tearing across the square, with a number of fighters inside and clinging to the sides, blazing away at the door of the longhouse where he had rammed the truck.

Danny threw up the grenade launcher to his shoulder and snapped off a quick shot.

Missed!

His second one didn't. It caught the leading truck smack in the middle of the engine block, and the explosion blew it twenty yards away.

The second truck skidded to a halt. He could see that firepower from his group in the longhouse was slamming into the vehicle as the fighters bailed out and started running away. Most of them didn't make it.

Danny didn't wait to see the outcome. He was already out the door and running towards the outline of Black Cloud's meetinghouse, his weapon at the ready.

Surprisingly, as all attention was out on the square, again, he made it across without attracting any enemy fire.

In the number one longhouse, where Bob's group were consolidating their defenses, there had been a moment of anxiety, when the enemy came tearing down on them with weapons blazing.

Little Bear and Bob coolly returned their fire, which didn't seem to be slowing them down. Then the first vehicle exploded and was blasted off to their right, bursting into flames and turning the square into daylight.

Little Bear shouted across at Bob.

"That's Danny. I told them that you let the tiger loose to hunt."

They both lifted up their weapons and started blasting away, supported by a half dozen of the prisoners, who had scavenged weapons and ammo that C.C. had, by then, pulled out of the crates and cartons.

There was a cry behind them as one of the roof defenders came hurtling down and thudded into the ground. Bob glanced up.

"Hell, Black Cloud's warriors are getting their act together. They must have spotted our positions up on the roof."

He dashed over and looked up, screaming, "keep your heads down on the roof. Don't give them a target."

Somebody waved back at him.

Danny crouched outside the meetinghouse, listening and watching for any sign of movement.

A small section of warriors came racing round towards the back of the longhouse where C.C., Bob, Little Bear and the released prisoners were digging in.

Things were hotting up.

One of the men who had bailed out of the truck in the square, came dashing up, firing sideways at the jammed truck embedded in the longhouse.

With his attention elsewhere, he didn't even see Danny, who cut him down with a short burst. At the same time a hail of bullets came skewering through between the logs behind him, and he dived to the floor.

Some fighters were inside the longhouse meeting room.

Conscious that he had to get off the street and out of sight, he pulled a grenade out of his confiscated pack, opened the longhouse door a fraction, pulled the pin and rolled it inside. Then he slammed the door shut.

There were shouts of panic inside, followed almost immediately by a deafening explosion. Danny knew to expect the unexpected when you started blowing things up.

The first surprise was when one of the logs from the longhouse went flying over his head into the square. The second was when a face suddenly appeared in the space where the log had been, followed by a weapon swinging towards him.

He hurled himself sideways and bullets mashed up the ground where he had been squatting a moment ago. He sent a burst back along the smashed log front.

At the same time he was wondering 'How had this guy survived a grenade explosion at such a short range?'

He didn't survive the exchange of gunfire that Danny sent ripping back at him. He leapt to his feet, grabbed the door and hurled himself inside in a forward roll.

He needn't have bothered. The room, where they had had their meeting with Black Cloud was empty, apart from the bodies of three warriors, caught in the grenade explosion and Danny's return fire.

Where was Black Cloud, he wondered, and started carefully testing a door that appeared to lead him to the rear of the longhouse.

For some reason, thinking of possible squaws back there, made him think of the media account of the Seal team taking out Bin Laden in Pakistan. The CIA had been spying on the compound in Abottabad for five months, waiting to catch a glimpse of him, and had spent 1 Billion Dollars on the task to kill him. Apparently at the last moment, a woman had tried to block the Seal team from delivering the fatal shot.

He hesitated about clearing the next room with a grenade, thinking that there might also be women inside.

Then he kicked the door open, staying well back in case any return fire came through.

Nothing.

He peered inside, and in the dim light, brightened occasionally by the flames from the square filtering through where the missing log had been, he could see that the room was empty.

He eased inside, eyes and body alert for any sound or movement, and moved to the next door. He had a feeling that he would strike pay dirt in the next room, apart from the fact he had understood that there were only three sections in the longhouse. He didn't believe there was an exit from the back of the building either, so if there was anyone in the building, they had to be inside this room.

He extracted a grenade and looked at it, thinking of the probability of women being inside. He shook his head, knowing that many of his SAS troopers had lost their lives through hesitation and analysis like this.

A compromise. He left the pin in the grenade, opened the door, tossed it forcefully inside and slammed the door.

There were screams inside, some of them female, and shouts of panic.

Danny opened the door almost immediately and jumped through, his muscle memory already pressing the trigger at the appearance of a group of warriors surrounding Black Cloud, now all in complete disarray as they tried to take cover from the anticipated explosion.

Danny's firepower ripped through them sending a number of them crashing backwards like rag dolls. Turning slightly he was aware of women screaming over to his left, crawling away from where the dud grenade had landed.

He factored in that no females were holding weapons and continued hosing the scrambling, terrified group of armed warriors in front of him. Some who, at the last moment, tried lifting their weapons and fighting back.

They were too late.

He stopped firing.

The screaming continued until the women looked across at the blood-spattered bodies, strewn across the room. Then they started wailing.

Almost as a reaction, one of the bodies was pushed aside and Black Cloud sat up.

Inexplicably, a grin started to creep across his face.

Danny had seen that look not too long before and dropped to the floor like a stone, rolling desperately to one side.

Bullets raked past the space that he had been standing in moments before, and tore into the head of Black Cloud.

As Danny swung round, his rifle was already spitting lead and Jeff, standing in the door with a pistol in his extended hand, was blown back out of the room.

The wailing started again as he got to his feet carefully, checking the room outside, to see if Jeff had brought reinforcements.

He hadn't, but he could see that Jeff was dead.

He checked the rest of the room.

All the warriors were dead. There was no doubt about Black Cloud.

His head had been blown apart by Jeff's handgun.

Just then the cell phone rang.

It was Bret Zeitner.

"What's the situation there Quigley?" he asked.

"Better make this quick. Where the hell are you guys?" he demanded.

"I'm still in the Capital Washington, on the East coast. Take too long to get out there to the West coast, even in an Air Force jet. However, we have the Washington State National Guard coming up in their choppers with a bunch of Marines they managed to grab. Washington State, as you may or may not know, being a Brit, is the closest to British Columbia. No problem with Canada. They have Special Forces flying out as we speak, from their training HQ in Ontario. It will be hours before they get there, but when they do, they can contain the area and chase down those guys. Brief me on what's happening?" he asked.

"We blew the longhouse with the suicide vests and IED's inside, and took over the other longhouse, where we're making our stand. The building's coming under increasing firepower, I suspect Black Cloud's people are coming up on the roof after them and I saw about a hundred warriors assembling about ten minutes ago, so we can't hold on much longer. The good news is that I just terminated their leader Black Cloud in his meeting house with a number of his guards and a hunting guide called Jeff, who was actually working with him and was in on the whole thing. Now, Bret, just how soon can you're guys get here?"

"I'm in communication with the leading chopper and they figure thirty minutes. If that longhouse is still burning, it'll bring them right to your location. Now where should they land Danny?"

"Right in the square. It's all lit up with a burning vehicle. They'll be coming in under fire, but I'll try to minimize that if I can. There's a small field outside the camp, but it would be too late for us. The Canadian Special Forces could use that.

Oh, and I'm wearing a white bandage round my arm, so tell those guys to watch out for me. Anyone outside the longhouse is fair game. I'm warned that those guys will fight to the end, so tell our guys to watch for tricks."

"No prisoners then.... well we need some survivors to figure out how all this got so far without anyone stumbling across it. We badly need intelligence on the targets for those fifty guys you saw leaving. We don't know if they managed to get any material across the border already, to support their operation. Could be 9/11 all over again. All the signs were there, but everyone asleep at the wheel. Right, enough said. It was decided that I would be the go-between for yourself and the attack group, just to keep it simple. Over and out Danny...stay safe."

He was alone again, but the wailing continued.

He threw them a disgusted look and went back up to the Chief's meeting hall.

A germ of a plan was sifting into his mind. He looked up and saw the typical opening in the roof. But being a smaller building, it was much closer to the ground.

Could he get up to it without a rope?

He doubted it. He sighed. Nothing but to go outside and try to climb up the same way he's done with the longhouses.

He went back and confiscated all the ammo magazines he could find among the dead warriors. He found another satchel of grenades and grabbed those too, then crept outside.

As he did so a number of warriors came racing past, firing across at the door of the longhouse. He could see that the vehicle he had rammed into the door was blazing away, which might add more urgency to the attackers' efforts.

They badly needed the contents of that building.

Danny could have cut some of them down, but it would have given away his position, so in the confusion, he slipped off around the Chief's longhouse until he was out of sight. Then he started climbing.

Much more difficult on a smaller building and loaded down with weapons and grenades but he made it.

Originally, he had thought of trying to seek out any ammo supplies that Black Cloud's men might have, back at the firing range. However, he doubted that he could make it there undetected. He had instead, sought the high ground where he could overlook the square and the entrance to the number one longhouse, now being held by Bob and his crew.

He maneuvered himself around and managed to find a foothold in a log inside the top of the building.

He laid out both weapons on the roof - the rifle and the grenade launcher along with his supplies of ammo and grenades.

He had also liberated Jeff's handgun, which was tucked into his belt.

He looked around at the battle area.

Two imminent dangers came to his attention immediately;

A squad of warriors had managed to storm across to the back end of the longhouse which had a second door, still locked. As they probably had the keys to open it, the group inside would be caught in crossfire.

Picking up the grenade launcher, he took aim and fired the first salvo, hoping as he did so that it wouldn't actually blow the door and make their entry even more possible. The grenade struck home in the exact center of the group, sending bodies flying. The survivors ran in close to the building, desperately seeking protection, and looking around for their attackers.

Danny fired a second grenade, and immediately switched the weapon to automatic and raked right along the side of the building as the second explosion went off.

The grenade had worked, but in doing so, it had blasted a small hole in the side of the building, which he saw some of the warriors scrambling through.

Most of the squad had been decimated, but he had just created an untenable situation for the group inside, and no method of communication with them.

They were now on their own, but he could help them elsewhere.

Out in the square, at the top end, the attacking Indians had pushed out one of the larger trucks, and were moving it steadily towards the longhouse. A large group of the warriors were taking cover behind it.

There wasn't even a driver in the cab.

From its side and the back of the truck, the attackers were pouring a steady stream of fire straight through the open door of the longhouse.

'Where's the sense there?' he wondered. 'They could blow up all the ammo packed in crates in there, which is what they desperately need'.

Perhaps logic had gone out of the situation.

He had seen it often. Young Rupert's (Officers), conditioned by theoretical training tactics, quite often froze when confronted with real action, and forgot everything.

He fired two grenades in quick succession, one catching the truck on the right front wheel, slewing it sideways. The other grenade flew off harmlessly into the woods.

One of the attackers raced round the side of the vehicle and jumped into the cab, grabbed the steering wheel, and despite the mangled wheel, the survivors continued to shove the vehicle forward.

Danny took direct aim and his next grenade appeared to go straight through the cab window, followed by a massive explosion.

A number of the attackers were blown to pieces.

Some who survived clambered dazedly to their feet.

Two others were looking back towards where the grenades had come from.

One of them pointed directly at Danny's position.

Shit, he thought, so much for protecting the incoming helicopters.

He'd be lucky to be alive.

He started picking them off coolly, one at a time as a small group raced towards the meeting hall.

Three of them made it around the side of the building, and moments later he could hear them directly below him.

He grabbed a grenade, pulled the pin, and lobbed it down.

The explosion that followed seemed louder than ever and the roof lurched down about three feet.

The grenade launcher slid off out of sight.

He still had his rifle and some spare clips of ammunition, plus four grenades left in the satchel…. and his pistol. He readjusted his footing and got his balance, wondering how the group were doing in the longhouse.

Meanwhile, the group inside was in trouble and they knew it.

With a burning vehicle blocking their entrance, and flames now licking up the side of the building, they were running out of options. They had heard the explosions at the back and assumed that Danny was somehow involved.

Moments after the second explosion at their rear, a series of shots sounded from behind, and three of the prisoners were hurled aside.

"Jesus, they've got in through the back somehow!" Bob gasped. "We have to stop them or we're finished."

He grabbed two of the prisoner group and started running back into the building.

Another prisoner fell from the rooftop and landed with a thump in front of them. The inside invaders had spotted them and were zeroing in on them.

Bob gestured and pointed to the stacks of crates off to one side.

They nodded and followed him as he scrambled up and started inching his way over the top, towards the back door.

The attackers had the same idea.

In front of him he spotted two figures lying prone, concentrating their fire on the rooftop. Bob and the two Indians with him dropped to their knees and raked them with bullets. He gritted his teeth, hoping there wasn't ammunition or explosive material in the crates underneath them.

As he got to his feet the two prisoners raced past him and leapt off the top of the crates onto a group of attackers below.

Bob braced himself on the edge of the boxes, trying to distinguish his people from the attackers. He managed to clearly get two shots in, then a few moments later, the scuffle ended below.

Scrambling down he helped his two ex-prisoners to their feet, now covered in blood.

"My God are you guys okay?" he gasped.

One of them grinned. "It's not our blood you see. We never felt better!"

Bob shook his head in amazement and then hurriedly looked around for something to plug the hole in the back wall.

As he stood there debating it, a face appeared in the gap and a rifle barrel was thrust through.

One of the Indians moved his arm like lightning, and a knife embedded itself in the attacker's forehead, sending him back out of sight.

"Quickly," Bob shouted. "Let's jam some of these crates in the hole and you two stay here and make sure no one else tries to break in."

He handed them some spare ammo clips, and in a few moments they had erected a passable barrier that might slow down any more attackers who tried to make entry.

He wasn't kidding himself.

Black Cloud had dozens of fighters who would just keep coming, and it was just a matter of time until they started using their superior numbers.

He raced back to the front of the building.

Danny in the meantime was bracing himself for more people coming at him when the cell phone beeped again.

"Yeah?" he shouted, knowing that Zeitner was on the other end.

"The choppers are incoming in five minutes and want you to be ready for them. What's the situation on the ground Danny?"

"Getting sticky as we speak. A truck is stuck in the center of the square but you could still get two choppers in. There's a firing range two hundred yards behind the main block of buildings. The other choppers could land there but they might run into some solid opposition as I think the firing range has the only supply of ammo left. Our group are still holding the longhouse but they may have to make a break out of it in the next few minutes as I mentioned, there's a vehicle burning in the doorway and the building's now caught fire.

Tell your guys to watch out for them. The good news is that the attackers haven't got their hands on that material inside. I'm on the top of a medium sized log meeting house, just off the square. Your guys are obviously coming in from the south so I'm directly north of the square. Remember I'm wearing a white armband. I'll be trying to neutralize any opposition that comes after the landing teams."

"Roger that Danny...over and out."

He smiled. Zeitner was falling back on some of the military jargon he's used when he was with Force Recon, the Marine Corps Special Forces. He'd confided that information to Danny when they met recently in New York State.

Then the familiar sound of incoming choppers came to him.

God, how many times had he been crouched behind the girth of a tree or hugging the ground, when that sound made him almost sob with relief. Especially, if he was holding a fellow trooper who had suffered a life-threatening wound.

Then the helicopters were over the top of the square and starting to drop down.

A fusillade of fire started coming up at them from the attackers on the ground, now surging through from the firing range direction.

Danny started firing, using full automatic, and taking aim at the leaders out front. He could hear the group in the longhouse opening up too. Then the heavy 50 calibers started stuttering from the choppers, cutting a swathe through the Indians, who kept coming.

The rifle clicked on empty and he grabbed another clip and shoved it in, jacking a shell back in the breech and continued firing.

Other choppers shot overhead. He could hear them landing further out and the heavy sound of their weapons bearing down on the opposing forces.

He continued firing, switching to bursts of three, and focusing on small groups of Black Cloud's people as they concentrated on the choppers.

Just as one of the choppers was ten feet from the ground, it was caught by a heavy burst of machine gun fire and burst into flames.

As it crashed, dozens of men leapt to safety from its buckled door and tried to scramble away. Some of them were caught in a fierce deluge of weapons fire and bodies started piling up.

Danny switched back to full automatic and started hosing down along the side of the square, where the attackers were crouched.

The second chopper landed with a thump just twenty feet away and the heavy machine guns swept along the edge of the square. Immediately the soldiers inside jumped out and ran into the square dropping down and covering the remaining soldiers as they dived out.

The next ten minutes, was a steady firefight as the disembarking soldiers, made their way forward, inch by inch, taking casualties, but pushing forward.

A group of at least twenty of Black Cloud's people came racing directly at the landing party screaming 'Allah Akbar'.

The major lying on the ground, blinked in astonishment.

"Hell, I thought we'd left all this shit back in Iraq."

Then he lifted his weapon and started blasting into the attackers.

Danny had used up his last clip of ammo.

He was reluctant to climb down in the middle of an intense firefight and possibly get cut to pieces.

As the firing died down out front, he heard a slight scuffle off to his left.

Grabbing the edge of the opening he tried to jump down and reduce himself as a target, but caught a blow on his right shoulder.

A hit! He'd taken a hit! God, he thought he was protected! Perhaps he was being reminded of his mortality.

He was now hanging on with one hand to the edge of the opening, when a face appeared above.

Danny stared mesmerized.

It was the twin, standing there grinning.

How had he climbed the meetinghouse with a broken arm? Perhaps hate had driven him. He'd never know.

The twin placed his boot forward, almost playfully, on Danny's hand. The one holding him up.

"I know I kill you one day. Tell me now before die...you kill Striking Hawk my brother?"

Danny stared back up into the hate-filled face and nodded. "Yes, I killed the rotten bastard...and now...I want you to join him!"

He fired the pistol that he had managed to pull from his belt, straight into the heart of the Pakistani above him, sending him flying back down from the top of the building.

Danny managed to crawl back out onto the roof and sat there with his head bowed.

There was only sporadic firing out front now, but back towards the firing range there was an intense battle still going on.

Suddenly a voice came from below, down inside the meeting hall, and a torch shone on him.

He looked down.

A Marine Major stood there with a group of fellow Marines beside him.

"You must be Danny Quigley, on top of a meeting house and wearing a white armband. We owe you a lot Quigley. Our casualties would have been enormous without your guidance and help. Let's get you down from there my friend."

Danny gestured. "The people in the longhouse?"

"They're safe, don't worry. It's them who are worried about you. One of your friends, Bob I think, had spotted you on top of the building and we also got your briefing from that CIA guy about your location."

The next ten minutes were taken up with getting him off the roof from the outside, with the help of two of the Marines.

One of them, a medic, slapped a compression bandage on his shoulder.

"You were lucky Quigley. Just a flesh wound. Any deeper and you would have had muscle damage. If you were in Afghanistan it might be your ticket home buddy."

The Major drifted over.

"The fighting at the firing range is almost wrapped up."

Danny stared. "But there were at least a hundred of them."

The Major nodded. "We were cutting them down like ninepins, and they were giving a good account of themselves. We suspect they ran out of ammunition, thanks to your guys holding that longhouse. They just upped and ran into that dammed forest. God knows where they are. We're going to let the Canadian Special Forces go in after them. They probably know those damn woods better than we do."

Just then, Pat, Bob and C.C. ran up and all gathered round, slamming him on the back and shoulders.

He winced as Bob grabbed his hand. "Danny, my boy, we fucking did it! Wait till I rejoin my unit and tell them I fought with the famous Danny Quigley!"

The Major stared. "You're Danny Quigley? Shit, you got a decoration from us for that work you did with a Delta Team in Afghanistan and fighting your way back out of the mountains."

He turned to a bunch of Marines. "This guy killed over a hundred and sixty Taliban and Al Qaeda in Afghanistan in about seven days. The fucking Israelis use his experiences in their escape and evasion training and for their Special Forces. So do the Brits!"

The Marines gathered round, staring at him.

It was the medic who said it all.

"Jesus, you're a dammed civvy now and you can still do all this shit!"

The Major put his arm around his shoulders...gently.

"Quigley, we have instruction to get you and your group down to Vancouver a.s.a.p. As you know we have about fifty terrorists who have slipped across the border and represent a real threat to the security of the U.S. We need to debrief your crew and get all the information we can out of you. That CIA guy Zeitner will be there to meet you when we arrive, so let's go. We have a chopper already for you and your group."

Danny struggled out of his grasp. "Wait a minute! We have other people in our group who aren't here."

The Major nodded. "Yes, we know about them and the sick prisoners. Your friend C.C. Courtney has volunteered to stay behind and lead us to them. Don't worry; we'll take good care of them. There are all sorts of support on the way, medical and otherwise. This mess will take a long time to sort out. You've done more than your share, believe me. Come on let's go."

In a short time they were on a chopper heading south.

# Chapter 45

When Danny arrived at his hotel in Vancouver, one of his first tasks was to telephone his ex wife Fiona and let her know that he was okay and that they had found C.C., who was now returning to the U.K. He enquired about his daughter Allison too but when Fiona asked him when he would be coming home, he was unable to answer because of the upcoming debriefing.

The de-briefing took three days.

It was held at the CSIS office where Danny had met the agent Leroy Heseltine, on his first trip into the city.

Already present were representatives from the FBI, Homeland Security, The National Security Agency, U.S. Defense Department, RCMP and Canadian Forces.

A tight security blanket had been thrown around the whole incident in the interim, to avoid warning terrorists who had slipped across the border. A dozen of them had already been stopped, and an alert had gone out to all police forces.

The media with their contacts were already sniffing around.

On the second day, C.C., Siobhan, Little Bear and Little Dove arrived and filled them in on the state of the ex-prisoners.

The four of them were hustled into separate de-briefings.

Danny was wearing a sling on his arm but mainly to help the stitches heal up. His only problem was trying to sleep on one side, though showering was tricky as well.

Finally Bret Zeitner pulled him, and his four colleagues, C.C., Pat, Bob and Siobhan, off into a separate room.

He didn't waste any time.

After they were all seated, he looked around the room.

"Now, it may take months to get the whole story on this incident, so anything I say in here is strictly confidential. It has to stay here, for a number of reasons. One is that an ally of the west, Pakistan, and particularly the United States, has initiated what amounts to an act of war, a planned and deadly attack on our country. Was it initiated by the Pakistan Government, or the hydra-headed Security Intelligence Service over there? Certainly a huge rift has opened up in the relationship between them and the U.S. over this. Will our President and Congress take this as a declaration of war and reciprocate in kind? Not my job to say…thank God! From the information we have culled from you guys, and the Canadian Government, it looks like the following happened;

Agents from Pakistan had infiltrated the North West of British Colombia and had probably selected this area from information passed on by those people running drugs into this part of the country.

They ran into extraordinary luck when it struck them that a certain First Nations tribe, looked uncannily like certain groups of Pakistanis - those with thin refined faces. Equally, they discovered that certain tribes still harbored great bitterness and hostility towards the white man, particularly directed at the United States. Somehow, they came across Black Cloud and the plan started to evolve. The next step was when a Liberian-flagged cargo ship came into that new port you Canadians had built up there.

It unloaded containers, ostensibly bringing in mining equipment for the First Nations on their newly acquired territory. Now whether the Canadian Customs were under-manned or didn't have the necessary x-ray equipment, we don't know yet. What we do know is that a regular flow of containers were brought in and transported off into First Nations territory. Oh sure, they did a good job disguising the stuff coming in, so the Customs people never found the hidden compartments where men, weapons and explosives were hidden. The Canadian Government was of course delighted with the new initiatives. Their investment in a new port was off to a revenue-rich start. What they didn't realize was that they had allowed a Trojan horse to land on their shores."

C.C. cut in. "So Black Cloud carefully selected people, real First Nations people, who started slipping into the camp and spreading sedition. Particularly with the young people, who were disgusted with years of false promises from governments about land rights and honoring treaties. When the time was right, he struck, with his trained Pakistani soldiers, who quickly rounded up those who didn't go along with their ideas and locked them up in a stockade, and I, an ignorant Brit, hadn't a clue what was going on all around me!

God, I must have been totally blinded by my vision of the utopia I thought I had created!"

Pat put her arm around him. "Hey look, don't be too hard on yourself...you weren't to know C.C., and you know what? You somehow got healed of your cancer in the meantime."

He nodded gloomily. "Yeah, but I should have known something wasn't right."

Zeitner looked around the room. "Whatever, probably because of you C.C., with the call to Danny in the U.K. sent by you under pressure from Black Cloud, the plan has fallen apart. Now we and the Canadian Government have one huge mess to clean up."

"What will happen to the First Nations up there?" Pat asked anxiously.

He shrugged. "I've no idea Pat. It's up to the Canadian Government to sort that one out I'm afraid. All I can say is that we have a bunch of starved Indians who were locked up because they didn't want to go along with that heinous plan. That must stand to them. Little Bear has given them the early events of the way the tribe was seduced, including himself, and I think he and his tribe will come out of this okay."

"I sure hope so," she whispered. "They're mostly good people."

"What's happening with the Pakistanis who ran off into the woods?" Bob asked.

"Being picked up in droves, starving and out of ammo. Your Special Forces were mightily disappointed. They'd been told that these were suicide bombers and wouldn't go down without a fight. Their leaders are already singing like canaries, some of them demanding political asylum in Canada. Can you believe that? Oh, by the way Bob, you were posted as AWOL by your unit, so we sorted that out for you as well."

The question and answer session went on for some time until finally Zeitner called a halt, and had them bussed off to a downtown hotel where a block of rooms had been reserved for them. Before they left the briefing room Zeitner pulled Danny off to one side.

"Little Dove is back at your hotel. Your friend in London, at MI5, Rebecca Fullerton, volunteered her sister, Ann, I believe is her name, to come across and babysit her. She's never been in a big city before. Apparently Ann was glad to have an excuse to skip class for a few days. A call from Leroy at CSIS did wonders. Oh, Rebecca, heard rumors, that you were giving back the insurance brokerage to C.C. She wants you to call her."

The group found them both in the restaurant with Little Dove, mesmerized by a huge menu and Ann Fullerton, hugely enjoying the experience.

They both jumped up when the group streamed in and there were hugs all round.

Little Dove held on to Danny, gently touching the arm that was in a sling.

"Are you okay Danny?" she asked.

He shrugged. "Just a scratch."

Strangely, it was the first real wound he had ever received in combat, and despite himself, he was pleased with her expression of concern.

Ann laughed. "Why am I not surprised that it's Danny Quigley who ends up getting shot. The stories my sister in London told me about you...."

Danny couldn't get away fast enough, dreading that she would bring up a litany of his past escapades, so on pretense, he caught Little Dove by the arm and hustled her out into the foyer.

She looked disconcerted. "What's wrong Danny?" she asked.

He breathed a sigh of relief and fudged the first reply that came to him.

"Just wanted to know how you are Little Dove...you know, swept up in a helicopter and before you know it, you're in a massive city, without all you've grown up with, the woods, quiet water, and so on."

She smiled. "Thank you Danny, but you needn't be concerned. Vancouver is a beautiful city and I want to see all of it, while I'm here. Ann is going to show me around for the next few days, and then I'll have to decide what to do for myself."

"What will you do Little Dove? I mean the quiet little village back up there will never be the same again. I hate to say it, but it will now be run by bureaucrats from the Government, who will think they know what's best for all of you."

"Yes, I know Danny, but my place is there as we go forward to a new life from this evil. My people need me there. Can you understand that?"

He nodded, giving her a long hug.

She smiled happily.

"You mustn't worry about me Danny. Little Bear is going to marry me."

"Little Bear! Does he know it yet?" he almost demanded.

Still smiling prettily, she replied. "Not yet he doesn't...but he will."

He stood looking at her for a long time and then folded her in his arms.

"I had one of the most incredible experiences of my life with you Little Dove" he whispered" and I will always remember you, always!"

She smiled and stood back, looking at him for a long time, then turned and walked back into the restaurant. He felt a physical wrench inside.

He knew he had said goodbye to something pure and precious.

He couldn't face the people inside right then.

Walking over he hit the elevator button and rode up to the 10th floor, still feeling sense of loss.

Opening the bedroom door, he walked straight to the balcony, opened the door, and stepped out. The fresh air felt terrific as he gazed at the incredible panorama of the city spread out below.

It sure was beautiful.

The phone rang inside his room.

Probably someone from downstairs looking for him.

He shrugged. Right then he just wanted to let the fresh air wash over him and cleanse him of the last several days.

Finally he stepped back in the room, grabbed a jacket, his room key, and stepped outside, almost bumping into Pat who was reaching for his doorbell.

She stepped back. "Hey, I was just coming for you Danny. I tried to call you a few minutes ago."

He glanced back at his room. "Ugh... ah.... anything in particular?" he managed to ask, feeling guilty.

She pursed her lips delicately. "Well, it's an old Indian thing really. You know when the warriors return victorious, the happy women would take them into their wigwams and help them celebrate...wind down, if you know what I mean" she said, peering up at him coquettishly, her lips slightly parted.

He stared at her, a smile starting to transform the hard lines on his face.

"That's absolute BS Pat, and you know it. When was the last time you even thought like an Indian and all that stuff?"

She grinned impishly. "It may be BS Danny, but right now, I can tell you like it"

She caught his arm.

"Come on my big chief let's go to my wigwam and I'll help you celebrate."

They walked off down the hall together.

It was a short walk.

At 8am the telephone rang in Danny's room, which he had returned to, in the small hours of the morning.

It was Bret Zeitner.

"Danny, we need to meet as soon as possible. How about I buy you breakfast?"

He was outside the hotel a half hour later, having showered, changed and given Pat a brief call to cancel their pre-arranged breakfast together.

Bret was already waiting in a taxi in the front seat and waved to him.

He jumped in.

As the vehicle sped off, the CIA agent reached back and shook his hand.

"Congratulations again Danny. What you pulled off.... just amazing! Talk to you more over breakfast."

It was some little nook that had the most incredible breakfast buffet that he had ever come across.

When he was finally sated, he sat back grinning.

"You know Bret, I can't help thinking of my mate, ah, buddy, Scotty McGregor, right now. We used to love our breakfasts, and when we came back to Hereford after an operation, we would go down town and have the most enormous breakfast that was on the menu. Probably our way of winding down."

Bret looked at him closely. "You miss it, don't you?" he prompted.

"I suppose that's what's coming across Bret, but you know, I couldn't hack the army life any more and I know it."

Zeitner chuckled. "Could have fooled me Danny, after that de-briefing. Someone, back down the line referred to you as 'a walking killing machine.' It might have been your MI5 friend Rebecca, who was quoting your old Commanding Officer back in the regiment.

They weren't kidding. You may say you couldn't hack it anymore, but the facts say otherwise. Your group would not have survived, back up in the woods, and down here, the U.S. would be knee deep in another terrible catastrophe. So thanks again."

Danny shrugged. "Whatever...you do what you have to do don't you? You've been there Bret, when you were in Force Recon in Vietnam. I bet if the chips were down, the old warrior would somehow come alive again and you could kick ass with the best of them. Some skills are like muscle memory and they jump back into your nerve ends."

Bret smiled. "I'd like to think so my friend. I actually hope I never have to test your theory. Hey, you should see the training that the Seals, Delta and the Green Berets get now. Miles ahead of what we got before they dumped us in the jungle over there. Anyway...." he finished lamely.

"You didn't just want to shoot the shit Bret. What's this all about?"

Zeitner made a face.

"On target again Danny. Look two things: one, I'm in the dog house with Langley right now for La Fonte's little incursion into Canada, and his attempt to murder you. Okay, I got caught on the edge but tried to redeem myself by warning you, however I'm still in the doghouse and on suspension, at least, until we get a copy of Rebecca's e-mails, which I sent her anonymously. Oh and our agency need to have a face-to-face with you in Washington."

"Oh God! I was hoping to head back to London tomorrow Bret. What about a Skype interview?"

He laughed. "I'm afraid not Danny. Langley has seen it all, and it's too easy to have a Skype interview, where someone with a weapon is standing out of sight and telling you what to do. No, they want to talk to you in person."

"Why Washington and not that big CIA headquarters out in Virginia."

Bret sighed. "Seeing me back there right now would start too many rumors. My reputation may be rehabilitated when this crisis blows over and I can be touted as someone who was undercover, if you like, and in some small way, led to its eventual exposure. You and I know of course Danny, that I played a very small part and almost got you killed in Canada."

Danny leaned forward. "Well, if it hadn't been for your speedy reactions at the end there my friend, we would have all been wiped out. So Bret, if you can play it that way, and save yourself and your career, that's fine by me."

"Thanks Danny, I appreciate that."

"You said two things, that you wanted to talk to me about Bret."

"I know of Pierre La Fonte's reputation and I have to tell you, he won't give up on you. That contract I would imagine is still on the table and he needs that money more than ever now that the DEA has tossed him out over this fracas. He might just want to even the score with you for screwing up the comfortable deal he had down on the Mexican border. That bastard is like a rabid wolf Danny!"

"Pardon me for saying this, but I haven't done anything to the guy. He came after me and sure, I shot up one of his choppers and killed three of his team. Apart from that I never even heard of him before he choppered in and hogtied our group, with the intention of murdering us."

Bret grimaced. "You have to factor in the twisted mindset of La Fonte. Because of you, he's in deep trouble and someone has to pay. I'm very much afraid you're it my friend. I hope I'm wrong, but I very much doubt it."

Danny raised his hands in defeat. "Okay, this is your stomping ground Bret. Now, what about the so called faceless people behind this, can they not be identified and warned off, now that La Fonte is a wanted man and may attract attention to them. If he's caught, he might sing like a canary and drop them in it?"

"If only it were that simple. Where did it originate from and by whom? We may never know. You killed the only one from our organization in Buffalo, some time ago, which was involved. The plan was to smuggle a nuclear bomb into Iraq and undermine any possible charges in the International Criminal Court, against certain people in the previous administration."

"Yeah, I recall there was some concern that Saddam's daughter would bring a case against them for killing her father and brothers in a war that many now say was illegal from the start. I mean, nothing's come of that, to date, as I understand it. Probably a rumor to begin with."

"These people spend twenty four hours a day protecting their so-called legacy. They're downright paranoid and remember, you were the guy who actually saw the nuke in the desert and led the Israelis to it. The Israelis won't talk, that's for sure.

By the way, La Fonte will never be taken alive. He wouldn't last ten minutes inside a jail cell, and he knows it."

Danny sat there shaking his head, a resigned look on his face.

"So where do we go from here? You didn't invite me here to tell me that it's only a matter of time before this bastard gets to me. You must have some sort of plan Bret, surely."

"Well, you're right Danny. We want this animal out of the game permanently. He's too dangerous to leave skulking around, and to be honest; the DEA knows that he can point to where too many bodies are buried. You better believe it. They want him out of the way as well. Okay, you won't like this...you know what a tethered goat is?"

He blinked. "Sure, any big game hunter would know that. You tether a helpless animal out there in a location where the big boys feed at night, and when they take the bait, the hunter takes them out. I gather I'm supposed to be the goat that will attract La Fonte to come and get me, and supposedly you and your vast organization, scoop him up. Am I right?"

"When you put it like that, well yes, but......"

"What other way is there to put it Bret?"

"Look Danny, with the vast resources of our organization, technical back-up that you couldn't even dream of, La Fonte wouldn't get within a mile of you before we scooped him up. I can guarantee you that your life wouldn't ever be in danger. I Guarantee it."

Danny's face registered some reservations. "Bret, you're talking to someone who's been there. I've seen the most elaborate plans go tits-up in a so-called sanitized locations, and you know very well that where there are people involved, human error can interfere, sometimes with devastating consequences... okay, tell me how you see this playing out."

"Quite simply, we get you set up in a tempting location that will attract La Fonte, and drop the word out in the street as to where you are. If he has his nose to the ground, he'll be on it like a buck in the rutting season."

"Hmm…. not sure I like your analogy, but anyway, I gather you have a place in mind?" Danny asked.

The CIA man hesitated. "Well yes, but you're not going to like this part."

"Quite frankly, I don't like any of it, so just spit it out Zeitner!" he demanded.

"The farm in South West New York State, where you stayed some time ago. We've scouted out the area and it's perfect."

Danny's face blanched. He stood up defiantly.

"You must be kidding! Bring all this crap down on top of Dianna, who has a teenage kid and a disabled sister… come on… no way MISTER Zeitner, just no fucking way!"

He turned to walk off.

The CIA man stood up and caught his arm.

"We already talked to her Danny. She said yes."

# Chapter 46

Danny's mind was in a complete whirl during the rest of the morning as he said goodbye to the various people in his group. A group which had come through so much together over the past number of days.

He was glad it happened so fast with the CIA man's vehicle waiting to whisk him off to the airport and on to Washington.

He had agreed to meet up with C.C. back in London the following week, to discuss the changeover of the business, hoping the La Fonte situation would be settled by then.

There was no opportunity to see Pat or Siobhan who had gone shopping with Ann, but left a farewell message for them with C.C.

Then it was on to Washington, but there was now a growing anger in Danny's heart about the arrangement, involving the farm being used as a trap for La Fonte.

He used the business class flight to go over the plan. Planning was one of the CIA's strong points and he grudgingly had to admit that they appeared to have thought of everything.

Still......

There was no social chitchat with Zeitner on the flight.

They broke for meals and then continued working on the details of the plan.

Then there was Washington.

This consisted of a number of meetings and de-briefings. Not just clearing Zeitner's name, but addressing the various agency's concerns about the Pakistani/Indian terrorists, now on U.S. soil.

These were an imminent threat to the United States, and they continued to pump him for further details. Details he had already given a number of times, back in Vancouver.

It seemed to go on forever.

Finally, he was off the hook and Zeitner arranged for an agency car to take him back to the airport.

His flight to Buffalo was already booked...first class.

He smiled crookedly.

When one is travelling to be staked out at the end of the trip, it was nice to travel in style.

Danny didn't know what sort of reception he would get at the farm. He'd left there several weeks ago after carrying out an action against a sinister world-wide company, Empire Security, based in Buffalo, in which several people were killed and a building blown up. He had been helped considerably in this action by Dianna Rayburn and Rory Hanlon, an ex Delta Force member.

All of them managed to leave the scene without being detected, and in Danny's case, making it back safely to the U.K.

He needn't have worried.

He was met at the airport in the late afternoon by Dianna, her sister Jennifer, and her son Kieran. He felt like a long lost prodigal son returning after a lengthy absence.

Finally when he extracted himself from the hugs and slaps on the back, he climbed into the vehicle for the hour's drive south to the farm. When they got there it was hugs all round again.

"Hey guys, I just left here several weeks ago! If I'd known you felt that way, I'd have come back sooner!" he said smiling.

They all crowded around, sitting on various chairs in the kitchen.

It was Dianna who put it into perspective for him.

"Danny, when you got here some time ago, Kieran had just been beaten up at school. You gave him some training and he whipped that bully's ass all round the schoolyard. In fact the family has since left the area. Jennifer had lost her voice as a result of a terrible tragedy in her youth and she started talking again, thanks, I believe to your intervention with Kieran. As for me. Well, I'll tell you more about that later, but suffice to say, you made me realize that I had buried myself here for the past three years, and that had to end. So... enough said?"

"Enough said? Well yes and no." He looked around the table. "Do Jennifer and Kieran know the real reason I'm here? If they don't, I believe they should" he said quietly.

Jennifer and Kieran looked at her.

"I broad-stroked the situation for them, and basically we all feel that we owe you a lot

Danny, and we want to be there for you. I understand you could be in considerable danger right now, so we wouldn't turn our backs on you at this point. I must confess, you'll have to fill us in on the total situation, when you've settled in. One quick question though. Are we in danger right at this minute?"

He shook his head. "No Zeitner's given me two days to scout the area, which they've already checked out, and make my own judgment about their plan. Then he drops the word in the street and we need to be on our toes from that moment on. I have to get you guys up to speed as to what could happen and what our options are."

Kieran grabbed his arm. "Are you going to show me some more stuff Danny? You know, how to disable people and that."

He laughed. "Nothing quite like that Kieran, though I might work with you on something else." He threw a quick look at the boy's mother. "I'll have to clear it with your Mom first though."

Dianna threw a suspicious look across at him. "Hey, I don't like the sound of this! If my son spends any more time in your company, he'll turn into a flipping assassin."

Danny thought he'd better put a stop to where the conversation was heading.

He slapped the table.

"Who'd like to go out for a bang up meal?" he asked.

It was hands up all round, including Dianna, who leaned forward and whispered "and the condemned man ate a healthy meal" raising her eyebrows.

He grinned, saying nothing.

They travelled for forty minutes before arriving at what they all claimed was their favorite eating place. Not a chain as he had expected at first, but an old world chateau, with an attached vineyard, where Dianna came to for occasional wine tastings.

The menu was extensive and really top end. Dianna apologized when they opened the menus and he saw the prices.

"Sorry Danny, but they just love the burgers here and the deserts are to die for."

Prices were the last thing in his mind right then. Seeing the family so energized and happy was reward enough for the moment.

Kieran settled for a root beer and the house burger, with fries and a salad, while Jennifer ordered a smaller burger and a salad and joined both her sister and Danny in a glass of the vineyards house wine.

Danny and Dianna went for the spare ribs, which looked delicious, roast potatoes and vegetables.

When the wine came they all sat back.

Danny picked up his glass and raised it. "To the Rayburn family, I salute you and wish you well."

They all drank to that including Kieran who raised his root beer and clanked their glasses.

For the first time, since he'd flown into Canada, several weeks ago, he felt himself relaxing down. There was closure on certain parts of his experiences, which helped; finding C.C. for example, but for the moment, he parked the challenges ahead.

Dianna looked over her glass at him.

"I know you don't want to fill us in right now on what's happening, but can you tell us what you've been involved in for the past while? Zeitner wouldn't tell me anything. Just muttered something about national security, and 'ask Quigley' when he gets there."

'What the hell' Danny thought. Perhaps in the telling, it might take some of the knots from his gut. In a way, it led into the present situation, so he led them through an abbreviated version, warning Kieran to avoid talking about it in school, due to the fact that there was still a news embargo on the full story.

The food came halfway through, so he halted the story and concentrated on the ribs.

He lifted his face, and looked across at Dianna.

"You weren't kidding, these are absolutely amazing!" he exclaimed.

She grunted in reply her face smeared with gravy from the ribs. "Yeah, to die for!" Then realizing what she'd said, she rolled her eyes. "Sorry! Wrong analogy right now."

When they'd finished they just sat back and started on a second glass of wine.

Jennifer raised her glass. "I drink...Danny" she said with a great effort.

He shook his head. "Oh man, you are coming on Jennifer! Way to go!" he said leaning forward and tapping her shoulder.

Dianna looked pleased. "Yeah, she's doing terrific. We're going to get a speech therapist to work with her shortly, so that should bring her on much faster. But yeah, it's a miracle Danny, thanks to you. Now, while these two eat deserts, how about filling me in on the rest of your exploits. I must say it sounds like something out of Hollywood, but then I know what you're capable of don't I?"

He noticed the glint in her eye and wondered if there was a hidden meaning in what she had just said.

They did have some history together after all!

He continued with his story, leaving little out until he came full circle.

Then he stopped and she was silent for a while.

Kieran and Jennifer, assuming they had heard it all, decided to go into a small room and play video games

Finally Dianna she stirred.

"You know, if Zeitner had told me the full story, despite the way I feel about you Danny, wanting to help you and so on, I may very well have said 'No', to him. Inviting a monster like La Fonte into our lives could be the most stupid mistake I've ever made."

He nodded gravely. "It's still not too late Dianna."

"No I wouldn't do that to you. But knowing Zeitner and his ilk, he would just drop the word out there anyway, if I called him tomorrow and told him I was cancelling out. It's all about the game Danny. The plots they weave, entangling other people's lives and generally messing them up. That's why I got out of the agency. You need to be very careful you don't get sucked into his maneuvers, and end up a scapegoat somehow."

"He explained that bit to me already. I was the tethered goat."

"All I'm saying is, keep a few cards up your sleeve. These guys operate in a sleazy world all their own. You know with the Patriot Act, they made thirty thousand phone taps on private citizens last year without having to go to a single judge for permission. This is a different world we live in now and I'm telling you, cover your ass on this one."

"But it's the FBI who will be covering this one. Zeitner will only be acting in an advisory capacity. Surely I don't need to try to second-guess the Feds?"

She looked him hard in the face. "My advice still goes Danny. Watch your back is all I'm saying."

As if in unison, they dropped the topic and spent the rest of the evening with small talk until Kieran and Jennifer returned, their eyes sparkling.

In good spirits they bundled into the car and headed back to the farm.

The following morning Dianna had a commitment in the city of Erie and Kieran was picked up early by the yellow school bus. Danny and Jennifer lingered over the breakfast table and he enjoyed some small talk, which she struggled through.

Then she headed out to do her chores with the animals, leaving Danny to pore over some maps supplied by Zeitner. He intended to walk around the four squares of the property

He could see immediately why the property would appeal to the CIA agent.

It was a corner site at a crossroads. The pastures behind the farm provided a clear area for helicopters to land, in an emergency; or after La Fonte was captured. Behind the pastures was a rising wooded area, which he discovered later, led up to another cleared pasture, a half mile further up, which, though further away, provided a secondary site for helicopters to land.

The farm itself was situated fifty yards back from the main road, and the building ran parallel to it. There was a small shallow creek between the road and the farmhouse. Across the main road, there were two houses, which he understood were owned by Amish families, running a logging business and a small livestock farm.

A gravel road ran past the side of the farmhouse and directly across this road, was a section of swampy land, where some Amish families lived.

He put a jacket on and started doing a recce of the different sections, which Zeitner had marked for him.

La Fonte had come in by helicopter in his attack on their group in Canada. The only possible close landing site for an attack, was in the pasture behind the large barn. The noise of any landing would, of course, alert the farm inhabitants. The FBI team planned to place two snipers up on a platform in the barn, which had hay bales in it at present. They would cut out some sections of the wooden wall to provide a field of fire, if La Fonte tried to come in that way.

Danny took forty minutes to work his way back up through the thick woods to the higher pastures, which the Feds had marked as a secondary landing site. It could equally provide La Fonte a place to land in a chopper, without alarming anyone in the farmhouse, and make his way down through the woods to the farm.

The thickness of the brush and trees though, would make it difficult to traverse down through the woods at nighttime.

If Danny was preparing to neutralize the attack himself, he would have placed some booby traps in various places through the patch of woods, but he couldn't risk it with the Feds involvement and local hunters moving through.

As it was, the Feds were planning to have a small team placed on the fringe of the upper pasture, back out of sight in the woods.

So, the lower and upper pastures were well covered, and if La Fonte came in either way, he would attract some powerful firepower.

Rather than returning through the woods he went out onto the gravel road, where a left turn would bring him back down to the farm.

He started walking, and made some notes of vehicle tracks leading off into the woods on his left. The tracks looked like they were possibly made by tractor-trailers, hauling lumber out. He investigated further and discovered a pile of cut logs further in. Looking down through the tree branches from there, he could clearly make out the side of the farmhouse. It was quite close.

Hmm... Checking Zeitner's plan document, he could see no mention of this section of the woods.

Back out on the gravel road again, he headed down towards the farm and stopped as he came to a small, gravel-covered road cutting off to his right, into the swampy land owned by some Amish families.

He debated whether he should investigate it as well.

Considering the imminence of a possible attack, it made sense to do so.

A hundred yards in, he tensed. Coming towards him was a man or a youth carrying a shotgun over his shoulders. Then he spotted the typical standard dress of the Amish, straw hat and dungarees, and relaxed, until, the two dogs with the man raced towards him.

Danny had a great respect for dogs.

Soldiers in enemy territory went in dread of such an encounter, which could rob them of any element of surprise. He'd seen some savage injuries from dog bites and even worse, was the risk of catching rabies.

However, unlike some people, he wasn't frightened of dogs and his lack of fear generally took the aggression out of the animal.

As he stood there holding his hands out invitingly, the dogs slowed down and eventually came in close, nuzzling him.

The Amish youth came up to him and stopped. He was a stringy lad with a lean spotty face and scraggly hair. His eyes looked pretty alert.

"Not scared of dogs I see" he commented.

Danny wasn't sure what to expect from an Amish person. Did they speak English or some mixture of Pennsylvania Dutch?

He reacted with some surprise. "Oh, yes indeed. Sorry I didn't mean to trespass."

He pointed backwards. "I'm staying with Mrs. Rayburn over there for a few days."

The youth nodded." You're English?"

"Yes.........it shows does it?"

He smiled faintly. "Well, anyone who isn't Amish is referred to by us as English. We like to keep things simple."

"Oh, right. Are you out hunting then?

The youth nodded, patting the gun barrel. "Yep, looking for my buck. I got one more tag to go. Spotted a big one out here yesterday. I wouldn't wander round this area at night, if I were you. Not right now anyway."

Danny wasn't sure if this was a warning or not.

He nodded to the youth and headed back down the small road.

Defensively, what did he make of that?

He wasn't quite sure. The dogs were a bonus for raising the alarm if anyone tried to penetrate the outer defenses of the farm at nighttime, from that direction.

The last site he looked at was the two houses directly across the other side of the main road. The Feds had approached the family with the logging business, for permission to install a team of snipers in the logging shed, but were met with suspicion and a refusal.

Authority always meant bad news for the Amish.

They didn't encourage killing on their land, and police with guns generally meant just that. Still, he strolled past, eyeballing the two buildings and spotting, as the Feds had, that it would have been a great place to slip in a sniper team to provide maximum cover for the farm and the crossroads.

The small creek, of course, ran between the Amish logging business, the main road, and the farm, but it wasn't much of a barrier to a trained assassin.

His last recce took him along the creek for a couple of hundred yards. It ran down to a dirt track, beyond, which was, situated a further smallholding. He discovered later, speaking to Dianna, that the small beehive sized wooden units spread around the slope were for keeping calves in and fattening them for the market.

It would be easy for the sniper team in the barn to cover this end, he thought.

He presumed that the dirt track ran up the far side of Dianna's property, up past the upper pasture, completing the square.

He headed back, just in time to join Jennifer for a large sandwich and hot coffee.

The recce had given him lots to think about.

He would contact Zeitner later to discuss his findings.

However, before his call, he tackled Dianna when she returned home a short time later, about some preparations he was suggesting: giving Jennifer and Kieran some basic lessons in handling and firing a handgun.

As he expected, she didn't react positively at all.

"Look Danny, I'm opening the farm up to a possible incursion by some very bad people as it is, and I'm recognizing already that, in my willingness to help you out, I may have been too quick to go along with Zeitner's proposition. I was and am reassured by the methodical approach to capture or kill this animal La Fonte. The Feds are shit-hot at that kind of work. In theory the CIA has no authority to operate in the United States, however since 9/11 all sorts of interaction has been happening between various law enforcement agencies. Now, the idea that it might come down to Jennifer and/or Kieran, having to get involved, and possibly to fire weapons...no way!"

He was taken aback by the vehemence of her reaction.

"Hey, I was only trying to factor in all the possibilities here Dianna. I didn't realize you felt so strongly about it."

"Look Danny, my son Kieran is still just a kid. Sure you taught him how to look after himself if he gets picked on in school, and I thank you for that, but teaching him to handle weapons at his age? Come on! As for Jennifer, she had a terrible shock as a child, which resulted in her being unable to speak for years, up to several weeks ago. Something like this, firing and handling weapons, could very well reverse that improvement. Can't you see that?"

Danny realized he hadn't thought this through carefully enough, nor was he fully aware of the health implications involved for Jennifer.

"Dianna, sorry.... I didn't consider all the possibilities here. Okay, I was probably carried away by how well they both adapted to the self-defense I worked on with them. Yeah, I can see now where you're coming from. In that context, would it make sense for you to send both of them to a friend's house as of tomorrow? A school friend for Kieran, and one of your acquaintances for Jennifer? In fact perhaps you would be better moving out as well, once Zeitner drops the word in the street tomorrow."

Her eyes flashed angrily. "Kieran and Jennifer, I'll go along with, but there's no way I'm deserting my own home just because some bastard might drop in and try some nasty stuff on us. Forget that my friend. Anyway, you have a short memory. I saved your ass up in Buffalo quite recently, and I may very well have to do it again, so I'm staying put, you hear?"

He lifted his hands.

"No argument here Dianna! And thanks! You are one tough and capable lady and I'd want you on my side in any fracas. I'm convinced that the Zeitner plan, which seems to cover all the bases, will net this bastard, without him getting close enough to harm any of us."

She reached across and touched his hand. "I'm not forgetting how close we got when you were here last Danny. I hope you weren't expecting a repeat performance after we came back from that amazing meal yesterday evening. Seeing Kieran and Jennifer having such fun, and so relaxed, I felt a wave of anxiety about what I was possibly bringing down on them. I know enough about these stakeout situations to be aware that you can never predict, with any certainty, how they can turn out. So, the mood wasn't exactly conducive to going tapping on Danny Quigley's door."

He didn't admit that in fact he had lain awake, wondering if she would pay him a visit, but not for long, as the hectic events of the past week caught up with him and he was out like a light.

They chatted for some time after that and he went over how the Feds were going to cover the various approaches to the farm. He made a passing reference to the young Amish youth he had bumped into.

She laughed. "That would be Jacob from across the way. His family is pretty poor so that deer he's hunting could see them through the winter. We've given them the occasional lift in to the hospital in an emergency, and I got the occasional pie left at the front door afterwards as a gesture of thanks. Those shotguns they use are ancient and highly dangerous, so they have a lot of accidents. That was good advice telling you not to wander round in the dark."

He stood up. "Speaking of which, is it okay to get some of your weapons from that cache up in the barn? When it gets dark I want to go back up to a place in the woods that I spotted earlier, where you had workers pulling logs out. I'd like to leave some stuff there, just for insurance."

"Oh yes, I sold a bunch of timber earlier this year, and they still have some to haul out. What about it? No problem with raiding the weapons cache Danny. Take whatever you want. What's bothering you though?"

He grimaced. "I'm not exactly sure Dianna. It's not on the Feds plan, and I want to check out the view with a night scope from up there. A sniper could possibly use that space to fire straight into the kitchen here. Probably I'm worrying too much, but what the hell..." he gave her a hug which developed into a long kiss.

She finally pulled away.

"Hmm... I could kill that La Fonte myself now. If it wasn't for him we might be spending an interesting afternoon together and scandalize poor Jennifer completely."

He grinned. Things were looking up.

The call to Zeitner was short. He briefly went over the recce that he'd done that morning, and expressed his approval and confidence in what was being planned.

The word would go out on the street tomorrow and the Feds would move their teams in, come darkness, that evening.

He felt a shiver going up and down his spine.

He hoped Zeitner and his colleagues in the FBI had thought of everything.

# Chapter 47

Danny slipped back into the house later in the evening, after scouting around for an hour outside in the darkness that had settled in. Jennifer and Kieran were horsing around as usual, and Dianna's earlier concerns appeared to be gone for the moment.

She glanced across at him, as she placed some soup bowls down in front of everyone.

As she was about to sit down herself, the front door bell rang.

She went over to the window and looked out.

"There's a State Police car outside. What on earth would they want at this time of night? Perhaps they've caught that guy and everything's off," she said hopefully.

There was a second ring on the doorbell accompanied by an impatient knock.

Danny stood up, but Dianna was closest to the door, and reached forward pulling it open.

Two big men stood there in State Police uniforms and the typical wide-brimmed hats, and side arms.

"Yes, Officers..." she started to say, but was taken aback when both policemen crowded past her inside.

One was a raw-boned, blonde-headed man, who was first in, holding an officious looking document in his hands. His colleague, a swarthy, overweight officer, crowded in behind him.

The first Officer looked across at Danny. "We have an arrest warrant for Danny Quigley. I gather you are the person we want. You fit the description. I'd advise you to come quietly and we can sort this out when we get to Headquarters."

Dianna gasped. "Arrest warrant! Whatever for? Danny just got here yesterday and he's...."

The policeman cut her off.

"He's under suspicion for the suspected disappearance of two Federal Agents several weeks ago, possibly murdered by Mister Quigley here."

Danny was taken by surprise.

"Federal Agents...several weeks ago. I haven't a clue what you're talking about Officers!"

But he did.

Zeitner had told him how Steve Walchuk had blackmailed him under threat of tying him to the disappearance of the two Federal Agents.

The question was, how did this filter out to two policemen in New York State.

Zeitner had told him that it was known to very few people.

He walked over to the two Officers and stopped in front of them.

"Officer, do you mind if my attorney takes a look at that warrant you're holding" he said, pointing to Dianna.

The officer held the document closer to his chest, glancing back at his colleague.

"Look, when you get to headquarters, you can make the one call you're allowed to make to your attorney. Our instructions are to bring you in right away on this warrant."

"Officer, is this the Buffalo HQ you're taking him to? Useful to know if I have to go in there and possibly bail him out" Dianne said.

"Ah, yes, that's the one" the blonde one answered.

"Oh, the station chief there is Josh Meadows, isn't he? Nice guy, I'm sure we can sort this out speedily" Dianna commented.

"That would be him Miss" he replied.

She glanced at Danny. "The station chief is Chuck Harrows Danny, not Josh Meadows. I just invented the name."

Things happened suddenly then.

Both 'policemen' jumped sideways, drawing their holstered weapons swiftly. One of them elbowed Dianna to one side sending her sprawling. Jennifer screamed and jumped up from the table, rushing across and helping her sister to her feet. Kieran stood up more carefully and moved across, standing by Dianna, and putting his arm around her, as she was getting up.

Danny recognized the professionalism in the actions of the two who stood to his left and right, covering him.

Despite the rising anger in him, he tried to look calm and relaxed.

"Well, well, here we are then. Can I ask you how you ended up here at the farm? It was supposed to be a secret."

The blonde one smirked. "We had a tail on your friend Zeitner. We thought he might lead us to you. That's the only reason he's still alive, unlike Walchuk. After all, he was sending you e-mails, telling you about our plans. He led us here. It had 'stakeout' written all over it. We thought we'd nip it in the bud."

The swarthy one moved across to the window and glanced out quickly, raising his thumb. Within two minutes there was the sound of vehicles racing past and heading down towards the back pasture.

Blonde chuckled again. "There's an old friend of yours dropping in to see you Quigley. Unfortunately, it will be a short reunion. He should be landing in that back pasture any minute now. He's looking forward to meeting up with you again... claims you screwed up his promising future."

Lights flared up suddenly through the other window, which faced back towards the pasture, to the left of the two policemen.

Blonde glanced sideways. "Ah, the landing lights from the jeeps. Right on time."

The swarthy one's eyes moved in the same direction and Danny moved.

First, a small slide forward with his left foot, followed by his right, which lashed upwards, sending the second 'policeman's' weapon flying up towards the ceiling. Blonde started to turn his weapon towards him.

Danny hadn't stopped moving, he slammed the swarthy cop in the face with his elbow and dived straight past him out the window, to the crashing of glass and a shattered window frame.

Blonde tore over and fired off a series of shots out into the yard. The swarthy cop jumped across the kitchen floor and groped around on the ground until he found his weapon. Then he joined his colleague at the window, firing out into the night. The lights from the pasture didn't reach the back of the house, which was in shadow.

Blonde turned and savagely pounded his weapon on the table, making Jennifer jump.

"Shit, shit, shit!" he mouthed. "That fucking French Canadian will be landing in minutes, thinking we've got Quigley. He's going to be one pissed off half-breed. What the hell do we do now?"

The swarthy one nodded to the two women and Kieran. "He's not going far. He'll be back for these, you betcha. La Fonte has his ways of getting people to do what he wants."

The blonde one's eyes were like gimlets, as he examined the three.

"We would have just put you down with a nice clean bullet to the head, but now I'm afraid you might all have a bigger role to play. Quigley's as good as dead, it's just a matter of time, and you lot will be following him soon after."

Dianna stared back defiantly. "I've seen Danny Quigley in action and I'll tell you something, it would take more than you two phony cops to kill him. It's you two who are as good as dead right now, because, one thing's for sure, he'll be back."

The blonde one went as if to strike her but the unmistakable sound of helicopter blades descending in the back pasture, stopped his fist in mid air.

La Fonte had landed.

Dianna was expecting some Rambo to enter the kitchen when a group of six hard-looking swarthy men, all dressed in black, straggled into the house.

'Mexicans' she thought. 'Probably the jeep drivers and the others who just flew in'.

Her first impression of La Fonte was that he looked like the skinny Indian from the reservation, with long greasy hair, who pumped gas into her car at the tax-free pump further up the highway...until she saw his eyes - like dead sharks.

She realized then that she was in the presence of real evil...the devil incarnate, and shuddered.

La Fonte recognized the fear in her and went across.

He grabbed her by the back of the neck and pulled her close.

"I know you, you're that CIA bitch from some years back...you never lose the stripe, do you?"

He shook her again.

"Hey!" Kieran shouted, moving to help her. Without taking his eyes off Dianna, La Fonte backhanded him viciously with his left hand, sending him crashing across one of the kitchen chairs. Jennifer ran over and crouched down beside him.

La Fonte shook Dianna like she was a small rag doll.

"Not much now without your big CIA organization are you? You were gonna use this crappy farm of yours to set a trap for old

Frenchy. Ha, Ha, big deal! When the Feds get here, there won't be much of the farm left." He looked around. "Or anyone else for that matter. The Feds won't be very happy with old Bret Zeitner, that's for sure."

Kieran sat up and pointed a finger at La Fonte.

"Talk's cheap you moron. You still have to get Danny Quigley. He's out there and he'll kick your ass." He looked around at the men watching "and this bunch of thugs you brought with you. You wait and see" he spat.

"Kieran don't." Dianna said warningly.

La Fonte let her go then strode across to Kieran and hauled him to his feet, almost effortlessly.

"Hmm, a boy with spirit. I like that." He reached forward and almost lovingly stroked his cheek. "If we have some time later I may test that spirit further."

"Oh God no!" Dianna moaned.

La Fonte laughed harshly. "Don't worry bitch, you won't be left out. Some of my men will be only too happy to make your last hour in life a meaningful experience."

Dianna was conscious of a row of dark eyes examining her.

There was no doubt what was in their minds.

She shuddered.

La Fonte turned suddenly and pointed to two of the men.

"Outside you two and check that Quigley isn't creeping around. Keep an eye on that police cruiser. Some of you still need it to get out of here," he snarled.

One man strolled across to the window.

"Hell, I can check from here" he said peering out.

The next moment he was flying backwards into the table, smashing it.

A second later, they heard the sound of a shot.

All eyes were on the man lying in the middle of the broken table.

The blonde one was the first to spot it.

"Jesus, he's shot plumb center in his forehead. Who could shoot like that at night?

Dianna was smiling now, her voice stronger. "That's Quigley out there, and he won't stop until he gets all of you. My advice to you bastards is to get out while you can."

The room suddenly came alive.

"Turn those lights off now!" La Fonte screamed.

The room suddenly went dark and the only sound was weapons being jacked, and people crawling around.

There was a loud explosion from the direction of the road, lighting up the front of the house.

"See what that is!" hissed La Fonte.

There was a scrabbling of feet and one of the men peered cautiously round the window frame.

He pulled back quickly. "The cruiser's just been blown up. It's in flames!"

La Fonte scrambled forward on his knees and grabbed Dianna by the hair, hauling her across to just under the window frame. He pulled an automatic out of an underarm holster and pressed it to her throat.

He knelt forward, with his head close to the open window and screamed.

"Quigley, I got your woman here. I'm going to blow her Goddam head off in ten seconds if you don't throw down whatever weapon you have and come out into plain view. You hear that? I'm starting to count...one...two...three...."

A loud explosion sounded from the direction of the back pasture.

La Fonte stopped counting.

"What the hell was that?" he asked.

Two more explosions came in rapid succession.

Dianna casually moved the weapon away from her neck.

"No good counting La Fonte. He can't hear you... he's obviously gone somewhere else by now."

There was light flickering through the kitchen from the flames of the burning police cruiser, and now fires blazing in the back pasture.

No one moved.

Then everyone jumped when there was pounding on the front door.

One of La Fonte's team sat up and fired through the door.

A loud scream came from the other side.

La Fonte jumped to his feet. "We got him. We got the bastard."

Just then the door slowly opened. A bloodied hand was clinging to the door handle, and a body fell face forward onto the floor.

One of the men leapt across and tipped the body onto his back with his boot.

The men stared.

"Holy shit!" one of them whispered, "It's the pilot."

La Fonte was on his knees in an instant grabbing the wounded pilot and roughly lifting his head off the floor.

"What's happened back there?" he shouted.

There was no answer. He shook him harder. "What the fuck's happened?"

The man's eyes flickered and opened for a moment. "He blew up the chopper... The jeeps as well..."

Then he slid sideways out of La Fonte's hands.

He was dead.

One of the men whispered. "Who the fuck is this guy?"

Dianna laughed back in the room. "He's an ex British Special Forces hardass, and I know for a fact that he's done the U.S. Marine sniper's course. Out there," she pointed, "he's in his element. Oh, you can threaten to kill me all you want, but he won't come in. He's a realist. He knows you're going to kill me anyway, when you're done here."

The blonde one shook his fist at La Fonte. "Just what the hell have you led us into La Fonte? This was supposed to be a cakewalk for Christ's sake!"

La Fonte automatic came up menacingly. "We're all in this together and we've come through worse shit than this. He's only one man after all and you guys are all seasoned vets who have been hunting people for years along the border. Now, get out there and do what you're trained to do. Find Quigley and kill him. Now go!" he snarled.

The men glanced at each other and their fear was turning from anger to determination.

They turned and ducked out of the door, moving fast and keeping low.

La Fonte grabbed Dianna and pushed her, Jennifer and Kieran across into the corner farthest from the door, and shoved them to the ground.

"Don't move from there," he snarled.

Moving a few paces, he swept some ornaments from a heavy dresser and pulled it across in front of him and the huddled group.

A shot rang out, somewhere in the area.

A few minutes later it was followed by another.

Almost in a conversational tone, Dianna started talking to him.

"I'm just adding up the numbers here La Fonte. Let's see. There's the two phony cops, then the two jeep drivers who I suspect were part of your group of five. That's seven…. you make eight and the pilot…nine in all. Now, math was never my strong subject but, let's see, you had two killed right here. "She raised her finger as if testing the wind. "I'd guess you just lost two more a minute ago. Danny fires single shots, unlike your own men. When they left here, they were so shit scared. They'll be blasting off whole magazines, if they spot any movement out there. So that leaves five…"

Another single shot sounded from farther away.

She turned to Kieran. "Help me out here…how many left now Kieran?"

He sat forward grinning. "Four for sure, … but…"

"But what?" snarled La Fonte.

"Well, he's very good using his knife as well...so.... who knows how many are left?" he said innocently.

La Fonte shook his automatic in their faces. "Shut up! Shut up for fuck's sake!" he screamed.

Dianna waved her finger. "Temper, temper," she cautioned.

La Fonte opened his mouth to say something, just as another shot rang out, followed by yet another.

It was Jennifer who spoke. "There's only one left out there now." There was a grim satisfaction in her voice.

Dianna and Kieran stared at her.

She had never strung such a long sentence together prior to this.

La Fonte leaned forward as if to say something, when the whole window on his right collapsed inwards, driven by a bloodied body that crashed onto the floor.

Kieran stared. "I was right. He did use his knife."

The man's neck had been sliced across.

Jennifer looked up at La Fonte. "Now you're on your own" she intoned.

La Fonte's back was to the wall, his eyes darting from side to side.

He didn't have long to wait.

A voice boomed from outside.

"I'm coming in La Fonte. Hold your fire, there may still be a way out for you."

Everyone held their breath. It seemed to go on forever.

Then the door where the pilot had been shot crashed open.

La Fonte tensed, pointing his weapon.

'He won't come in that door' Dianna thought but he did, striding through a second later.

There was a collective gasp from the room.

Whether it was the lighting from the myriad of flames flickering from outside, or their over-active imaginations, but Quigley looked massive standing there. A shifting glow seemed to encase his whole shape. His head moved around the room taking in every detail then he focused his gaze on La Fonte.

"Your time is up. I've come for you," he whispered.

"But you said..." La Fonte wheezed.

"I lied... now"

"No!" La Fonte shrieked, grabbing Dianna by the hair and lifting her to her feet, he thrust the gun under her ear. Then he dragged her across to the door where Danny was standing.

"Back, back, or she dies right here now" he screamed.

Danny shrugged, stepping aside slowly.

La Fonte hauled Dianna through the door and turned, his dead eyes focused on Danny.

"I came to kill you, now I will." He raised the weapon.

Dianna drove her elbow back into his face, sending him sprawling.

The weapon fired harmlessly into the air.

La Fonte scrambled to his feet and started running in the only direction left for him straight across the road into the Amish property where Danny had met the youth out looking to get his deer quota earlier in the day.

La Fonte looked back desperately and saw Quigley coming after him. Strangely he didn't seem in any great hurry.

The half-breed was panting now, his breath coming in great gulps.

'I can still beat this' he thought. Then he saw a dark figure looming up in front of him.

The last thing he heard was the loud bang as an ancient, but still deadly shotgun, which tore a large hole in his heart.

Danny stopped and watched the Amish youth fall to his knees beside the still body on the track.

Then he started crying hysterically. "I swear I saw a deer.... I tell you, I saw a deer..."

Danny helped him to his feet and slowly led him back to the farm.

It was going to be a long night.

It took three days.

Again loads of interviews and interrogations.

The same questions being asked over and over again.

The weapons were a tricky one.

Oh, he found them in the chopper before he blew it up.

The fact that the CIA was a shadow behind an FBI investigation helped, as did a concerned telephone call from Rebecca at MI5 in London.

He was finally allowed to go, but was required to return for a full enquiry at a later date. Again, Zeitner guaranteed that he would appear, whenever this happened.

The rest of the Pakistani/Indian terrorist Force were been tracked down in the U.S. and that enquiry was still ongoing.

It was Zeitner who put it into perspective.

"For some reason Danny, every time you come here, lots of people get killed. We just want you out of here so we can go back to normal stuff, like fighting the drug trade and solving crimes. Though I must say, you provide an inexpensive method of sorting things out. No lengthy court cases or bad guys spending thirty years in jail postponing the death penalty. A lot to be said for it buddy."

They were at Buffalo airport and Zeitner gave him a long handshake.

"I owe you a hell of a lot Danny. I won't forget it." he said, looking him directly in the eye.

Then he turned and left.

Danny heard his U.K. flight being called.

He turned and put his arms around all three of them: Dianna, Jennifer and Kieran.

They clung to each other.

Finally Dianna stepped back and looked closely at him.

"What happened to you that night Danny? You looked almost like an apparition when you stepped through that door. And not just me... we all saw it."

He shrugged. "No idea...the stress, the excitement of the moment, the flames throwing their shadows, who knows?"

"But, when you were chasing La Fonte, you looked like you knew what he was running into. You seemed so casual. I just don't understand it Danny."

He looked away, a puzzled look creasing his face.

"I guess I did somehow... know... that my role was finished. I can't explain it any more than that."

The boarding call sounded again.

Dianna gave him a last hug.

"Look Danny, I know that you're going back to your own family in London. Just remember, you have a second family here and you will always be welcome. In fact, we'll be chasing you to come back over soon. Oh, that idea you had for Kieran and Jennifer" she made a movement as if firing a pistol, "that might be a good idea, when you're over here next time."

They watched him walk away.

"I want to be like him when I grow up Mom." Kieran said fiercely.

She hugged him.

"You could do a lot worse Kieran. I remember an old western that ended with someone saying about the hero, 'He's the kind of man that every kid wants to be like when they grow up, and every man wishes he had been, at the end of his days.'

Yeah, that's Danny Quigley!"

# THE END

# Acknowledgments

I have to acknowledge help and guidance from the following people:

Bob Beach in Randolph, NY for his proof reading efforts, advice, and access to his excellent graphics artists Tom Rickert at www.registergraphics.com. (i.e. the cover)

My daughter Suzanne for her reading efforts and valuable insights.

As ever, my wife Marie for her eagle eye in spotting grammatical errors. Not to mention the support and opinions of my 6 highly talented, grown up children, Lynn, Suzanne, Heather, Michael, Peter and Posie.

Last but not least I have to mention the computer skills of my grandson Morgan Coates who handled seemingly insurmountable obstacles with ease and competence

# OTHER BOOKS
## BY
# RUSS MCDEVITT

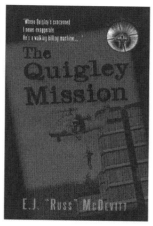

AVAILABLE THROUGH **RUSSMCDEVITT.COM**
AND OTHER LEADING BOOK SELLERS

ALSO AVAILABLE ON:

**amazon**kindle

26262706R00261

Made in the USA
Columbia, SC
11 September 2018